GUN FOR HIRE

Circle-D Saga

NANCY M. WADE

GARNAN Enterprises, LLC

ISBN: 978-1737699873
ISBN: E-978-1737699828

Published in the United States by GARNAN Enterprises, LLC of Ohio.

Also By

Works of Nancy M. Wade

Circle-D Saga Trilogy:
Endless Circle – book 1
Moment in Time – book 2
Gun for Hire – book 3

Meadowood Mysteries Series:
Scarecrows and Corpses – book 1
Reunion With Death – book 2
Deadly Bones – book 3
Berry Little Murder – book 4

Reflections: A Sentimental Journey
Frontier Heart
Courtship of Laura

Contents

GUN FOR HIRE

Prologue

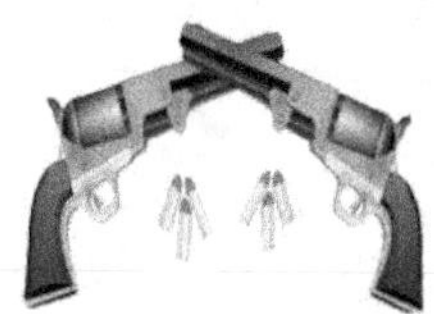

"You understand you'll be on your own?" questioned the director of the Secret Service.

"Yes sir, I understand," replied Cody Jarvis as he stood at ease in front of the director's heavy oaken desk, feet apart in a parade rest stance with his hands clasped behind his back.

"If you get into trouble, the agency will disavow any knowledge of you or your actions."

"Yes sir. I'll manage."

"Jarvis, your knowledge of the region and past military experience make you the perfect candidate to infiltrate and uncover the land fraud and counterfeiting in Wyoming."

"I'll do my best, sir," Cody answered.

His eyes shifted to the scene outside the office window. A woman sitting atop a buckboard wagon with a young child beside her, a boy no more than four or five years old, argued with a soldier on the street below. Memories suddenly flashed through Cody's mind of his own mother on their Missouri farm. His father gone, serving with the Union Army. Cody witnessed his mother argue for her life with a Confederate bushwhacker ransacking their home. Her screams had seared his six-year-old psyche.

"Are you listening, Jarvis?"

"

Mentally shaking himself, he returned his attention and focus on the solemn expression of his director.

"The President wants this matter taken care of before he can support territorial Wyoming's bid for statehood. Where are you planning to start?"

"Cheyenne... where my reputation precedes me," said Jarvis, his lips set in a firm line.

"Just get the job done."

Cody placed his Stetson firmly on his head, saluted the director then spun on his right heel and strode out of the room.

Part I - Chapter 1

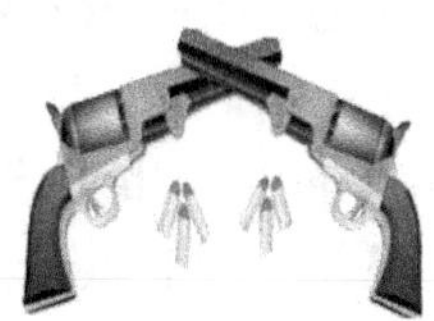

Deer Springs 1884

Wide prairies stretched for miles across the Wyoming plains, striped with deep ruts gouged into the land by oxen-pulled wagon trains crossing the Oregon Trail. The rugged countryside waved a sea of grass across its Great Plains, then ended in fierce mountains with towering peaks that rose sharply on the distant western horizon.

The wild land offered a home to roaming buffalo and longhorn cattle that grazed on the open range. At least it was until settlers dotted the landscape with their sod huts and rough-hewn log cabins as they staked claim to parcels of the rich land.

To encourage the western expansion, the federal government had passed the Homestead Act which granted parcels of public lands, normally one hundred and sixty acres, to any United States citizen willing to farm or settle on the land and reside there for a minimum of five years. As long as a person was at least twenty-one years old, they could file an application for deed to the land, make improvements, and claim it for their own. Women had the opportunity to own land and were motivated to relocate to the territory that had provided them with voting rights in 1869.

A constant train of hopeful pioneers and immigrants in heavy Conestoga wagons trekked westward looking for the promised land or fame and fortune. Many gave up; many died along the way. Many more simply settled wherever they broke down and took advantage of the land grants if they could. It was a situation ripe for opportunity and also ripe for corruption in the hands of the right person.

Cody Jarvis sat back in his saddle as he paused and scanned the horizon before him. Waves of heat radiated off the torrid earth. The hot air stifled both man and beast. He pushed the brim of his hat off his forehead with the tip of a forefinger and wiped a sweaty brow with the cuff of his sleeve. Dragging fingers through thick black hair, he pulled the bandana off his neck. He was tired and dirty, covered in over a week's worth of grime from riding the trail between Cheyenne to Ft. Laramie and onto Deer Springs. Cody scratched his itchy cheek, dark with a thick growth of black beard. He looked every bit the lone outlaw gunslinger.

He studied the rough shod town of Deer Springs that rose out of the prairie like a boil on the backside of humanity. The horizon contained outlines of haphazard wooden buildings of varying sizes and heights; two large tents also provided temporary shelter. Crude sod huts and a few roughly constructed log structures dotted the surrounding land. A few head of cattle grazed nearby.

"Probably homesteaders staking a claim," thought Cody as he surveyed the frontier dwellings.

"Come on, Lightning, just a bit farther." He nudged his horse forward with a thump of his heel and steered clear of the homesteaders by circling around unseen, north of town. After a month's investigation, he had followed the trail of money in Fort Laramie, and now that trail had led him to this God-forsaken frontier town.

Jarvis slowly crossed a wide pasture of parched grasses. He neared a shallow stream and had no problem coaxing his thirsty bay forward; dismounting, both horse and man gulped the cool rippling water. Cody stretched out on his belly at the edge of the stream; splashed his sweaty face then cupped his hands to drink more of the clear water. He rinsed his bandana in the cold water and tied it around his neck again. Forcing himself to his feet, he slapped his hat against a chap encased leg, knocked a layer of dirt and dust from the brim, then mounted up. He settled the Stetson low on his forehead to shade his blue eyes from the glare of the setting sun. Perhaps in another hour or so he could slip into town unnoticed in the dark; find a place to bed down and get some much-needed shut eye.

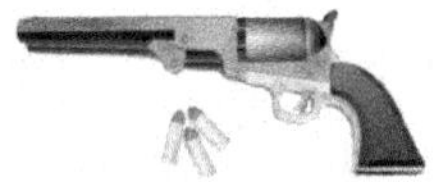

An off-key piano played loudly behind the closed doors of a saloon at one end of the street. Raucous laughter and loud cursing floated out an open window of the local bawdy house. Cody listened as he surreptitiously slipped into the north side of town where the buildings sat further apart and little light shone between. If it was possible, Deer Springs appeared worse up close than from a distance. The town, if you could call it that, appeared to be a haven for every kind of low-life drifter and criminal type with little evidence of any law presence.

Cody clung to the shadows. His hand rested on the butt of his revolver, eyes searched murky shadows, as he slowly walked his tired mount. An empty stable beckoned. One door hung open, and Cody made his way into the dark structure. He tied Lightning in an empty stall, unsaddled him, then dumped his saddle blanket and rig onto the hay covered ground and soon followed it. Stretching out, he rested his head on the saddle's apron and placed his gun within easy reach then closed his eyes. He was asleep within minutes.

Faint morning sunlight filtered through cracks in the wooden walls; flies buzzed within the horse stalls. Years of living rough, with his life depending on his instincts and gun, caused Cody to waken immediately when he heard the barn door creak, followed by muffled footsteps. His hand curled around the grip of his Colt, a finger on the trigger as he feigned sleep and listened carefully. The footsteps neared then stopped.

"Hey there, young feller, you can't sleep in here," a hoarse voice warned as he nudged Cody's booted foot with his own.

Cody peered through narrowed eyes. What he saw was an elderly man, back humped with age and years of hard living, sparse gray hair barely covered the bald head. The man's face wore grizzled whiskers over leathery skin, weathered and wrinkled, but with eyes still alert and watchful. Cody exhaled and relaxed his grip on the revolver; he perceived no danger from the old cowhand. He rolled to his side and slowly got to his feet.

"Sorry pardner. No harm done. Got into town late and didn't know where else to bed down," Cody Jarvis informed the man.

The man studied Cody; his eyes traveled from the soft leather chaps and denim pants to the shirt covered in sweat and grime. His eyes stopped at the gun belt strapped low on the hip and the pair of smooth-handled Colt .45 six-guns resting in their holsters.

"This here's my place. I don't want no trouble."

"I don't plan on starting any. This town got some place where a man can get a decent night's sleep without interruption?" Cody asked as he slapped the rim of his hat against his leg.

"Maybe. Come far?"

"Far enough. Can I board my horse with you? I'm willing to pay two bits for a bucket of water and feed."

"Yeah, I reckon that would be okay." The old codger paused and sized up the stranger again. "You take yourself down to Clara's boarding house just past the mining office; tell her Clem sent you. She'll set you up with a bed and place to wash up," the old man rasped.

"Thanks. Much obliged. My rig safe to leave with you?" Cody asked as he hefted his saddle and blanket and slung them over a stall partition. He removed his saddle bags and rifle; tossed the bags over his left shoulder and carried the rifle with his left hand. His right, gun hand, he kept free.

"Sure 'nuf. Don't believe I caught the name," Clem stated with a lift of his eyebrow.

"Don't believe I tossed it. It's Jarvis. Cody Jarvis. And this here's Lightning. Thanks Clem," he replied as he flipped a silver quarter to the man's out-stretched palm.

He left the stable and slowly headed out of the alley then stepped up onto a raised wooden boardwalk that traveled past store fronts and taverns. This early in the morning, only a pair of settlers and their womenfolk moved about. Cody tipped his hat to one of the bonneted ladies as she entered the general store. Pausing, he glanced inside before he passed. Barrels of grain, flour and sugar sat among burlap sacks of feed and farming implements. Shelves and boxes filled one entire wall of the store; bolts of colorful cloth, ready-made clothes, canned goods and mason jars, buckets of nails and screws crammed every open space. The center of the floor space contained two tables laden with fresh produce, a couple baskets of eggs, pungent cheese, and salted meat.

The clerk stared at Cody as he lingered by the door; a frown wrinkled his brow as he gave Cody the once over. Cody nodded and moved on. He scanned the painted signs as he strolled past various buildings and noted the sheriff's office across the street from the Silver Spur saloon. Finally, he spotted a narrow structure with a single glass window in front; a small placard propped in the window's corner proclaimed Deer Springs' Mining Office.

Moving past the office, Cody knocked on the next wooden door. The chipped blue paint stuck to his knuckles with each loud rap. Cody rubbed his hand on the seat of his pants and waited for the door to open.

"I'm comin', hold your horses," bellowed a woman's gruff voice seconds before she cracked the door open and peered out the narrow slit. "Who're you? Whatcha want?" she asked suspiciously.

"Morning ma'am; name's Cody Jarvis. Clem down at the stable said you might have a room to rent."

A heavy-set woman, with matted gray hair pulled back into a severe bun and wearing a plain dark dress, swung the door wider. She looked him over. "Come on in. If Clem sent you, you must be all right."

"Thanks. Feel like I'm wearing half the Wyoming territory on these clothes. Got a tub I can soak in; remove some of this grime? Been awhile since I've had a hot bath," said Cody. His eyes scanned the one large room. The place was clean yet sparse, with only mismatched seating for four around the wooden table that graced the center of the room. He noted the faded but clean gingham tablecloth and the threadbare woolen rug on the floor. The smell of strong coffee hung in the air.

"Yeah, I can fix ya up. How long ya stayin'? And you can call me Clara. We ain't too formal here."

"Thank you, Clara. If it's all right with you, I'll stay awhile. Don't know yet how long, maybe couple of months."

"Well, seein' as you're fixin to stay awhile, I'll charge you only six dollars a month for the room and board. I normally charge more. I cook what vittles I find for breakfast and supper. You ain't one of those fussy eaters, are you? And I don't take none of that paper money, only silver or gold. Okay?" Clara asked unblinking, her eyes studying him, waiting for a reaction.

"Sounds fair to me." Cody reached into his front pocket and withdrew three gold dollar coins and offered them to the woman. "Here's two weeks' worth; I'll pay the balance of the month later. That do?"

Clara accepted the coins, smiled at Cody, then tested one coin by biting it with the few teeth she had left in her mouth. Satisfied that the gold was genuine, she opened a drawer in a small desk that stood in one corner, removed a key and handed it to Cody.

"Top of the stairs, second door on the left is yours. I'll heat some water for that bath."

Cody clasped the key in one hand as he hoisted his rifle and saddle bags then climbed the stairs. He glanced down the upper hallway and made note of the number of doors before unlocking his own room. His eyes quickly scanned the meager space, taking in a lone chest of drawers and a single bed that supported a mattress with more lumps than a bowl of oatmeal. At least the blanket and pillow appeared clean, albeit a bit frayed.

Cody crossed the wooden floor and moved to the narrow window that overlooked the dusty street. Standing to the side, he cautiously lifted the yellowed and cracked window shade to peer across the street and both sides of the building. He had a good view of the Silver Spur and could look down onto the entrance of the mining company office. Cody smiled to himself, pleased with the location.

Now to see to that bath. He hung his hat on the bedpost and unbuckled his gun belt, withdrawing a Colt and laying it on top of the chest within easy reach. The gun belt followed his hat to dangle from the other post. He shucked his boots and wiggled toes that hadn't been free for over a week. Felt good to stretch. Cody peeled off his shirt and bandana, socks and belt, but left his jeans on. He tucked the wad of dirty clothes under his arm as he grabbed his Colt and sought the location of the tub awaiting him.

He padded down the stairs and found Clara in a small alcove located off the rear kitchen. He watched her pour a large kettle of hot water in a copper hip bath already half full. Steam rose from the inviting bath water.

"Can I help with that?" he asked as the woman bent to pour the heavy kettle.

"That ought to do it. You holler out if you need more," Clara told him. She paused in her chore to ogle the man's bare chest with its thick black furring that led in a line below his belt. Clara noted a thin scar crossing taut muscles. Her brow raised along with her curiosity, but she knew better than to ask. Still, she wasn't so old that she couldn't appreciate the sight of a handsome, able-bodied man.

"I'd like to use this water when I'm done to wash up some clothes, then I'll empty it for you if that's okay," Cody said. He laid his gun on the floor next to the tub within easy reach.

"Suit yourself," Clara replied as she left the tiny room and closed the door.

Cody stripped off his jeans and lowered himself into the hot water. He had to pull his knees up to his chest to fit within the tub but at least he could soak most of his body. A bar of lye soap and a rag waited on a stool next to the tub; Cody reached for the harsh soap and scrubbed away miles of thick trail dust.

Steamy hot water relaxed his tired body as Cody allowed himself the rare luxury of letting his mind drift. He'd been following the money for weeks, tracking smugglers and leads that kept pointing to one man. And now he felt close. He was sure of it. Time to put his plan into action.

Chapter 2

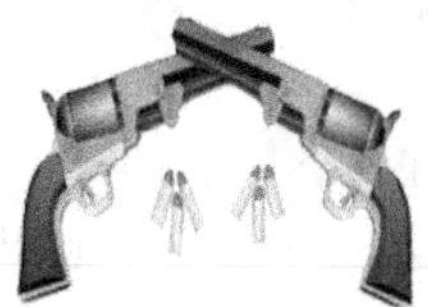

Logan

Cody browsed through the stack of denim pants on the shelf of the general store, selected a pair his size then turned his attention to a rack of cotton shirts. Female twittering caused him to look about the shop. His eyes found a pair of young girls staring at him unabashedly, their cheeks blushed prettily as their eyes locked with his. Cody raised a palm to rub his own pink, clean-shaven cheeks and wondered if that was what the teens snickered over. Perhaps just a young woman testing her wiles on an older man? The girls appeared to be barely out of the nursery. Shaking his head, he returned to the task at hand and felt positively ancient in their company.

Cody laid the pants and black cotton shirt on the counter, added a pair of cotton socks and on impulse, selected a peppermint stick candy to his purchase. The clerk behind the cash register coughed lightly and raised an eyebrow but said nothing.

"How much?" Cody asked as the clerk bundled the clothing in brown paper and tied it with a string. Cody picked up the peppermint, sucking on one end; he clenched it between his teeth.

"That'll be four-fifty, mister."

"Here you go," Cody said as he handed the clerk both coin and paper currency. He watched the clerk count the money carefully before he dropped it into a cash drawer under the counter.

Cody tipped his hat to an older woman and smiled at the two young girls who twittered and giggled as he left the store. A woman with a brood of children clinging to her skirts marched toward him on the narrow wooden boardwalk. Cody stepped down into the street to allow her to pass unhindered. Hot, noon day rays bounced off the storefront's glass, shooting arcs of white light. Cody tilted his Stetson forward on his brow to block the sun's glare from his eyes. He started toward the Silver Spur saloon then stopped midway when he heard his name shouted.

"Jarvis! You yellow-bellied snake, turn around," a loud voice snarled. The cowboy stood in the middle of the dusty street and stared defiantly at Cody.

Cody turned to face the threat. He recognized Boyd Wilson, a low life criminal... hard to forget. Cody had been responsible for sending Wilson to prison ten years ago when they both had served in the army. The problem now was what Wilson was doing in Deer Springs. The last thing he needed was his cover blown.

People paused outside stores; a couple of wranglers stepped out from the saloon to watch the drama unfolding in the street. Swirls of dust blew up, a lone tumbleweed bounced against the wooden walk while the sun beat down mercilessly.

"I always knew I'd find you one day," growled Wilson. His hand slid to his gun holster. His fingers hovered above the hilt.

Cody narrowed his eyes and coolly studied the man before him. His own right hand hung deceptively relaxed while his left still held the tied paper package. The stick candy protruded from his lips.

The glare of the sun pierced Wilson's eyes. He blinked then reached for his gun. It was over in a split second.

Smoke spiraled from the barrel of Cody's Colt, still pointed at the man lying crumpled on the street before him. He slowly slid the revolver into its leather holster and calmly walked toward the saloon, pushing open the swinging doors. He didn't bother looking back at the dead man.

The wranglers watching outside followed him in. A few heads turned his way. Most men were unconcerned and resumed conversations or their drinking. Four men seated at a round table in the corner concentrated on their poker game and never bothered to look up at the intrusion of the stranger. Death in Deer Springs was a common occurrence.

Cody found an empty chair at a lone table, positioned the chair back against the wall and dropped his package onto the floor. He flicked the last piece of peppermint candy into a nearby spittoon. The bartender sauntered over, a bored expression on his face.

"What can I get cha?"

"Beer for starters. Got any food?"

"Guess I can fry you up a beef steak and some taters if you're hungry," the man offered.

"Sounds good; make that steak medium rare but bring me the beer first," Cody ordered.

"Comin' right up."

Cody leaned back, pushed his Stetson off his forehead and surveyed the men scattered about the room. His eyes shifted to the saloon doorway as three more men entered. Two hung back, mincing their steps as they followed their leader—from all appearances, the man in charge. He didn't dress like a common cowboy. He wore a fitted waistcoat with dark trousers and a white shirt. Oil slicked back his black hair but the temples and walrus mustache both displayed signs of graying. The clothes and hair reminded Cody of a southern plantation owner or perhaps a riverboat gambler but the cold steel evident in his eyes betrayed the first, more civilized image. He paused and regarded Cody. His two minions stopped short, nearly running up the heels of the man. He turned and scowled at them; they shriveled in his glare, stepped back, then hurried over to the bar.

Cody watched the fancy dressed dude strut toward him. Steely eyes studied Cody as he slid a chair over to the table and made himself at home. Both men faced each other, silently sizing each other up.

"Mind?" His attitude clearly stated he didn't care if Cody did.

Cody calmly struck a match on the underside of the table and lit a cigarette. He took a couple pulls and exhaled slowly, then stretched his legs out before him and stared at the man.

"You're new in town." It was a statement not a question as he scrutinized Cody's appearance.

"Just got in."

"You cost me a good man, mister. What's your name?"

"Jarvis, Cody Jarvis. That piece of scum worked for you? Can't say much for your choice of employees," he sneered and flicked his cigarette ash onto the floor.

"He had his uses. You owe me, Jarvis. What are you going to do about it?"

"Depends. Who are you? You offering me a job?" Cody asked as he studied the speculating gleam in the other man's eyes.

"Seems I've heard tell of a gun for hire down in Laramie, or was it Cheyenne, by the name of Jarvis. That you?"

"Maybe. Like I said, who's asking?"

"I'm Zachary Logan. I run things in these parts. People usually check with me before stirring up any trouble."

"Wasn't much time to ask permission; if you know what I mean? Next time I'll try to ask first." Cody said in a low voice and only took his eyes away from Logan's face when the barkeep set his beer down. Cody took a thoughtful sip of warm beer then broached Logan.

"So, you run things around here, huh? What, like the mayor or sheriff?" Cody scoffed.

"Hardly. I've got a cattle ranch west of town, the Diamond Bar. Plus, I own this saloon and the mining office. We're a small town and don't like it when strangers come in and cause trouble."

"Sorry, but Wilson and I just settled an old beef. I didn't even know the cowpoke was here."

"Hmm, well, I could use a man like you, somebody good with a gun."

"Why? Cattle ranching doesn't normally involve shooting."

"We've, ah, had some problems with rustling. My men keep watch on the herd and oversee the sale of those beefs. Lots of money can change hands around here; I have to protect my interests," Logan stated as he stood. "Think it over Jarvis. You want a job? Come see me."

Cody nodded as his plate of food arrived. "I'll do that. Get back to you in a few days."

He watched as Logan joined his men at the bar, swallowed a shot of whiskey then walked toward a rear door of the saloon.

"Hmm, maybe Logan's office?" speculated Cody. *"Bears looking into."*

Chapter 3

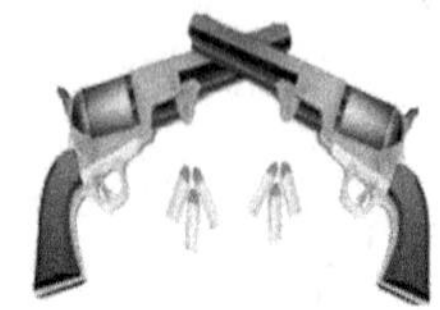

Sheriff Connor

Boyd Wilson's body lay on the planks of a rickety buckboard wagon. Two men measured his length for the undertaker then scratched a number on the sole of Wilson's boot with a piece of chalk. A single horse slowly dragged the wagon toward the end of the street where a pile of wood spilled out of a three-sided lean-to. Deer Springs' idea of a funeral parlor.

Cody watched the lumbering procession as he left the Silver Spur, scanning the street and the movements of the town's citizens. He looked up as windows were thrown wide open on the second floor of Dollies Darlins, its red painted clapboard siding leaving no doubt as to the nature of its business. Feather ticks hung across the open frames, airing in the hot sun. A scantily clad female leaned against the bedding, waved invitingly to Cody below then giggled as he tipped his hat to her.

He stepped off the boardwalk, headed to the stable, when a door slammed loudly. Cody spun about by reflex, bent at the waist; his hand reached for his gun. A short man wearing a tin star on his chest rushed toward him. Cody paused, straightened, and waited warily.

"Stop right there, mister. You responsible for that?" he demanded with a finger pointed toward the creaking buckboard.

Cody quickly studied the flushed face, heavy jowls and balding head, then took note of the portly belly hiding the man's waistline and the gun belt hanging below. He waited for the fella to catch his breath before turning to answer him.

"Yeah, I shot him. It was self-defense; he drew first."

"I'm Sheriff Ned Connor. I run things in this town; I don't like strangers causing trouble and shooting respectable citizens. What's your name?"

"Cody Jarvis. Like I said, he drew first." Cody peered at the lawman and spat onto the dusty street.

"You got witnesses to back up that story?"

A crowd gathered along the boardwalk to watch the theater before them, hoping for more gun action to liven their dreary day. Cody spotted Zachary Logan among the onlookers. Logan casually leaned against the saloon wall, one foot propped on a wooden bench as he too watched the sheriff and the gunslinger.

The sheriff noticed the growing throng then nervously glanced toward Logan.

Cody caught the movement from the corner of his eye and saw Logan imperceptibly nod to Connor. *Hmm, like that, is it?*

The sheriff took a deep breath and exhaled slowly, as if he were making a big decision.

"Well, seems like there might be enough people to back up what you say is true. I'm gonna let you off with a warning. But I won't tolerate any more bloodshed. You got it?"

The sheriff flexed his shoulders and pulled himself erect. Connor tried to increase his stature and provide an imposing impression on the crowd and the cock-sure whelp before him.

"Got it. Is that all, Sheriff?" Cody asked as he tried to keep the disgust out of his voice. Without a doubt, he just witnessed who ran this town, and it wasn't Connor.

"I'll be watching you, Jarvis. Remember that."

Cody turned, ignoring the man, and continued his way toward the stables to check on his horse and maybe have a conversation with old Clem. As he entered, the cool shade of the stable felt good and was a welcome respite from the scorching heat of the afternoon. Cody took a moment to allow his eyes to adjust to the shadows of the barn. He moved over to the stall holding his horse and dropped his parcel onto the floor. The loyal Morgan bay snorted and nuzzled Cody's outstretched hands. Cody lovingly stroked the horse's nose and caressed its head.

"How you doin' boy? Clem treating you good?"

"Sure am, young fella."

Cody turned at the sound of the old man's voice.

"Just finished brushing him down. Don't he look good?" Clem guffawed then continued on more seriously, "Here tell you had some excitement."

Clem stepped out of the dark and stood next to the stall. The bay snickered as Clem opened his palm to reveal a slice of apple. The horse chomped his treat appreciatively.

"News travels fast," Cody said as he rubbed Lightning's head and scratched behind his ears.

"Yeah, well, I don't imagine folks will shed any tears over the likes of Boyd Wilson. Good riddance, I say... just one less Logan henchman."

"Hmm, Logan, I met the man. What can you tell me about Zachary Logan? He seems to be the guy in power around here." Cody studied Clem's face, waiting for a response.

"The man's a weasel. Cheats honest folk and hires a bunch of outlaws to take what he wants," Clem declared and spat on the stable floor as if to emphasize his point.

"What do you mean, he cheats honest folk? He told me he ran a cattle ranch and the saloon. He been in Deer Springs long? Sounds like he's just a smart businessman," Cody said, trying to rile Clem.

"If you think stealing land and killing some of those sod-busters is just good business, well fella, then you ain't the person I thought you were."

"Hold on now Clem. Just who do you think I am?" Cody asked. His eyes continued to study the old man.

"I think you've come to clean up this town, that's who. You got that lawman look about you. I can spot 'em a mile away," Clem stated and stared Cody in the eye, daring him to deny it.

Cody shifted his stance, patted Lightning again, and gazed at the dust motes floating above shafts of sunlight, then turned to Clem, making a decision he prayed he would not later regret.

"I need your help Clem."

"I knew it!" Clem exclaimed as he slapped his thigh with his battered hat then cackled in glee as he danced a little jig in the scattered straw.

"I'm trusting you to not tell a soul. My life depends on it. As far as you know, I'm just one more gunslinger. Got it? I may have to do things you won't like or even understand, stuff that won't sit right, but I've got to get close to Logan to learn what kind of operation he's running."

"What can I do?" asked Clem.

"Just keep your ears and eyes open and your mouth shut," Cody instructed.

"What do you need to know?"

"When did Logan arrive in Deer Springs?"

"Um, dunno, maybe about three or four years ago. Him and two other dudes rode into town. Next thing I heard tell, he had won the deed to the Silver Spur in a poker game with Joe Peterson. Just took over the place; lock, stock and barrel."

"Where's Peterson now? I'd like to talk with him."

"Dead. Logan shot him. Ole Joe accused Logan of cheating in that poker game, said he wasn't going to give over the Spur. Joe drew his gun on Logan and that was that."

"Uh huh, I think I get the picture. That kind of *transaction* happens frequently, I take it?" Cody asked.

"Decent folks don't stand a chance. Settlers that file a claim and try to build up a homestead, they wind up losing the land and move on, or get buried under it."

"Thanks Clem. Guess that's what I needed to know." Cody flipped a coin to the old codger and gave Lightning's nose one last rub. "Give him an extra bag of grain tonight, Clem. He's the closest thing I have to family."

"Be careful out there, young fella."

Chapter 4

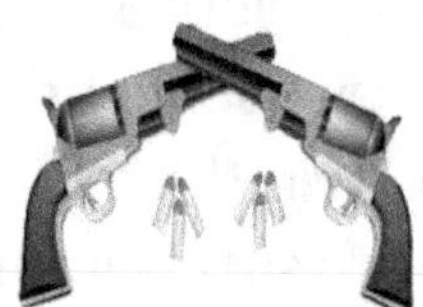

Mining Office

The smell of flapjacks on the griddle and bacon sizzling in the pan greeted Cody as he descended the boarding house stairs the next morning. Clara poured him a mug of coffee and slid a full breakfast plate in front of Cody.

"Smells delicious, ma'am, fit for a king. Thank you," Cody said with a smile for the woman.

"Eat up; there's plenty more. Reckon those clothes of yours are dry on the line by now. I'll leave 'em in your room," Clara offered.

"Thanks."

Looking pointedly at his black shirt and creased blue-jeans, Clara commented, "Of course, those new duds you're wearing look mighty fine." She laughed as she set the coffee pot back on the stove.

"Everyone else already eat?" Cody asked, choosing to ignore her mention of his clothing. He glanced around the empty room.

"Just got one other boarder, a schoolmarm who ate and hurried over to the schoolhouse this morning. Had one other gent staying here, but he left. Said he didn't want to stay under the same roof with no gunslinger." She raised an eyebrow and gave Cody a meaningful stare.

"Sorry you lost business on my account; promise you there won't be any gun play here. I don't plan on bringing trouble to your doorstep," apologized Cody with a sincere look.

Clara studied Cody's face and decided she would trust him. She nodded, then headed toward the washroom and outdoors. Clara picked up the clean clothes, stiff from drying in the blistering sun yesterday and folded the pants and shirt. She gathered up some of her own things, noticed the dining room was empty and Cody's plate sitting in the sink, then proceeded upstairs. Knocking once, in case Cody was inside, she eased the door of his room open. A quick peek confirmed the room was empty. She placed the folded clothes on the bed.

"Humph, sure is tidy for a gunslinger," voiced Clara to the vacant room. Bed made, clothes hung on the peg and just a single hairbrush rested atop the chest. "He don't make no fuss."

She shut the door, clicked the lock and went about her business.

Cody entered the mining office next door. The narrow room barely had enough space for a battered desk and two chairs. A map of the region hung on one wall and a pair of dented metal filing cabinets stood against the other. Cody noted a squat safe tucked into the corner behind the desk.

He moved to study the map with its red and blue markings and circles drawn across the land. A slight sound behind him drew his attention to a thin, gray-haired gentleman wearing a stained shirt that might have been white at one time and loose-fitting trousers held up by suspenders clipped to his waist and draped across bony shoulders. He stood in the door-way leading to a back room.

"Can I help you?" the man asked. Sweat glistened on his forehead; his beady brown eyes, framed by a pair of wire-rimmed spectacles, scrutinized Cody.

"Howdy," Cody greeted in a too loud voice with a broad grin. "I'm fixin' to do some prospecting." He held his hat behind him and bounced from side to side.

"That so?"

"You the man I speak to about available land and filed claims? Wouldn't want to be accused of stealing or claim jumping," Cody stated as he turned his back on the gentleman and returned his attention to the map on the wall. "What's this blue circle mean?"

"I'm Clyde Olson; I run the mine office. The blue circles are legal claims filed with this office."

"Hmm, reckon you're the right person to see then. What do the red lines mean?" Cody asked as he held his hat in hand and scratched his head, pretending to be baffled.

"Red lines indicate potential veins ready to prospect."

"Whoa, I gotta get me one of those!"

The clerk silently snickered at this dumb cowpoke standing before him. He'll make the perfect sucker. Clyde could already hear the praise Zachary Logan will heap upon him for unloading another parcel of worthless land and producing a huge profit in the bargain. This yokel, in his unmistakably new store-bought clothes, had to be the perfect mark.

"What do I gotta do?" asked Cody. He grinned at the man then peered at the map, running his fingers along the red lines, squinting to read the identifying landmarks.

"Just sign this here agreement and pay the asking price for the land. We've got some very promising parcels just waiting for the right person to work them. Why, I bet you'd strike gold or silver in no time at all," Olson went into his sales pitch persona.

"Gosh, that sure sounds excitin'. I'll have to chew on it a spell," Cody said. He pumped Olson's hand and left the mining office before the clerk could digest what had just happened.

Cody slipped back into the boarding house and took the stairs two steps at a time. He hurried into his room and opened the bottom chest drawer, withdrew a rolled-up map then spread it open upon his bed. He grabbed a pencil and began recording the marked parcels he had memorized from the mining company map. Some of the land designated for sale appeared to be located on Arapaho Indian reservations. Cody realized that Logan not only swindled settlers out of their homestead claims, but he was also selling pieces of federal land reserved under Indian treaties. No doubt many a poor un-suspecting miner forfeited his money, claim and possibly his life when the Arapaho expelled him off their property. Logan's operation encompassed more than Cody had realized.

Cody rolled up his map, tucked it inside his shirt, and locked his door behind him. He stepped into the alley between Clara's and the mining office and headed toward the stable, keeping to the seclusion of the back streets. The sun burned a hole in the sky overhead; a heavy haze hung in the air enough to take a man's breath away. The heat was oppressive. Cody entered the barn from the rear, startling old Clem with his silent entrance.

"Scared me half to death. You move as quiet as an Injun," Clem complained.

"Sorry Clem. I just came to get Lightning; didn't see the need to announce it to anyone in town that might be watching."

Cody approached the horse stall and patted the stallion on his nose. The scent of sweet green hay clung to the cool shadows of the barn. He brushed the huge bay then tossed a blanket onto his back, followed by his saddle. He buckled the girth and snugged the cinch. Lightning stood still, accustomed to his tack and the touch of his master. He snorted once; eager for the freedom to run and flex his muscles.

Cody chuckled and patted his steed affectionately. "All rested up and raring to go, huh fella? Well, let's explore some of this territory. See you later Clem."

Cody led Lightning out the rear door of the stable then swung up into the saddle and with a nudge of his heel, horse and man trotted off.

Chapter 5

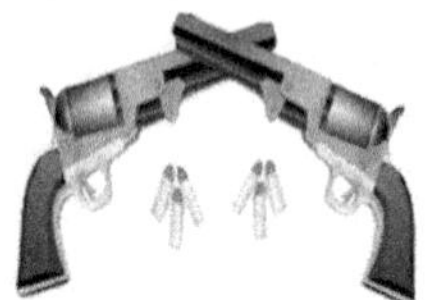

Jergen

Cody circled Deer Springs, giving it a wide berth, then headed north toward the foothills. Lightning stretched his thick muscles and galloped freely across the open land; Cody gave him his head until they had covered several miles. He was curious to have a look at some of the land marked on his map. The more distance he put between himself and the town, the more relaxed he felt. He sat back in the saddle and scanned the horizon. To his east, he saw cattle grazing in small herds; a split rail fence created a horse corral attached to a barn that looked more like kindling wood than anything solid.

He steered clear of the homestead with its log cabin; smoke curled above the chimney and laundry hung on a rope line. He respected the folks who put down roots and sacrificed their all to build a life for themselves in this wild land. Maybe some day he'll own a ranch, have a family, but that future seemed decades away. Assuming he survived this mission.

Cody stood in the saddle and peered across the vacant space. The land stretched as far as the eye could see. The Wyoming Territory resembled his time spent with the Army at Fort Lyon in Colorado on the Frontier, fighting Indians and trying to maintain order with a handful of soldiers spread over the vast terrain. Living off of baked beans and hardtack or whatever game a man could snare, it was a hard life and a lonely one for a soldier.

Cody shook his head to clear the cobwebs and the path his mind was taking. No time for dreams. He rode further north, stopped once to check the landmarks indicated on his map, then got his bearings and continued. The afternoon wore thin, and dusk colored the horizon when Cody spied a cluster of tents gathered around a wooden sluice in a small stream. A trio of placer miners worked the land with pickaxes and shovels. They sifted the dirt and rocks into the water sluice, as they searched for nuggets of gold or silver ore.

"Hello in the camp!" Cody called out as he rode into their camp. In the twilight, he appeared as a dark shadow. "Howdy. That coffee I smell? Can you spare a cup?"

Without waiting for an invitation, Cody dismounted and tied his horse to a tree branch near the stream where Lightning could drink his fill. He sauntered into the open circle of firelight and approached one of the grizzled prospectors.

"Pot's hot, pour your own. I'd tell you to make yourself at home, but you seem to have done that already," one man stated with a smirk.

The gray-haired, prospector held out his hand to Cody. "Hank Jergen. This here's my son Willum." He pointed to the man climbing up the riverbank and walking into camp. "That's my partner, John Woods."

Cody shook the man's hand, scrutinized his face and the other two men. "Nice to meet 'cha. Cody Jarvis." He turned to shake the other man's hand.

"You lost, mister?" asked John Woods indignantly. He scowled at Cody as he reached for his canteen of water.

"No, not exactly. Just trying to get the lay of the land so to speak. I heard tell a man might get lucky around these parts. They say there's gold and silver ripe for the picking. That true?" asked Cody as he studied the faces before him.

"You're a fool. Think we'd be digging all day like slaves if them there riches were just scattered on top the ground? Somebody been telling you lies, buddy," said Willum.

"Well, I'm right sorry to hear that, boys," Cody said. "Reckon I've been told a tall tale."

The three men glared at him suspiciously. Cody squatted by the campfire and poured coffee into a tin cup. He took one sip, swallowed hot liquid that tasted more like tar than chicory and coughed hard.

Hank Jergens laughed and slapped Cody on the back, "Bit strong for you? That pot's been cookin' for three days now. Makes a man's hair stand on end, but it keeps us awake during the night and that's what we need."

"What makes you want to stay awake all night, old timer? You afraid of claim jumpers?" Cody asked.

Before the man could answer, a bullet whizzed past Willum's head and struck one of the burning logs. Chunks of wood exploded, and sparks flew into the air. Cody automatically drew his gun and rolled to his side while the three miners ducked for cover behind anything solid. Cody peered into the fading daylight and listened. No sounds of approaching riders or men crawling stealthily toward camp could be heard. He slowly slid his Colt back into his holster and turned to the others.

"Think that just answered my question. Happen often? Do they ever hit anything or just harass?"

"John got hit in the shoulder once, but we don't scare off. This is our claim, and we aim to keep it," said Hank.

"So, I see. Somebody must think you've got a valuable mine if they keep trying to scare you fellas off."

"We do all right. Like I said, it ain't lying around. You gotta work for what silver you find." John Woods spat onto a burning log, his saliva mixed with tobacco juice sizzled and crackled in the embers.

"Maybe I ought to rethink this mining stuff; appears to be hard work and dangerous to boot," Cody said with a laugh.

"You don't look the type to scare off easily," Willum commented.

"I'm not, but I'd like to think I have enough common sense not to risk my neck for a piece of rock."

"Humph, what are you really doing out here, mister? You ain't lookin' to stake a claim," John Woods stated as he stared at Cody, refusing to break eye contact with him.

"Like I said, boys. I'm just exploring the area."

"You don't say," Hank said in a dry tone.

"Well, thanks for the coffee and the company. Reckon I'll move along," Cody said. "Good luck to you."

Cody untied Lightning and mounted up, turning south, back toward Deer Springs. It was late when he hit town and left the bay in the stable. He needed a hot meal and a good night's sleep to consider what he saw and learned today. But first a visit to the Silver Spur was in order.

Chapter 6

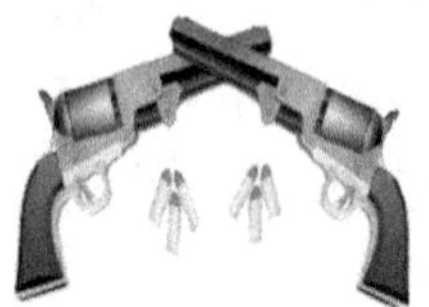

Diamond Bar

A thick layer of cigarette smoke clung to the fetid atmosphere of sweaty, unwashed bodies milling about the bar and within the confined interior of the saloon. A full day's sweltering heat had intensified the stench. Cody swallowed hard, wished he didn't need to breathe briefly, and narrowed his eyes against the stinging smoke as he stepped up to the bar.

"Beer," he ordered. The bartender, Kelly, filled a pilsner glass with the frothy ale and slid it across the wooden surface. Kelly studied the stranger, trying to recall where he had seen the man before, sure his face was familiar. It'd come to him.

Cody took a large gulp of the lukewarm liquid then wiped his mouth with the back of his hand. He rested one foot on the brass bar rail as his eyes scanned the mirror hanging behind the bar, allowing him to watch the commotion at his back.

"Jarvis, just the man I was looking for," Zachary Logan stated as he closed the rear office door and strode toward Cody.

"Why's that?"

"Have you considered my offer?" Logan asked. He struck a match and lit his cigar, peering at Cody through the spiraling smoke.

"Maybe. Let's just say, I'd like to hear more."

"Come out to the ranch tomorrow morning; I'm about five miles west of town. I've got a small spread, only sixteen hundred acres, but I plan on expanding."

"I'm not a cowhand. I don't really know what use I could be to you on the ranch," Cody said, his eyes never leaving Logan's face.

"Well, let's talk about that tomorrow, shall we?"

"Right. See you then," Cody said as he finished his beer and slid the empty glass toward the barkeep. He felt Zachary Logan's eyes on his back as he walked through the swinging doors of the Silver Spur.

Clara, bless her heart, had left a plate of warm food, covered with a tea towel, on top of the pot belly stove. Cody carried the plate upstairs to his room where he finished the mashed potatoes and roast chicken in short order and vowed to thank the landlady for her kindness in the morning. He kicked off his boots, hung his hat and gun belt on the bed post then dropped onto the lumpy mattress to get some rest. Morning and his meeting with Logan would be upon him in far too short a time.

Dawn sunlight pierced the cracked window shade and sent a shaft of bright light across the face of Cody Jarvis. He threw a forearm across his eyes to block the unwanted disturbance. Cody took a deep breath that ended in a raspy cough, forcing him to sit up. *Too damn much cigarette smoke,* he thought and coughed again until he spat a wad of phlegm into the spittoon sitting by the door.

"Argh, time to get up. Need to figure a way into Logan's inner circle," Cody told his mirror. The image before him agreed. He poured clean water from a porcelain pitcher into a wide bowl that sat atop the chest of drawers, compliments of Clara again, then splashed his face and washed his hands with a sliver of soap. He stroked the two-day growth of whiskers along his jaw and decided to leave it. No need to be clean shaven.

Cody stretched stiff muscles as he finished dressing. He yanked on boots, strapped on his gun belt then with hat in hand and his empty dinner plate in the other, headed downstairs. Upon entering the dining room, it surprised him to see the timid schoolmarm daintily sipping her cup of tea. He nodded politely to her as he pulled out a chair at the table.

"Mornin' miss."

She glanced at him nervously, her eyes skimming his attire before replying, "Good morning, sir."

"Clara, thank you kindly for the supper plate last night. I sure did appreciate it."

Clara took the soiled dish from him and added it to her dishwater. She set a plate of fried eggs with a slice of ham in front of him as she poured a steaming mug of coffee. Cody smiled and nodded his approval. He reached for a basket of biscuits from the center of the table.

"Miss, have one?" he offered the woman the basket before helping himself to the warm dough.

"No thank you."

"Clara makes a mighty fine biscuit. Would be a shame to waste them." Cody held the basket out to the shy teacher again as she reluctantly selected a flaky treat.

Cody caught Clara's eye and winked to her. He hoped his gentlemanly manners would calm the schoolmarm and guarantee her continued residency for Clara. He didn't want to cause any more income loss to the woman.

The teacher dabbed her mouth with a napkin and rose from the table. She nodded to Cody then turned to Clara. "Thank you for a delicious breakfast."

"You're welcome, Miss Barton. You have a good day now," Clara said as the schoolmarm quietly left.

Cody gulped the rest of his coffee then cleared his throat, "I may be gone a day or two, Clara. Don't bother making any more meals for me until you know for sure I'm back. Wouldn't want you to waste good food." He left two bits on the table for the landlady then headed out.

Cody strolled down the sidewalk past the mining office, glancing in the window as he passed, he tipped his hat to a startled Clyde Olson. The general store bustled with activity this morning. Cody had to quickly sidestep or be run over by a pair of farmers toting large bushel baskets of corn through the door.

He noticed the sheriff lounging in front of the jail, his chair leaned back on two legs while his feet rested atop the horse hitching post. The man was good for nothing except whatever Zachary Logan told him to do. Cody snickered at the sight and continued to the stable. Today, he made sure to put on a show of riding out of town and headed toward the Diamond Bar.

Cody rode leisurely, in no great hurry to meet Logan. His mind reviewed the facts he had learned in the mine office dealings, certain Logan used the office to assist in his land swindles and perhaps more. If he could just discover his counterfeiting operation, he'd haul Logan's sorry ass down to Fort Laramie to the authorities and charge him with both crimes. But he must bide his time and gain more information.

The heat of the day rose as the sun climbed the cloudless sky. Ripples of heat radiated above the prairie ground as Cody wiped a bandana across his damp brow. He finally rode alongside a line of barbwire fencing erected to mark the perimeter of Logan's spread. Cody continued further until he encountered a split rail wooden gate with a carved sign hanging above that declared the Diamond Bar ranch. A large herd of cattle grazed on the sparse grass. The dirt road wound further onto the property until finally Cody spied a wooden two-story house ahead with a stable and barn built behind it.

Cody rode into the yard; he counted three men inside the stable and two others with rifles positioned near the corners of the house. Seemed like a lot of fire power for a simple cattle ranch. He casually dismounted and tied his horse to the rail as his eyes darted to the armed men then shifted to movement behind a window's filmy glass. He knew he was being watched and took pains not to make any sudden actions.

He strode up to the door and rapped lightly, then stepped back. Cody gazed about and noted the visible hired guns; they didn't bother to hide their presence.

A woman cautiously opened the door. She hesitated then looked to someone behind her as if seeking permission or guidance.

Cody studied the silent woman; a sense of defeat and hopelessness clung to her like the fine, muslin gown that she wore. It wasn't the fading bruise beneath her right eye, but rather the lack of emotion in her hollow hazel eyes that illustrated her resignation. Cody recognized the same blank stare he'd witnessed on fellow soldiers after the horrors of war and wondered what despair caused this woman's bleak expression — perhaps her marriage?

"Sarah! Allow Mister Jarvis entry," barked Zachary Logan from a side room.

The woman waved Cody forward, then silently glided up the tall staircase and disappeared. He stared after her for a few seconds before he turned and entered the side parlor to greet his host.

"See you found the place okay," Logan stated the obvious as he shook Cody's hand. "Have a seat."

Cody shook the man's hand then resisted the urge to wipe his palm on his pant leg afterwards. Something about Zachary Logan made him feel unclean.

Chapter 7

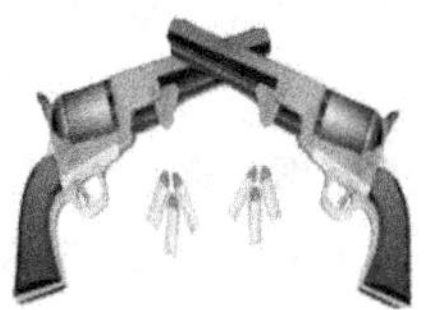

Hired Gun

"Given any more thought to my offer?" asked Logan as he moved to a sideboard and picked up a decanter to pour himself a shot of whiskey. He held a second glass before him, silently offered it to Cody, who shook his head in the negative.

"Too early for me. Thanks anyway."

"Well?" Logan persisted with his first question.

"What's in it for me?" Cody made his own inquiry. "You've got plenty of gun hands from what I saw riding in. Why me?" Cody leaned back against the sofa cushions and nonchalantly draped an arm along the back of the chair, watching Logan.

"That's just it, they're gun hands. Oh, don't get me wrong; they're good loyal men, but I want a big name. Someone with a reputation. Like you. I want a name to be reckoned with - tied to me that folks will know the Diamond Bar means business."

"And you think that means me? I think you're misinformed."

"My contacts in Laramie say otherwise, Jarvis."

"Like I said before... what's in it for me?"

"Greed! I like that in a man. I can understand greed." He raised his glass in a silent toast. "I've got a sweet operation going on here. I plan on growing it bigger and I need someone like you," Logan stated as he stared out the window, envisioning his empire.

Cody studied the expression on Logan's face and realized he had struck a chord. The man saw himself as some sort of king, ruling his domain and the people around him. Cody encouraged him to talk about his dreams. He'd learn as much information as he could right from the source. Maybe given enough rope, Logan will hang himself too.

"Some day I'll own this land as far as the eye can see."

Logan moved away from the window and turned his attention back to the taciturn gunslinger lounging before him. Their eyes met in silent assessment. A tug of war. Each man daring the other to blink first. Logan narrowed his eyes as he tried to read the thoughts behind Jarvis' unflinching, cold blue orbs. Like ice.

Abruptly, Logan strode out of the room. Cody listened to sounds of a door opening and closing in the rear of the house then other muffled noises before Logan returned a few minutes later holding a small leather pouch.

Logan tossed the pouch to Jarvis, who caught it with one hand. Jarvis hefted the weight of the pouch in his palm, judging the amount of its content.

"Fifty dollars in gold coin," confirmed Logan.

Jarvis raised an eyebrow and shrugged noncommittally. "What do I have to do?"

A grin slowly spread across Logan's face making his walrus mustache dance incongruously. Greed! He knew he'd judged Jarvis correctly. The man could be bought; it just took a smarter man like himself to realize it and know how much. His grin widened at the thought of his own cunning.

"Let's say you're my enforcer. Be available when I need you, that's all."

"I'm not staying out here in the middle of no where. I live in town, just so we're clear on that."

"I don't give a damn where you live, so long as I can find you when I need you! Do I make myself clear?" Logan growled in an irritated voice.

"Crystal," stated Jarvis as he rose and tucked the leather pouch into his pocket.

Logan watched Jarvis head out the door.

"This whelp might be harder to control than I thought."

Chapter 8

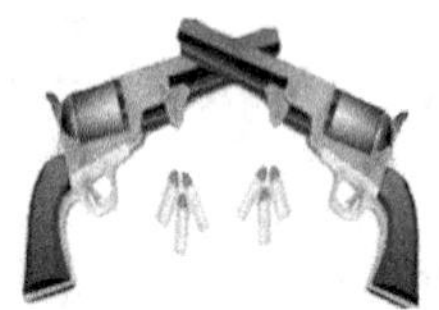

Confrontation

Three days later, Cody sat nursing a beer gone flat inside the Silver Spur saloon. He propped his feet on the chair beside him and tipped his hat forward across his eyes. At a glance, he appeared asleep in his suds. He was anything but. His shielded eyes watched the action at the bar and the men who came and went from Logan's rear office. He listened to snatches of conversation among the bar patrons, picking up odd pieces of information and filing them away in his mind.

Two of Logan's flunkies entered the saloon; the same two that Cody previously witnessed running up the heels of the man. Now they sauntered around the room, pretending to be important, until someone says "boo". They spotted Cody in the corner, elbowed each other in the ribs as they pointed to him.

"Go on, you tell him," whispered the tall, slim wrangler to his heavy-set, shorter partner.

"Me? Why can't you do it?" objected the squat man. He rubbed his scruffy beard worriedly as he stared at the sleeping gunslinger.

"Aw right, we'll do it together. C'mon," the slim guy agreed as he pulled on his right ear lobe.

They inched closer to Cody then jumped nervously when Cody's feet hit the floor. Cody raised the brim of his hat with one finger and stared at the two clowns. His right hand stayed deceptively close to the holster of his Colt.

Slim coughed, cleared his throat, and summoned his courage. "Logan wants to see you, Jarvis." He took a step backward.

"That's right," added his round friend. "You gotta come with us." He took two steps backward to stand behind his partner, not that he'd gain much protection behind his twiggy frame.

"Where?" Cody asked as he rose from his seat, stretched his arms and flexed his shoulders as if he had just woken from a sound sleep.

"Just follow us over to the mine office," Slim told him, feeling a little braver now and determined to act in charge. "You've got work to do."

Cody followed the two flunkies out of the saloon. *Wonder what Logan's up to now? Whatever it is, I've got a bad feeling about this.*

Zachary Logan conferred quietly with his mining agent, Clyde Olson. He looked up at the sound of the door opening and closing then resumed his discussion and survey of the land map spread across the desk.

Slim and Scruffy, as Cody mentally nicknamed them, shuffled their feet nervously as they waited on their boss. Cody moved toward the window, nonchalantly glanced outside while he tried to concentrate on the map's image reflected on the window glass. He chewed on a toothpick, appearing bored and unconcerned. He waited on Logan and wasn't surprised when that man issued an order he had suspected coming.

"You... 'bout time you earn your keep. Take Ike and Abe here out to this spot," Logan commanded as he pointed to a place on the map. "A pair of prospectors refuse to listen to reason and accept my generous offer to buy their claim. I need you to convince them otherwise. This time maybe with your *persuasion* they'll learn what's best for them. Make sure they do," snarled Logan as he shoved the map toward Cody.

Ike and Abe snickered, grins spread across their grimy faces, their excitement barely contained.

Cody studied the map and had a feeling he knew who's claim it would be. Just like he thought, he had a bad feeling about this job.

"Right. Just as long as these clowns stay out of my way," Cody stated as he brushed past the two men and left the building. He strode into the stable and saddled Lightning, silently nodded to Clem then rode out.

They headed north. Ike and Abe rode abreast leading the way and slightly ahead of Cody. He preferred to keep them in front of him and safeguard his own back. Despite the lateness of the afternoon hour, the sun burned in the sky above, blistering the parched earth below. Cody tilted the brim of his hat lower to shield his eyes as he watched the pair of riders and contemplated what he'd do when they reached Jergen's claim hours later.

Hank Jergen stirred a pot of soup resting among the hot coals of the campfire. The sound of horses turned his attention to the horizon and a possible threat. Hank tapped his son Willum's arm and pointed to the three riders coming into view. At first he relaxed, recognizing Cody Jarvis among the group, until they came closer, and he saw the company he kept. He'd had a run-in before with that pair— Logan's flunkies. Hank motioned Willum to seek cover, then cautiously waited.

As they neared the camp site, Cody spied the older man and his son by the fire. He watched Willum casually move behind the buckboard wagon while Hank stayed close to his Winchester rifle. The old-timer wasn't taking any chances. Cody was glad to see it. He didn't mean the old man any harm but couldn't be sure of the actions of Slim or Scruffy.

"That's close enough, Jarvis," shouted Jergen. He watched the trio of riders halt, the setting sun to their backs cast their faces in shadow.

"Jergen!" Ike shouted back, "Mister Logan says he has business with you."

"Just as I thought. Well, you tell Logan I don't want any *business* with him. I ain't selling."

"Be smart, Hank. Listen to the man's offer," Cody suggested as he leaned forward across Lightning's neck.

"I didn't figure you for running with this bunch, Jarvis," grumbled Jergen.

"You know how it is; gotta go where the money is," replied Cody. He sat back and studied the old man, his eyes shifted to the son, then darted to a new figure.

Just like before, Hank Jergen's partner, John Woods, hurriedly climbed the riverbank and approached the campfire. One glimpse and he took in the scene before him. Dropping his tin pan, he moved next to Jergen.

"Humph, knew we couldn't trust Jarvis. I told you. He's a hired gun to the highest bidder," Woods growled. His hand clutched for the six-shooter stuck in his waistband.

"Don't try it Woods," warned Cody. "You don't want to be dead, and I don't want to shoot you. Don't be stupid."

John Woods' anger flared at the insult. His eyes narrowed as he stared at the three men on horseback, especially Jarvis.

Cody read the man's body language, realizing his hand would be forced into doing something he didn't plan on. From the corner of his eye, Cody suddenly spotted Ike raising his rifle to aim at Woods. Cody immediately kneed Lightning, forcing the stallion to sidestep and bump into Ike's horse with a loud oomph. Ike's horse squealed in fright and reared up. The action caused Ike to flail his arm and fire wildly. The bullet ricocheted harmlessly off a nearby boulder.

Woods chose that moment to shoot at the intruders. Jergens yelled a warning. Ike almost fell out of his saddle as he tried to gain control over his frightened horse, and Scruffy watched with wide-eyes the mad commotion happening around him.

Cody had sensed the threat from Woods. In a split-second, he drew his own gun and returned fire, hitting the prospector in the right shoulder. Woods fell backwards, dropped his gun and rolled in agony as he clutched the wound, his fingers splayed to stop the bleeding. He was injured, but he was alive. Part of his mind realized that fact. Later, he would wonder why Jarvis hadn't killed him.

"What the hell, Jarvis! Can't you control that nag of yours?" spit Ike as he pulled back on his reins, the bit cruelly cutting the horse's mouth.

"Let's get outta here," whined Scruffy.

"Did you kill him?" asked Ike as the three turned their back on the mining camp and rode south toward Deer Springs.

"No. Wasn't necessary. He got the message okay."

"The Boss ain't go'in to like this, Jarvis," Ike mumbled.

Chapter 9

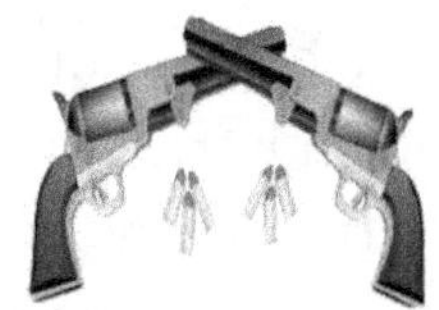

September 1884

Zachary Logan paced the narrow room. He ground the end of his cigar into a small dish setting on the corner of his desk then turned to the three men.

"Two old men and a boy...and the three of you couldn't take care of them?" he sneered. "I expected better of you, Jarvis. You're supposed to be some hot-shot gunslinger, yet you couldn't take on a pair of old men! What excuse do you have?" His voice rose in volume and fury with every word until he was shouting in the confined space of the rear office. No doubt the bartender and any patrons in the Silver Spur heard him clearly through the thin walls.

"They got your offer. It's better this way. They've been warned and know the threat to them if they don't sell. This way it'll be all legal-like. If I killed them and you claimed the site, you could be accused of stealing. Didn't think you'd want the transaction under that kind of close scrutiny," Jarvis explained in a deceptively soft, calm voice as he glanced around Logan's office, studying all the details.

"Humph. Maybe you're right. But I say who and when. You hear me? I make the decisions around here, not you. Go on, get out of here, all of you." Logan slammed down a ledger book on his desk, causing a poof of dust to rise from the surface. He turned his back on the men. His arms crossed; he stared out the small window overlooking the back alley.

Cody had developed a daily routine—a lazy one to the casual observer. After breakfast at Clara's, he strolled down to the stable to check on Lightning and spoke with Clem to learn the latest gossip. Some days he rode out of town and was gone for hours, then he returned to wander into the Silver Spur and joined whatever poker game was currently in progress. He became known as a shrewd gambler who ruthlessly called out the occasional cheat, not giving that fool a chance to regret it. Some days he rode with Ike and Abe back and forth to Logan's ranch when the whim struck Logan's egotistic need to declare his authority. Cody couldn't see any reason for the show of guns, but he guessed Logan enjoyed the display.

Three weeks had passed, and Cody still couldn't find any evidence of the counterfeiting operation that the bureau suspected Logan to run. Twice, Cody tried to slip into Logan's office at the Spur only to quickly move away when the bartender Kelly turned his scrutiny on him. Frustrated, he promised himself to wait until night and try again.

Kelly walked over to Cody's table and dropped the plate of food in front of him. "Here's your beef, just the way you like it," Kelly stated as he studied the gunslinger. He didn't trust him. Where'd he come from? He couldn't understand why Logan put so much stock in this guy.

"Thanks, Kelly." He picked up the fork and knife to cut into the thick steak then paused. Cody set the fork down, his right hand still clutched the sharp knife, and raised his eyes to the man hovering by his table. "Something on your mind, Kelly?"

The room suddenly hushed; the piano player stopped banging on the off-key ivories and three men sitting at the poker table paused in their play. All eyes turned to the silent drama building between the two men.

Kelly glanced about the room then turned his eyes back to the man before him, sitting deathly still. He took a step backwards, his better instincts warring with his emotions and dislike of the arrogant man at the table. Kelly swallowed. "I don't like you Jarvis. I don't know what you're up to, but I'll be watching you."

"Fair enough. I'm not exactly a big fan of you either, but it took guts to speak your mind and I respect you for that. You just mind your own business and I'll tend to mine."

Noise in the room came alive again as Kelly turned and walked toward the bar; he felt Cody's eyes drilling into his back with every step. He grabbed a bar towel and wiped the beads of sweat from his forehead before he nodded to Sam at the piano.

Cody returned his attention to his meal. His senses were attuned to every sound and nuance in the room as he pretended to ignore the bartender, knowing full well he would need to watch the man and tread more cautiously lest he tip his hand.

Cody stood before Logan's desk waiting on the man to speak. He'd been rudely awakened by Slim and Scruffy hammering on his bedroom door at five-thirty in the morning with their demands to come quickly, and now he waited. His patience was wearing thin.

"Jarvis, I need you to ride shotgun on a shipment of silver down to Fort Laramie. Ike and Abe will accompany Olson to transport the ore, but I want that load protected. Kill anyone that comes even close to that wagon. Do I make myself clear?"

"Got it. When do we leave? Your clowns rousted me before I had time for breakfast. It's a long ride to Fort Laramie; I'd rather not make it on an empty stomach," Cody said. His eyes locked with Logan's until the other man blinked and nodded his acquiescence.

"You've got an hour. That should give the men time to load the wagon," Logan said.

"Right." Cody exited the office and headed back to the boarding house.

Clara placed a plate of eggs and bacon on the table when she saw Cody walk through the door. "Thought you might need some vittles," she said as she poured a large mug of coffee from a tin pot.

"Sorry about waking up the entire house. I won't let it happen again," he told Clara as he reached for the strong coffee. "Thanks for the breakfast too; tastes really good. Looks like I'm gonna be gone for about a week or more, so don't worry about any meals for me for awhile." He reached into his vest pocket and withdrew six silver dollars and handed the money to the landlady. "This oughta cover me for next month's rent. Hold my room for me, would you Clara?"

"That room is yours as long as you need it," she said as she pocketed the coins and returned to her cooking on the stove.

The heavy wagon lumbered ahead with Abe holding the reins. Next to him, Clyde Olson clung to the side of the hard wooden seat, his bony frame jarred with every turn of the wheels. Ike rode alongside the wagon on the left and Cody chose a short distance away from the conveyance to the right, clear of the dust stirred up by the pair of horses pulling the load. It was a clear route between Deer Springs and Fort Laramie, but at this slow pace, it would take three or four days to reach the larger town.

As Cody rode along, he let his mind consider the silver being transferred to a Fort Laramie bank and what Logan's actions meant. Just when Cody had hit the proverbial brick wall in uncovering evidence against Logan, Logan threw this trip in his lap. Was it a gift or a trap? Cody didn't believe Logan trusted him unquestioningly, hardly, more likely Logan was testing him. He had to be careful, play the hand that was dealt, learn as much as possible while being patient before he sprung his own trap.

Cody had to chuckle to himself when he recalled Olson's reaction at seeing him among Logan's men. His eyes had widened as he gasped. But the man wisely chose silence rather than question why the bumbling prospector that had previously visited his office was now the gunslinger riding shotgun protecting his precious cargo.

They rode on past dusk until the sky darkened and the wan moonlight prevented them from venturing further. The shorter autumn days provided a relief from the intense heat but not the drought that still plagued the land. Abe pulled the wagon into a short clearing. Ike and Olson prepared a campfire while Abe watered and fed the horses, leaving their traces and harnesses on the team.

Cody strung a rope between two scrub trees as a string for the horses; tying Lightning's reins to the line, he unsaddled and rubbed down the stallion. He spoke softly to the big bay as he fed him a handful of grain. The bay snorted and shook his head as if in agreement to his master's words.

"I'm taking the first lookout. Cody, you got the late watch while I get me some shut eye," Ike stated in a commanding voice, daring Jarvis to contradict him.

Cody eyed the cowhand, then shrugged as he threw his rig onto the ground and stretched out beside it. "Suits me. Wake me around one," he told Ike. Chewing on a piece of beef jerky, he sipped water from his canteen then propped his head on his saddle and lowered his Stetson over his eyes. His Colt stayed near his right hand as he caught a few winks of sleep.

Cody heard it before he saw it, despite the loud snores coming from Abe's side of the campfire. He tightened his grasp on the Colt and carefully raised the brim of his hat. His eyes quickly and thoroughly scanned the ground near him. Olson tossed and turned, restless in his sleep, kicking a burning log. Cody listened intently and heard again the distinctive rattle. He raised to his knees, peered into the dark, then fired. Exploding gunshot shattered the silent night; sound echoed off the surrounding boulders. The decapitated head of the rattlesnake flew into the air and landed near the feet of a screaming Clyde Olson. The snake's body continued to quiver and sliver without its head, the rattle noise finally dying. Acrid smoke rose into the chilly night air from the barrel of Cody's gun. He slid it back into his holster just as Ike came running back into the camp from where he had wandered off to relieve himself.

"What the hell?" shouted Abe as he wiped the sleep from his eyes and jerked free from his tangled blankets.

"Is it dead?" asked Olson, as he jumped away from the fire perimeter.

"Yeah, it's dead," Cody answered as he kicked the snake head into the fire where it sparked and hissed. He bent to pick up the body of the snake stretched next to Olson's bedroll. Two seconds later and its fangs would have found the restless man. Cody held up the length of snake and showed it to the frightened Olson. He tossed the snake to Abe. "Good eating. You cook us up some breakfast while I take the watch and Ike here can get some sleep."

Ike scratched his head and hiked up his britches. He looked over at Abe, whose hand held the snake carcass as far away from his body as his arm could stretch.

"Well, I'll be," Ike whispered. He turned to Abe, "You heard the man. Cut up that meat and throw it into a pan. I'm gonna get a few hours of shut eye before dawn."

The camp site silenced as Olson cautiously shook out his blankets and examined the ground around him before nervously lying down. Ike pulled a blanket up over his shoulder and tilted his hat across his forehead before giving in to a much-needed rest. Abe pulled a tin pan from his saddle bag and went to work slicing the snake meat into portions. Cody found a comfortable spot near the edge of the clearing where he could overlook the campsite and the stand of horses as well as keeping an eye on his fellow travelers or watching for any intruders.

Chapter 10

Laramie

They rolled into Laramie four days later. Abe pulled the wagon team to a halt behind a wooden two-story building. Ike dismounted and strode to the closed door, pounding his fist on the portal.

"Hey! Open up. Logan sent us," he shouted to the occupant on the other side of the wooden door.

The door creaked open a few inches. The narrow crack permitted Cody to make out a man's face peering from the other side; his beady eyes scrutinizing their motley group. Satisfied that he recognized at least one of the group, the man stepped out to speak with Ike.

"We got business to do," Ike told the man with a sweep of his hand indicating the iron stronghold box in the wagon bed.

The man glanced at Cody still on horseback then back to Clyde Olson as that one swung his legs over the side of the wagon to drop onto the ground. He directed his comments to Olson, "The usual transaction?"

"Um, yes, yes. The usual. Let's get this box inside, makes me nervous having it exposed where anyone can see," Olson said as he wiped a soiled bandana over his grimy features and ran a hand across his sparse hair in an effort to tidy up.

"You boys haul that box inside."

Abe crawled into the back of the buckboard and grabbed hold of a leather handle on the side of the iron box. He tugged with both hands until the heavy box slid forward where Ike could reach the other handle. They both pulled the box forward until they could lift the heavy container off the edge of the wagon then strained to carry it through the open door. Cody heard the thump of the box being dropped onto the floor or whatever table surface was inside.

Cody left Lightning tied to the back of the wagon then moseyed over to peer into the shadowy confines of the small room. Was this another one of Logan's mining offices or some kind of bank? His curiosity raced and he struggled to maintain an indifferent attitude and blank expression on his face. His eyes became accustomed to the room's dark interior as he took in a large vault that took up one wall, and opposite, a long table cluttered with ledger books and papers against the other wall. The largest scale that Cody had ever seen sat in the center of the table. Wide bowls hung from chains on each side of the pedestal and cross beam. One bowl was empty and the other contained lead weights. On the wall above the table, shelving held various sized bottles of chemicals, droppers, and tools. Cody studied the purpose of the room and knew the answer to his own question—an assay office.

Cody didn't expect a legitimate assay office. What was Logan up to? He knew better than to trust the man to make an honest transaction. There had to be a catch somewhere. He simply hadn't figured it out yet. Cody watched as Ike removed the lock on the stronghold box and lifted the heavy lid.

Olson stood next to the accessor, Adam Trent, while Abe and Ike stepped back. Cody remained near the door as he watched the careful operation. Trent lifted the glass globe and turned up the flame of an oil lamp, flooding the room with light, before he dropped chunks of ore into a rectangular pan. He donned a pair of gloves then reached for the dropper and a vial. A cloudy liquid dripped onto the rock, sizzled and ran off into the holding pan. Trent scraped the lump of ore with a tiny rock hammer and nodded in approval. He placed the nugget of silver ore into the left hanging scale and added weights until the two trays balanced. Opening a ledger book, Trent wet the end of a pencil with spit before he recorded the quantity on the ledger page. His assay office would measure and grade each sample of silver ore before stamping a hallmark symbol into the silver to identify the ingot as pure and tested. Next, Trent would ship the marked ingots to the larger assay office in Denver, Colorado. Laramie was only a branch of that office. Denver would eventually sell the ingots to the United States Mint.

"This is going to take a while. You boys go find yourself a saloon or some place to wait. I'll stay here with Mister Trent until we have a final tally," Olson told the men with an air of dismissal. The timid little man puffed up his sense of importance; he was in his element within the assay office.

"Yeah, I can use a beer right about now. C'mon Abe," said Ike as he sauntered to the door and brushed past Cody. "You comin' Jarvis?"

Cody shrugged, took one more look around, and closed the door behind him. "Something to eat and drink makes more sense than standing around watching a pile of rocks. Maybe I'll scare up a poker game."

Abe and Ike headed to the nearest saloon while Cody strolled the streets of Ft. Laramie in no particular hurry. Compared to Deer Springs, Laramie was a thriving modern metropolis. Once an important stop for the Pony Express, now the railroad connected Cheyenne to Ft. Laramie and points west, bringing the mail into the territory by train instead of horseback. The Overland Stagecoach still routed passengers through the town on its way west, providing passage for folks that couldn't afford the higher train fare.

The linking of the Union Pacific and Central Pacific railroads at Promontory, Utah in 1869 opened the continent to travelers across the nation, but it couldn't help those homesteaders seeking to claim land in the Oregon Territory. Making the arduous journey from St. Louis, Missouri across the wide plains and Rocky Mountains, carrying all of their life's possessions, still required a Conestoga wagon and a team of oxen and most still passed through Fort Laramie. Cody paused in his walk as a trio of loaded wagons lumbered down the street, headed northward, out of town.

"Hope they aren't intending to travel far. Damn fools are making a late start in the season. Likely get caught in a snowstorm in the mountains," Cody mumbled to himself as he watched the ragtag group—men driving the teams, women clinging to the hard wooden seats, and kids peeking out of the rear porthole in the canvas covering. *"God bless them. They've got a harsh road ahead."*

Cody turned the corner and wandered down a side street. He spied the telegraph office sign hanging in a window, then quickly looked around to see if anyone might be nearby who could witness him entering the office. Satisfied that the street was deserted, Cody cautiously entered the telegraph office and approached the counter.

"Need to send a telegram," he told the clerk. With pencil in hand, he deliberated and painstakingly chose his words before sending a brief message to his director. He slid the form back to the clerk.

The clerk read aloud, "ZL our man. STOP Details later. STOP signed CJ. STOP. That it?"

"Yeah, that's it. How much?"

The clerk counted the number of letters in the short missive. If he recognized the address for the recipient, he didn't comment. "Reckon two bits should cover it. Want it to go out today?"

Cody handed the coins over to the telegraph clerk. "Send it today."

Cody went to the door and after carefully checking that no eyes watched, he left the office and resumed his walk back towards the main street and the rowdy saloons.

In his mind, he was certain that Zachary Logan was their man. Logan's business dealings were as crooked as the day was long. All Cody needed was proof. There had to be more to this silver transaction than met the eye. It didn't seem logical that Logan would simply sell the silver ore and not make some kind of profit or manage to swindle folks in the process. It wasn't in his nature to be honest.

Cody pushed open the swinging doors of the Red Garter saloon. Both soldiers from the fort and cowhands filled the crowded, smoky room. Four dance hall girls pranced across a raised stage to the lively tune coming from a player piano that sat in a corner near the stage. The music frequently produced a discordant sound as the player mechanism rolled over the paper roll perforated with bullet holes and not musical notes.

He spied two separate card games in progress at tables positioned along the opposite wall from the stage. One man stood, hurled his cards onto the center of the table and stomped toward the bar. Cody calmly walked over to the table and took the empty seat.

"Howdy fellas. What's the bet?" he addressed the three players.

One man silently raked in the bets, then shuffled the cards and dealt a hand all around. He wore a red garter around the sleeve of a dingy white shirt and gave a tight-lipped grin as the game began again.

"Seven-card stud, mister. Opening bet is two bits," the dealer told Cody.

Cody nodded and tossed his coins onto the center of the table. He picked up his hand and read the cards then placed them face down on the table as he nonchalantly studied the faces of the players around the table. A nervous twitch of an eyebrow on the face of the cowhand sitting to his left, beads of sweat on the pot-bellied gentleman sitting to his right, and stone-cold eyes giving nothing away from the dealer playing for the house. No emotion. No tells that Cody could recognize. His own face wore a similar image.

They silently played three hands as bets were ante upped and called. The pot-bellied player tossed his cards on the table and slowly pushed his chair away from the table.

"I'm done. Deal me out."

The dealer raised a questioning eyebrow to Cody and the cowhand, who tapped the table in front of him to demand more cards. He was in. Cody shrugged and placed his next bet; might as well play a little longer. It'll be awhile before Olson and Trent finish the count of that silver ore.

Raucous noise increased as more men poured into the Red Garter. Cowboys, tired and thirsty from bringing in a herd of cattle off the trail and into the stockyards, pushed their way to the bar. They shouted and demanded service as they tossed hard-earned coin onto the bar. The more whiskey consumed, the louder the volume of voices rose.

A woman screamed indignantly as hands mauled her and pulled her off the stage. Cody turned to watch a drunken cowboy manhandle the dancer and her attempts to slap away his hands. Pushing his chair away from the table, Cody strode toward the couple. Within seconds he managed to separate the woman from the man's clutches then drew back a fist and cold-cocked the drunk. The man flew backwards and landed on the floor, out for the count. Two of his friends rushed forward intending to confront Cody. They came to a sudden halt at the sound of a gun being cocked.

Cody pointed his Colt at the two men. "You tell your friend he needs to mind his manners. I don't abide by the mistreatment of women."

They nodded then bent to their unconscious friend. The dance hall gal rubbed a bruised arm as she walked past Cody. "Thanks mister."

"Ma'am," Cody said as he tipped his hat to her. He frowned at the rest of the rowdy bunch then turned his attention back to the game at hand, sliding into his seat.

"Now, where were we? I'll see your five and raise you another five dollars," Cody said as he tossed a handful of silver dollars into the pot. He raised his eyes to the dealer's face and saw a flicker of uncertainty.

The cowhand threw his cards down and held his hands up, "Too rich for my blood. I fold."

"Looks like it's just the two of us, mister," the dealer stated. "I call." He flipped his hand over, face up, and revealed a full house.

Cody leisurely turned his cards over and watched the grin on the dealer's face disappear. A winning straight flush, all spades, lined up like little soldiers from the ten-card down to the six. Cody reached for the pile of money in the center of the table. A hand pressing down on his halted him.

"You're a cheat," the dealer growled.

Chairs scraped the wooden floor as men nearby rapidly backed out of the way. Cody slowly stood and faced the poor loser. His right hand rested near the hilt of his gun. He studied the man's expression.

"That's a lie. I'm just the better player. You're the cheat. I watched you deal yourself cards from the bottom of the deck," Cody stated in an ominous voice.

The dealer worriedly looked about. The crowded room had grown quiet, a few mumbled comments reached his ears. He stood alone facing the stranger. The specter of death hung between them. Making his decision, he lifted his hands palms upward and stepped back.

"Take it," he nodded toward the pot of money. "If I draw on you, you'll kill me."

"Probably." Cody picked up his winnings.

He handed the astonished cowhand his original ante before stuffing the rest of the money into his pocket. "Choose your games more wisely," Cody told the cowhand as he tipped his hat then cautiously backed out to the door. He waited ten minutes on the street to make sure no one followed before he walked away in search of Ike and Abe.

Chapter 11

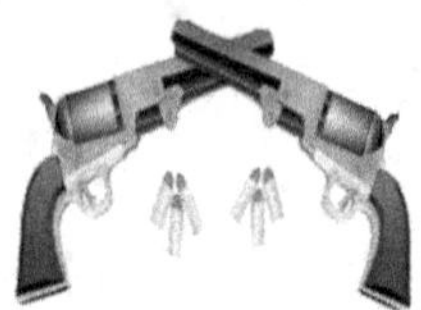

Assay Office

Adam Trent meticulously counted the currency in stacks of hundreds as Clyde Olson looked on and annotated his ledger book. Trent bundled the silver certificate bills and held them together with paper straps then scribbled the total amount on each strap.

Cody watched the procedure from his position near the door. Abe and Ike stood to one side; their eyes gleamed at the thought of so much money. When the assay officer finished, he handed a form to Olson to sign. The entire procedure appeared to be legal and handled correctly. So why did Cody think he was missing something?

Olson packed the bundled currency into the same iron stronghold box and snapped the padlock closed. He held out his hand to Ike.

"The key please," Olson demanded as Ike produced the skeleton key to the lock and Olson tucked it into his waistcoat pocket.

"I found us some rooms for the night. We'll leave early in the morning to head back," Ike told the group.

"Perfect. I'll need a private room and the box stays with me," Olson stated.

"Figured you say that. C'mon let's go."

Abe hefted the iron box, much lighter without the silver ore, and placed it on the wagon seat. Olson climbed up next to it with Abe once again taking the reins. Cody and Ike both mounted their horses and followed the wagon as it traveled through town and turned onto a side street away from the saloons they had visited earlier.

A large two-story house sat alone across from the black-smith's forge. Abe pulled the wagon into the yard and climbed down. He waited on Olson to jump to the ground then hoisted the iron box to his shoulder and climbed the steps to the front door. A wooden painted sign, nailed to the wall, read *Boarders.* He rapped lightly on the portal as the men joined him on the steps.

Cody and Abe had tied their horses onto the hitching post near the wagon. Lightning immediately began chomping on the long grass bordering the edge of a wilted flower garden. Cody would see to his water and feed once he got himself settled.

A middle-aged woman with a young child on her hip opened the front door wide and ushered in the men. She gave them a quick perusal and nodded.

"Thank you kindly madam for your hospitality," Olson said as he handed the woman a silver dollar. "I trust this will cover the cost of two rooms for the night?"

"Yes sir. I have a small room ready for you with one bed and the other gentlemen can share the larger room with two beds at the top of the stairs and to the left." She reached into a pocket of her apron and produced two room keys. "This key is for the single room," she said as she handed the key to Olson and the other to Abe.

"Thank you. We need to leave early in the morning. Would you have any coffee ready at that time?"

"I can fix a plate of biscuits and gravy and a pot of coffee," she said.

The men murmured their thanks and climbed the stairs to find their quarters. Abe opened the door to the large room and noted a single bed along one wall and a wider double bed under the window.

Cody immediately claimed the single bed and placed his saddle bag and rifle on the foot of the bed. He raised an eyebrow and shot Logan's men a look that dared them to question the sleeping arrangements. They grumbled but turned away.

Dawn brought bright sunlight through the bedroom window, waking Abe and Ike with the light on their faces. Abe grumbled and rolled over, but Ike pushed him out of bed. He hit the floor with a thud and a curse.

"Get up! We've got to get a move on," Ike commanded.

Cody hung his legs over the side of his bed and stretched then slid his feet into his boots. He buttoned his shirt then walked over to the bowl and pitcher of water setting on the washstand. Splashing water onto his face, he wiped the sleep from his eyes. Cody dragged fingers through his hair in a half effort to comb the thick locks then picked up his hat. The smell of hot coffee drew him downstairs, where a pot and mugs were waiting on them as promised.

A plate of flaky biscuits and a bowl of thick gravy sat in the center of the table. Cody placed a biscuit with a spoonful of gravy on one plate and poured a mug of coffee. He had just taken a forkful of the delicious food when Olson stumbled into the room, still half asleep.

"Grab yourself a mug, the morning will look a heap better to you," Cody suggested to the little man.

Abe stomped into the room, the stronghold box in his arms. He deposited it on the floor near the doorway with a thud, then moved to the table and rubbed his hands together in anticipation of the food and drink.

Ike growled as he entered the dining room and grabbed a cup of the hot brew. "Aargh, hardly slept a wink with this walrus snoring in my ear all dang night. And you better wipe that grin off your face, Jarvis! I ain't gonna bed down with this clown no more."

Cody couldn't contain the chuckle from behind his coffee mug as he listened to Ike's complaint. Personally, he had a good night's rest despite Abe's loud snoring, however; he was grateful he'd slept on the other side of the room.

Ike was in a foul mood as he tossed down a biscuit and swallowed his coffee so hurriedly. It had to burn his throat on the way down.

"C'mon, saddle up. Let's get going," Ike growled again and headed out the door.

Cody laughed and slapped Olson on the back, "Looks like it's gonna be a long day."

Two hours north of Fort Laramie, Cody turned in his saddle and listened to the sound of riders coming up fast behind them. Swirls of dust filled the air as a trio of riders galloped closer to them.

Ike spotted the approaching men too and signaled to Abe to whip those horses and speed up the wagon.

"We can't outrun them," shouted Cody to Ike. He spotted an outcropping of rocks ahead with a slight rise.

Cody rode alongside the wagon and gestured to Abe, pointing to the spot ahead where they could take cover. "Get into that outcrop and get down off that wagon. Be ready to fight."

They galloped toward the meager protection, Abe shouting to the team and Olson clinging to the wagon seat for dear life. Cody and Ike spurred their own horses forward.

The trio of bandits wore bandanas across their faces and kept coming faster and closer. One rider in the lead drew his gun and fired a shot at the fleeing wagon. The bullet struck the wooden tailgate of the buckboard, splinters flying.

Abe pulled hard on the reins of the team and turned the wagon sharply. It careened and tilted dangerously before righting itself and grinding to a halt. Ike and Cody jumped down from their mounts and crouched behind a grouping of boulders in the narrow ravine.

"Get behind those rocks or under the wagon," Cody shouted to Olson as the frightened man jumped off his seat and stood frozen, uncertain of what to do. A bullet whizzed past his head, too close for comfort, making the poor man fall to the ground and roll under the wagon bed. Olson covered his head with his arms, curling into a fetal position.

Satisfied that Olson was safe, Cody turned to the matter at hand and took aim at the charging riders. His shot hit the arm of one man, causing that person to slouch forward although he managed to keep his seat in the saddle. The other bandits fired as they raced toward them, bullets ricocheted off the surrounding rocks. Abe and Ike launched a hail of gunfire. Thunderous noise and acrid gun smoke filled the air. Their volley struck another of the would-be robbers. Cody moved behind a protruding rock and took careful aim at the leader of the pack as the lone bandit circled around to renew his attack. Cody's bullet hit the man dead center in his chest; his body fell onto the ground. The remaining wounded bandit turned tail and galloped away; his life, the only reward he would claim that day.

Abe and Ike slowly rose from their crouched positions and joined Cody as they walked toward the fallen men. The man Ike had shot still breathed, but barely alive; his eyes fluttered open. Cody kicked the gun away from his hand and pulled down the makeshift mask to expose his face.

"You know these men?" asked Cody. Abe and Ike both shook their heads no. "How'd they know about the money? They sure as hell planned to rob us."

Abe flushed a deep red and shuffled his feet as he stared at the sprawled bodies then looked away. Ike swung a fist at Abe, glancing off his jawline.

"Who'd you talk to, Abe? You stupid son of a bitch, you were drunk and shot your mouth off, didn't you? You could'a got us all killed," Ike swore at his partner.

"I dunno, maybe. I don't remember," Abe whined.

"All right. It's done. Pick up the weapons and let's get back on the road. We need to put some distance between us and Fort Laramie before someone else tries their hand at getting that money," Cody said.

Olson crawled out from under the wagon. His body trembled, but he took a deep breath then dusted off his clothes before climbing back up onto the seat. He checked the stronghold box, still secure sitting on the floorboards. Abe shifted the burlap bag of provisions in the back of the buckboard and tossed the two recovered gun belts and six-guns onto the bed. Shoving his hat further onto his head, he climbed onto the wagon and pulled on the reins to turn the wagon toward the trail once more. He knew he'd be in trouble when Logan heard about the incident.

Chapter 12

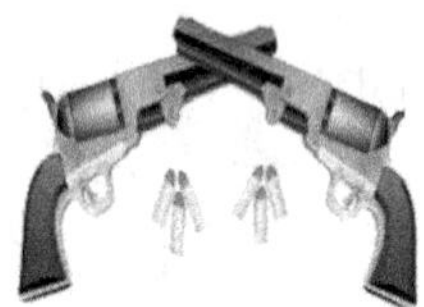

Counterfeit

Three days later, they rode into Deer Springs. There were no more incidents of hijacking attempts, but Cody decided not to chance it. Men and beasts were now both close to exhaustion from having pushed themselves to cover the distance in a shorter amount of time.

Abe pulled the wagon into the alley behind the mining office. Clyde Olson jumped down and opened his rear door; his cluttered office never looked so good. Abe followed him inside, hefting the iron box and tossing it onto a pile of papers littering the desk.

"Jarvis...thanks for getting us back in one piece," Ike said, the words bitter in his throat. His raspy voice reflected his level of fatigue and he reluctantly offered to shake Cody's hand.

Cody shook the man's hand and nodded in acknowledgment. He recognized the effort it took for Ike to thank him.

"No problem. You did some fancy shooting back there, too."

Cody slowly walked alongside Lightning, headed toward the stables at the end of the street. The stallion tossed his head, eager to be home in his stall.

"Howdy Clem," Cody greeted the old-timer as he unbuckled Lightnings cinch and removed the saddle and gear. He patted the horse's rump and rubbed the stallion's nose as the horse snickered and tossed his head, enjoying the affectionate touch. "How's it going?"

Clem scratched his head and pulled on his suspenders before he hung a fresh pail of water in Lightning's stall and added a bag of grain.

"Been quiet in town. Where'd you run off to? Haven't seen them Logan men hanging around either."

"Yeah, well, I rode down to Fort Laramie with Ike and Abe. Guess you could say I provided protection for a transfer of silver ore and cash."

"Humph. That a fact." Clem spit tobacco juice onto the floor of the stable. "Well, I guess you know what you're doin'."

"All part of the game, Clem. Give Lightning a good rub down, won't ya? He deserves it. Keep me posted if you hear anything of interest. I'm gonna climb into a hot bath; I smell like an old goat."

"You do at that," chuckled the old man.

Cody reached for the heavy kettle of hot water and waved Clara off. There was no need for the woman to do more heavy work. He could carry his own bath water. He poured the hot water into the tub already half full then carried the kettle back into the kitchen to fill it again from the water pump. The muscles in his arm rhythmically pumped the handle up and down until the water flowed freely and the kettle was full once more. Cody set the heavy iron kettle on top of the stove.

"You'll be wanting some food when you're done," Clara stated. "I'll fix you a plate and leave it on the table for you."

"Thanks, Clara. Appreciate your kindness. Right now, I just want to soak some sore muscles and get rid of my own stench."

Cody closed the door to the bath and peeled off his clothes then lowered himself into the waiting hot water. A sigh of relief escaped his lips as he closed his eyes and rested his head on the edge of the tub.

He was too tired to think. It had been a long trip to Laramie and back. Cody didn't feel any closer now to discovering Logan's counterfeit operation than before. What had he learned? Silver ore got transferred to an assay office in Laramie for cash. So what? Nothing wrong with that transaction. There had to be more. What was he missing?

Cody groaned his frustrations as he finished lathering himself with soap; his mind still mulling over the puzzle. He wrapped a towel around his hips, the thin cloth barely covered him. With one hand gripping the towel and his Colt, the other juggled the plate of food as he quickly headed upstairs to his room before he encountered and shocked any of the resident females.

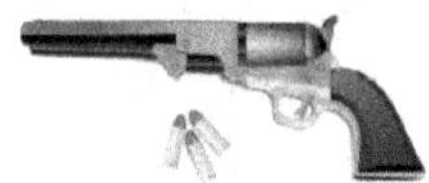

After wolfing down his food, Cody sauntered over to the Silver Spur. Standing at the bar with one foot propped on the brass rail, he casually surveyed the room and its occupants. As he sipped his beer, Hank Jergens entered the saloon and ordered a whiskey, tossing a dollar bill onto the bar. Kelly picked up the currency and rubbed it between his fingers.

"This bill is so crisp, it crackles. Fresh off the printer, Hank?"

"Yeah, right. Fresh from the bank, you mean. Me and my partner just got paid by Olson for a load of silver ore. Took us over a year to mine that," Hank explained.

The appearance of the crisp bill caught Cody's attention. He listened to Hank's comment and thought of the money he had witnessed being counted and loaded into the stronghold box in Fort Laramie. That currency wasn't newly printed; it showed creases and dirty smudges with a few torn corners like most circulated money.

Cody reached for the dollar bill before Kelly could slide it into the cash drawer. Kelly started to object, but Cody's hand was faster.

"Never seen a new bill like that. Relax Kelly, I'll give it back." Cody turned the bill over and studied the engraving and portrait on the money. The printing looked good, but it was counterfeit. He was sure. Where would Hank Jergens get a counterfeit bill?

He handed the money back to the bartender without another word and downed his last swallow of beer. Nodding to Kelly, he turned and headed out the saloon doors. Cody ambled across the street, stepped onto the wooden sidewalk and passed in front of the mining office as he headed toward the boarding house.

A single oil lamp burned in the dark mining office. Olson sat at his desk working in the shadows. Stacks of money were piled neatly in three rows across the desktop. Cody stood to one side of the building and peeked into the window to watch the scrawny man transfer bank straps from each pile of worn currency onto a new crisp bundle. Olson placed the old money into a box and the newly printed currency went into a tray within the squat vault.

Cody heard voices coming from the Silver Spur, so he rapidly moved away from the window and hid within the alley shadows between the buildings. His mind raced to conclusions about what he had just witnessed. Olson and Logan ran legitimate money through the mining office and substituted it with counterfeit money when they paid out the vouchers given to prospectors. The miners wouldn't suspect the money given to them and the bogus bills would circulate around town. That had to be the game. The problem was how to prove it and where to find the printing press creating the funny money.

Chapter 13

Midnight Search

A sliver of moon peeked from beneath a carpet of thick gray clouds. The portent of winter weather moved onto the land. Temperatures had dropped overnight, and the pre-dawn hour remained bitter cold and dark.

Cody turned up the sheepskin collar and huddled within his heavy coat as he crept into the alley separating the mining office and Clara's boarding house. Before moving forward, he paused to listen. A cloak of silence had shrouded the town. A lone wolf howled in the distance.

He felt along the side of the building, peeked into a single narrow window set high on the wall to insure all was dark inside, then made his way to the rear door. Cody knelt to insert a thin rod into the keyhole and carefully jiggled the doorknob as he worked to pick the lock. A satisfying click and the knob turned. He stepped into the blackness and gently closed the door behind him.

"Umph," Cody muttered as he bumped into the corner of a table jutting out from the wall. The cramped office definitely had no room for a printing press or any other device unless it sat underground. He peered into the pitch darkness, searching for a trap door to a lower level. Cody crawled on hands and knees, running his hands across the wooden floorboards seeking a hinge or loose boards that would lead to a basement. Nothing. All he got for his trouble was a splinter in the palm of his left hand.

Cody stood and brushed off his pant legs then listened by the door. All quiet. He slowly eased the portal open and slipped out into the night. Dashing across the street, he moved to the rear entrance of the Silver Spur and Logan's office. Maybe if he hurried, he could finally get a look inside before morning dawned and folks roused.

Cody edged toward the door, glancing all around, then jumped suddenly as he stepped on the tail of a sleeping cat.

The cat screeched indignantly, "Rroww!"

The shrill sound was enough to wake the dead. Cody shrunk back into the shadows; his heart thumped in his chest as he tried to calm his breathing. He looked up at the pale blush painting the sky as the sun began to rise. Another failed attempt. He'd have to wait again to explore Logan's office and look for a possible hidden basement.

A cigarette ember glowed red in the early morning light and a pair of watchful eyes looked down on a fleeting figure sneak across the street and slip back into Clara's boardinghouse. Ike stood in the bedroom window of the bordello; he scratched his whiskered jaw and wondered what Jarvis was up to. Should he mention anything to Logan or wait and play that chip when he needed it? Maybe he'd just wait and see.

A lone Conestoga wagon limped through town pulled by two exhausted oxen ready to collapse at any moment. The man and woman clinging to the high wooden seat beneath a torn canvas didn't look much better and appeared to be all done in. Their faces wore a defeated expression that Cody had seen too many times in the past. Standing on the sidewalk outside the general store, he shook his head as he watched the wagon creep past and head out of town. Another disappointed dreamer on the way to Oregon; obviously left behind as their caravan went on without them.

"Hope they find shelter somewhere before winter weather hits us; it won't be long now," Cody spoke his thoughts out loud.

He turned and entered the store. Browsing through a copy of the St. Louis Star-Times, only three weeks old, Cody read about the exploits of Wyatt Earp and Doc Holliday in Tombstone and the outlaws known as the Cochise County Cowboys. The reporter who wrote the story focused on the friendship between the lawman and the gambler gunslinger. Cody read the account, lost in thought, and didn't notice the store clerk until he spoke behind him.

"Just got those newspapers in. Ain't that something? Sounds like that there place in Arizona is really wild. Sure glad we don't have that kind of trouble here in Deer Springs," Morgan exclaimed as he pointed to the tintype picture of Wyatt Earp on the front page.

"Yeah, it's an interesting story," Cody agreed as he picked up one issue to buy. He added a plug of tobacco and papers for rolling cigarettes and a pair of woolen gloves. Cody placed his items on the counter and watched Morgan tally the cost.

"Reckon you owe me one dollar and seventy-five cents," the clerk said as he checked his math and nodded once more. "Yep, that'll do it."

Cody paid the clerk, stuffed the cigarette makings into his pocket and tucked the rolled newspaper under his arm. He glanced up as several people entered the store and he stepped out of the way to make room for a mother and two children followed by a pair of soldiers. He nodded to both groups, then left the store and crossed to the Silver Spur.

Several horses were tied to the hitching posts in front of the saloon; all wore trappings and brands of the US Army. Cody entered the saloon and noted four soldiers gathered by the bar. They wore the dark blue wool uniform with insignia and Hardee hat of the cavalry. Deciding to steer clear of them, he headed over to the table where Logan sat, his back to the wall, watching over his realm.

Cody slid into a seat next to Logan. "Busy today. Looks like we've got some visitors from out of town."

"Hmm, looks like we do. Keep an eye on things, Jarvis. Make sure there's no trouble while our men in blue are in town. Don't give them any reason to stay longer. Understand?" Logan commanded as he twirled the ends of his mustache and studied the soldiers speaking with Kelly.

Cody caught the bartender's eye and pointed at the table. Kelly nodded and brought over a pilsner of beer. He set it down in front of Cody then paused, looked back at the soldiers then stared at Cody again.

Snapping his fingers, Kelly spoke in an accusing tone, "I knew I'd remember where I'd seen you before...Ft. Lyons. Yeah, you were in the Army. Seeing those soldiers made the connection."

Logan studied Cody; his expression wary as he silently waited for his explanation.

"Yeah, well, everyone gets to be a sucker at least once in your life. The Army and me parted company years ago," Cody stated as he leaned back in his chair, a sneer curling his lips.

Logan gave a humorless laugh. His eyes never left Cody's face as his mind considered several possibilities, none to his liking.

Chapter 14

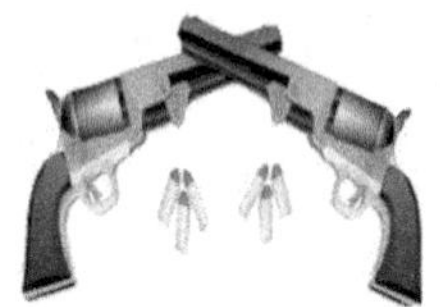

Clem

Deer Springs was bustling and growing day by day as more men moved into the region searching for gold and silver. Some of the wooden clapboards still wore that bleached look from freshly milled lumber, the older establishments wore weathered or painted fronts. A new dry goods store had opened next to the barber. A bank had recently been added along with a land office for recording deeds of acreage to the new homesteaders. Residing over it all was Logan's stamp of approval or claim of ownership, or it didn't get built.

Cody pulled up his collar against the cold winds blowing down the street. Ominous looking clouds filled the sky with the threat of the first winter storm on the horizon. He walked into the Silver Spur and had to elbow his way up to the bar among the crowds of men standing about.

Some men bragged about their mining claims, others voiced plans for building big ranches. Most were pipe dreams that would fail soon enough when the demands of the land or the harsh climate defeated the unprepared dreamers. Cody raised an eyebrow and shot Kelly a questioning look as he heard the bartender charge an unusually high price for beer. Kelly shrugged in reply to Cody's unspoken question. He nodded toward Logan's office, as if that said it all. Boss's orders.

Cody rapped on the office door and entered at Logan's muffled reply. He was surprised to find Ike and Abe both waiting on the boss' instructions. What was he up to now?

"Heard tell we got another one of those foreigners staking claim to some land north of here. Go find out what you can about them. They claimed a rich parcel that I had my eye on. See if you can convince them to move on," Logan insisted. He leaned back in his chair and stroked the ends of his mustache then turned his attention to the ledger book in front of him. They'd been dismissed.

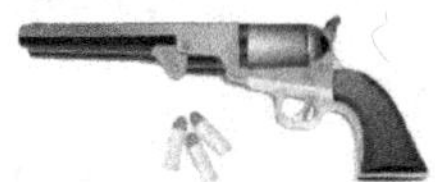

Clem shoveled the muck from the stalls and started raking the loose straw when four men entered the stable. His hunched back and elderly appearance belied the agility and strength he showed as he turned suddenly to confront the men. Clem waved the rake menacingly, his only weapon at hand.

"We need answers, old man. You tell us what we want to know, and you might live to see tomorrow," one man growled.

Clem took a step backwards, his back to the empty stall, holding the rake before him like a lance as the men slowly advanced.

"Give it up old codger."

"You're mighty friendly with Cody Jarvis. When did he get to town? Where's he from?" asked the taller of the men. Clem recognized him as Fuller, one of Logan's gun hands.

"I dunno. I just stable his horse for him," Clem stated defiantly. He waved the rake again, but the heavy-set goon yanked it from his grasp.

"Who's Jarvis working for?" demanded the ugly, pock-marked thug. He punched Clem in the gut.

Two horses in the stable stomped their hooves and snorted angrily at the perceived threat. Clem's mare whinnied and kicked at her stall.

Clem bent over, as he tried to fill his lungs with air. "I told you; I don't know nothing about the man," he wheezed.

The heavy-set man punched Clem in the face. "You better start telling us what you do know."

"What's he doing in Deer Springs?" asked Fuller.

"Working for Logan," spat Clem.

Fuller stood back and nodded to the men to continue. The other three thugs punched and kicked the poor old man until he lay curled on a pile of hay unconscious, bruised and bleeding.

"We ain't gonna get anything from him," complained pock-mark.

"Jarvis is staying down at that boarding house. Let's have a look at his room. Maybe his landlady will be more cooperative," Fuller snickered as he stomped out of the stable.

The men followed him, leaving the stable door wide open. Frigid wind and snowflakes blew into the opening, scattering chaffs of straw. The horses strained at their ties, grunting and snorting as they broke loose.

Fuller pounded on the faded blue door of Clara's boarding-house. He pushed it wide open as soon as Clara had unlatched it. She stumbled backwards.

"Hey! You can't come in here that a way. What do you want?" Clara demanded in an outraged voice.

"What room belongs to Jarvis? Stay out of our way, woman, and you won't get hurt," Fuller told her as he and his goons climbed the stairs. "We'll search every room up here until you tell us."

Clara wrung her hands as she watched the men storm up the stairs. Deciding she couldn't risk losing the schoolmarm's income if she left, she called up to the searching men.

"Second door on the left."

"Now you're being smart. Unlock it or we'll kick the door in," warned Fuller.

Clara hurried up the steps with her ring full of keys. Her hand shook as she unlocked the bedroom door and stood back.

The four men rushed into the room. One man tore off the blankets from the bed, flipped the mattress over and searched underneath. Finding nothing, he tossed the bedding onto the floor. Clara watched from the doorway as the taller man pulled open the chest drawers and rummaged through the few belongings stored by Cody.

"Ah ha, what do we have here?" Fuller made a satisfying sound as he pulled out a rolled map from the bottom drawer. He brandished it about like a prize of war. "C'mon, there isn't anything else here."

He stomped out of the room followed closely by the other men. The pock-marked thug pushed Clara out of the way as he stormed down the stairs and out of the house.

Clara heard the front door slam shut, then surveyed the damage the ruffians had caused. The porcelain wash bowl and pitcher lay busted in two; the washstand reclined on its side. The drawers were all pulled out of the chest and strewn about the room. They had pulled away the chest from the wall and turned it over. Cody's clothing, what little there was of it, tossed onto the floor.

"Damn them!" Clara shook her head disgustedly. Suddenly a new thought came to her ... Clem. He had befriended Cody.

She ran down the steps, threw a cloak over her shoulders and rushed out into the howling wind and snowfall that began covering the ground. Clara dashed to the stable and found the doors hanging open, the sound of angry animals greeted her.

"Clem!" she called out as she searched the barn, gasping when she spied booted legs extending out of a stall. "Oh my

God, Clem. What did they do to you?" Clara cried as she bent to her injured friend.

The mare stood in the stall next to Clem's body. She nuzzled Clem's head and shoulders and whinnied softly. Clara patted the mare's head and pulled gently on her bridle.

"C'mon now. He'll be okay. I'll get him fixed up. Move back now," she told the horse. She tied the mare into the stall next to Clem before she ran outside again, braving the winter storm, to seek help.

The first person that Clara saw was the madame of Dollie's Darlins standing in the doorway of the bordello. Clara latched onto her arm.

"Maizie, have you seen Doc Porter? Clem's down at the stable beat up bad. He needs help."

The woman took one look at the worry on Clara's face and nodded. "He's here. Upstairs attending to one of my girls that got abused by a heavy fist. I'll go get him. You go back to Clem."

"Thank you! Tell him to hurry. I just hope we're not too late."

She left the woman looking after her as she dashed back to the stable, her cloak flying behind her like the sail of a great ship.

The doctor joined Clara in the stable ten minutes later. He knelt down next to the injured man and examined the injuries as best he could. Clara tenderly rubbed a wet cloth across the grizzled face to clean away the dried blood.

"Can you hold that lantern closer?" asked the doctor. "That's good. How long ago did this happen?"

"I don't rightly know. Not long, I think. I think the brutes who did this ransacked my place. When they left; that's when I thought of old Clem. I hurried right down here and found him like this." Tears sprung to her eyes as she stared at her dear old friend. "Is he gonna make it, Doc?"

"He's hurt bad. Can he stay with you? We need to move him. He's gonna need round-the-clock nursing for awhile. I don't like the looks of that head wound. I hope he comes to soon," the doctor said as he listened to Clem's thin breathing.

"I'll keep him and look after him, but how we gonna get him to my place?"

"Go ask Maizie for help. She oughta be able to find a couple of strong lads," the doctor suggested.

Clara stood and wrapped her cloak about her shoulders then ventured into the blowing snow again. She rapped on the red door and called out for Maizie. The woman opened the door just wide enough for Clara to squeeze through, shutting it quickly against the blast of cold air.

"Doc needs help. Round up a couple of strong men to carry poor Clem to my place. Can you do that?"

"Yeah, there's a pair of fellas upstairs. I'll go roust them and tell them to put their britches back on," Maizie said with a chuckle as she climbed the stairs and called out to her girls as she gained the upper hallway.

"Candy! Tell that cowpoke I need him. If he lends a hand he can have a free one. Git him out here now."

She pounded on the next door and offered the same deal then returned to Clara waiting by the front door. Two men stumbled down the stairs, buttoning their shirts and shrugging on coats. One man had a pock-marked face that Clara recognized and the other was a stranger. Clara stared at the ruffian who had left her house, their eyes held until the thug had the sense to look away. Clara held her tongue and made no accusations. She needed this man to carry Clem, but she'd remember him all right.

Clara led the two men back to the stable where Doctor Porter waited. The doctor had wrapped Clem in a cocoon of horse blankets to protect the injured man. He glanced up as Clara joined him and nodded at the two men.

"Careful now, one take his head and shoulders, the other hold his legs. Lift him up. Try not to jostle him too much. Clara you lead the way," the doctor ordered.

Clara ran ahead and prepared a cot near the fireplace in the dining room. She pushed the table and chairs over to the side to make room for the makeshift bed where she could keep Clem close to her.

The men laid Clem onto the bed. The pock-marked man turned with one last look at the landlady and the doctor before he hurried back to the bordello. Doctor Porter and Clara were too busy unwrapping Clem from his blankets to pay him any mind.

The doctor ran his hands across the old man's chest and received a grunt of pain from his patient. He checked for any open wounds on his body but found only ugly bruises.

"I need some strips of cloth. I'm afraid Clem has a couple of broken ribs and the only thing I can do for him is to strap him up tight to prevent movement until they heal. Poor codger suffered some well-placed kicks."

Tears filled Clara's eyes, but she swallowed to hold them at bay.

Clara ripped a sheet into long lengths then helped the doctor wrap the cloth around Clem's narrow chest. Clara applied a bandage to his head. The cuts and scrapes on his face were cleaned and a soothing salve added. Now all they could do was wait.

"I'll be back tomorrow to check on him. When he wakes, just give him some water and maybe a thin soup to eat. Keep him lying still."

"Thanks, Doc," she said as she closed the door behind him and latched it secure.

She stood looking at her friend who lay asleep, his chest rising and falling in shallow breaths. Clara's anger simmered with a determination to see the scoundrels that did this to her friend brought to justice and made to pay for what they did. Just wait. Their time would come when Cody Jarvis learned of their dastardly deed. Where is that man?

Chapter 15

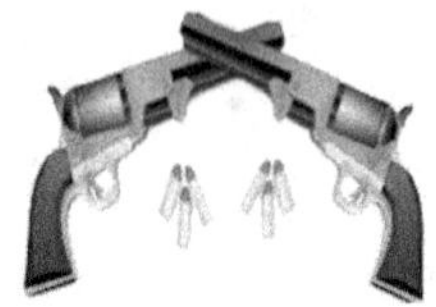

Dunlap

Wind howled and snow continued to fall on the plains. The three riders pushed forward, hunched over their horse's necks. Each man pulled down their hats low on foreheads and turned up heavy coat collars to fight the frigid temperatures.

Cody turned in his saddle and narrowed his eyes as he tried to make out the shapes of Ike or Abe in the near white-out conditions of the snowstorm. They were supposed to be riding to his left, but he couldn't spot them now. Couldn't make out any shapes. Where were they?

This was a foolish idea to ride out to some homestead in this kind of weather and threaten them to move out. Logan must be crazy, and he must be even crazier to have gone along with the hair-brained scheme. Winter was no time to force a land grab. Cody's thoughts swirled in his head like the snowflakes swirling around him. He had just decided that he'd had enough of this foolishness when he heard a shot ring out and felt the blow of the bullet smashing into his chest.

Cody tried to hang on as his world turned black and he tumbled from the saddle, fingers curled around Lightning's reins. His last conscious impression was the cold, wet snow seeping through his clothes as the heavy snow buried him in its white blanket.

James Dunlap and his new Irish friend, Michael Canavan, struggled to get home in the heavy snowstorm. A deer carcass lay draped across the rump of Michael's horse. The two men had gone hunting to put meat on the table and had traveled far afield from their homesteads before they managed to kill the lone deer. The storm had developed swiftly. Temperatures plummeted, forcing the hunters to give up their plans of bagging more game and seek shelter.

Their horses plodded through the deep snow. Ahead, a dark object appeared on the wintry horizon. The object moved, shifted slightly.

James Dunlap rubbed his eyes and looked again. Surely the storm was playing tricks on him. He peered into the snow-filled distance and tried to determine if the image was real or just his imagination.

"Do you see a big horse ahead?" he asked his friend.

Michael Canavan stared in front of him, concentrating on identifying the object. As they shortened the distance between them, he pointed and coaxed his own horse forward.

"Saints preserve us. It's a horse, to be sure." The wind carried away his words.

James Dunlap and his wife, Margaret, had left their Scottish home back in March. They had traveled over two months by ship then an arduous overland coach to Independence, Missouri, where they joined a wagon train to head westward for the promised land of Oregon. The trek was fraught with late spring rains and flooded rivers, impossible to cross then weeks of walking and driving their oxen across the wide prairies only to break down in early September with a broken wheel axle and exhausted animals in rugged Wyoming. The arduous journey had worn down their spirits as much as it destroyed their team. Their dreams of reaching Oregon had dissolved as they watched the wagon train roll on without them.

The green horn immigrants would have perished where they dropped if not for the generosity and charity of another immigrant family. Michael and Rose Canavan were a young family that had also arrived in the New World a year earlier from Ireland. They took the Scots under their wing and advised them to file for a homestead grant of one hundred and sixty acres. Michael and James cleared a small parcel of the land, cut the timber then Michael taught James how to erect a crude log cabin for shelter. The women worked to mix the adobe mortar then packed it between the log chinks, filling gaps to keep air from whistling through the cracks. They covered the packed dirt floor with wooden planks salvaged from their Conestoga wagon and a large stone fireplace provided heat. It was a sturdier structure than the sod houses built by other homesteaders found along the trail.

James and Margaret rationed what provisions they had packed within the covered wagon, praying it would be enough to last the brutal winter months. It was too late in the season to grow any food, but James hoped to supplement their meager food with small game he caught in snares. Come spring, they would plant a vegetable garden.

Michael had suggested to James that they go deer hunting and would divide the meat between their two families. The men had left three days earlier before the storm had struck. Now they approached the dark stallion standing in a snow drift.

James dismounted and slowly approached the abandoned horse. He was a magnificent animal. As he extended his hand to the stallion to sniff, James noticed the pair of reins that dangled from the stallion's head and ended in a hand partially concealed in the snow. He almost jumped back at the sight.

"Michael! There's a man buried in the snow. Come quick," shouted James.

Both men bent to the pile of snow and dug with their hands to uncover a wounded man, more dead than alive. Red blood soaked the front of the man's coat; however, it appeared the cold snow had stopped the bleeding. As they dug him out and attempted to lift him, his coat crackled from the frozen blood and ice encasing him.

It was a mercy he felt no pain in his unconscious state. They laid him across the saddle of the huge horse and tied him in place. Michael mounted his own steed then took the reins of the big horse to lead him away.

Margaret Dunlap jumped up, startled by the door thrown wide, the sewing on her lap fell to the floor. A rush of cold air and snow flurries filled the space. James and Michael half dragged - half carried a man into the cabin. She raised questioning eyes to her husband; he only shook his head.

"Give us a hand, Margaret. We found him buried in the deep snow. He's wounded and lost a lot of blood. Doubt he'll survive through the night, but we couldn't leave him on the plains for the wolves to gnaw on," James explained.

They laid the frozen man on a pallet of blankets near the hearth. Ice crystals encrusted his hair and beard while his skin wore the color of ash. Margaret knelt next to him; her fingers worked to pry open the ice-encased coat buttons, while James grunted and pulled to remove frozen boots and pants.

"I'll be going to my own home now before the snow deepens. As soon as I butcher that deer, I'll be back with your share of the meat," Michael said as he looked at the man lying deathly still. "I feel I know him from somewhere, but I can't be sure." He shrugged and pulled his collar up.

James nodded then saw Michael to the door. "You be careful out there," he told his friend with a wave of farewell before he latched the portal closed against the storm's fury.

Margaret placed several flat rocks to heat among the burning logs then drew them out with the fireplace poker and positioned them alongside the wounded stranger to help warm him through the layers of thick blankets. She feared there was little she could do for him except to keep his body warm and comfortable. Margaret took a cloth, wet it in warm water from the kettle, and began to gently clean her patient's face. She blushed slightly as she realized the train of her thoughts. *He could be a handsome man if the thick black beard was removed along with the grime.*

Cody lay in a deep sleep while a high fever ravaged his body. He thrashed about. Nightmarish dreams filled his head even as his mind struggled to rise from stygian depths.

Margaret and James took turns watching the feverish man. Margaret cursed her lack of real medical knowledge and could only provide common sense nursing applications. She cooled his burning forehead with handfuls of packed snow and wrapped a tight bandage around his chest then prayed the bullet wound would not tear open with his violent movements. At least his skin had returned to a normal color.

After two days, the fever broke. The wounded man's sleep became more restful. Margaret breathed a sigh of relief as she neared her patient.

Was this heaven? The most beautiful angel hovered over him. Her light scent filled the small space. She bent over and placed her hand on his brow. Cody watched her through half-closed eyes. *He must be delirious.*

Margaret moved about the confines of the small cabin, tending to a pot cooking over the hearth or mending a ripped garment. Cody's eyes followed her movements, watching her.

She jumped at the sound of his hoarse voice as he tried to speak. She rushed to the pallet and held a ladle of water to his parched lips, quenching his thirst, then smiled, returning his studious gaze.

"Where am I?" Cody's deep baritone voice questioned.

"Lie still. You're in my home and you're safe now. I fear you were near death's door."

"If that be true, dear lady, then it must be your gentle hands that have pulled me back. Might I know the name of my savior?"

"Margaret Dunlap. My husband, James, found you in the storm."

"I'm grateful, Maggie. I'm forgetting my manners. You've introduced yourself and I haven't even told you my name. It's Cody Jarvis, ma'am, and I can't thank you and your husband enough for saving my life."

Cody tried to raise himself to a sitting position, wincing as he did so. He knew Margaret saw the flicker of pain cross his face when she hurried to place a pillow behind him. She wrapped her arm across his bare shoulder to support him; the intimate contact seared both of their skins, electrifying where they touched. Cody finally scooted back and leaned against the solid cabin wall, his face registering the astonishment he felt.

Margaret's face flamed. She shrank away. Her hands fluttered and she nervously fidgeted with dishes on the table.

Cody watched the woman and read the fear in her eyes. One look about the tiny two room cabin verified that her husband James was gone, and they were very much alone. Cody could only guess that James' absence and his presence were disturbing his angel of mercy.

"Do you feel strong enough to eat some solid food? You must be hungry. I've got some stew simmering." Margaret cautiously stepped near him, ladled a small amount of stew into a bowl and handed the steaming food to him.

Cody accepted the bowl and balanced it on his lap while his other hand reached for Margaret's, holding it tenderly. He studied her face as he said, "You don't have to fear me, Maggie. I won't hurt you."

She pulled her hand free from his light grasp and nodded, removing herself to a chair on the opposite side of the cabin, placing as much room between them as possible.

Chapter 16

Survival

The strain of sitting up took its toll, causing an exhausted Cody to lie back down again. He fell into a deep sleep and only woke once when the door opened to permit a gust of frigid wind to blow across his pallet.

James had returned home. The hour was late as he dropped a brace of rabbits on the floor near the hearth and glanced at the sleeping man near it. He climbed into his own bed and gathered his wife close. Margaret laid her head on her husband's shoulder, feeling joy and relief at having him near and calming the nerves that were on edge at having a stranger in the house. His heavy breathing moments later told her that any questions or thoughts to be shared would have to wait.

The early morning brought chores for the Dunlaps that could not be neglected if they meant to survive in this rugged land. They had quickly learned what needed done on the frontier in order to see another day. James fetched a bucket of fresh water from the nearby stream then carried in an armload of firewood. He stacked the split wood neatly as Margaret began cooking breakfast. Their visitor lay awake watching their toil.

"Good to see you awake, lad. How are you feeling?" James inquired in a booming voice.

"Better. I reckon I owe you and your missus my life. Thank you. We haven't been properly introduced yet, but I presume you're James Dunlap. I'm Cody Jarvis." He leaned forward and stretched out his hand to James in a firm shake that pulled on his injured shoulder.

Margaret sat listening to Cody's friendly words and glimpsed the smile that touched his face but noticed it didn't extend to his eyes; they were still distant and wary. She wondered if she had imagined the tenderness he had exhibited yesterday.

Where Margaret had been reluctant to question their guest, James had no such compunction. He poured himself a cup of coffee then offered one to Cody as he turned his chair to directly face the man.

"How did you come to be shot and left all alone, Mr. Jarvis? Were you jumped by bandits or Injuns? What line of work are you in? Did you say you live around these parts? The wife and I just settled here about three months ago, ourselves. We don't know too many people yet." James paused to let the man start explaining.

Cody choked on his swallow of coffee as James began his list of questions and he tried to cover the sound with a short laugh. James and Margaret both waited for his answer.

Cody tried to think of a plausible story.

"I was on my way back to Deer Springs from a cattle-buying trip to Denver. When the storm started, I decided to make camp and was just hunkered down by the campfire when these four cowboys came riding into the light. I reached for my rifle, but I guess I must've been too slow, 'cause the next thing I felt was the bullet hitting my chest. They took my bankroll and lit out. Reckon you know the rest."

"So, you know cattle then?" James eagerly jumped on the one fact of Cody's explanation that interested him. "I'm think-ing to get us some cattle and turn this into a ranch instead of a farm, course we don't have much money to spend right now."

James scratched his scalp as he let the idea sink in and began to relish the prospect. Excitement shone in his eyes. James was always dreaming of a more prosperous life and a quick, easy way to achieve it.

Margaret shook her head then gathered up the soiled dishes, placing them into a bucket of soapy water. She packed away the precious oatmeal and reached for the flour to begin the process of baking bread. She half listened to the conversation going on around her as she worked.

Cody studied James and recognized the gleam in his eyes and saw the abrupt decision for what it was. "You don't need a lot of money to start a good herd if you round up the mavericks in the spring. Then you only need to buy a good breeding bull." He began to spin his tale.

James leaned forward in his chair, the back legs rising off the floor in his excitement. "Just what are these mavericks you're talking about?"

"Unbranded cattle, strays. Come spring there are plenty of cows that roam the prairie, and their calves are unbranded until claimed by some cattleman. I'm just saying that the early bird gets the worm if you know what I mean? Why shouldn't you be the one to pick up a few calves here and there? The mothers will probably wear a brand and it's considered cattle rustling if you try to include them in your herd, but the young calves are easily separated." Cody knew his words would snare the naïve dreamer.

"Oh, I see what you mean. So, tell me, Mr. Jarvis, have you a home you were heading to? If you've nowhere to go, you're more than welcome to spend the winter with us," James offered.

Cody looked up; he couldn't believe his ears. He needed a place to lie low to heal, and now he had one. Cody glanced between the husband and wife. James was clearly excited about the prospect, but he read uncertainty on the wife's face. His eyes met Margaret's. Was that fear in her eyes? Cody nodded his head ever so slightly, then smiled graciously.

"That's a very kind offer, Mr. Dunlap. Please, call me Cody. The winters in Wyoming can be fierce and I'd just as soon not be out in them. And as soon as the weather warms a bit, I'll be glad to help you round up some of those mavericks."

James looked very pleased with himself. It was written all over his face that he thought he had maneuvered Cody into staying and helping with a spring round-up. Margaret nodded to her husband as he turned a jubilant face to her, but the intense stare from the blue eyes across the room really held her attention.

Near the end of November, Cody's wound had healed nicely. His strength had returned enough to allow him to help with some of the lighter chores at the homestead. He tended to the animals outside and quietly moved about the cabin; several times his cat-like walk and nearness caused Maggie to jump. Cody sensed her nervousness but couldn't stop himself from seeking her presence. He felt drawn to the woman in a way he'd never been before; it was a new and unsettling experience.

James constantly sought Cody's company. Acting like long-lost friends, the two men talked for hours on end about all their big plans, spinning dreams. James did most of the talking while Cody sat silently listening and watching. Now, James intended to go out hunting again come morning. Cody could see the idea made Maggie anxious, but he was at a loss how to reassure her.

Dawn broke. The meager sunlight shined through the cabin window. James dressed and packed some rations to carry with him for the planned hunt. Cody lay still on his pallet, feigning sleep to give the couple some semblance of privacy. He could hear their whispered intimate words and even their conversation from outside the cabin.

Maggie grabbed a shawl and wrapped it around her shoulders as she walked outside with James. He stuffed the food into his saddlebags and slung the rifle across the saddle then turned to kiss her good-bye. Maggie tried to hug him closer through the thick layers of his wool coat. He kissed her a second time then laughed at her desperate expression.

"I'll be home in a day or two, Margaret. Now stop your worrying. Cody is here to protect you. You'll be fine."

"Oh James, you thick clot. It's Cody that scares me. I don't like being alone with him."

"Now don't act like a silly woman. The man won't harm you. He's our friend and I'll be glad of his help with the ranch. Go inside before you catch a chill. Keep the fire stoked good and hot. With any luck, we will roast some elk when I get home."

Three days later, James had not returned. The weather had turned colder and now the moist air tasted like new snow.

Cody spent the morning chopping wood and stacked it by the hearth. He watched Maggie look out the window every few minutes and run to the door at every sound, only to find it was the wind or the cabin creaking. Her worry and anxiousness over James' delay home hung in the cabin like a palpable thing.

Reaching a decision, Cody reached for his gun belt and strapped it around his waist. He checked his Colt, spun the chamber then slid the revolver into its leather holster. Shrugging into his heavy sheepskin coat, he stood next to the door, one hand on the latch.

Cody turned to Maggie, the wind outside drowning his words, "I'll find him for you, Maggie. I owe you and I always pay my debts."

Maggie ran to the door to beg him to be careful and to bring James home, but he had already left, galloping off into the swirling snowflakes.

It was past dusk when the pounding on the cabin door brought Maggie out of her seat. James and Cody stumbled forward through the sturdy portal. Snow encrusted both men. Cody's hands shook from the cold as he unbuttoned James' wool coat, then discarded it. He carried him, unconscious now, to the couple's sleeping alcove and dropped him onto the bed.

Maggie quickly checked James for signs of blood. She raised concerned eyes to Cody as she asked, "What happened? Is James hurt? Are you? You better get out of those wet things too."

"I'm all right, just need to get ww...warm. Think his horse threw him. May have broken his right leg, not sure. I need some of that hot coffee. My teeth are chch...chattering so hard, I can hardly talk."

Cody wrapped his hands around a mug of the strong brew then collapsed into a chair near the hearth. The heat from the fire brought the color back into a face blue with cold.

Maggie bent her full attention to James as she ran hands along his body, feeling for injuries. The right leg lay oddly twisted, clearly broken below the knee. It would need to be straightened and splinted. It was a blessing that James lay unconscious, oblivious to the pain.

"Cody, I need you. I don't know what to do and can't set this leg by myself. I'm afraid I don't have the strength to hold him or pull it into place." Her eyes mirrored worry and fear as she beseeched his help.

"Get an old blanket; we'll need some wood for splints and let's see..." Cody scanned the room until he spotted the freshly tanned hides. He unsheathed his sharp hunting knife and cut four long strips from the hides. Seeing her puzzled expression, he quickly explained as he dipped the hides into a pot of boiling water that hung over the fire. "These will hold the splints in place; the wet leather will dry and tighten like bands."

His calm and commanding manner allowed Maggie to follow his instructions and assemble the necessary items. Cody hurriedly split two small logs with the axe and shaved the bark, smoothing them as best he could to make splints. He glanced at Maggie.

Maggie swallowed hard and nodded for him to begin.

They removed James' boot and Cody slit the length of James' pant leg along the seam with his knife blade. Cody held James' foot and ankle firmly while Maggie pressed down on his shoulders. A quick pull and the leg straightened, but not without a bellow of pain from poor James. He writhed and twisted in Maggie's grip as Cody labored to position the blanket-padded splints. Steam rose from the leather bindings tied in place.

Cody stepped back to survey his work. Maggie gently stroked James' forehead and murmured soothing words. She kissed his cheek and patted his shoulder, covering him with a warm quilt as he slipped into a more normal sleep.

Maggie smiled and reached for Cody's hands, clasping them warmly between her own. "Thank you. I don't know what I would have done without you. James would still be lying in the wilderness, as good as dead, I'm sure."

Cody returned her smile, his mercurial mood swaying from a melancholy to a yearning tenderness for this woman and desire for her loving care that he had witnessed with her injured husband.

"I'm glad I was here for you, Maggie. James would have done as much for me – he has in fact!"

Cody had fallen into the habit of addressing Margaret as 'Maggie', and she seemed to accept the casual informality between them. Cody got the impression that her fears and misgivings about him were dissolving. She was less skittish around him, and it pleased him when she sought his help.

James slept fitfully, thrashing about throughout the night. Twice Maggie awakened Cody to help hold him still. The leg pained James badly and Maggie didn't know what else to do.

"Do you have a bottle of whiskey in the house? A good stiff drink will alleviate the pain," Cody suggested.

She nodded and rummaged through a small chest then withdrew a bottle of Scottish whiskey brought from their homeland. Maggie held the cup of whiskey to James' lips as he coughed and sipped the burning liquid.

"I don't abide by drinking spirits, but the whiskey does seem to put James to sleep and for that I'm grateful. At least he's lying quiet now and not moving the leg," Maggie told Cody.

She repeated the dose twice more during the long dark hours.

The thick whiskey fumes filled the tight confines. Maggie almost swooned as she breathed in the unaccustomed spirits. Wrapping James' heavy wool coat about her, she stepped outside into the crisp morning air. Her breath appeared in tiny vapors in the cold air, floating upwards into the bright blue sky.

A peaceful serenity lay upon the sparkling snow glistening over the land. It was a beautiful scene.

The cabin door eased shut as Cody moved forward until he touched Maggie's shoulder. He stood studying her; drawn to her in a way that couldn't be explained. Maggie's scent lingered in the cold air, blending with the smells of the farm and the woods as Cody drank it in. They stood in each other's nearness with no fear or desire to move. Calm, safe.

Cody's eyes burned with the intensity of his feelings as he looked at Maggie. It startled her. She looked away then spoke to break the spell.

"Thank you for all you've done for James. I know I've said this before, but words don't seem to be enough." She swallowed hard and her face flushed. "I owe you an apology," she admitted.

Cody shot her a quizzical look and started to speak, but she pressed her finger to his lips to stop him. "No, let me finish. I haven't behaved very nicely to you. You frighten me sometimes and I'm ashamed to say that I still don't think you're always truthful with James and me."

His expression closed to a blank mask. Cody stepped back, putting a tangible distance between them that seemed to stretch into a chasm. He needed to get hold of his emotions and remember the mission. Whatever softening growing between him and Maggie Dunlap had vanished.

Chapter 17

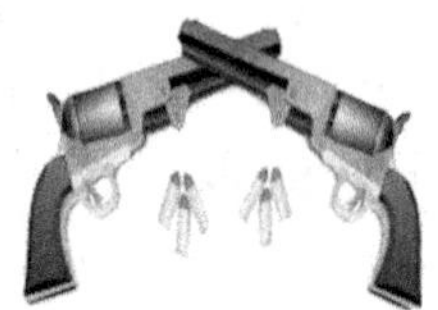

Christmas 1884

James' disposition grew worse. He became cranky and restless at being confined to his bed. The winter stranglehold upon the land kept everyone imprisoned with little chance of going outside.

Cody continued to venture out in search of fresh meat for the cabin. Each time he rode away from the cabin, he kept a look out for any of Logan's men that might be in the area searching for him. That was an issue he would need to confront soon. Could Abe or Ike be the ones that shot him? Somehow he doubted they'd have the courage. In the snowy white-out conditions that day, it was possible that another rider may have done the deed.

Some days, Cody and James sat and talked of plans for the spring, but lately, James appeared to have lost his enthusiasm. Maggie and Cody both tried to tell him that his leg will mend, it was a clean break, if only he'd be patient.

Maggie began making preparations for a Christmas celebration. The calendar date had little significance for Cody. In his life, it was just another day. Still, he enjoyed listening to Maggie hum her Christmas carols and watch her try to decorate the shabby cabin with holiday greenery.

Early the next day, a loud knocking drew all of their attention. Maggie and James both wore apprehensive expressions as Cody waved his hand and cautioned them.

"Stay back. I'll see to the door," he said as he drew his Colt and moved to unlatch the door to crack it slightly open.

Voices in greeting called out to the Dunlap family. Maggie, recognizing her dear friends Rose and Michael Canavan, threw the door wide open and gestured them to come inside.

Maggie and Rose hugged as Maggie welcomed her friends. "What are you doing out in this terrible weather? How have you been? Come in; come in out of the cold!"

Cody moved to sit unobtrusively by the hearth, where he could observe the guests.

Rose glanced toward Cody then her eyes fell on James' splinted leg. "Whatever happened to you?" she exclaimed as she hurried to James' bedside, where he reclined against the headboard, a blanket wrapped around his shoulders and his legs stretched before him.

Michael was at her heels as they both began asking questions at once. Their presence rallied James from his stupor. James laughed out loud for the first time since the accident. The Canavans' arrival had made a commotion, like a fresh storm blowing through the log cabin.

James answered his friend, "I'm fine, be up and about soon. Damn horse threw me; that's all. Cody here hauled my butt home."

Michael looked over at where Cody still sat quietly, studying him rather quizzically. "Cody, is it?" Extending his hand, he made his own introductions, "Michael Canavan, sir, and my dear wife, Rose. I didn't catch the last name..."

Cody shook the other man's hand briefly and hesitated before replying, "Jarvis, Cody Jarvis."

Maggie rushed forward to explain to her friends. "Cody is the man you helped rescue; don't you remember? He's been staying with us ever since he recovered from his wound and has offered to help James this spring with the ranch." Cody listened to her voice change from loud and exuberant to a dwindling whisper as the two men faced one another. She glanced questioningly between Cody and Michael.

Cody shrugged his shoulders and leaned back against the hearth.

Michael's demeanor visibly changed. His voice hardened. "I've heard that name in Deer Springs. Jarvis, a gunslinger and low-down murderer, as I recall." He faced Cody and waited for his reaction to the insult.

Cody's eyes met Maggie's across the crowded space. His expression was blank as he arose deliberately. The chair legs scraped the wooden floor as it slid back. Michael stepped backwards; uncertainty written on his face. Tension in the room grew.

"Maggie, I'm going outside and see about that firewood we need for tonight and check on the animals."

"Thank you, Cody," Maggie whispered.

He gave a curt nod, leaving no doubt that her 'thank you' was meant for more than firewood.

As soon as the door closed behind Cody, Rose turned to her husband. "Michael! Are you crazy? Are you trying to make me a widow?" She threw up her hands then flounced onto the edge of the bed, jiggling the mattress. James groaned in agony at the sudden movement, causing Rose to jump up guiltily. "Oh, I'm sorry James."

"Michael, are you sure you know Cody Jarvis?" James finally asked. "What makes you think he's this gunfighter?"

"The name's well known in town. Fella hangs around that rough bunch from the Diamond Bar Ranch, especially Zachary Logan. You folks havena' been here long and don't know the trouble we've had in Deer Springs."

James shook his head in disbelief. "Have you seen Cody with this Logan man? What type of problems are you talking about?" James glanced between Michael and Maggie, torn between his feelings of loyalty to his two new friends. Maggie reached across the bed and patted his shoulder, trying to comfort him and convey her understanding, while her own feelings careened crazily.

"Well, no, I havena' seen the two exactly together...but there's been talk. Logan's a bad sort. I heard Logan killed a man to get that big ranch of his and that saloon, of course no one can prove it. His riders are all outlaws outside of the territory. Decent men willna' work for him."

"But that's no proof that Cody is mixed up with those criminals. Just because a man carries a gun doesn't make him a killer." Maggie tried to defend Cody. Rose looked up sharply at her outburst.

"How much do you know about the man? Has he told you anything about himself? I don't like the idea of you two being alone with him. Do you think it's safe... and James laid up like he is, too?" Rose fretted and wrung her hands, her eyes beseeching her husband to do something to help protect her friends.

"I suppose I could ride over once or twice a month and see how you're getting along. We only came today to wish you both a Merry Christmas. What with the heavy snow, I didn't think we'd have a chance to visit again for some time."

Michael suggested a plan he hoped his wife would approve of, although Maggie had doubts as to whether such trips would be possible when the winter snows deepened and the temperatures dropped even lower. Michael's danger would be far greater. She tried to remind him and Rose of the risk Michael would be taking and reassured them that they'd be fine. They insisted that Michael would be able to do this. The argument continued for a few more minutes, but it was of no use. Michael would come or not; only the weather could prevent it.

Maggie served her guests hot tea and sweet rolls that she had baked specially for the coming holiday. They talked of trivial matters and tried to forget the serious worries of the past hour. The time sped by in their friends' company. Afternoon light dwindled as the Canavans prepared to depart. As they hugged each other and bade farewell; Michael repeated that he'd return in two or three weeks.

Cody stepped out of the lean-to and observed the couple riding away. He felt chilled to the bone but knew his presence would have made Maggie uncomfortable and he wasn't prepared to divulge his life story and association with Logan. Let them think what they will.

Chapter 18

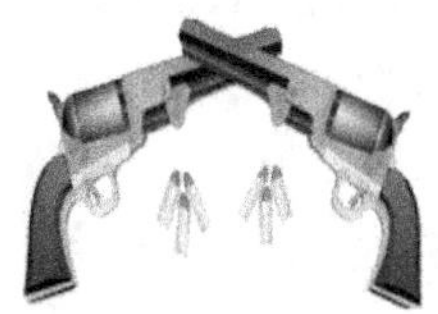

Entanglement

January 1885 brought the new year with the fury of more snow. The wind rattled the roof planks, knocking one loose and dumping a pile of the wet, cold snow right in the middle of James' bed. He, of course, bellowed loud enough to wake the dead, scaring Maggie. Cody calmly picked up his coat and wrapped Maggie's heavy woolen scarf about his head and neck, then prepared to go out into the storm.

"Do you have a hammer? I'll do what I can."

The meager Dunlap tool collection filled a canvas sack that hung on a hook. Maggie reached for the bag and handed it to him, her hand lingered on his.

"Be careful up there. Don't you go falling off and giving me another invalid to care for," she jested.

A brief smile touched Cody's lips and his eyes narrowed as he studied her for a long minute before he patted the top of her hand in reassurance. "Don't worry Maggie. I'll be all right."

Aware that James was listening intently to their conversation, Maggie moved hastily away and began to prepare a meal for everyone. Cody grunted with the exertion of climbing onto the roof while his cautious moving about caused more snow to fall through the cracks. James sulked and attempted to get out of bed, standing on one leg. Maggie hurried to prop her shoulder under his to lend support while he hobbled over to the chair by the hearth. The bed covers quickly became soaked and she struggled to pull them off the heavy feather tick.

Cody swept away piles of snow to expose the warped shingles then hammered the loose nails, pushing the slats closer together. Maggie watched his efforts as the amount of daylight shining through the rooftop diminished. The chilly whistling of the wind seemed to lessen too, thanks to his attentions. She stopped stirring the porridge and glanced to her husband while she listened to Cody work on the roof. Maggie shook her head, trying to make sense of her confusing thoughts that twisted and turned in her mind, that trapped her heart in a tangle of emotions and divided her loyalty.

Cody stomped back into the cabin, his cheeks and nose colored bright red from the cold. Maggie laughed when she saw him.

"You look like Saint Nicholas! Look at that red face."

"Well, that's a fine way to thank a man for risking his life to keep you warm and dry."

Maggie looked at him shame-faced but could see the laughter in his own eyes now and relaxed. Their jovial mood was in sharp contrast to James' sullenness.

James waited uncomfortably in a chair. It wasn't a joking matter to him. He was forever in a sour mood. The fall had broken more than his leg; it had broken his spirit too.

Maggie shook out the heavy quilt, and tried to restore the bed to a warm, dry condition.

"Cody, can you assist James back to bed while I serve the food?"

"Here, James, let me get a shoulder under you. How's that leg feeling today?" Cody asked, as he supported the weaker man.

"Oh, just dandy ... no thanks to the nonsense I have to sit and listen to. A man could starve around here. Where's that bottle of whiskey?"

"Do you really need it? I thought the leg was mending?" James liberally helped himself to spirits ever since the night of the accident. It was a rare day when Maggie saw him sober.

"And I say it hurts. I should know if I need it, not you!"

"All right, here." Maggie reluctantly handed him the whiskey bottle and his breakfast tray. She had baked more sweet rolls and added one to his tray along with the bowl of porridge to please him with the treat. They used to be his favorite.

Cody watched the interaction between husband and wife and heard the audible sigh from Maggie as she turned away.

He lifted the two steaming bowls of porridge from her hand and carried them to the small table.

"It's all right Maggie. He'll get over this." Cody's voice held a note of tenderness in it.

Or was it pity?

Maggie shrugged and chose not to comment. Cody watched her focus her attention on the plain but nourishing breakfast that was becoming their mainstay.

Silence filled the room as they all ate. Cody cleared his throat; the sound echoed off the timbered walls, startling Maggie.

"I'll be going out to hunt again and if the snow's not too deep, maybe go into Deer Springs. We could use some supplies from town. I was thinking of leaving in the morning."

It was the first time he had suggested going into town—a confrontation that no longer could be avoided. Cody had to know what awaited him in Deer Springs, and truth be told, he didn't trust himself around Maggie any longer. His growing fondness and attachment to the woman were foreign to him and he didn't know how to cope with these new emotions.

"All right, I'll make a list of what we need the most; bring back whatever you can find. I'll trust your judgment on what's a fair price. There isn't much money."

"I'll do the best I can, Maggie. Don't worry about the cost."

James snarled from across the room, "Don't forget to pick up another bottle of whiskey. It's the only thing that helps kill the taste of this slop my wife feeds me!" James hurled the bowl of half-eaten porridge across the room. The stoneware shattered and the sticky oats plastered the wall and floor. He slumped back upon his bed, clutching the near-empty bottle to his chest.

Maggie bent to pick up the pieces of the broken bowl. James with his temper plus the wintry isolation were too much for Maggie. She sat down in the middle of the debris and cried, sobbing so hard, her shoulders shook. She couldn't seem to stop.

Cody's strong arms lifted her and held her against his stalwart chest. He stroked her hair and patted her back until the crying lessened. Maggie raised her head from his tear-soaked shoulder and searched Cody's face.

His eyes gazed into hers, delving into her soul, then his lips lowered as he kissed her ever so gently. Cody held her face in his callused palms as he kissed the tears from her closed eyelids, her cheeks, and the tip of her nose then returned to her waiting mouth. Maggie returned his kiss with a yearning that shocked both of them. Breathing heavily, she pulled away from his embrace as shame washed over her. Maggie quickly looked to where James lay, snoring loudly, fearful that he had witnessed her sin.

Cody dropped his arms and watched her face mirror a myriad of emotions and thoughts. She was still breathless as she turned to him.

"I think you better see if you can stay in town when you get to Deer Springs. Please try to understand, Cody. It'll be better."

"Who is going to take care of you if I'm not here? That drunk? Think about what you're saying, Maggie." His anger colored his words and he regretted them as soon as they were out of his mouth.

"Don't call my husband a drunk. I'll be all right. I need time to think; you're confusing me. Please..." She paced the narrow floor and wrung her hands. Hot tears slid down her cheeks.

Cody nodded his acceptance of her decision. He would go.

Maggie's face reflected her warring emotions. *How can they face each other every day, feeling as they do? What of her marriage vows? Yet how can she face every day without him? And tomorrow he leaves.*

Chapter 19

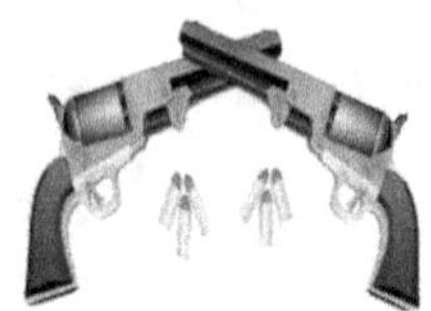

February 1885

Deer Springs waited eerily silent, like a ghost town frozen in a wintry storm. Snow blanketed the streets with tall drifts and rooftops creaked under the weight of the white stuff. No one walked about the streets. The dull glow of lamp light shone through a few filmy windows. Cody cautiously rode down the main street as he headed toward the stable. Glancing up at one of the second-story windows of Dollie's Darlings, he caught a movement behind the frosted glass. He continued slowly to the stable then dismounted and swung the door open wide enough to allow him and Lightning to enter.

Cody paused and looked around the empty stable. Clem was no where in sight and all the animals were gone. *Strange. Wonder why the place is empty?*

Cody led the bay into his usual stall and the horse snickered his appreciation for being back inside a warm enclosed shelter. Cody hung a bag of oats on the wall of the stall and filled a trough of water. He tossed his rig across the stall gate, retrieved his rifle, and with one last rub of Lightning's nose, he headed back out.

The wind whipped down the empty street as Cody ducked his head and turned his collar upward. He leaned into the fierce gusts and headed to the boarding house.

He rapped on the blue door, tried the knob and found it locked, then knocked again. Stomping his feet to knock off the accumulated snow, he waited for Clara to open the door.

"Who's there?" Clara shouted through the solid portal.

"Cody Jarvis," he called out in a loud voice over the howl of the wind. "C'mon Clara, open up. It's freezing out here."

She cracked the door open a few inches and peered one eye through the narrow slit before standing back and allowing him entry. Clara shook her head and touched his arm, wanting to make sure she wasn't seeing an apparition.

"Wasn't sure these old eyes weren't playing tricks on me. Where've you been, boy? I gave you up for dead."

Cody shrugged out of his coat and brushed the wet snow from his hair and face as he turned to the landlady. "That's a tale for another day."

A cough from the corner of the room drew his attention. He turned and walked toward the sound and the heat radiating from the wood-burning stove. Surprise registered on his face as he recognized Clem lying on a narrow cot.

"Hey, old-timer. Find a cozy spot to wait out this storm?" he jested. His joke fell on deaf ears.

Clara walked up to Clem and laid a comforting hand on his shoulder as she adjusted his quilt.

"I've been taking care of Clem for the past two, almost three, months now. He's slow to mend, but he's getting there."

Cody frowned in concern and genuine affection for the man. He crouched next to the bed and stared intently at Clem's face, noticing for the first time the fading yellow bruises that covered his jaw and hairline then streaked downward to color most of his collar bone. He squeezed Clem's hand.

"What happened? Who beat you, Clem?"

Clara answered his query, her voice seething as she plopped onto a wooden chair, "Logan's goons. Lily-livered cowards...four of them beat and kicked him til he was unconscious and close to death. Broke three of his ribs. Doc Porter and me didn't know if poor Clem here was goin' to make it."

"When? Did you know the men? Tell me their names." Cody asked through gritted teeth. Clara was right; only cowards would pick on someone weaker and older with no defense.

"Don't know all their names, but I remember what they look like. Reckon it was the same day that you left town. One of the fellas was called Fuller. After they finished with Clem, they came here and busted up your room searching for something. Big lug with a pock-marked puss took a map you had in a drawer. Seemed to me they were disappointed and expected to find more," Clara explained as Cody listened intently. His unreadable gaze shifted between the woman and the injured man.

"This is my fault. I'm sorry. I promised I wouldn't bring trouble to your doorstep and it appears it followed me anyway. I'll make it up to you Clara." He looked at Clem again as a deadly expression filled his eyes. "I'll find the men who did this to you, old friend; I promise they'll pay for this."

Cody doggedly climbed the stairs and sought his bedroom. The temperature of the room felt much cooler than downstairs. Drafts from the window caused a layer of frost to glaze over the glass. Cody lifted the edge of the yellow window shade and tried to peer into the street below. Still empty. Only his tracks appeared in the snow while the wind slowly erased the evidence of his passing. Come morning, he planned to make his presence known and learn just who his enemies were.

Clara had breakfast on the table when Cody made his way downstairs. Clem sat at the table, a blanket wrapped around his thin shoulders as he sipped hot coffee and ate a plate of food.

"Good to see you up, Clem," said Cody as he pulled out a chair next to the old man. "Now, want to tell me what Logan's men really wanted from you? They didn't just take it into their heads to beat the crap out of you for nothing."

Clem coughed then wheezed as he took a deep breath before locking eyes with Cody. "You... they wanted to know information about you. Kept asking me who you were working for and where you'd come from." He laughed, a brittle sound that set off another coughing attack before he continued. "I told them you worked for Logan and that's all I knew. Reckon they didn't like my answer."

Cody nodded and clasped the old man's hand. "You had my back, old timer. You did good, and I'm real sorry you had to pay a dear price on my account. I won't forget this."

"What kept you away? Rumors around town said you were dead."

Cody finished his food and sat back in his chair. Clara wandered over and joined the two of them. She and Clem were silent as they waited for his explanation.

"Those rumors were almost true. Remember the day the first snowstorm hit? I got shot and left for dead, buried in the snow. Luckily, one of those new homesteaders found me. That's where I've been."

Clara and Clem exchanged looks. "I think you angered Logan and got on his wrong side. Any idea why?" Clara asked.

"Maybe, not sure, but I plan on finding out." Cody stood and gave his two friends a long, thoughtful look. "Thanks for believing in me." He grabbed his coat and walked out the door.

Cody's footsteps echoed on the hardwood floors of the vacant Silver Spur as he strode toward the bar. Kelly stopped his chore of polishing the mahogany wood surface and glanced up at his first customer of the day. His cloth paused in mid-air and his mouth hung open, the greeting on his tongue unspoken. He blinked twice and tried to recover his composure.

"Boss in?" Cody asked, as he observed the bartender's nervousness.

"Er, uh, no. He's riding out the snowstorm at his ranch."

Cody turned abruptly at the sound of a door closing and a grumbling voice. Abe and Ike entered the saloon from the back room. Abe stumbled forward as he hitched up his britches then stopped in his tracks as he spotted Cody by the bar. The color drained from his face and he just stood there. Ike showed the presence of mind to appear embarrassed or at least nervous.

"What's the matter, Abe? You look like you've seen a ghost," chided Cody as the pair came closer.

"You're supposed to be dead," Abe squeaked.

"Shut up, moron," Ike spat on the floor and shot Abe a warning look.

"Guess you're not that good a shot," Cody said as he gave each man an icy stare. He locked eyes until each one turned away, refusing to face him.

"I didn't shoot you. You can't blame that on me," whined Abe.

"Um, we kinda lost you in that storm. Couldn't see my hand in front of my face. Yeah, we, um, didn't know you were hit," Ike tried to explain.

"So, you left me for dead. I oughta drill you both right here," Cody growled. "Give me one good reason why I shouldn't. Now, you're gonna tell me who beat up old Clem in the stables. Start talking. My patience is running thin."

Ike and Abe exchanged worried looks. Abe's only concern was Cody standing in front of him, not Logan's other man who wasn't even in town.

"Fuller. That's who you want. He gave the orders to beat Clem," Abe sputtered. "He may have been the one that shot you, but I can't be sure. You gotta believe me; we weren't part of that."

"Why Clem?" Cody bent his knee and placed a foot on the bar rail, he leaned forward, his left arm resting on his knee, his hand dangled free. He narrowed his eyes in a menacing look.

"I dunno. How could we know? We was with you, remember?" Abe cried. "That Fuller's a mean one. He don't need no reason to kill someone. He enjoys it."

"Who else was with him? I know you must have heard all the details when you got back."

Ike decided he would not risk his hide for the slime that Logan had hired. They weren't even in town anymore. "I'm not sure of their names. They only work for Logan once in a while, you know? One is Woodrow– you can tell him by his pock-marked face, really bad scars on his skin. A short, pudgy dude goes by the name Mueller. That's all I know."

"Where can I find Fuller and these men?" asked Cody as he straightened up.

"Heard tell they left town and went down to Fort Laramie," Abe said."

Cody straightened back up and glared at the two men. It was a start.

Chapter 20

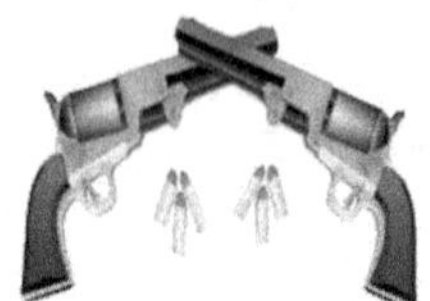

Cody

Cody and Lightning trudged through the deep snow, at times up to the horse's belly, as they made their way south. The weather had cleared enough for the journey but not the brittle cold temperatures. Man and beast alike welcomed the sight of the town ahead and the warm shelter it offered.

The livery stable provided a place for Lightning with dry hay and a bit of warmth among the other animals. Cody flipped the livery boy a couple coins then unsaddled the horse and brushed his coat before venturing out to find his own lodging for the night and perhaps word of a certain group of men.

He walked past the gate of the Army fort then headed down the main street, stopping to peer into the odd storefront here and there. Eventually, his steps took him into the Red Garter saloon that he had frequented before. The same player piano produced haphazard notes but tonight there no dancing girls were on stage. Cody scanned the room as he approached the bar.

"Beer," he told the bartender. He took off his Stetson and ran fingers through his hair then shrugged to stretch stiff shoulder muscles.

One of the dance hall girls sidled up to him, looking him up and down. "I know you," she said. "You were here a few months ago. Yeah, I never forget a face. You punched some drunk that was trying to manhandle me."

Cody turned to her. He thought he remembered the incident, but one saloon looked like another and he couldn't be sure. She was an attractive gal and in the past he would have considered giving her serious attention. Now, however, when he looked at the woman, all he saw was a haunting reflection of Maggie's face and luminous eyes smiling back at him. He shook his head to mentally banish the image from his mind.

"Got an available room for a night's stay?" asked Cody.

The woman smiled enticingly, "You can stay in mine if you want. All our other rooms are rented."

"I just need a place to sleep. Sorry, but I'm not suggesting anything more."

"All right, big fella. Like I said, you can stay in my room and if you happen to change your mind ... well that's okay too."

She crooked her finger and led the way upstairs to a door at the end of the hall. She opened the door into a pleasant room crowded with a pair of upholstered chairs flanking a small round table and a wide bed that took up most of the floor space. Red velvet curtains hung at the narrow window and a worn tapestry carpet covered the wooden floor.

"I'm Scarlet, by the way, and you're...?"

"Cody." He took one of the chairs and stretched his legs out before him. "Help me off with my boots, won't you darlin'?" he asked with a tired smile.

Scarlet knelt on the floor in front of him and tugged on his leather boots, stiff with the cold. One hard tug and the boot came off in her hands but the effort knocked her off balance and she landed on her rump with a thud.

She laughed, "Oof! Wasn't expecting that. Okay, let's try the other one." She pulled with both hands and the second boot came off without as much fight.

Cody laid his hat and coat across one chair. He shucked his trousers and shirt, added them to the pile, but left his long-johns on. Trying not to yawn too widely, he looked longingly at the soft bed then raised an eyebrow at Scarlet.

"What side do you sleep on? I'm all tuckered out, Scarlet, or I'd enjoy your company." Cody plopped down on the comfortable mattress.

Scarlet admired what body she could glimpse beneath the pieces of clothing and sighed. *Maybe after a good night's sleep he'd be more receptive to some pleasure.*

"You can take the left. Hey, before you crawl under the covers, how about helping undo some of these hooks on the back of my dress?"

She moved to stand between his legs as he sat on the edge of the bed. Scarlet presented her back to him and held her hair out of the way so he could reach the row of tiny fasteners. He made short order of the task as she felt the material fall away. Her bodice gaped and she slid the shoulder and sleeves of the dress downward.

"Lovely," commented Cody as he admired the slim woman clad only in chemise and corset. He shoved his legs under the blankets and laid his head on the feather pillow. Cody heard Scarlet move away from the bed. He closed his eyes. Seconds later sleep overcame him.

A groan of pleasure escaped Cody's lips as the soft body of a woman pressed against his back, snuggling under the warm blankets. His mind gradually surfaced from exhausted depths. Eyes sprung open and took in his surroundings as he recalled where he was and the identity of the soft body cuddled next to him. She sighed and inched closer, trying to melt into him. Cody enjoyed the warmth and contentment until he felt a wandering hand leave his waist and creep lower. He gently removed her questing hand as he threw back the covers, swung his legs out, and managed a sitting position.

"Hmm, don't go," breathed Scarlet. She lay in that mystic realm between sleep and wakefulness, missing the warmth of her male bed mate.

Cody slid out of bed, made use of the commode hidden discreetly behind a screen, then hurried to dress. When he turned toward the bed, Scarlet was awake, lying on her side in a very provocative pose.

She smiled at him seductively. "Good morning."

He returned her smile. She presented a pretty picture any man would appreciate, and he was no different. "Morning. Sorry if I woke you."

"I hope you weren't planning on running off without breakfast or even a goodbye."

His stomach chose that moment to growl loudly. "Um, guess breakfast would be a good idea."

"Let me throw on a robe or something and we'll see what we can find. Too early for any business downstairs but I think I can put together some food from the kitchen," Scarlet said as she slid out of bed. Her smile and eyes told Cody that she caught his thorough perusal of her body encased in nothing but a sheer chemise. She tilted her head and glanced toward the bed. "Sure you want to eat ... food?"

Although his body said otherwise, he nodded and moved to watch out the window while Scarlet dressed. The townsfolk of Laramie were beginning to move about; maybe he'd find the men he was looking for. Cody reminded himself to keep the mission in mind, but at times it was a difficult task.

"You never did say, what brings you to Laramie?" Scarlet asked as she whipped eggs in a bowl and heated a skillet on the stove top. She sliced a piece of bread and spread it with jam then added it to Cody's plate. A slab of bacon sizzled in the skillet; she turned the meat over then poured in the scrambled eggs to cook.

The enticing food smells filled his nostrils as Cody waited on the promised breakfast. It would appear that Scarlet knew how to please a man, both with her charms and her cooking. What was she doing wasting her life in a place like this? Cody sat pondering that question as she served him the delicious meal.

"Mmm, this is delicious. Thanks. I didn't realize how hungry I was."

"So? What brings you to town?" persisted Scarlet.

"I'm looking for a couple of guys. Heard they were here."

"Who are they? Maybe I've seen them."

"One's a tall guy, mean face with a thin mustache, goes by the name of Fuller. The other man is called Woodrow; you'd know him by the pock-marks and scars on his face. They usually travel with a third guy, but I don't know much about him," Cody said as he chewed a mouthful of bacon and eggs. He drank his coffee and waited on her answer.

Scarlet sipped her coffee, her gaze pensive as she stared into the recesses of her memory. She turned to Cody with a nod of her head, "Yes. I think I did see a man with a badly scarred face, scruffy hair… accompanied by a short, pudgy guy. Didn't speak much, but he was free with the hands, if you know what I mean. He gave Priscilla a hard time. She's one of our waitresses."

"Yeah, that sounds like him. Do you remember if he was with Fuller, the taller man?"

"Gee, I'm not sure. Hey, what'd they do?"

"I just need to find them. Let's just say we have some unfinished business," Cody told her as he slid his empty plate across the table and rose.

He pressed a kiss on her cheek. "Thanks for putting me up last night. Appreciate it plus the meal. I've gotta go." He left a five-dollar gold piece on the table and left.

Late in the afternoon, after visiting numerous taverns and shops, Cody wandered into a two-bit, run down saloon on the edge of town. A handful of men filled the dingy, smoke-filled room. Cody studied the appearance of two men standing at the bar; their backs leaned against the plywood bar top as they sipped tankards of beer. Both men noticed Cody simultaneously. The short, pudgy fellow turned white while the pock-marked man's eyes widened and he dropped his drink as his hand groped for his gun then paused.

Ice cold eyes glared as Cody spoke in a menacing voice, "You Woodrow? Heard you wanted a piece of me, or are you only brave with women and old men?"

Woodrow gulped; his hand trembled as it slid to his gun belt once again. "To hell with you, Jarvis," he spat, then dredging courage from the bottom of his soul, he drew and fired.

Smoke spiraled from the Colt's muzzle as Woodrow's body collapsed onto the dirty floor. His face lay in the puddle of his spilled beer. Woodrow's partner backed up and held his hands out, palms up.

"You tell Fuller that I'm looking for him. Got it? He's next," Cody stated in an ominous voice. He turned on his heel and strode out of the saloon. Anger simmered below the surface, his fists clenched and unclenched, as he walked toward the livery stable. He had found one man who'd beat Clem so critically, but not the one he wanted the most— Fuller. He owed Fuller for more than just Clem's injuries.

Chapter 21

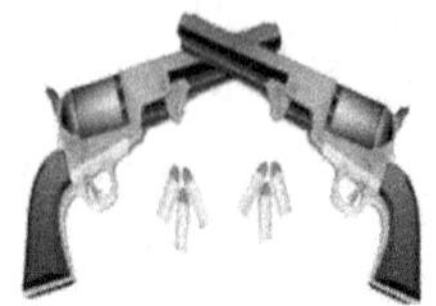

Fury

Maggie chopped and split wood for hours, and yet the stockpile appeared meager. They'd burn most of it in one night if the temperatures continue to drop. James blamed her for sending Cody away and for making him do without his whiskey. He'd become cruel and petty; the fanciful dreamer she had married was gone. Maggie didn't know if he suspected the real reason Cody left or if he believed the story she had told him. She was at a point where she didn't care anymore what he thought.

She kept telling herself that things will be better come spring. They could both begin life together anew. Isn't that what spring is for, fresh beginnings? If only spring would arrive in this god-forsaken land.

Maggie paced the confines of the cabin, fearful she was losing her mind and hearing things - like now, hoof beats in the distance.

The sound grew louder. She ran to the door to identify the approaching rider in the distance. He sat tall in the saddle and even bundled in his thick sheepskin and leather coat; she could tell that he wasn't a heavy-set man such as Michael Canavan. Only one other man would have cause to visit the Dunlap home.

Cody reined his horse to a halt and dismounted quickly when he spied Maggie standing in the open doorway. He tied the stallion in the lean-to and hurried to the cabin.

Maggie studied his face. Had she been on his mind as much as he had dwelled in hers? Cody reached for her hands. She watched his eyes take in her appearance, not missing the tiniest detail.

"May I come in, Maggie?"

"Cody. I didn't think I would see you again."

Maggie watched him scan the dark interior of the cabin. She'd tried to conserve the lamp oil and candles, only lighting them in the evening hours. Now the fire had burned low, with only a few logs stacked within the hearth. James sat in the middle of the bed playing solitaire with a worn deck of cards, his favorite pastime. Suddenly, Maggie saw her home through Cody's eyes as he took in the soiled dishes and the dried food still on the floor from where James had thrown his previous meal. The expression on Cody's face when his eyes came to rest on her was her undoing.

"What happened, Maggie? Did James hit you?" He questioned as his fingers gingerly caressed her bruised eye and swollen cheek.

She had ceased to care how she looked and now was ashamed of her own filthy clothing and battered appearance. Dirty hair hung down her back in a tangled mess and even her skin wasn't clean. What had happened indeed?

She shook her head in the negative, not knowing how to begin or even if she should. How do you tell another man that the man you married had changed into a sullen, dark individual? She felt like she was living with a stranger and now the man who had entered her life as a stranger meant more to her than she was free to say.

Cody reached out to touch her again. Maggie took a step backwards, rejecting the touch she yearned for. It can never be and she must not let herself dream of something that she could not have.

Cody read the despair on Maggie's face. He strode purposefully toward James as she watched in a detached way. Cody grabbed James by the arm and pulled him off the bed. James looked startled. Maggie realized that he hadn't noticed Cody before that moment.

"James, stand up man! You need some exercise and I'm going to see to it that you get out of that bed and back on your feet. Your wife deserves better, and by God, you're going to provide it. Get up, don't even think of sitting back down."

Cody held his anger in tight control. He propelled James toward the door with an iron grip on his arm that would not loosen, reaching for James' coat as they left.

The brittle air hit James smack in the face and sobered him like nothing could. He hurried to don his woolen coat and stood stomping some warmth into his feet.

"Where the hell have you been? What gives you the right to come back here and drag me out into the cold? Are you crazy?"

"Here, put this to work and it will warm you right up."

Cody thrust the wood axe into James' hands and pointed to the dwindling stack of logs that needed splitting. Seeing James adjust his stance to maintain his balance on the still splintered leg, Cody nodded, satisfied and walked back to his horse to retrieve several parcels. He had bought supplies and now carried them into the house.

"Maggie, I brought you a few things. You never did write out that list, but I chose a couple of items I thought you could use."

Maggie looked among the packages to discover a dozen candles, a bar of scented soap, a tin of salted pork, several canning jars of beans, bags of flour, sugar, and oats. Cody handed her one last bundle wrapped in brown paper. She opened it carefully as he watched closely. A cloth bound book rested atop folded blue fabric. When she picked up the cloth and shook it out, she realized Cody had brought her a ready-made, store-bought dress. The soft blue cotton was adorned with tiny white flowers, with a lace edged collar and leg-of-mutton sleeves. The wide skirt billowed with yards of fabric that would swirl when she walked. Delight over his gift shone on her face as her hands lovingly caressed the dress.

"Oh Cody! Where did you get everything? But I can't accept; the dress is far too lovely."

He disregarded her feeble protests and leaned towards her to whisper, "The dress is a late Christmas present. Please, I insist. When I saw it in the store at Laramie, I knew that no one but you could wear it. The book is to help keep you company."

"But Cody ..."

"Take it as my way of an apology then, Maggie." He glanced around and waved his hand toward the filth, "To see you like this, I can't forgive myself for letting you come into harm's way. I should never have left you, but I couldn't stay away."

His words warmed her heart and soul. If only it could be so. The sound of wood chopping caught Maggie's attention, and she shot Cody an inquiring look.

"I put James to work. He needed the fresh air; he'll never get better by lying about that bed all the time. Are you going to tell me what happened around here while I was gone?"

"Not now, maybe later, when I find the right words."

"All right Maggie. Can I see you in that dress?" he asked as his eyes skimmed her from head to toe.

"I'm afraid I need a good scrubbing before I'm fit to touch something so fine." Embarrassed, Maggie pushed her hair back behind her ears and rubbed at the dirt clinging to her arm.

"Well lady, fill a kettle with water and I'll bring in the firewood to heat it. This cabin isn't much warmer than outside. What were you thinking of, to let things get so run down? Never mind, I won't harp on the subject." He reached out to lightly stroke the side of her face; his hand dropped to linger on her shoulder. "Thank God I returned when I did. Scares the hell out of me to think what I might have found if I had waited until spring," he said in a voice filled with concern.

He turned and went back outside to carry in armloads of firewood. Maggie filled a hip bath with some water and put the kettle on to boil more. Suddenly, the simple idea of a hot bath appealed to her senses and made her feel more alive than she had in weeks.

She draped a long quilt over a clothesline to create a makeshift privacy screen at one end of the cabin then began disrobing as soon as the tub was filled with hot water. The water soothed both her bruised body and tortured mind as she soaked in its liquid heat. A light lavender scent drifted from the rare bar of soap. Maggie's memories of formal gardens and moonlit summer nights floated on the sweet fragrance. A happier time remembered—filled with future dreams and promises. It seemed so far away now. *Where was the young girl that had blushed with her first kiss and vowed to honor a marriage promise agreed between two old families? Had she perished on the trek westward, or had she simply matured to face the realities of life?*

"Maggie? You didn't drown in that tub, did you? If I don't hear any sound soon, I'm coming in to check on you." Cody said in a devilish threat.

Cody's humor was infectious. She splashed the water for an answer. Cody laughed, then glanced up at James entering the cabin.

"She still in that bath? I'm getting hungry. Hurry up Margaret." James hobbled over to sit in a chair by the fireplace and enjoy the hot blaze licking at the fresh supply of wood.

"Here James, have some of this chewing tobacco. I brought this special for you. You know, we ought to take off that splint and let the leg finish mending on its own. You don't need that crutch," Cody said as he pointed to the wooden splint.

"Since when did you become a doctor? I think I liked you better when you were gone."

"James, how can you say such a thing? After all the help that Cody has been?" Maggie's words chastised him through the curtain as she reluctantly abandoned the watery haven and carefully rubbed dry her bruised arm and side.

James had definitely regained his strength all right, especially when fueled with liquor. She shuddered slightly at the memory of the ugly fight they had and the cruel beating afterwards. She vowed silently that Cody must not see the purple marks; his patience with James was dangerously deceptive. She wouldn't know how to control him if he unleashed his rage.

Sliding back the quilt, Maggie stepped from behind the curtain to display her lovely new frock. The dress fit her as if it had been custom made. A high collar accentuated her slender neck and the fitted bodice clung to her round breasts in what appeared indecent without the benefit of a proper corset. The wide skirt swirled around her legs, making her feel regal with every step.

Cody nodded approvingly; an admiring smile lit his eyes. She stood in the center of the room and slowly turned to model the beautiful gown. For that split second Maggie looked young and alive again, admired by her beau. It was an exhilarating moment.

James snorted in disgust, "Still playing lady of the grand manor? A pity your face spoils the dress." He swung his arm wildly, intent on backhanding his wife, but stumbled sideways instead.

The joyous smile on Maggie's face vanished at the cruelty of his words. Her fairy tale had burst.

Cody reacted in a lightning swift movement. His recoiled fist connected with James' jaw with a solid impact that sent James sprawling flat. A red haze consumed his mind; he saw once again his mother lying in the dirt. Squeezing his eyes shut, he shook his head and blinked away the image. Cody stood with legs spread apart, one hand dangerously fingered the butt of his Colt revolver, as he waited for James to move.

"Touch her again and I'll kill you." He spoke in a deadly calm.

"Cody, no! It doesn't matter; it isn't worth a life." Maggie tugged on his arm, moving him away from James.

She had viewed the silent play in horror. Cody's stark, violent temper frightened her far more than James' abuse. The joy of seeing him again instantly shattered. This was an ugly side of him she had never witnessed before.

"Get out. I won't have a gun wielding murderer under my roof. Take back your gifts too."

With trembling hands, she unbuttoned the gown and slipped it off her body, standing before him in nothing but a chemise and petticoats. She thrust the dress into his arms and pointed toward the door.

"You're making a mistake." His face returned to its cold, chiseled look. "This is twice that you've banished me from your life."

"No, I'm trying to fix a mistake. I should never have given you my trust and affection," Maggie said is a voice barely above a whisper.

Cody studied her face then nodded. No emotion shone behind his icy blue eyes; only a small tic in his cheek gave evidence of a clenched jaw. He turned and slowly walked away.

The door shut behind him. Maggie stood in the center of the room, staring at the closed portal, listening to the sound of her heartbeat drumming in her ears. Cold shivers finally broke her reverie, and she dragged on her old clothes.

Now, she had to drape the pieces of her life about her like a worn coat, shabby and ill fitting, but serviceable. Any happiness that Cody offered was an illusion. Her marriage to James was her harsh reality, and it would take some mending.

Chapter 22

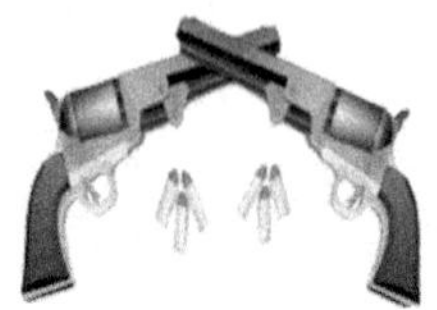

Retribution

Spring had finally arrived. Warmer temperatures filled the days while buttercups and prairie bluebell flowers dotted the fields.

James and Michael Canavan went off rounding up as many stray calves as they could find—the mavericks that Cody had foretold. James had benefited from the fresh air and exercise, appearing healthier than before.

Maggie devoted her time and efforts to preparing a plot of earth for a vegetable garden near the cabin. As she scratched away in the hard soil, she watched James cross the yard. He favored his good leg and walked with a slight limp, although he tried to hide it. He caught her watching him, frowned angrily, then turned away. James blamed her for the limp; she saw it in his eyes but she and Cody had done the best they could to properly set his broken leg. Neither was a doctor; it wasn't their fault.

Maggie and James planned to ride into Deer Springs and waited on Michael and Rose Canavan to join them so they could ride to town together. Safety in numbers.

Maggie had not been to town since last September. She worried about what would happen if she saw Cody again, yet the excitement of seeing people and the hustle and bustle of town life after being so isolated all winter overrode those fears.

"Rose, I can't thank you enough for all that you and Michael have done for us these past weeks. We would have perished without you, I know it," Maggie told her friend as she climbed atop the buckboard wagon.

Rose reached for her hand and squeezed affectionately. "You make too much of it. We didn't do all that much. I'm just happy we could help, especially now, with you in the family way and all." Rose's smile spread across her face.

Maggie hastened to admonish her to lower her voice. "I haven't told James yet that I am pregnant. I'll have to tell him soon, but not now."

"All right, Margaret. I don't understand all the secrecy. Won't he be happy about the baby? Michael would be fair to splitting his britches over the proud accomplishment. Men! You'd think we women have nothing to do with it at all," Rose continued in her observations and again Maggie had to remind her to hush.

The couples enjoyed the mild weather on their long ride into town. A light breeze prompted both women to remove their bonnets and allow the sun to warm their faces and lift their hair. It was grand just to be alive and free after the long winter confinement.

As they neared Deer Springs, the changes surprised the Dunlaps. The town had doubled its size with new buildings springing up along muddy streets like weeds in a meadow. They passed the cemetery on the outskirts of town and then rode past the livery stable. The rhythmic pounding of a hammer on an iron anvil rang out as they neared the blacksmith.

Some of the wooden clapboards still showed that bleached look from freshly milled lumber. The older establishments wore weathered or painted fronts. Maggie pointed out the dry goods store next to the barber. A bank had recently been added near the land office where they had first filed their claim for the ranch.

"You and Michael go ahead, James. Rose and I will meet you outside the mercantile. I need so many things. You men can take care of your business without the pair of us tagging along."

James readily agreed. He and Michael headed for the first saloon as soon as Rose and Maggie entered the general store.

Magically, Maggie felt like a child again as she stepped through the door, thrilled by all the wonderful sights and smells that beckoned and urged her forward. A rainbow of colorful fabric bolts drew her to the back corner and she fingered the lovely materials, remembering the soft blue gown that she had thrown back into Cody's face. She chased the image from her mind and turned to search for Rose. Her friend was reaching into a deep barrel, scooping corn seed into burlap sacks.

To her left, Maggie spied a wall of shelving laden with mason jars of all sizes and filled with an assortment of vegetables and fruits. Whoever had put up the canned peaches and spiced apple rings had done an excellent job; they looked delicious. She decided not to leave without at least a jar or two. The store bustled with activity as four more women shopped for dry goods and a couple of men argued with the clerk over the price of feed. Maggie measured twenty pounds each of flour and sugar. She looked longingly at the dress material, but knew she couldn't afford it, then added two jars of the precious fruit to her basket. James had given her two dollars to spend, and she was trying to stretch it as far as possible.

He never told her where he found the money. She was afraid he had won it playing poker with Michael Canavan. James fancied himself quite the card shark; he had spent all winter lying about playing with that deck of cards. She hated the thought that her friends might suffer by their hand. Heaven only knows, they could ill afford the loss. But James would only become angry if she questioned him and she had tried so hard to smooth the relationship between them. Now, with a baby on the way, she must hold her tongue and not rile him.

Maggie waited patiently by the cash register and nodded politely to an older woman. Maggie observed the elder woman extend her hand as the clerk painstakingly counted her change into her palm. The woman's sharp eyes watched his every movement.

"That's right, young man. And you tell Mr. Morgan that if he expects to continue doing business with me, he'll lower his prices. I recognize highway robbery when I see it and so will everyone else if I write an article in the paper about his unscrupulous ways!"

"I'm sorry, Mrs. Fitzhughes. But you really need to talk to Mr. Morgan. Gosh, I'm just a clerk."

Maggie watched her gather up her parcels and snap her purse closed. Then she surprised Maggie by giving her a quick wink and a nod before spinning on her heel and walking briskly out the door. Maggie almost laughed but caught herself in time as she realized the woman preferred to have the clerk think her stern. Maggie was immediately drawn to her sly humor and forthright manner.

"Who was that lady?"

"Mrs. Fitzhughes, she publishes the Gazette. I don't know what she thinks I can do."

"Does Mr. Morgan really gouge his prices?"

"Ah... I really wouldn't know, ma'am."

Maggie laid her selections on the counter and watched as the young clerk scratched some figures on a piece of scrap paper, adding the numbers twice, and twice coming up with a different total. She bit her lip, anxiously awaiting the outcome, praying she had enough money. She smiled at him lamely, as he nervously began again.

"Uh, that'll be two dollars and twenty-eight cents."

"Are you sure? Would you consider taking a little less for the peaches?"

"Well, gosh ma'am. I don't know if I can."

"I only have two dollars. Really."

He looked up at her and must have taken in her worn apparel and decided that her pleading was genuine because he smiled back and started packing the foodstuff into a large sack.

"Two dollars it is."

"Thank you very much." He would never know how much that moment of kindness meant to Maggie. She gathered up her purchases and went outside to wait upon Rose and the men.

A murmur of voices rode the light wind blowing down the dusty street. Maggie shaded her eyes from the noonday sun as she tried to see the source of the commotion. A group of men gathered in front of the Silver Spur Saloon. Two men stood apart and even from the short distance, she could make out the figure of Cody Jarvis. Maggie recognized that stoic stance as he stood alone while the crescendo of angry voices rose all around him.

"Been looking for you. Glad you got my message," Cody stated in a dangerous voice. He faced the gunman, locking eyes.

Fuller stared down the other man. Reckoning day had come. "Nothing personal, Jarvis. It was just a job."

"You made two mistakes, Fuller. One... you tried to kill me and two... you attacked a friend of mine. I don't take kindly to either."

"Let's settle this," Fuller challenged, his eyes never leaving Cody's.

Cody and Fuller stepped into the center of the empty street then deliberately backed away from each other until a short distance remained between them. The street became deathly silent, even the wind ceased, then a deafening noise split the air and a trail of gray gun smoke spiraled upwards. A man lay crumpled in the dirt while the spurs of the other jangled as he crossed the length between them.

Cody kicked the gun away from an outstretched hand lying in the dirt, pivoted, and strolled back toward the saloon. He didn't even bother to check if the man might still be alive. Finally, he had taken care of the last man that had tried to kill him and had attacked Clem. He had kept his promise.

The Sheriff came running out of his office and charged across the open space. He glanced at the dead man then ran up to Cody, grabbing his arm to turn him around. Cody stopped mid-stride and turned an evil eye at the puppet lawman.

"Leave it alone, Connor," Cody growled, pulled his arm out of the sheriff's grasp and continued toward his destination. He never noticed the achingly familiar face that had witnessed the deadly fight from across the street.

Maggie's eyes stung from the acrid smoke and unshed tears. Seeing Cody so near yet so far, watching him face danger, tore at her already fragile composure. She didn't hear James and Michael approach, so engrossed in her thoughts. James' question startled her.

"What?"

"I said, 'who got shot?' What's going on?"

"I don't know James. It just happened." Maggie put her hand to her forehead and closed her eyes.

"Well, you were right here watching. You must have seen something," James insisted, excited by the gruesome gun play.

"I don't know the man and neither do you. It doesn't concern us. Let's go. I'm not feeling well."

Only one thought was on her mind now, to get home and away from here. She did not want Cody to find them.

"I don't understand what you're so upset about, Margaret. Like you said, we don't know the man. You better get used to things like this; we're in the West now."

"I can't help it; murder distresses me!"

"Come on, James. Can't you see that Margaret really isn't well?" pleaded Rose. Rose looked at Margaret's pale face and turned worried eyes to Michael, silently beseeching her husband's help.

"Oh all right! Did you get everything you wanted in the store? I wanted to spend some time looking around too," James complained but relinquished.

"You can come back on your own another day," Maggie suggested to appease him.

Two days later, James returned from town. He was excited about an idea he had learned on how to increase their land holdings and build a bigger ranch. People would respect him if he owned more land; they wouldn't laugh at the drunken cripple behind his back.

Maggie still hadn't told him about the baby, fearing it would anger him. Her poor baby had not been conceived in love, but more likely during the night James had forced himself on her while in a drunken stupor. In her mind, Maggie knew God punished her for giving her heart to another and betraying her vows.

Chapter 23

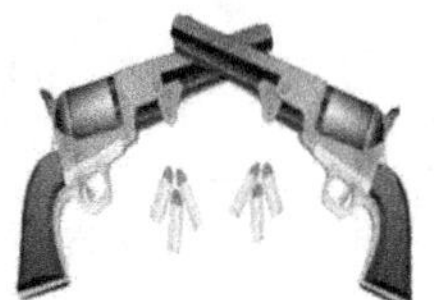

Olson

Cody entered Logan's office at the Silver Spur and stood before the large desk. He didn't pretend to hang on every word spoken by Zachary Logan or grovel at the master's feet. Cody studied the papers on the man's desk and tried to read them upside down. He deciphered figures listed on an invoice of silver ore then shifted his gaze to other papers. One document caught his interest; it partially covered a crude area map with parcels of land drawn and labeled. The Dunlap name jumped out at him. Why was Logan studying land grants? Did the land somehow relate to the silver claims?

Logan finally deemed to grant Cody his attention. Looking up from the papers on his desk, he leaned back in his chair and stared at the gunslinger.

"You've got more lives than a cat, Jarvis, and you've cost me several valuable men... men who did as they were told. Unlike you, they completed their assigned tasks," Logan said as he ground his cigar into a glass ashtray. He glared at the insolent man before him.

"Maybe we should part company then. I don't appreciate my boss sending men out to kill me. Was that one of your assigned tasks? Fuller and Woodrow got what they deserved," Cody answered in a lethal voice.

Logan would neither confirm nor deny he had ordered the killing. The two men continued to stare down one another, until Logan finally blinked and broke eye contact.

"Our business is done when I say it's done. Stay in town. I might need you to make another run to Laramie with Olson."

"When?"

"When I say," Logan snarled, then turned his back on the man.

Cody spun on his heel and left without another word. Maybe he could learn more about the counterfeit operation with more time spent with Olson. A trip to Laramie just might help. He was running out of options.

Scarlet smiled broadly as Cody Jarvis entered the Red Garter saloon. She hurried to his side as he stepped up to the bar.

"Hello stranger. What brings you back to town? I hope it was to see me." Scarlet rubbed her breasts against his arm invitingly and smiled, dimples deepening at the corners of her mouth.

Cody eased his arm away from Scarlet's pressing body and returned the smile. "Nice to see you too. How's it been around here? Been busy?"

"About the same. Spring weather has most of the farmers staying in their fields. Guess they're either too tired or too occupied to come into town; makes my evenings slow, but I'll get by."

"I'm sure you will, darlin'."

"Hey, did you ever find those men you were looking for?"

"Yeah, I found them." Cody sipped his beer and looked into the long mirror behind the bar.

The tone of his voice alerted Scarlet. Goose bumps danced along her arm as she saw the finality in his icy eyes. She read death in that blank stare and knew enough not to question more; she'd survived this long among cowhands and gunslingers by recognizing when to stay silent.

Cody finished the mug of beer in one gulp, then slid the empty glass across the bar surface.

"I'll be seeing you," he said.

"Can you stay the night?" asked Scarlet. She reached out a cloying hand, her voice desperately pleading.

"I don't think so. Take care." Cody kissed her cheek and gave her a brief hug then left Scarlet standing at the bar as he walked out the swinging doors.

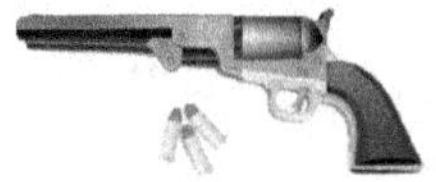

Like before, Cody stood in the doorway watching Olson count the dollar bills being paid for transferring raw silver ore to the assay office. The only difference this time was that Olson traveled with Cody alone due to the smaller quantity of ore carried in a leather pouch instead of the heavy stronghold box. They had made the trip to Fort Laramie on horseback, without the need of the buckboard.

Adam Trent opened his ledgers and wrote the ore quantity and percent of purity in his records. Satisfied, he closed the book and placed the ore into his large vault.

"Pleasure doing business with you, Mr. Olson. This last lot contained a much higher grade of silver. I'll be transferring it directly to the U.S. Mint in Denver."

"We hope to have similar deposits in the future." Olson nodded politely as he placed the currency into the leather pouch and secured its flap. "Good day, sir."

Olson and Cody untied their horses and mounted up. Careful to not draw attention to themselves, they rode slowly through the back streets of town toward the comfortable two-story boarding house they had frequented before. Missus Andrews greeted them at the door in the late afternoon.

"Hello, nice to see you gentlemen again. Will you be needing two rooms or just one?" She glanced between the two men.

Olson spoke up first, and since he was paying, Cody let him make the decision. He didn't care either way.

"Two single rooms would be best if you have the vacancies, ma'am," said the normally timid man as he cast friendly eyes on the widow and smiled.

"I can manage that. Would you like to join us for supper? I'll be serving shortly for a small additional charge." The widow met Olson's appreciative look, returned his smile then lowered her eyes.

That was all the encouragement that Olson needed. Suddenly, he stood taller and straighter, preening, his chest puffed out. Cody had to hide his grin behind his hand, coughing lightly, amazed as he watched the transformation of the little man.

"We will, of course, accept your gracious invitation to dine. I'm sure whatever you cook must be delicious," Olson replied politely.

The woman withdrew two room keys and handed them each to Cody and Olson.

"Your rooms are both on the right, at the end of the hall. If you want to freshen up, come downstairs in a few minutes. I'll start serving supper."

"Thank you, Missus Andrews," Olson said as he held her hand a fraction longer than needed when he grasped the room key.

Cody and Olson climbed the stairs, and each entered their comfortable and clean bedrooms. Cody sat on the side of the bed and heaved a sigh of relief. It felt good to unwind and have time to think. Now all he had to do was get Clyde Olson to spill the beans about that counterfeit money.

Cody washed up and made his way downstairs to join one other boarder and Clyde Olson who had hurried his ablutions and now grinned like a schoolboy at the widow Andrews. She shyly returned his smile and heaped a generous serving of food onto his plate as she made her way around the table. Cody watched the courtship with amusement and a raised eyebrow. Did every man look as foolish when he was smitten with a lass? His mind returned to thoughts of Maggie Dunlap and her well-being. He had promised her he'd stay away, but he knew in his heart he would break that promise. With that decision made, Cody relaxed and turned his attention to the delicious food in front of him.

They departed early the next morning. Olson's face beamed with a wide smile as Missus Andrews presented him with a small parcel of food for the journey and placed a light kiss on his cheek. There was no doubt in Cody's mind that the man wouldn't wash that cheek for days, maybe never again. He silently chuckled to himself.

After riding for hours, Cody took advantage of Olson's mellow mood by trying to pry some information out of him.

Cody glanced over at the man riding alongside him. In a casual, conversational voice, he asked, "When we get back to Deer Springs, how soon will we swap the counterfeit money for this currency?"

"Hmm? Same day probably," answered Olson, still in a dreamy mood. He immediately reined in sharply and stared in horror, realizing what he had just confessed to Cody. "You know about the operation?"

"Oh sure, that's why Logan had me come along with you. Don't worry, your secret is safe with me." He presented a passive expression to the diminutive man, hoping it would re-assure him.

"Oh. I didn't know. Um, he never said, but I guess it makes sense."

"There wasn't much ore in this transfer. Was this just one transaction? One miner?" asked Cody and held his breath, waiting to see if Olson continued to answer or would clam up.

"Um, yeah, Jergen's claim is the only one that consistently produces."

"That's what I thought. They work that site hard."

Both men fell back into a lapse of silence as they continued trotting toward Deer Springs. Cody glanced at Olson again and tried to gauge the man's thoughts. Would he mention to Logan the topic of their conversation, or would he just assume it natural and on the up and up between Cody and Logan? It was a gamble Cody had to risk.

The day after they returned to Deer Springs, Logan called Cody into his office.

"Jarvis! Get in here," yelled Zachary Logan when he spotted the man in question enter the saloon.

Cody sauntered over to the back office and waited in the doorway.

"Come in and close the door."

He did as he was told then waited. Seconds later, his mis-givings were confirmed.

"Olson and I had a little conversation; seems you asked him about some counterfeit bills. What gives you that idea?"

"Huh, a blind man could see the difference in touch and look of real currency versus that funny money you're printing. It didn't take much to put two and two together," Cody stated defiantly.

Logan studied the other man's face. "Suppose it's true. What're you going to do about it?"

"Nothing ... as long as I get my cut," Cody said. He was smart enough to know that Logan only understood greed; he'd be suspicious of any other motive.

Logan nodded then laughed out loud. "And here I was thinking you might be turning into a choir boy. Well, well. Let me think about it. I assume you know to keep your mouth shut."

"Naturally. Wouldn't want to kill the goose that lays the golden eggs. You've got quite an operation here, Logan. Why shouldn't I enjoy a piece of it?" With that comment, Cody turned and left Logan to think over his proposition. *What was that old saying? If you can't beat them, join them. Maybe he could learn where the press and plates were located by being part of the operation.*

Chapter 24

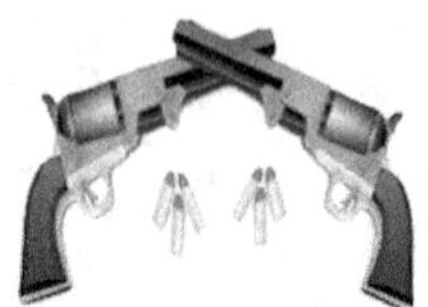

April 1885

Maggie paused in her work, rubbed the minor ache in her lower back, and enjoyed the sights and sounds surrounding her. The spring sunshine had renewed life after its winter hibernation, causing the land to bloom. Everywhere she looked, wildflowers waved their soft white and pastel colored heads in the gentle breeze blowing across the meadow. Pretty white flowers, hollyhocks, and penny grass dotted the plains.

Their life had taken on a pleasant routine. Maggie rose early and scratched around in her little vegetable garden then fed the handful of chickens in the nearby pen. James was up and out early, tending to stock and mending fences. She marveled at what a difference a few months had made. They had been so down on their luck at the beginning of winter and now she felt almost prosperous – a house, fenced corral with 2 horses, chickens, cows, and cattle on the range. Their ranch was becoming a reality. James had even made improvements on the cabin. He had promised to build on another room, and with Michael's help, repair the roof once and for all.

She wondered if maybe now she could tell him of the baby. Maggie had caught him looking at her with speculating eyes. She tried to convince herself that their life together could be happy.

Approaching riders interrupted Maggie's musings; two men rode toward the house and one other galloped from the direction of town. She recognized Michael and James as they crossed the western meadow. She shaded her eyes to better spy the identity of the lone rider in the east. Cody Jarvis— She couldn't believe it. Cody reached the yard first, dismounted, and quickly walked to her side, still holding the reins of his horse.

"How are you?" His eyes spoke volumes as he studied her appearance, searching for signs of abuse. He remembered too well his last sight of her.

"I'm fine. What are you doing here? I told you to never come back."

"I keep breaking my word where you're concerned. I worry about you. Don't hate me Maggie."

"I don't, but..." she stopped as she watched James leap off his mare and stride angrily toward them.

"Would you look at the two of you? First time my back is turned, I catch you playing around. I oughta ..." James' hand whipped across Maggie's face with a stinging slap. She stumbled backwards and fell onto the garden hoe.

"Dunlap, I warned you before what I would do to you if I ever caught you hurting her. You deserve to be shot down like the dog you are." Cody's hand slid to his gun holster.

Maggie crawled the few feet separating Cody and James. Her mind was in a whirl—she hesitated between the two. James saw her dilemma and sneered.

"What's the matter, Margaret, can't decide between your husband or your lover? You whore! Do you think I don't know what the two of you were doing when I was abed?"

"James, you're wrong! Please, please stop this. I'm going to have a baby!" she blurted out, beseeching both men to be reasonable.

Cody relaxed his hand on his revolver. He smiled at her tenderly, hauntingly, before turning cold, watchful eyes to James.

"Am I supposed to believe that's my baby? You lying bitch!" James kicked at her viciously, striking her abdomen, causing Maggie to double over in pain. He drew back his foot to plant another kick, but halted in motion as an ominous click filled the air.

Cody stood with his gun drawn and pointed menacingly at James. "I warned you. I've given you more chances than any man deserves."

"Cody, please, no. Think of me and the baby," Maggie sobbed. "Please go, for my sake." She held her breath as she tried to read his expression and the thoughts behind them.

Cody looked down at Maggie, pity or love on his face, she couldn't tell. He gradually lowered the gun's hammer then reached out in a lightning fast move to pistol-whip James across the side of his head. James crumpled to the ground unconscious. Cody smiled with satisfaction then knelt to Maggie. He lifted her and carried her lovingly into the house, gently placing her on the bed.

Maggie was sore and battered and gave herself over to his tender ministrations. His hand caressed her face, stroked her cheek and smoothed back strands of fallen hair.

"Are you all right? Should I get you something?" He was at a loss as to what to do. Cody held her hand, pressing it between his own.

"Just go. I'll be okay. Can't you see that every time you come back, it makes it that much harder for me to endure? I have to make a life here with James. I have no choice."

He sat on the side of the bed, taking Maggie into his strong arms and kissed her with a gentleness that exploded into a fiery passion. She clung to him and kissed him back for all eternity.

"I love you Maggie Dunlap. If you ever need me, I'll come running." He released her back onto the pillows, then stood up and turned to go.

Tears slid down her face as she whispered, "I love you too." She didn't know if he had heard her or not as her eyes locked on his silhouette standing in the open doorway.

When Cody walked over to his waiting horse, he saw Michael Canavan tending to his friend.

Michael scowled at Cody, "You better get out of here, Jarvis. You've caused enough trouble for one day. Good thing James and me is tolerant, or you'd be the one on the ground!"

"Humph." Cody looked at the pathetic pair. "Maggie could use your wife's help, Canavan."

Later that night, Maggie hemorrhaged. Rose Canavan sat with her, trying to stop the bleeding with packing between her legs. It was no use. Her baby daughter was born and died in the morning; poor little thing, conceived in violence and brought into the world by violence. James wouldn't need to worry about the father's identity now. Maggie named her Anna after her own mother. She buried her tiny form among the tall elm trees near the cabin.

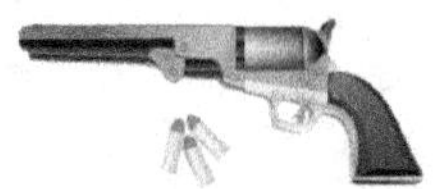

Maggie wiped the sweat from her brow; hands and nails encrusted with dirt from hours spent toiling in her vegetable garden. She proudly harvested the fruits of her labors in the hot, late August sun: carrots, onions, and potatoes filled several baskets. Work on the ranch was never ending; always wood to chop and stack or meat to salt and cure to be stored in the newly dug root cellar along with her vegetables. Maggie had learned that when work consumed her body, it gave her mind no time to linger on thoughts of what ifs.

James and Michael had struggled the past month to dig a root cellar beneath the new room addition. Wooden planks lined the cellar walls and floor to keep the earth from caving in and provided a dry, cool environment to store their precious food stuffs that must see them through the winter months ahead. Their accomplishment pleased Maggie, plus the added benefit of James' sobriety while he concentrated on the exhausting job.

Unfortunately, with the project done, James had returned to his habit of visiting town to gamble and drink for hours on end. Today was no exception. The sun had gone down hours earlier, and the cabin was silent save for the occasional scratching noise of Maggie's pen on paper as she sat writing in her journal. She allowed herself one small luxury, a lantern lit at night to see to her sewing or to indulge in the joy of writing. The glimmer of light illuminated her small corner of the dark cabin. The scrape of the door opening and closing made Maggie look up. She watched James stagger into the cabin.

She didn't need more light to tell that he had been drinking; the liquor fumes were stronger than the stench of sweat and horse on his clothes. He dropped his hat on the table and struggled to kick off his boots, cursing as he hopped on one foot while trying to maintain his balance.

Maggie clapped her hand across her mouth to stifle any sound, but he heard the small gasp and turned toward her. His eyes glared in hatred. His mouth twisted into a snarl that turned his face into a cruel mask. This evil shadow of a man loomed in front of her. Where was the husband that she had married? Was he gone forever?

"What are you looking at? Still scratching in that damn book?" James sneered. "Think you're so smart, well you just wait ... people are going to respect James Dunlap. I'm gonna make this ranch bigger than Canavan's or even Logan's place. And I found out how to do it all legal like too. Just need to stake out parcels of land for every one of my sons, and you, madam, are going to provide them."

She stared at him, dumbfounded. He must have been thinking of this idea for some time, but her mind rejected the notion of ever sharing a loving marriage bed again. James had not come near her since before April and the loss of Anna. She couldn't believe he was planning a family and a future for them.

A moment later, she was right to doubt his *loving suggestion.* There was no love in his expression as he approached the bed and threw her onto her back.

"Spread your legs, whore, like you did for Jarvis. I'm going to take what is mine. By God, I need a son and you're going to give me one if I have to take you every night."

His rough hands shoved her nightgown up about her hips; dirty fingers groped her flesh painfully. She screamed in protest. Maggie pushed against his chest and twisted and turned, but her thrashing only aroused him more.

"Go ahead and scream. Who do you think will hear you?"

He laughed drunkenly, reveling in her panic and fear. His meaty fist connected with Maggie's left cheek and eye; pain shot though her head, making the room spin. She blacked out just before he thrust into her—again, and again.

Maggie's marriage had turned into a nightmare of rape by her own husband night after night, until her body was numb and her spirit broken. She was nothing more than a potential brood mare to him.

Was this to be her punishment for giving her love to another? She'd been physically faithful to James, although he would never believe her, but God knows she could not control her heart's desire.

By the end of September, Maggie was as certain as a woman could be that she was indeed pregnant again. James had succeeded in his plans to own more land. She prayed now he would leave her alone. If they survived another winter, her baby would arrive sometime in June.

Chapter 25

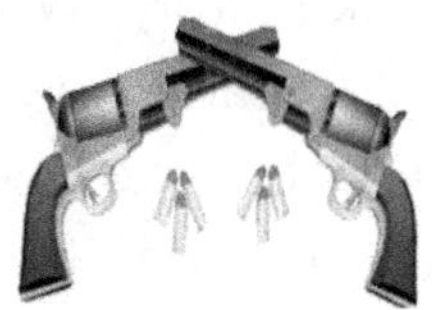

Discovery

Cody sat at the table; one hand gripped the handle of his glass beer mug and the other loosely held his cards. His mind drifted, paying only half interest to the poker game in front of him. He watched Kelly move about the room lighting oil lamps as dusk deepened and shadows grew in the saloon. Cody reclined back in his seat; his front chair legs rose from the floor, the backrest supported by the wall behind him. He regarded the players at his table, but the commotion at the poker table across the room really drew his attention.

James Dunlap slapped his cards onto the table and bellowed loudly, "I call. Try and beat that hand!" He reached for the handful of chips in the center of the table and dragged them toward his pile.

Cody kept the drunken Dunlap under observation as the noise at that table became louder, the level of boasting expanded, and the threat of danger heightened. Cody scrutinized the three men playing against James, all were gun hands he recognized from Logan's ranch. He doubted they would put up with Dunlap's behavior much longer, and that would spell trouble for the man. He watched and waited, debating whether to step in, then decided against it.

Disgusted with listening to the obnoxious Dunlap brag about his card skills, Cody tossed his own hand onto the table. He slid his chair backward and stood.

"Deal me out. I'm done for the night," he said as he carried his mug over to the bar and slid it toward Kelly.

"Haven't seen Abe or Ike lately. Where'd they get to?" He asked Kelly as he rested a forearm on the bar, one foot on the brass bar rail and turned his back to the room.

"Dunno. Logan probably has 'em working at the ranch."

Cody gave a short laugh, "Can't see the two of them punching cows. They must have gotten on Logan's bad side. Well, see you later."

"Yeah, you do that." Kelly turned his attention back to wiping a cloth over the top of the bar and poured the remains of half-empty mugs into a slop bucket.

Cody walked along the wooden sidewalk that stretched in front of the Silver Spur toward the land office and barber shop just past it. He stood lost in thought, stared at the night sky and watched a shooting star streak across the horizon.

With no actual destination in mind, Cody wandered down the street, his footsteps taking him into the stable. A lantern hung from a rafter and Clem sat working on a frayed saddle cinch. So intent on his work, Clem didn't hear Cody enter.

"Harumph," Cody cleared his throat to announce his presence. He studied Clem's figure and realized the man appeared more frail, older now, since the beating he had taken. His wounds might be healed, but the old timer wouldn't be the same again. Pity. Cody missed the defiant rascal.

Clem put down the leather punch and awl then looked up at Cody as he walked into the circle of light. "What're you up to, roaming around in the night?"

Cody straddled a small bale of hay to sit near Clem. He dangled his hat between his legs; the brim gripped between thumb and forefinger of his left hand. Cody dragged fingers through his hair with the other hand, silent, eyes not focusing on his immediate surroundings. His mind in turmoil.

"I don't know what to do, Clem. It's been well over a year and I'm no closer to nabbing Logan than the day I arrived. Hate to admit it, but I think Logan has outsmarted me. I've seen counterfeit money being passed around town and I can't do anything about it. Hell, I witnessed the swap of real money for counterfeit in the mining office, but I don't know where it's being printed. If I can't prove Logan is behind it, I can't arrest him." For the first time in his career, Cody felt defeated.

"That so? You know for sure this here money is phony? Doesn't surprise me. I always wondered how Zachary Logan had so much money to buy up land and businesses around town. Makes sense if he's making his own," Clem said as he scratched his bald head.

"I'm sorry Clem. I know you thought I was some big hero that was gonna swoop in and clean up Deer Springs. I'm not that guy. I hate to disappoint you. Nothing has gone the way I wanted."

"Well, seems to me, the first thing you need to do is climb out of that self-pity hole you dug for yourself." Clem stared at Cody. Their eyes locked. He leaned toward him and punched the younger man on the shoulder. "Look at you. You're young and healthy. You've got your whole life ahead of you. Quit wallowing and start doing."

Cody considered the words of the older man. He admitted it; he was feeling sorry for himself. When he watched a drunk like James Dunlap, he thought of Maggie— the wife Dunlap didn't deserve and the woman he loved but could never have. And then there was Logan and the injustice of it all. It was too much.

"You're right. Guess I just needed someone to kick me in the butt. Thanks old friend," Cody said. He nodded and patted Clem's arm affectionately as he rose. Settling the Stetson back onto his head, he walked over to Lightning's stall and saddled up the stallion.

"Going somewhere?" asked Clem as he watched the younger man move with a determination that had been missing before.

"Yep. I've searched the saloon and the mining office and came up empty. Just one more place to look. Think I'll check out Logan's ranch a bit closer."

"Be careful out there," warned Clem as he picked up his tools and returned to his task.

The half-moon cast a pale glow, barely illuminating the dark out-buildings surrounding the main house of the Diamond Bar. It had taken close to two hours of riding from town to gain access to Logan's ranch and now Cody studied the night sky trying to judge how much time was left before sunrise. He tied Lightning in a copse of trees behind the barn then crept on foot toward the cluster of buildings.

The sound of loud snores coming from one narrow building confirmed the bunk house. Cody laughed to himself as he recalled the freight train that emitted from Abe's mouth when he slept. Yep, he was in there all right. No light shone through the window; no one appeared to be awake.

Cody moved on toward the next building and peeked inside. A tack room filled with extra harnesses, bridles, and saddles. He poked around at a couple of boxes stacked in one corner; lifted the lid of one box and was surprised to see ammunition. Cases of bullets for both handguns and rifles were stored next to the tack, enough to start a minor war by the looks of it. What was Logan preparing for?

Located furthest away from the house, the massive red barn sat with wide double doors. The doors were closed but not latched as Cody inched one open just wide enough to slip inside, carefully closing the door behind him. He stepped lightly in the dark expanse of the barn, his footsteps muted by the layer of straw covering the floor. His eyes peered into the blackness. He tried not to arouse any of the animals as he passed their stalls. One side of the barn held a row of horse stalls, all occupied. A horse whickered faintly as he walked past; Cody froze and listened for any sounds or movement from a stable hand. Hearing none, he proceeded.

The other side of the huge barn contained a couple of milk cows in one large stall connected, by the smell of it, to a pigpen at the far end. He listened to tiny piglets rooting for the sow's tits as they nursed; the mother grunted softly as she rolled to a more comfortable position.

The rear of the barn contained bales of hay stacked from floor to ceiling, like most farms and ranches, but as Cody moved toward the wall of hay, he noticed one thing different... this wall held a gap between the wall of bales and the outer wall of the barn. Cody felt along the hay bales, groping in the dark until he could determine the open space then squeezed into the gap. The hay had created a secret corner in the barn. As he stepped forward, he bumped into a massive piece of machinery. The black iron blended into the darkness of the night.

"Ow," Cody cursed silently and rubbed his shin bone where he had bruised it on the heavy iron. Even working in the dark, blind as he was, he was sure. Cody ran his hand along the lines of the machine and smiled to himself; he had found the printing press. Feeling along the wooden and metal contours of the press, he crouched down to look under it and along the sides, then moved about the narrow corner searching for printing supplies. He found no boxes of paper, ink, or anything that appeared to be the counterfeit plates. All he had was the press.

If he confronted Logan with his findings of a printer press, Logan could claim he had planned on starting a newspaper or some other innocent occupation. Without the engraved plates for currency, he had no case to prove counterfeiting.

A faint glimmer of light suddenly shone through cracks between the hay bales. So involved with studying the printing press, Cody hadn't heard anyone enter the barn. All his senses sprung alert. Cody stood still. He strained to listen as footsteps shuffled in the straw; if he didn't move, he'd be caught within the confined corner. He slipped out of the tight opening and moved into the last horse stall to hide in the dark, holding his breath as he eyed the movement of the swinging light. Someone held a lantern; it swayed as the person walked.

Cody crouched low behind the gate. The mare wasn't happy about sharing her space and stomped her front hoof.

"Easy girl," whispered Cody. He patted the horse's nose and tried to calm and quiet her.

He peeked through the narrow hinge opening of the stall door and glimpsed Abe stumble about, half asleep or drunk. He held a lantern with a low burning candle inside that produced a shallow circle of light in the pitch darkness of the barn. Abe turned toward the sound of the mare then jumped in fear as the sow snorted and let out a loud squeal in her pen. The lantern swung precariously as a startled Abe spun around, his feet twisted, then he ran from the demon in the dark. In his haste, he dropped the lantern near a bale of hay. The hay ignited into a ball of flames and tumbled onto the printing press.

Cody sneaked out of the horse stall. The mare whinnied angrily at the smell of smoke and bolted through its gate. All the horses began to stomp and snort then kicked at their stall doors and walls. In the blackness and commotion, Cody escaped the barn and slipped into the stand of trees where Lightning fretted nervously.

Sarah Logan stood in the upstairs window, like an unseen ghost, she observed the turmoil below her and recognized the lone figure escaping into the trees. Her lips curled into the slightest of smiles.

"Fire! Fire!" Voices cried out as men ran from the bunkhouse and lights blinked on in the main house. Animals stampeded in a panic from the barn; men grabbed buckets of water to throw on the growing fire as bedlam erupted. In the chaos, Cody galloped away supposedly unseen and headed back to town.

The next day, Cody was talking with Kelly at the Silver Spur when Ike and Abe both straggled in. Their clothes were coated with black soot and smelled of smoke, burnt straw, and manure. Abe's face wore streaks of soot and other brown stains; one of his eyebrows appeared to be singed. Cody took one look at the pair and laughed out loud. The pair halted in front of him, bristling.

"What happened to you guys? You look like you've been playing in a coal mine," Cody said, trying not to laugh again.

Logan, upon hearing the commotion, came out of his office and walked over to the group.

"We had a fire in the barn last night. You wouldn't happen to know anything about that, would you?"

Cody looked him square in the eye, "No. Why would I? Anyone injured? Have much damage?"

"Harumph, just some equipment and bales of hay. We got all the animals out in time," Logan stated.

"That's good," said Cody as he faced the pair of men. "You two need a good scrubbing."

With one last glare at Cody, Logan stomped to his office and slammed the door.

Chapter 26

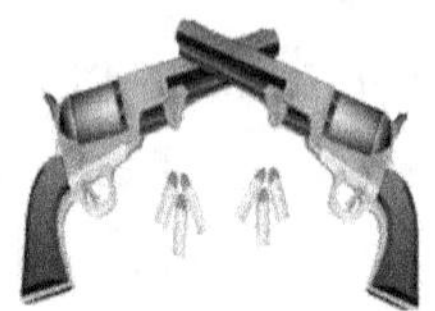

January 1886

Winter blew in with a vengeance, brutally cold and cruel. Cody sat before the pot-bellied stove in the corner of Clara's front room. An upended barrel held a board and set of checkers between his knees and Clem's. Both men studied the board for their next move, taking their time, in no hurry to finish the game because that would mean venturing out into the snow. Animals waited in the stable and the men delayed their feeding while they warmed their hands and behinds near the hot stove.

Clem moved his red checker piece and jumped two of Cody's black disks before he paused. "Ha, betcha didn't see that move coming!" he chortled.

"Hmm, you're right, but did you know you just left your flank unprotected?" Cody asked with a grin as he moved one of his pieces in a zig-zag pattern across the board, jumped and claimed three of Clem's disks. "Crown me," he said as his player gained the square next to Clem.

Clem scratched his balding head, "Well, I'll be."

Cody laughed and pointed to the board, "You're running out of men. Better make your next move a good one."

Clara shook her head at the pair then poured them each a fresh cup of hot coffee before she joined them near the heat, her mending on her lap. She glanced at the front window. The glass rattled in its frame as strong winds howled in the snowstorm.

"Looks like that storm is whipping up into a real blizzard. Sure don't like the looks of it," commented Clara.

"Haven't had a blizzard in the past five years; gonna have some dead cattle on the plains if the temperatures drops any more," Clem said as he sipped his coffee then sat back and sighed. "Reckon I better see to the stable before it gets any worse."

"I'll lend a hand, Clem. Need to see to Lightning."

"Guess we'll finish this when we get back," Clem said as he slowly rose and limped toward his coat and hat hanging on a peg by the door. His old bones took longer and longer to work out the kinks after sitting for awhile and the cold didn't help none. Clem shrugged on his coat and wrapped a thick scarf about his neck, pulling the wool up over his nose and mouth. He pushed a wool knit hat down over his ears and pulled on a pair of gloves before reaching for the doorknob.

Both men bundled up against the storm, but when they stepped outside, a gust of wind hit them with a force that almost knocked them over. Cody took Clem's arm and they clung together, leaned into the ferocious gale, as they made their way toward the stables. The enclosed barn offered protection from the snow and wind, but not the bitter cold. Clem took a hammer and broke up a layer of ice on top of the water buckets for each horse. He poured a generous amount of oats and grain into the feed bag for Lightning and his own mare, then generously fed the cankerous nanny goat.

"Hey boy, how you doin'?" Cody spoke to Lightning as he brushed his coat then draped two long blankets across his back and hindquarters. "This ought to help keep you warm."

Lightning shook its head and neighed. He nuzzled Cody's hand, looking for his apple treat that Clem always gave him. "Sorry boy, no treat today."

Clem neared the stallion's stall and pulled a withered carrot from his pocket and held it out to the large black horse. Lightning readily chomped on the special treat.

Grinning at Cody as both horses greedily ate the dried carrots, Clem explained, "Best I could find in Clara's root cellar were these old carrots, no apples left." He rubbed Lightning's nose then turned his attention to his own horse, covering the mare in a couple heavy blankets. "Wish I could do more to keep them warm. Guess this'll have to do."

"At least they're dry and out of the wind. Maybe you ought to let that nanny goat join the horses in their stalls; she looks awfully lonely over there. Let her share the warmth. I don't think Lightning will kick up a fuss over the goat nearby," Cody said as he stroked the stallion's head.

"Reckon you're right."

"Hey Clem, I've been meaning to ask you; have you noticed a decrease in currency around town? Seems like I've seen more coins being used at the Spur and less paper."

"Now that you mention it, Morgan, over at the general store, was counting out silver coins the last time I was in. Some prospectors were buying food stuffs and paid more with coin and only a couple of paper dollars."

"I'm thinking that barn fire destroyed a certain printing press and may have put a stop to Logan's funny money, at least for awhile. I just wish I could have found those engraving plates; without them I don't have a case."

"Hmmm, I don't know nothing about plates like you call 'em, but if I were Logan, I'd keep something like that close at hand. Know what I mean?"

"Yeah, wouldn't surprise me if he slept with them under his pillow! C'mon, we better be getting back or we may have to spend the night in this barn," Cody said as he checked on Lightning's water and feed levels one last time then prepared to venture outside again.

They held onto hitching posts and door frames between the stable and Clara's boarding house as they bucked the snow squall and headwinds. Cody's thoughts turned to Maggie, praying she was safe and warm in this blizzard. That drunken fool husband of hers better take care of her or he'd have to answer to him.

The town of Deer Springs and the surrounding plains remained under a blanket of deep snow for months. It was early spring before the first thaw came and with it the dead, frozen carcasses of cattle spotted across the land. Every ranch and homestead were affected; some felt the loss more than others. The established ranches with large herds suffered the loss better than the small homesteaders with a few head of cattle that were now all gone.

Cody stood at the end of the bar and watched a pair of down on their luck homesteaders shuffle toward Zachary Logan, standing by his office door. Their dragging feet and threadbare clothing that hung on emaciated frames gave evidence of their situation. The wife's gaunt face and haunted eyes mirrored the defeat of the husband as he approached Logan.

"Mister Logan, sir, can I talk with you?"

Logan stepped into his office and gestured for the couple to follow. "What can I do for you...?

The couple stood in the open doorway, nervous, afraid to step into the office. Cody could see and hear them from his vantage point at the bar.

"Carver... Jake Carver and my missus. We want to sell our homestead. We're pulling up stakes. I hear tell that you buy land."

"Well, Mister Carver, where's your place located?" Logan pulled out a rolled map of the territory. Blue and red squares drawn across the region marked the Diamond Bar ranch boundaries and the parcels of neighboring spreads. He pointed at the map. "Which of these is yours?"

Jake Carver studied the map before him; the lines and words on the paper made little sense to him. His wife had more book learning than him. He whispered in her ear and nodded to her to take a look. Logan watched the pair.

The wife stepped forward; her voice trembled as she pointed to a red square drawn on the map. "Our place is east of the Canavan ranch. So I guess, if this spot says Canavan, I'm thinking this must be us," she said uncertainly as her finger rested on the paper.

Logan studied the parcel of land and its location. Yes, that would do nicely. He glanced up at the couple. The husband wrung his hands and the wife waited meekly to hear his decision. He almost felt sorry for them, almost, but not quite.

"Blizzard hit you hard?"

"Yes sir, we lost all our livestock and most of the crop we had planted. We've got nothing left. The wife wants to head back East," Carver said in a meek voice.

"We all took a hit from that storm. I can give you ten cents an acre, that's all. Take it or leave it."

"But we paid two dollars an acre for that piece of land. It's rich soil, good for farming, and the river runs through it. I gotta have more," argued Carver desperately.

"I'm offering you sixteen dollars cash, Mister Carver, that ought to pay train fare to get back East. Like I said, take it or leave it. We can go over to the land office now and close the deal. All you have to do is sign the deed over to me and I'll pay you on the spot."

"Can we think it over?"

The couple stepped outside the open door and huddled close together, discussing their options in frantic whispers.

Logan waited with arms crossed and a cigar dangling from is mouth. He studied the map in front of him and salivated in anticipation.

"Don't do it," Cody said in a low voice.

The husband's head jerked up. He stared at Cody. "What did you say?"

"Don't do it. I'll offer you a better deal for your land." Cody slid his beer mug along the counter, putting some distance between them and the open doorway. He turned his back to Logan's office and pretended to study the room.

The husband and wife hesitated then stepped closer. Carver nervously glanced back toward Logan inside his office and shot Cody a questioning look.

"I can't give you what you paid for your land but I can give you a dollar an acre, gold; that ought to help you make a fresh start," Cody stated.

A timid smile curved the wife's lips and a glimmer of hope filled the man's eyes. Cody nodded at the pair and for the first time noticed the woman's tummy bulge; she was expecting a child. His thoughts immediately turned to Maggie as he looked at this desperate couple. *How was she? Did she survive the brutal winter?*

"We'll take it."

"Meet me at the land office, just across the street. And this transaction stays between the two of us. Okay? You just tell Zachary Logan that you changed your mind."

Cody heard the angry growl explode from Logan's office after the Carvers rushed out of the Silver Spur. He smiled to himself, satisfied, knowing that at least for today, he prevented Logan from cheating another desperate homesteader. This one parcel of land won't be added to the Diamond Bar empire. Cody finished his beer and left the saloon. He was about to become a landowner.

Chapter 27

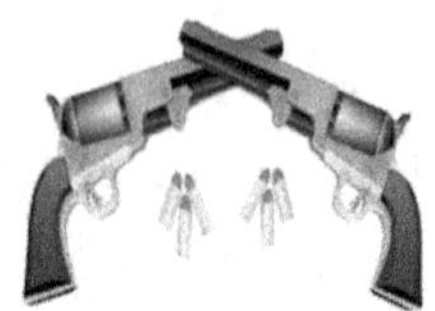

June 1886

Maggie Dunlap reclined against her pillow, exhausted from the difficult birth of her son. Hours of labor and unbearable pain ended when she heard the lusty wail of her son's cries.

She finished nursing the baby and laid him in the cradle next to her bed when James stumbled into the cabin. He walked over to the cradle and lifted the blanket to peer at his son. James' hair appeared wet as if he had bathed in the river attempting to sober up, but Maggie could still smell the whiskey on his breath and his clothes reeked of tobacco.

"We need to name him. Do you have any ideas?" she asked James.

"He looks mighty small. Are you feeding him right? I got big plans for my boy."

"The doctor and Rose both said he's healthy and looks like any normal baby. I'm taking care of him the best I can. It would help though if I had more fresh milk to drink. Can't you find time to at least milk the cow while you're home?"

"Are you going to nag me again, woman? I'll get your damn milk when I can. Do something useful; put down this name in that book of yours... Alexander John Dunlap. That's what I want him called."

"Alexander. I like it. All right, we'll name him Alexander John."

"When are you getting out of that bed? Who's going to cook my supper?"

"Rose made you food. Look in the pie cabinet; she left you a plate. The doctor says I have to stay in bed until the bleeding stops. James, I'm not well."

"Humph, just acting high and mighty, if you ask me. Don't think you're going to be pampered like some duchess; you're still nothing but a whore in my eyes."

James grabbed his plate and slammed the cabin door as he stormed out. The baby began to cry and Maggie cuddled him to her breast. Tears filled her eyes.

A month later, James returned from town with a packet of papers to file for a parcel of land in Alexander's name. He strutted around the cabin, bragging about how big and important he would be with these extra hundred and sixty acres as a landowner in the territory.

Maggie listened to his empty boast and studied the filthy, dirty smelling man before her. James expected to make his mark on the land and demand people's respect. Why can't he understand he could earn more respect if he would stop being a drunk?

James paced the floor, took a swig of whiskey from the bottle ever close at hand. His eyes glazed over as he relished the land baron he would become.

"What are you looking at?" he demanded as he caught Maggie's studious look.

"Nothing," she said and realized that she felt no affection for the stranger he had become. The wedding vows she had pledged so long ago imprisoned her, and now she must face a future filled with no love; her son her only happiness. Sometimes she dared to allow herself dreams and memories of Cody and thought ... if only.

James was told he needed some kind of improvement to the new land, either buildings or farming to satisfy the grant and make it legal. Lumber purchased from the mill in town was costly and cutting down your own trees was back-breaking work, so construction of some type of building was out. James had thought of a better and easier way.

"We'll plant fruit trees," he told Maggie. "I found a local man that will trade me apple tree saplings for one of our steers."

Maggie raised an eyebrow at this bit of news, but wisely chose to say nothing. Barter had become their way of life. Cash money seemed to be always at a minimum unless James needed a poker stake and then it seemed he miraculously managed to find some coin.

Her normal daily routine included tending to the three Guernsey cows and chickens that produced milk and eggs, which she bartered for flour and other staples at the general store. She was proud of the thick cream and butter that she made to sell along with her eggs for the much needed goods. The milk and eggs also provided nourishment for herself and baby Alex when other food stuffs at home were scarce.

Maggie packed up jars of cream and wrapped butter pounds then waited on James to hitch up the buckboard wagon to drive them into town. It was her first trip into town in months, certainly since the baby was born. For once, the weather was mild with a pleasant breeze and Maggie looked forward to a visit to Deer Springs and the chance for social contact after the long, lonely days spent on the ranch. Alex napped peacefully in her arms; hopefully he would not awaken and demand a feeding until she concluded her business in town.

"Well? Let's get a move on," James commanded as he carried the packed basket outside.

Maggie climbed up into the wagon; the baby clutched in one arm while she pulled herself onto the wooden seat. She covered the baby's face with a thin cloth to protect him from the swirling dust kicked up along the well-worn trail as they began their trek. The sway of the lumbering wagon and the warm sun on her face lulled Maggie into a light doze. She jerked awake at the sudden noise of voices shouting, a blacksmith's anvil clanging, and the commotion of town.

As they neared the mercantile store, several boisterous men stumbled from the wooden sidewalk and nearly fell into the path of their wagon. They cursed violently and shot pistols into the air as James jerked on the reins to guide the horse and wagon away from them. Maggie screamed and the baby cried, adding to the bedlam. Her composure was badly shaken as she climbed down from the rickety buckboard. She stood a moment on the walkway, clutched Alex against her left shoulder, juggled her bag and market basket with the right hand while she took deep breaths to calm her fright. Just when she thought she had her emotions under control and could take a step forward, Maggie looked up to find familiar blue eyes staring at her, drilling into her very soul.

His penetrating gaze took in every inch of her appearance. He noticed the lines of worry and stress that now etched corners of her eyes and on her face.

Maggie stood immobile, unable to think, as Cody Jarvis sauntered toward her. He took in the scene with some amusement. A small smile curved his lips. His right hand rested atop his gun holster, ready to spring into action as he studied the drunken cowhands. Satisfied that no harm was imminent, he relaxed and turned his attention to the baby still crying in Maggie's arms.

"How old?" Cody inquired of Alex as he reached out to remove the blanket from the baby's face.

"My son, Alexander, about a month old." Maggie jostled him back into position on her shoulder, still encumbered by her other burdens.

Cody quickly perceived the dilemma as he lifted the market basket and tote from her hands. Maggie patted Alex on his back; the baby soon found his fist to suck on and quieted. Cody watched her ministrations and smiled warmly again, his blue eyes twinkling. Maggie averted her eyes lest he think she wanted his attention.

James strode angrily toward them. "What do you want Jarvis? He's not your brat. I made sure of that."

"James! Please. People are staring." Maggie tried to reason with him as her embarrassment grew and she feared an awkward moment would turn into something ugly and dangerous.

"Well Dunlap, I see time hasn't changed you any, still as even-tempered as usual." Cody turned his back on the man, focusing on the woman before him and quietly asked, "Are you well Maggie? Do you need anything?"

"I'm fine. Please... I think it best if you leave." She looked into his eyes, silently begging him to understand and not provoke a fight. She had no doubt he would be the victor, but could she live with herself if she was the cause of James' injury or death? Or worse, could her heart bear to see Cody hurt?

He nodded to her ever so slightly.

"Don't push me Dunlap," Cody growled, his jaw clenched.

He stood facing Maggie a moment longer, regret showing in his eyes as he touched the brim of his hat and spun about on his heel to walk away.

James gave a harsh laugh as he picked up the basket from where Cody had set it and then grabbed Maggie by the elbow, propelling her forward.

"Well! I guess I told him! He can't push me around, not James Dunlap. He's not so tough. And I better never see you cozying up to him again."

"I did no such thing. He was only politely asking about the baby."

"Yeah, well, I don't want him sniffing around you again. Get about your business, Margaret. If you want time to do your shopping, you best get to it. When I say we're leaving, you better be ready or you can walk home."

Maggie nodded to Mr. Morgan as she entered the general store, glancing over her shoulder to witness James push open the swinging doors of the nearest saloon.

Maggie stretched her arms above her head, trying to ease the ache in her back from the long hours spent bent over as she and James worked to plant rows and rows of little apple trees. They labored throughout the summer months and into September; their dear friends Rose and Michael Canavan worked by their side. If not for their help, the chore would have been impossible. Maggie glanced at Rose and realized what a loyal friend she was and thought of how many times the woman had come to her rescue since their arrival in this wild land. They were closer than sisters.

James talked of pledging the troth of their children in marriage, linking the two families and properties in the tradition of the old world. Rose's daughter Katie was just a year older than little Alexander. Maggie considered the idea; perhaps Alexander would find happiness in his future married to someone from such a fine family like the Canavans.

Only a handful of trees remained to be planted to complete the orchard, but the ground was growing harder to dig with nightly frosts and autumn temperatures dropping. The men struggled to complete the planting and protect the young trees while the women returned to chores on their own homesteads.

Maggie spent her time milking her precious cows and tending to the flock of chickens. For once, she was glad for the solitude as Alex napped while she churned cream and prepared her butter molds.

Suddenly, James rushed into the cabin, his excitement a tangible thing. Maggie paused in her task to stare in amazement as he did a little jig in the middle of the cabin.

"I'm going to be a rich man, Margaret! Would you just look at this silver? I tell you we struck a vein and a deep one! You should have seen Michael's eyes when his pick axe splintered that large rock and the silver shined beneath!"

She watched him rub the stone and polish it to see the sparkle of the ore. Digging in the earth to plant trees had yielded more than apples. James appeared deliriously happy, but Maggie worried when she saw the greed shining in his eyes and his growing obsession with the silver.

"You need to share that silver with Michael Canavan. After all, it was his efforts that found it."

"Well, it's my land so that makes it my silver. Do you think I'm daft, woman, to be giving away my riches?"

"You owe Michael. It will make up for the money that I know you stole from that poor man. He's too loyal to you to ever accuse you of cheating at cards, but I've seen you, James."

James' hand shot out quickly; his knuckles grazed her cheek with the full impact of the back of his hand. "How dare you accuse me of being a cheat? It's not my fault if a man does'na keep his wits about him with cards in his hand and stakes on the table. He knows the risk; I didn't force him to play."

Tears stung Maggie's eyes and her cheek burned as she moved away from him to the far side of the cabin. Her blackened eye had just recently faded to yellow. She was still recovering from their last *family discussion* and her husband's cruelty.

Chapter 28

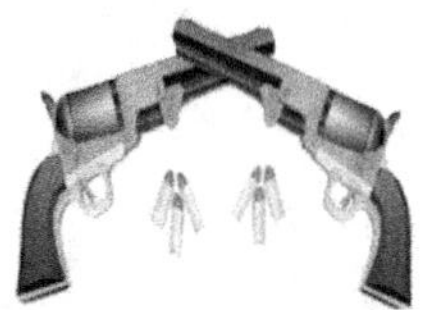

January 1887

"I don't know why I still keep you on my payroll. I don't like being disrespected. I'll give you one more chance; don't screw it up. There's a parcel of land that I want; some guy named Dunlap filed ownership on it, take care of him." Logan ground his cigar ash into the dish.

"No. Do your own dirty work," Cody said as he strode out of the room.

It was no secret around town; James Dunlap had been bragging every time he came into Deer Springs about the vein of silver that he struck. Cody had heard Dunlap proclaim how rich he was going to be, usually when he was deep in his cup of whiskey and gambling whatever money he had on him. It was just a matter of time before Zachary Logan's appetite for silver would be whet.

Cody tossed a thick blanket onto the stallion's back before adding his saddle and rig, tightening the cinch, and mounting up. The day was cold, but clear. Lightning and he both needed time out on the open range to stretch legs plus clear his mind. Cody headed east out of town, intending to inspect his newly purchased land.

As he passed the cemetery on the outskirts of town, he recognized James Dunlap and Michael Canavan riding in. *Wouldn't*

Canavan be surprised when he learns who his neighbor is now? The thought made Cody chuckle as he coaxed the bay into a gallop. The big horse snorted and bunched his muscles, reveling in the play and the crisp air filling his nostrils.

James had complained of being cooped up with cabin fever. He was determined to ride into town during a break in the weather. Maggie stood in the doorway and watched him ride off.

Relieved to see the sun shining and the clear day, Maggie planned to take advantage of the respite to wash clothes and hang them outside to dry. Never-ending chores filled her day.

The cabin felt peaceful without James' constant grumbling and ill moods. She was relieved to have him out of the house for awhile, although Maggie suspected he hurried to a card game and a bottle of whiskey. Even little Alex sensed his father's anger when he was home and seemed happier when he could crawl about the room without James shouting at him.

James did not come home that night; no doubt he had found a card game to his liking or had become too drunk again to ride the distance to their ranch. It had happened before. Maggie had just finished feeding Alex his breakfast when she heard pounding on the cabin door.

Expecting to see James stumble in, she was surprised to find Michael Canavan standing with his hat in hand and two horses tethered close by. She studied his expression and knew he was the bearer of bad news. She quickly turned to the waiting horses, seeing for the first time the blanket covered body draped across the saddle.

"Is that James? Is he sick or just drunk?" she asked Michael.

"I'm sorry Margaret. James is dead, shot down by that murdering thief Jarvis!"

"No! You're wrong! Cody wouldn't do such a thing."

Shame washed over her as she realized that her first thoughts were of Cody Jarvis and not her husband lying dead. Maggie looked at Michael and then at the draped form. She lifted the blanket from her husband's face; his eyes were open and blank. She reached to gently close his lids. Their promise of a life together, a marriage, and the adventure of the frontier had died long ago, yet as Maggie looked upon her dead husband, tears slid down her cheeks. Not for the man but for the life that could have been.

Michael helped carry James into the house and laid him on the bed. Maggie's mind went numb. What was she to do? Could she manage on her own? What happened? Why would Cody shoot James? He had promised her that he'd never hurt James. She had no answers to the questions swimming in her head.

Maggie stumbled to a chair and collapsed into it. Cradling her face in her hands, she cried softly, rocking her body in a slow motion to help calm jangled nerves. Michael sat silently, allowing her to grieve and to come to grips with the situation.

She raised her eyes to his. "You better tell me what you know."

"Well," Michael began his tale, "me and James had come into town yesterday. He met up with some wranglers from the Diamond Bar. There's always a card game going on at the Silver Spur saloon and it didn't take James much time before he grabbed a seat at a poker table." He hesitated, awkward talking about his friend to his wife.

"It's all right Michael, you aren't telling me anything new. I've suspected over the past year that he's been gambling heavily."

"I guess he stayed at the table for hours and into the night. I dunno, I had left, only rode back into town this morning to pick up some dry goods for Rose. I heard of the gunfight from Morgan in the store and rushed over to the saloon to see for myself."

"Was James already dead when you got there?"

"Gun smoke filled the room, hanging above the card tables and stinging my eyes, as I tried to find James. It took me a minute to get used to the dark and then I spotted James lying on the floor surrounded by a group of men and dance hall girls."

"Did you see Cody Jarvis?" She had to know if he was involved and yet dreaded hearing any confirmation that he was.

"Well, no, but when I pushed aside the cowpokes standing around James' body, they were all from the Diamond Bar and everybody knows Jarvis does Logan's killing. He's the hired gun. So it had to be him that shot him. There was a lot of money at stake riding on that poker game; James had bet the ranch on that last hand."

"What do you mean, he bet the ranch? I don't understand. Am I going to lose my home? Oh my God, I can't believe this is happening! It's a nightmare," Maggie cried in anguish.

"I only know what I heard, Margaret. I saw some papers on the table, looked like James had signed something, but I can't be sure."

Her mind tried to come to grips with this latest horror, dreading what she needed to do.

"I am going into Deer Springs and speak with the sheriff. I want some facts. Michael, can you please ask Rose to come and stay with little Alex while I go into town? I'll do what I can to prepare James for burial and then ride into town come morning. Can you please bring Rose back here in the morning?"

"Yeah, sure. We've got a pair of young boys boarding with us and working the farm. I'll bring them back with me to help dig the grave."

Maggie thought of the monumental task that lay ahead of her.

Chapter 29

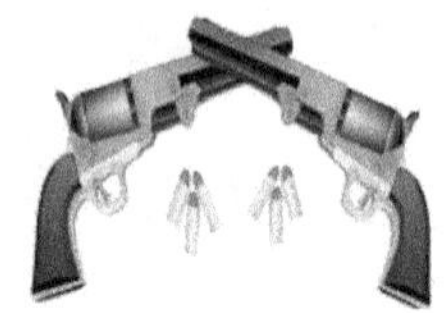

Maggie's Resolve

Rose knocked on the door with one hand as she turned the knob with the other and entered Maggie's cabin. Michael, carrying baby Katie, and his two ranch hands were close behind her.

"Where do you want the grave dug, Margaret? We brought shovels and our pick axes. I guess we can hammer together a coffin from whatever wood we can find in the barn."

Maggie draped a woolen cloak about her shoulders and led the men outside to a spot away from the cabin, but on the edge of the flower garden she had planted last summer. It would be a fitting place for James' grave. She liked the idea of knowing there would be fresh blooms gracing his resting place. Her love for the man had died long ago, but as his widow she would honor his memory and the life they had planned in their youth so long ago.

The grave dug; the men slowly lowered the wooden casket into the cold earth, sliding it down long ropes like a pulley. When it was done, they all stood in silence; a hawk screeched as it soared overhead. Rose produced her Bible and started reading the Lord's Prayer. Maggie wished a minister had been there to say a few words, but Deer Springs didn't include a church when it had experienced its growth spurt during the past year.

They rode in silence to Deer Springs and stopped in front of a row of one story clapboard buildings. Michael helped Maggie down from the buckboard wagon and tied the two horses to the hitching rail before proceeding to the sheriff's office. Maggie nervously opened the door, her resolve slipping. Unsure how to start or what to say, she approached the lawman seated behind the small desk.

"Sheriff Conner, my name is Margaret Dunlap. I need to find out what happened to my husband, James."

He waved toward a pair of rickety chairs and indicated for her to sit. Maggie sat on the edge of the hard wooden seat; her hands clasped in her lap. She glanced at Michael Canavan standing near the door. He nodded to her, reassuring her as she waited for the sheriff to answer her inquiry.

"What is it you want to know? All I can tell you is that the man was shot during a poker game. He was drunk and cheating at cards and one man at the table didn't take kindly to that."

"Do you approve of that behavior? A man gets shot for cheating at cards?" His callous words horrified her.

"Excuse me Sheriff, if you could perhaps explain how it happened or give Mrs. Dunlap more details ... she has a question about her ranch," Michael interjected.

The sheriff turned his attention to Michael, "Who are you?"

"Michael Canavan, sir. I'm neighbor to the Dunlap family."

"Humph. Well, I wasn't there, of course. I entered the Silver Spur after I heard the gunfire. Your husband was drunk, Mrs. Dunlap, and pulled a gun on young Jimmy Ryan when he was accused of cheating."

"That just doesn't make any sense. Oh, I can imagine James drunk all right, but not starting a gun fight. So was it this Jimmy who shot him?"

"No, it was someone else, one of Zach Logan's men. There were several at that poker game playing with both Mr. Logan and your husband. All you need to know is that I ruled it self-defense. It was a fair fight. I'm sorry for your loss." The lawman sat back in his chair, looked at Michael and Maggie then folded his arms across his chest as if to imply the matter done.

Maggie sat in silence, stunned by his words. Her eyes burned with unshed tears.

"What about my ranch, sheriff? I was told James had pledged a deed to our land at this poker game. Is that correct? Can such a thing happen?"

"You're new to our country, Mrs. Dunlap, so I can see where you wouldn't understand that money and land often change hands when men gamble. It's common practice. If your husband ran out of money, he probably bet the ranch; he'd been bragging all over town about the rich silver vein he struck on that land. I don't know who has the deed. Maybe Mr. Logan can help you."

"And where would I find this Mr. Logan? I'd like to see some proof that James signed over our ranch. I can't believe that even in a drunken state, James would do such a thing."

"Well, Ma'am, if that's how you feel, maybe you better wait on the arrival of the territory circuit judge. He'll listen to your case if you don't believe me in the matter of your ranch. I reckon he's due here some time next month."

"I think I will do just that, sheriff. Thank you for your time." Maggie nodded to him and rose to leave when his parting words stopped her in her stride.

"You do that; of course, since he's Logan's brother, I don't think it will matter much."

They stepped outside as Maggie tried to collect her emotions. A brisk wind lifted her cloak and stung her face, bringing her back to stark reality. She glanced about as a few people hurried across the wooden sidewalk, women entering small shops and men heading for saloons. Maggie didn't recognize anyone. She was alone; swept away in a tidal wave of events she had no control over. It was a long silent ride home.

Maggie turned to her friend, "Michael, how can I go about hiring a ranch hand like you have? Do you think there is a young lad who would work for me and live here for room and board? I won't be able to pay much until spring when we have some crops and animals to sell. I intend to work this ranch and live here until that circuit judge forces me to leave. This is my home and I'm staying."

"We'll help you all we can. Our hand, Jacob, has a cousin that may help you. He's still living with his parents and they have a large family. I'll ask. Margaret, won't you be taking a chance that Zachary Logan will put you out? If he owns the land now, what can you do?"

"I'm going to fight him; that's what I'm going to do. I plan to plead my case to this so-called judge, even if he is Logan's relative. The sheriff said James was shot in self-defense. But Michael, I cleaned the wound ... James was shot in the back."

Cody entered the corral and looked at the small lean-to then walked to the sturdy log cabin to inspect his new home. It was a solid structure, two rooms wide with windows cut into both ends of the building. Oil cloths covered the windows; he'd have to eventually replace those with glass. Cody nodded as he ran his hands along the surface of the large stones facing the fireplace and chimney. The Carvers had done a fine job building this place; no wonder they were heartbroken to give it up.

He had taken a full day to ride the perimeter of the land, noting the shallow stream that ran through it, enough water to provide for animals and crops alike. The soil was rich bottom land and would yield a plentiful crop of oats or wheat when planted. Cody sat in the saddle proudly surveying his land—the slight rise of hill and the thick copse of cedar trees lining one bank of the river. It was fertile land.

He tied Lightning in the lean-to then spread his bedroll out on the floor of the cabin. Daylight was gone. Cody lit a fire in the hearth then stretched out on the floor. He'd spend his first night in his own place. Cody let his mind dream of the life he would have here one day. Maybe it wasn't too farfetched to plan a future and a family.

Late afternoon of the third day, Cody returned to Deer Springs and heard the news about James Dunlap being shot.

Chapter 30

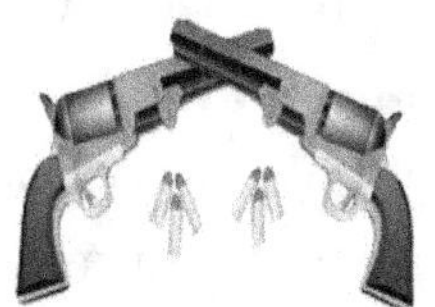

Trial

In mid-February, Maggie received word that the circuit judge had arrived at Deer Springs. She had to speak with him and resolve the uncertainty of her home and future. Not knowing whether or not she would be evicted made her jump at every knock on her door.

The young farm hand promised by Michael, Aaron Yoder, offered to help Maggie with the spring plowing and seeding when the soil thawed and the last snow was gone. Until then, Aaron, a quiet, industrious lad, stayed busy in the barn mending leather straps, sharpening the plow blade, or caring for the animals. Maggie approved of the lad, who performed more work in one day than what James ever did in a week. Tomorrow, Maggie planned to leave Alexander in Aaron's care while she traveled into Deer Springs to confront the judge.

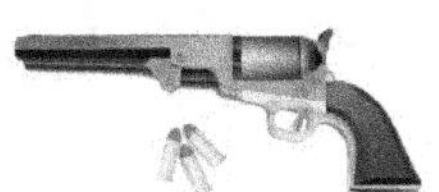

Zachary Logan leaned against the bar, chewing on an end of his cigar; he tapped his pencil impatiently. Logan straightened as he saw Cody walk through the saloon doors and head toward him.

"Took you long enough," Logan barked.

"I was eating breakfast. Got here as soon as I could after Ike gave me your message. What's going on?" Cody scanned the room and gave it a quick check.

"The circuit judge is in town. I'll be in court this afternoon and I need you to watch my back. Connors warned me that Dunlap's crazy widow plans to fight me for that scrap of land that fool husband of hers lost in a poker game. I don't know what she might do. You make sure you're there in case of trouble."

Cody fought to keep a passive expression on his face as he listened with interest to the news that Maggie would be in town and close by. He hadn't talked to her in months; he had planned on waiting a respectable amount of time after James' death before calling on her. Now, the chance to see her again warmed his spirit. It was all he could do to simply nod to Logan's request while his heart wanted to soar.

"Got it. I'll keep an eye on things."

"Good. See that you do. Court will be in here starting at one."

Cody waited in front of the Silver Spur. He kept searching for signs of Maggie Dunlap arriving in town. He paced back and forth on the wooden walk then took a deep breath and let it out when he spied her buckboard wagon slowly traveling up the street. Cody watched as Maggie reined in the single horse and steered the wagon into the alley next to the Spur. He noticed she had driven herself into town and was surprised that she had come alone. Before he could approach her, though, a group of rowdy cowhands jostled him and he found himself pushed behind their numbers.

Several men stood outside the Silver Spur saloon talking and milling about when Maggie pushed past them. They laughed at her efforts. Maggie pretended not to notice, but her face blushed red in embarrassment having to enter a disreputable saloon. The Silver Spur had been turned into a court room for the day. A large table had been placed along the back wall with a single chair behind it. More chairs created three rows in front of the table with an open aisle in the center space. Maggie slowly walked up the aisle and took a seat in the front row, waiting for the arrival of the circuit judge. She sat silently as more people straggled in to fill the empty seats. She noticed one man even brought some livestock; he tethered two goats to a rope wrapped around his left hand.

Cody squeezed into the saloon and stood in the back of the room to observe the proceedings. His eyes never left the image of Maggie Dunlap from when she entered the saloon to where she sat still and prim-like in the front row.

Sheriff Conner touched the brim of his hat and nodded toward her as he approached the head table. He tapped a wooden gavel on the table top.

"All right, quiet down everyone. The Honorable Judge Thomas Logan presiding."

With that announcement, a tall, lean man strode across the room and took his position behind the table. He opened a worn leather case and withdrew two thick books, placing them to his left on the table.

Cody saw Maggie jump as the judge loudly banged the wooden gavel on the worn makeshift desk.

"Come to order, please. The first case on the docket this morning is Henry Jones versus Robert McFadden. Will Mr. Jones and McFadden please stand? Now then, Mr. Jones, what seems to be the trouble?"

Cody listened as the man complained about the sheep grazing in his pastures and why he felt justified in shooting the animals. Then Mr. McFadden jumped up to argue that his sheep were not taking grass away from Mr. Jones' cattle and he demanded payment for his slaughtered sheep. Judge Logan appeared to be weighing the concerns of each man before he spoke.

"Mr. McFadden, this is cattle country. I'm restricting you to grazing your sheep only on open range. Mr. Jones, you are within your rights to remove the sheep from pastures within your ranch boundaries but must compensate McFadden for any killed sheep. I fine you an amount of thirty dollars for the dead animals." He rapped the gavel on the hard surface, then wrote some notes on a piece of paper.

Cody spotted Zachary Logan sitting in the front row. He caught the slight imperceptible nod between Logan and the judge before the magistrate began the next case.

"Logan versus Dunlap. Who's here representing Dunlap?"

Maggie raised her hand. The color washed out of her face as the judge studied her and looked her up and down insolently.

The judge nodded in Logan's direction then spoke again. "Zachary Logan, I see you possess a deed transferring ownership of a particular parcel of land. What can you tell the court about this transaction?"

Cody's head snapped up; the announcement grabbed his attention. He strained to see the document in question. How could he be so stupid as not to recognize that Logan would covet the Dunlap place after James foolishly bragged to everyone within earshot about the vein of silver found on the land? He didn't realize the scrap of land Logan had mentioned was the silver claim. That parcel was located close to Hank Jurgen's claim; it seemed logical the silver vein ran through both properties.

Zachary Logan stood by his chair and touched his finger to the brim of his hat in respect for the judge as he began to speak. His demeanor was calm as he stepped forward, tugging on his tailored coat.

"Judge, the land in question contains two parcels that I won during a poker game with James Dunlap. Unfortunately for Mr. Dunlap, there was a disagreement during that game and a gunfight occurred that sadly caused Mr. Dunlap's demise. Sheriff

Conner can provide you with the details; it was a fair fight in self-defense with plenty of witnesses."

"That's a lie!" Maggie blurted the words as she jumped to her feet. People in the courtroom gasped at the verbal insult thrown at Logan.

Cody's hand hovered above his holster, ready to defend Maggie; his eyes scanned the room for possible trouble caused by her words.

The judge turned to Maggie as he said, "And you are? Mrs. Dunlap, I presume? What is your version of what happened?"

Maggie nodded then swallowed, her throat dry. "Margaret Dunlap, your Honor. My husband was no gunfighter. I cannot believe that James would pull a gun on Mr. Logan. I have asked the sheriff for details but have not been told who even shot my husband; just that it occurred during some poker game."

Logan turned toward Maggie, a false expression of sympathy on his face. "My condolences to you, Mrs. Dunlap, but since you were not present and I was, you will just have to take my word for what happened. Your husband cheated all during the game. When my foreman accused him, he pulled a gun. Naturally, the man had to defend himself," Zachary stated.

"What about the deed? When was that transaction completed?" Judge Logan questioned.

Cody was curious about that too, and so it seemed, was Maggie. Cody wondered if James would have been foolish enough to bet their ranch on a turn of a card. They both waited to hear what Zachary Logan had to say.

"Well, sir, I believe it was the round of cards just before the shooting when Dunlap pledged his ranch against a bet. When he lost, he signed a paper transferring the ownership. He probably wanted to get his land back, so he resorted to cheating. I don't pretend to know what he was thinking; the man was drunk and angry," Logan proffered in an arrogant voice.

"Do you have the signed deed with you now?" asked the judge.

Zachary Logan handed a rolled document to the judge. He sat back down and stared at Maggie. Cody, seeing the expression on the man's face, had the urge to wipe off that smug leer.

"Mrs. Dunlap, what do you have to say about this matter?" Judge Logan waited to hear her side.

"My husband did drink and could become angry. I admit that to be true, but I do not believe my husband would pull a gun on someone. He wasn't that brave. A wife shouldn't say that, but it's true. May I see the papers he signed?" Maggie approached the judge's table. She reached for the document, but he pulled it open and laid his hand on the paper, keeping it displayed on the tabletop.

Maggie examined the words on the paper. She read out loud the description of the ranch; both parcels were listed: the one containing the cabin and the second parcel claimed under Alexander's name. Her eyes widened as she read the name 'James Dunlap' in a tiny, crimped signature. Zachary Logan's name appeared in a strong swirling script and two other men had signed as witnesses, both Logan's ranch hands, no doubt.

"My husband never learned to read or write. That is not his signature. I cannot accept this deed as true," she stated in a clear, but shaky voice.

"Mrs. Dunlap, I can understand that you are upset about the loss of your ranch, but this court only has your word on whether this is your husband's signature. Do you have any proof to your claim that he could not read or write? Mr. Logan says this is a valid deed and he has witnesses."

Cody clenched and unclenched his fists as he listened with disbelief... the court appeared to be aiding in the swindle of the Dunlap spread. Should he step forward and testify to help Maggie prove James was illiterate? He never saw the man read or write. Was that proof?

She shook her head and stammered, "It wasn't self-defense like this man says. James was shot in the back."

A second, stronger murmur passed through the courtroom spectators once again at her words. Maggie looked around. She clasped her hands; her teeth gnawed on her bottom lip. Evidently, no one had ever dared to defy Zachary Logan before, and she realized she had just called him a liar for the second time.

The judge and his brother exchanged looks. The judge motioned to Logan to stay seated, then he turned his attention back to Maggie and smiled briefly.

"Again, Mrs. Dunlap, do you have proof that your husband was shot in the back? It's not what the sheriff says and Mr. Logan has witnesses."

"I buried my husband, so of course, I don't have proof unless you dig up his body. What was I supposed to do, keep him on ice until you came to town?" Her voice sounded strident, angry. She flounced down upon her seat and crossed her arms.

The judge pounded his gavel once more. Maggie leaned back in her chair, awaiting his next words.

"I think I've heard enough facts in this matter. I believe I can make my ruling now and all parties will be bound by my decision. The matter of the shooting of one James Dunlap will remain as a justified shooting in self-defense since Sheriff Connors of Deer Springs did testify to that fact and I have no evidence to the contrary. As for the disposition of the land parcels, I believe a compromise is in order. The parcel of land containing the homestead and ranch buildings will remain in the Dunlap name, but the unimproved parcel of land will be forfeited as legal gambling winnings as indicated by James Dunlap's signature and shall be transferred to Mr. Zachary Logan's ownership. Are you both in agreement to this?"

"Yes, your Honor. I have no desire to see a widow and child put out in the cold. She can keep the ranch land. I'm satisfied to keep the other parcel as my just due."

Both men looked at Maggie and waited for her answer. They didn't give her much of a choice. She nodded, "Yes, thank you judge."

Cody could see that she was trying to appear meek while she controlled her temper. He had to grant her a grudging respect for standing up to Logan. She never glanced his way as she marched out of the saloon and the makeshift court.

Cody shook his head, disgusted by the slick proceedings. Logan had just gotten away with fraud again and there wasn't anything he could do about it. Justice wasn't met today, but at least Maggie still owned her ranch. He didn't have to worry about her being put out of her home. Cody rushed out of the saloon, intent on trying to talk with Maggie, but he was too late. Her wagon raced down the street, out of town.

Zachary Logan rose and walked back to his rear office. His lips curled slightly into a smug smile; he had gotten what he wanted. The land and the silver vein were his, all nice and legal. He'd have to buy his brother dinner as a thank you for his ruling.

Chapter 31

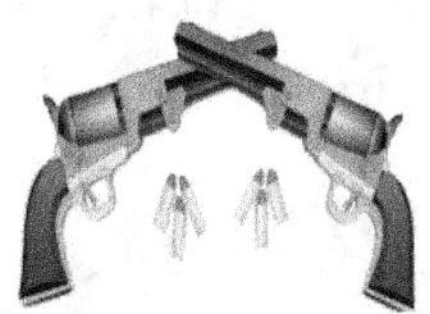

Cody read the telegram again. The director was not happy; he hadn't even bothered to encrypt the message. Cody had expected it, but somehow it still felt like a shock. He turned and left the telegraph office and wandered down the dusty street in Fort Laramie. His footsteps led him to the Red Garter. As he looked around the crowded room, it appeared the same as before, except no Scarlet.

"Give me a beer," he told the bartender. The mug slid towards him. "Where's Scarlet? She upstairs?" Cody asked the bartender.

"Scarlet's gone. She left about four months ago."

"Hmm, too bad."

Cody slumped into a chair at a corner table to study the telegram for a third time. The director was thoroughly dissatisfied with Cody's work. He pointed out that it had been three years and Logan had not been arrested. The counterfeit operation had stopped, but only because of the press burning, not because Cody had seized the engraving plates. Cody dragged his fingers through his hair and took a long swig of the beer. He had failed. He couldn't find a single case where he could prove fraud on Logan's part; all his land transactions had been approved legally by the circuit judge. How was Cody supposed to fight that? The fact that the damn judge was Logan's brother obviously aided Logan, but was it illegal?

The director demanded Cody return East for reassignment. Cody sat staring into the suds of his beer. He didn't see himself returning to Washington; maybe it was time he and the service parted ways. The idea kept bouncing around in his mind while a precious face kept floating in his vision. Maggie.

Alex seemed content to sit tied in his blanket swaddling, wedged between Maggie on one side and the large market basket on his other as the buckboard wagon bounced along the dirt road into Deer Springs. He waved his tiny arms excitedly as he babbled in that baby talk that only a baby can understand.

Maggie pulled up on the reins and managed to bring the buckboard wagon close to the wooden walk in front of the general store. She climbed down from the wagon and stepped onto the elevated platform before turning to untie Alex and lift him into her arms.

Cody stepped forward from the shadows of the storefront and placed a hand on her elbow to steady her; her scent and nearness filled his senses. His eyes sought hers.

"Hello Maggie." His warm breath caressed her nape as his softly spoken greeting reached her ears alone.

"Cody! I need to talk to you." She answered him in the same hushed voice, glancing about to see who had witnessed their exchange.

"What are you doing in town and alone?"

"I have business to attend. Is there somewhere private where we can meet?" Curious eyes were on them, drawing more attention the longer they stood there.

"The Silver Spur has added hotel rooms upstairs and some dining tables in the side room. Meet me in the side room when you're done with your business," he whispered to her then stepped back and made a show of touching the brim of his hat in salutation and walked away.

Maggie shifted Alex in her arms as she toted the market basket and entered the general store. The bell tinkled as she closed the door, announcing her arrival in the store. Mr. Morgan climbed down from his ladder where he was stocking shelves and moved behind the large counter to greet her.

"Good morning, Mrs. Dunlap. What can I help you with today?"

"Hello Mr. Morgan. I've got some fresh eggs and churned butter that I'd like to sell. I need sugar, flour, and perhaps some dry goods in exchange, if we can agree on a price." She placed the basket on the counter and shifted Alex onto her other hip.

"See you have the little fella with you today. Let's have a look in your basket. How many eggs do you have?" Mr. Morgan tickled Alex under his chin, smiling at the child, as he poked among the wrapped butter molds and counted out loud the eggs in the basket. "Hmm ... I make it three dozen eggs, if I haven't missed my count."

"Yes, that's right. I was keeping my fingers crossed that none broke during my ride into town. I tried to cushion them as best I could. So what do you think?"

"Well, ma'am ... how about three dollars? That ought to buy enough supplies for you."

"Can you do three dollars and two bits? Those are really large eggs plus the butter is freshly churned. I'm sure your customers will appreciate the quality." Maggie bartered for a better price. Mr. Morgan seemed to expect some haggling before agreeing on a mutual bargain.

"You drive a hard bargain, Mrs. Dunlap, but I agree. You go ahead and scoop out how much flour and sugar you need and whatever else you want. It's a pity your husband didn't have your business sense."

"What do you mean by that remark?" Sparks flew from her eyes.

"Oh, just that he wouldn't have lost your ranch, that's all. I didn't mean no insult."

"I still own my ranch, Mr. Morgan. Only our extra parcel of land was deeded to Mr. Logan, not that it's any of your business."

"My mistake ma'am." Morgan coughed and tried to appear busy at the register.

His attitude surprised her. Is that what folks in town were thinking?

Maggie sat Alex on the floor to toddle about as she went about the chore of filling sacks with the food stuffs. Her thoughts kept returning to the store clerk's comments as three more customers entered the store. She recognized Mrs. Fitzhughes from the newspaper, but not the two men.

One man poked his friend in the ribs and pointed to Maggie as she reached into the flour barrel. "Isn't that Jarvis' whore? Lookee there, his brat is crawling under foot," he laughed.

"Yep, spittin' image of him. I heard tell she had Jarvis kill her ole man too," the friend sneered.

Maggie stood there, speechless. Her outrage rose like a thermometer on a hot day; she couldn't believe the cruel falsehoods that were being said. She spun about to confront the two men and stomped her foot on the wooden floor.

"How dare you say such lies about me and my baby? Urgh!" Her frustration was such that all she could do was sputter in anger and stomp her foot again. This resulted in more laughter from the two filthy cowhands.

Maggie turned her back on them and placed her parcels on the counter. Alex whimpered, frightened by the shouting and commotion. She scooped him up and cuddled him against her breast.

"It's all right sweetie. Mama's here."

"I'm sorry, Mrs. Dunlap, for your trouble. If you say those lies ain't so, then I believe you." Morgan tried to reassure her, but there was doubt written all over his face.

"Just give me my purchases, Mr. Morgan. Good day, sir." Maggie's face blazed as she left the store. She placed the sacks under the wagon's seat and strode down the sidewalk in search of the Silver Spur.

Maggie avoided the wide swinging doors in front of the saloon and headed for the more private side entrance at the corner of the building. The room was dimly lit and it took a minute for her eyes to adjust to the darkness. Cody was seated at a small table in the rear.

"Really Cody, couldn't you have thought of some other place to meet than here? Have you no care for my reputation? There's already gossip flying around town. And of all places, the very saloon where James died. I must be crazy for agreeing to see you here."

Cody stood as she approached the table and held out a chair that would place her back to the room and nosy saloon patrons. A slight gesture of consideration. Alex sat on Maggie's lap, content to study this strange place and the man across from him.

"He's getting big," Cody commented as he smiled at the baby and lifted his eyes to Maggie.

"Are you aware that people in town are saying he's yours? I just had a very disagreeable run in with some men in the store. They called me a whore!" Maggie shook her head, trying to stop the tears that threatened to spill.

Cody's expression turned angry before he shrugged it off. "I'm sorry Maggie. I can't control what the scum around here say. I wouldn't worry about it."

"Easy for you to say! What will happen when my son is old enough to understand these cruel barbs and questions me about his father? Should I tell him he was conceived by rape or let him think he's a gunfighter's bastard? A poor choice, don't you think?"

She wiped away tears she could no longer control with the back of her hand. Maggie hugged Alex closer and kissed the top of his head—his dark hair so much like James' and so much like Cody's.

"I don't have an answer for you. What would you have me do? Shoot them?" Cody questioned.

"No! Anything you do now will only add fuel to the talk around town. Just tell me one thing ... did you kill James?"

She had to know. He had promised her in the past, even when provoked by James, that he'd walk away. Maggie waited for his answer.

Cody's eyes narrowed as he looked at the woman so dear to him, "No, I did not. Believe me or not, it's your choice."

"I've heard people say you were there; that you were the shooter."

"I wasn't. I can't tell you where I was that night. It had nothing to do with James. You'll just have to believe me."

Now it was Cody's turn to give the ultimatum. Did she trust him?

Maggie reached for his hand across the table.

They each studied one another's eyes; searching for a flicker of hope or love ... something. Cody read the doubt and fear in her eyes while Maggie hated his closed expression.

"If you didn't do it, why won't you tell me where you were?" Maggie kept probing for details; her mind and heart were at war with each other. She needed to know the truth.

Cody pulled back his hand, breaking their grasp. "I can't and I won't. Why does it matter where I was? Did you consider that I might have been making plans for our future? You know how I feel about you, Maggie. I made you a promise once. Why can't you trust me?"

Maggie shook her head, tears filled her eyes as she told him, "I must think of my son and his future. I can't build a life with someone who may have murdered his father. If you can't tell me the truth of what happened to James, then I never want to see you again. I'm sorry."

Her words shattered the fragile dream that he had held close in his heart. Cody turned cold eyes to her and wore a callous expression. His jaw clenched, only a small tic moved in his cheek, evidence of the wound her words inflicted.

"Believe what you must, Maggie. I'll only say this once. I do love you and will always be there for you if you need me." His brittle tone belied the tender words he spoke.

"Goodbye Cody." She turned and marched out of the room without looking back.

He remained seated and withdrew a packet of playing cards from his vest pocket. Cody mechanically shuffled the cards as she walked away. Her words drove a dagger into his heart, hardening any softer emotions now frozen in time, encased in ice like the gun for hire that he had become.

Part II - Chapter 32

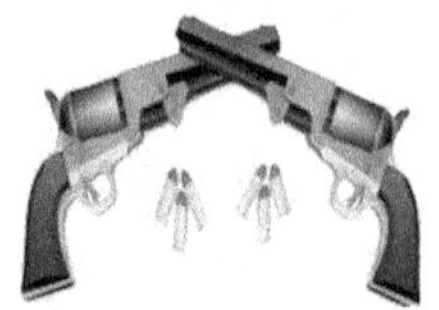

Eastward Bound

Clem wrapped Cody in a bear hug, sniffled slightly, then stepped back to shake his hand.

"I'm gonna miss you, boy."

Cody returned the firm handshake. He studied the wizen face and unexpectedly felt his throat choke up. He coughed once before trying to voice his thoughts.

"You've been a true friend, Clem. I'm sorry I was such a disappointment to you. Sure will miss our checker games," Cody said in a hoarse voice.

"Don't beat yourself up; you're only one man against Logan and his entire operation. You did what you could."

"You and I both know it wasn't enough," Cody murmured with a sense of guilt. "Maybe some day, I'll be back and will take care of that bastard."

Clara was next as she gathered him in a tight hug. She nodded, then smiled. "You take care of yourself. If you ever come back this way ... your room is waiting."

"Thanks, Clara. I want you to have this," he said as he placed a bag of gold coins in her hand. She shook her head and tried to give it back to him. "No, please take it. For all the lost income I caused you and the boarders that moved out. I owe you and I always pay my debts."

"All right. I have to admit, it'll help, but it wasn't necessary."

"I know. You keep it for a rainy day." Cody smiled and hugged the woman, then gathered up his saddle bags and gear.

Lightning waited, tied to the hitching post in front of the boarding house. Cody fastened his gear onto his saddle and checked the cinch again before mounting up. He touched his fingers to the brim of his hat in a farewell salute to Clara and Clem standing in the doorway of the house then he trotted past the Silver Spur and headed south toward Laramie and the train headed East. High time he left Deer Springs; there was only one thing he would miss and regret leaving behind... Maggie. He'd never forget her.

Cody watched the train chug into the station. It blew its whistle and the tall stack belched a plume of smoke while steam hissed from under its piston rods. People crowded the platform as they waited to greet arriving passengers or prepared to board the outgoing train. With the building of the depot and the addition of Fort Laramie as a stop on the Union Pacific line, Laramie business thrived and the town expanded.

Stepping over to the ticket window, Cody approached the agent. "One ticket to St. Louis in the passenger car plus fare for my horse in one of your stock cars. How much is that?"

"Let me see now," the agent said as he pulled on his bushy eyebrow and consulted a train schedule. "That will be the Atlantic Express, eastbound to Omaha. You'll have to change trains in Omaha to continue to St. Louis. Hmm, that'll be sixty-five dollars. Yes sirree, the Express will get you to Omaha in just four days. Sure beats the ten or twelve days riding by stagecoach. Why, by next year or sooner, the Overland Flyer will save even more time." The agent grinned broadly, so proud of the future of rail travel.

"Hmm, is that a fact? Reckon that will be something," Cody commented as he counted out the steep cost and handed the money to the agent.

"Thank you, sir. Have a pleasant journey," the agent said as he handed the ticket to Cody.

Cody untied Lightning from the hitching post and led him toward the stock cars at the rear of the train. Three stock cars were coupled behind the line of passenger cars. Their slotted sides would provide ventilation for the animals riding inside. Cody coaxed the big stallion up the ramp attached to an open boxcar and into the car. Four stalls filled the boxcar. Two horses occupied half the car, as Lightning stepped into an empty stall. Cody removed his saddle then draped the blanket and his rig across the top rail of the stall. He brushed the bay's back and hung a feed bag inside the stall before going in search of a bucket of water.

He found an empty bucket in the corner of the boxcar then carried it out to the platform where he spied a full trough of water. Cody filled the bucket to the brim then carried it carefully up the ramp, trying not to spill the water, and back inside the stock car. As he placed the water bucket inside Lightning's stall, he observed a petite woman maneuvering her mare into the last, available stall. The horse stood at least two hands taller than her. He watched her unsaddle the horse and attempt to toss the heavy rig across the stall gate.

"Can I help?" he asked.

She turned suddenly at the sound of his voice. Her hand flew to her neck, touched the ruffled lace at her throat, then smiled shyly. "Goodness, you startled me. Yes, I'd appreciate your help. So kind of you to offer," she said in a soft, lyrical voice.

Cody stepped forward, hefted the saddle rig, and draped it across the railing. "May I be of any other assistance?" he asked politely.

"No. Thank you. I'll be fine." She lowered her eyes and modestly held out her hand.

Cody didn't know whether to kiss the hand or shake it. He decided a light shake would be in order.

Touching his forefinger to the brim of his hat in a light salute, he turned to go. He stepped off the ramp and made his way down to the passenger cars. With one last glance back toward the stock car with the young lady inside, he climbed up into the passenger car and walked down the aisle to claim an empty window seat toward the rear of the car.

As he settled into his seat, he observed the petite woman climb the two steps into the passenger car. She smiled sweetly at the conductor as he held her tapestry carpet bag and escorted her to a seat in the left front of the coach. Her green silk skirt rustled as she moved down the narrow aisle; the matching fitted jacket buttoned up the front, ending below the froth of lace at her neck and cinched in a narrow waist. The hem of the jacket stopped above a modest ruffled bustle at the back.

The lady had drawn the admiring attention of several males riding in the car and a few envious stares of the female patrons. Cody watched as she removed her hat and gently lifted a lock of auburn hair off the back of her neck. Her coloring and shape reminded him of a porcelain doll that he had once seen in a store window.

With a jolt, the cumbersome train lurched forward, gradually building momentum as it started down the tracks. Cody watched the ladies within the car grab hold of chair arms or window frames, lest they bounce unceremoniously off their seats as the engine labored forward. Most men simply hooked a booted ankle around the seat leg in front of them to secure their position.

The conductor opened all the windows of the passenger car to capture any cooling breeze against the oppressive summer heat experienced on the plains in late July. Travel in the summer by any means was a hot, sticky affair. Cody would have preferred to leisurely cover the distance on horseback, not cooped up inside a rail car, but he had orders to report to St. Louis in four days hence.

He relaxed in his seat, tilted his hat forward to cover his eyes, and allowed his mind to drift—constantly returning to the unresolved situation left behind in Deer Springs. His failure to prove Zachary Logan's guilt churned like acid in the bottom of his gullet. The man swindled unsuspecting homesteaders out of their parcels of land, buying acreage cheap when those folks were down on their luck. It was despicable, but not illegal. Logan's gun hands threatened people and "encouraged" them to sell, but in the end, it was the farmer's choice. It wasn't fair, Cody knew, but how could you fight that when the circuit judge approved the transactions in court?

Cody's thoughts turned to Maggie. The corners of his mouth curled into a grin as he recalled the image of her standing defiantly before the judge and fighting Logan to keep her ranch and land. She had bravely stood her ground; Cody had been so proud of her.

James Dunlap never signed any deed over to Logan, but how could that ever be proven? Cody didn't know how a court would decide in Maggie's favor based on her word alone. Unless she had some kind of written proof or document showing James' true signature, Cody knew that Zachary Logan had gotten away with land fraud; all sanctioned by the court. Food for thought. Cody ground his teeth and dragged a hand across his whiskered jaw. He'd never felt so powerless, and now he had to explain himself and his lack of action to the director.

Chapter 33

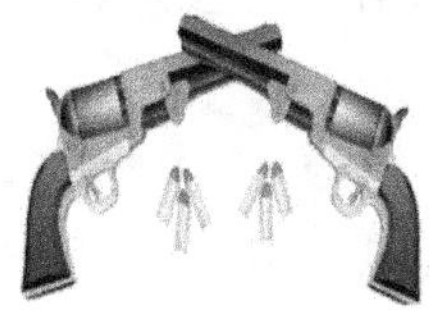

Miss O'Hara

The engineer blew his whistle as the Cheyenne depot came into view around the curve. Cody shifted in his seat to gaze out of the window at the impressive, two-colored sandstone structure with its tall clock tower. Carriages lined up within the tunnel portico of the building as the wealthy patrons waited in shady comfort for the arrival of the train. Removing a pocket watch from his vest pocket, Cody checked the time. Not bad; a tad over four hours covered the distance between Laramie and Cheyenne that would have taken him all day on horseback.

He stood to stretch his legs and noticed several passengers doing the same. The next leg of their journey would be considerably longer with fewer breaks. The train belched steam and rumbled to a stop alongside the wooden platform of the station. Cody jumped down from the car and strode back to the stock car with Lightning. He slid the door back as he hopped up into the boxcar and was greeted by neighs and whinnies from its occupants.

"Hey boy," Cody rubbed the bay's neck and scratched the top of his head. "How you doin'?"

Cody reached for the water bucket, now half empty, and sought to fill it again. He jumped down from the stock car, found some fresh water and hurried to place it back in Lightning's stall. With a final pat on the horse's flank, he left the car, sliding the door closed. Time to seek his own call of nature and some refreshment before the train left him behind.

"All aboard!" called the conductor as he waved his lantern back and forth then removed the wooden steps leading to the passenger cars.

Cody had returned to his seat just minutes before as the engine lugged forward, pulling its train cars out of the station. He noted all the passengers in his car had resumed their original seats with the addition of one new rider; no one had departed at Cheyenne. The petite gal in the front row sat gazing out the window while she cooled herself with a delicate lace fan. Cody studied her mannerisms, more appropriate for a fancy drawing room back East than a dusty train out West. *What brought someone like her to Wyoming?* He amused himself for the next hour by speculating answers to his question.

"Folks! Dining car will serve supper now. Space is limited so I'll be allowing one passenger car at a time to dine," the conductor announced as he walked down the aisle. "We'll start with this car for anyone wanting to eat."

A murmur of voices and people getting to their feet, then shuffling steps as passengers tried to keep their balance in the moving train as they stepped through the connecting door into the dining car. Narrow tables, seating two, lined the sides of the car. Couples quickly filled most tables, leaving solitary passengers to share remaining table space.

"May I?" asked Cody, as he placed a hand on the chairback of the empty seat.

The lady glanced up, nodded silently, then resumed her perusal of the printed menu. Beads of perspiration dotted her forehead and the day's heat caused a flush to her pale cheeks. She dabbed a napkin to her moist skin as she tucked loose tendrils of auburn hair back into place. Lying the menu aside, she raised her eyes to her companion.

"Not very many choices," she commented.

"Hmm, see what you mean. Looks like cold beef sandwiches or beef stew, which is probably the same beef just heated up with potatoes." Cody laughed as he turned the paper over, "by tomorrow only beef stew will be offered."

She smiled shyly and agreed, "You're probably right."

"We met briefly in the stock car. I'm Cody Jarvis, Miss ...?"

"O'Hara. Rosalyn O'Hara. Nice to meet you Mister Jarvis."

"Traveling far, Miss O'Hara?"

"Back to St. Louis. I'm afraid I'll be riding this train for several days," she said.

"Really? I'm also going to St. Louis. Long trip, but it's better than making the journey by stage coach. You'd be weeks, not days."

"Yes, I suppose you're right."

The attendant stopped at their table with pencil and paper in hand. "What can I get you folks?"

"Guess I'll have the beef sandwich. What do you have to drink?" Cody asked.

"Today I have coffee, tea, and beer."

"You can bring me a beer with my meal."

"Very good sir. And you Miss?"

"I'll have the beef sandwich with tea, please."

"Be just a few minutes, folks," replied the attendant as he moved to the next table and took their order.

Rosalyn laid a book of poetry on the table; a narrow pink ribbon dangled from its margins. She slid her finger between the pages, finding the ribbon bookmark. One hand rested on the open pages as she lowered her eyes and focused her attention on the prose.

Cody watched her silently reading the poetry. She reminded him of Maggie. How many times did he watch Maggie writing in her journal or reading by candlelight? Simple, quiet enjoyment. He frowned as his thoughts took him to a dark place. Maggie wasn't part of his life any more. She'd told him goodbye and he had to learn to honor her decision.

"Is something wrong?" asked his dining companion.

"What?" Cody shook away his mental cobwebs.

"You're scowling. You look quite ferocious," she said as she placed the ribbon on her page and closed the book.

"Sorry. Just thinking of something in my past."

"I apologize for intruding."

"None needed."

They sat awkwardly with silence between them growing as they stared at the passing landscape.

Cody cleared his throat, the noise discordant in the narrow space. "So, tell me Miss O'Hara, what brought you to Wyoming? You mentioned you are traveling back to St. Louis?"

"Yes, St. Louis is home." She folded her hands in her lap as she directed an inquisitive gaze on the man across from her. "What about you? Is it business or pleasure that takes you East?"

Cody paused as he thought of her question. "I suppose you could say business, but I have personal reasons as well."

"I see."

They fell quiet again as their food was served. Cody sipped his beer and regarded the woman seated across from him. *Who was she, really? Why would a refined lady, of obvious class, travel alone? She never answered why she was in Wyoming.*

The thinly sliced beef resting between pieces of thick, crusty bread tasted delicious. Cody reached for a bowl of beef broth and ladled a spoonful onto his sandwich. He chewed slowly as he glanced around at the dining car's occupants. Most people ate in silence, some conversations could be overheard, a few folks had finished their meal and returned to the passenger car.

Cody noticed one man sitting alone, toying with his food and sipping a mug of beer. He recognized him as the guy who had boarded in Cheyenne—who now anxiously searched the horizon through the open window with a hand resting on his gun holster, then moved to nervously drum fingers on the tabletop. The stranger's actions pricked Cody's lawman instincts.

Miss O'Hara laid her napkin on the empty plate and rose from her seat. She glanced at Cody; his expression seemed preoccupied.

"Thank you for your company," she said as she moved down the aisle toward the passenger car and her original seat.

Cody rose and tipped his hat politely, but his eyes never left the stranger seated alone.

The train engineer blew the whistle and a belch of smoke filled the evening sky as the locomotive prepared to round the hairpin curve of tracks leading toward Gering. Hurtling downhill from the higher Cheyenne range, the train approached the lower elevation of the Nebraska plains. The engineer applied his brakes to slow the heavy train and prevent a runaway before it entered the dangerous curve. As the engine crawled to a near halt, three horses and two riders galloped toward the train.

Chapter 34

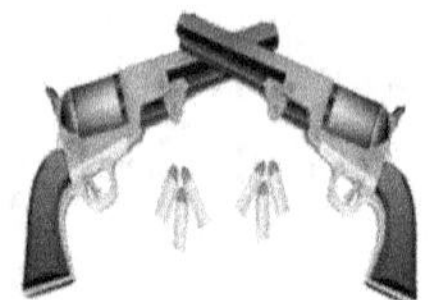

Bandits

"Everybody stay where you are!" shouted the stranger traveling alone. He stood in the entrance to the car and gestured with his drawn gun, waving it in front of him. "Hand over your money and jewelry."

The passengers reacted as one—women cried, men mumbled objections, fear hung over their heads. A general murmur ran through the car. People looked at one another uncertainly.

"You heard me," he warned and started walking down the aisle to collect his loot.

Looking out the open window, Cody spied one rider swing onto the tender car behind the engine. He couldn't see where he went after that but could speculate when the locomotive blew a hiss of steam and abruptly lurched to a stop. Their passenger car jerked forward and backwards. The sudden movement threw the gun-wielding stranger off balance. It was all Cody needed to jump up and rush the man, tackling him to the floor.

One woman screamed while others sat immobile staring at the tussle. A young boy wearing farmer overalls jumped out of his seat and grabbed the robber's gun from where it had been kicked away. The bag of loot fell and spilled onto the floor.

The two men rolled and wrestled before Cody connected a solid punch to the robber's jaw as they struggled in the narrow aisle. Jerking the culprit to his feet, Cody yanked the man's arms behind his back and forced him through the connecting door into the dining car. He pushed the would-be robber onto a chair, all the while holding his own Colt on the culprit. He took a quick glance around the car. Curtains decorated the windows of the dining car, held back with golden tasseled cords. Cody grabbed one of those cords and used it to tie the robber's wrists together.

The man grunted, "Who the hell are you?"

"Somebody that doesn't abide two-bit criminals like you. Now, shut up," Cody demanded. He slugged the man again, knocking him out. "*That ought to hold him*," he said out loud then rushed back to the passenger car.

Rosalyn sat clutching her purse on her lap. Another woman crawled on the floor, seeking to retrieve the stolen possessions. The young farmer had taken the seat next to Rosalyn. The boy still held the six-shooter in his two hands, turning it over and studying the piece, a look of amazement on his face.

"I'll take that from you now, son," Cody said in a calm voice as he reached for the gun. "Thanks for your help." He looked into Rosalyn's face as he questioned, "You okay?"

She fluttered her eyes and sighed, "My goodness. It all happened so fast."

"Well, it ain't done yet." Cody faced the passengers in the car. "You women get down and hide between the seats in case of gun fire. I think another robber boarded our train. Men, keep these connecting doors closed and locked. Don't let anyone in."

He handed the confiscated gun to a muscular man sitting with his wife. "You, go into the dining car and keep watch on the fella I tied up. Don't let him get away." The man gulped and nodded as he held the six-shooter and entered the dining car to stand guard.

With his own gun holstered, Cody moved from their car and stepped into the next passenger car as he made his way toward the engine. His eyes scanned the occupants of the car; the same fearful mood radiated among them.

"Lock both connecting doors," Cody commanded.

"...what's happening?"

"...why are we stopped?"

Cody ignored the comments and questions as he left that car and cautiously opened the connecting door to the passenger car first in line behind the tender. He peered inside the silent car. Every man and woman sat ramrod straight with their hands gripping the seat back in front of them, their heads facing forward. Quiet tears rolled down the faces of several women. Frustrated anger glowed in the eyes of the younger men while apprehension colored the worn faces of the older ones.

He stepped into the car and paused. *Where was the gunman?* Cody studied the passengers again. Hostages. He took a couple steps down the aisle then stopped. A mother with a baby in her arms raised her eyes to him; she shifted her eyes furtively to the left and nodded slightly. Cody's gaze followed her direction and spotted a man seated next to a trembling, elderly woman. His clothes were covered in dust and sweat coated his brow. A crocheted shawl wrapped the old woman's shoulders and draped her arms; it hid the gun under it and the man's hand pointing it at Cody.

Cody took a step backwards. He scanned the group again, his eyes locked with the eyes of the bandit. The confines of the coach were not the setting for a gunfight. People would get hurt. The last thing Cody intended was to force a challenge here.

"Looks okay in here," he announced. Pretending all appeared well, he smiled and made to leave.

He slowly opened the rear door, never turning his back to the bandit and stepped onto the connecting platform, closing the portal behind him. Cody noiselessly jumped to the ground then dropped to his knees to peer under the train car. Clouds of hot steam filled the air around him as the locomotive belched pressure from its valves while the engine idled. Cody inched forward in a crouched position until he spied the trio of horses waiting by the engine, their reins in the hand of one man who held a threatening gun on the engineer. He rolled under the tender car and crawled out on the side near the gunman.

As Cody stood, the horses snorted, alerting the robber. He turned abruptly and confronted Cody. Both men fired their weapons. Gun smoke joined the rising steam. The shots brought passengers to their feet, rushing to the windows inside the three cars. The remaining robber jumped up, pushed past people, knocked over an elderly man, and rushed out the door onto the connecting platform between the cars. He tried the door handle of the center passenger car and found it locked. Looking left and right, he decided to abandon the plan and his buddies, jump off the train, find the horses, and make his getaway.

Cody stood within the entrance to the cab. The train engineer hid behind him as they both waited and listened for the approach of the last robber.

"You get that steam built back up so we can get out of here as soon this is over," Cody told the engineer.

"Count on it." The man nodded and began to read his gauges and turn valves. The big locomotive started to spring to life.

Cody leaned out of the cab. He squinted to see through the puffs of steam. The dead robber laid on a bed of cinders next to the track. Horses fretted and pawed the dry earth where Cody had tied them to clumps of scrub brush further away from the track. A darker image emerged from the steam cloud, furtive movements of the lone bandit creeping forward.

Departing his concealed cover, Cody stepped away from the train and climbed the slight incline next to the tracks. He spotted his target.

"Give it up!" shouted Cody over the increasing noise of the locomotive. "Surrender and save your life."

The robber turned toward the sound of Cody's voice. He spied him at the same time that he realized the horses he needed were out of his reach. Fight or surrender? He chose fight.

Pivoting, the robber swung around and drew his gun, firing off two rounds before his body felt the impact of a bullet exploding in his chest. He dropped to his knees and fell over. Lifeless eyes stared upwards.

Cody moved towards the dead man, sliding his Colt into its leather holster. His right hand pressed against the wound in his upper left arm; blood ran down his sleeve and trickled onto his hand. He picked up the revolver lying in the dirt and shoved it into the waistband of his pants. Cody grabbed the reins of the three horses and led them to one of the empty stock cars. He struggled to drop the gangway into place then coaxed the horses to climb into the car. Tying their reins on stall gates, he left them to fend for themselves. Jumping out of the car, Cody knocked the gang plank to fall onto the ground, too heavy to lift one-handed. The door slid closed with a resounding thud.

"Let's get going. Stop at the next town with a sheriff so we can unload our prisoner back in dining," he told the engineer as he strode back to the third passenger car and climbed aboard.

Rosalyn hurried to unlock the car door as she recognized Cody standing on the platform. Alarm filled her eyes as she saw his bloody arm.

"Sit down. Let me help you. How do you feel?" she asked anxiously.

"Like I've been shot."

Cody tried to unbutton his vest with one hand, but his fingers were quickly brushed away as Rosalyn completed the task. He slid out of his vest and allowed her to unbutton the shirt beneath it.

"I can just tear the sleeve to get to that wound," she suggested.

"Not on your life. This is a new shirt. I'll take it off," Cody said firmly as he shrugged the material off his shoulder and arm, wincing, but silently bearing the pain.

"If you insist."

"I do. It's just a scratch. Flesh wound. Bind it up and I'll be fine."

He leaned back against the seat. The breeze coming through the window, as the train began to pick up speed again, felt good on his bare chest. His eyes closed as he relaxed under the ministrations of the lovely Miss O'Hara.

Chapter 35

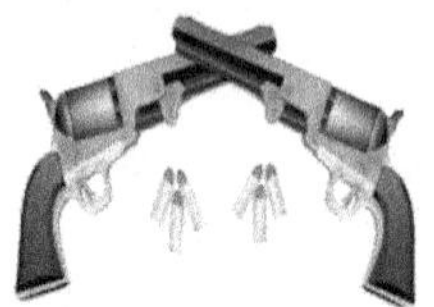

Respite

A wooden sign painted on the station wall proclaimed Gering, Nebraska. The huge locomotive blew its whistle and belched a plume of steam to announce its arrival as it crawled to a stop.

Cody laid a hand on the arm of the conductor, halting him in his stride. "Tell the station master we need the sheriff here, right away."

"Yes sir, I will," he said as he hurried to open the exit doors and lower steps in place. That task accomplished; the conductor ran into the station. Cody could see him through the window, gesturing excitedly and talking loudly, his head bobbing with each exclamation.

Minutes later, the town sheriff climbed aboard, followed by the engineer and the train conductor. He stood inside the passenger car and surveyed the handful of people still aboard and the others who had departed to the station. The sheriff moved to stand next to Cody's seat. He took in the bare chest with shirt and vest hanging open, a bloody bandage in view, then threw a questioning look at the cowboy.

"Wanna tell me what happened?"

The train engineer spoke up, his voice boomed in the quiet car, his voice and hearing accustomed to loud engine and boiler noises. "Had a bunch of robbers hold us up, right after LaGrange when we started into dead man's curve."

"That's a bad spot, all right. Did they get away?"

Cody said in a level tone, "You'll find one bandit tied up back in the dining car and his two partners are lying in the dust, food for buzzards. Their horses are in the first stock car."

The sheriff nodded and studied Cody's face before speaking. "You do the killing?"

"Yes, I defended myself and the passengers."

The sheriff glanced between the engineer, the wounded cowboy, and the quiet woman seated next to him. The remaining passengers near him all nodded in agreement as to how the events occurred.

"Hmm, reckon that's all I need to know. Show me where this fella is being held," the sheriff said as he indicated for the conductor to lead the way. "You folks can leave the train now. Go find something to eat and a place to spend the night."

The engineer spoke up, "We'll have a layover until eight o'clock tomorrow morning. Anyone traveling further East, be back onboard then."

The sheriff hauled the bruised and battered robber off the train car, relieving the tired passenger of his guard duty. The bandit's hands were still tied behind his back with the tasseled curtain cord. He didn't appear very brave as the sheriff tugged him toward the jail. Another deputy guided the captured horses toward the town livery.

Passengers climbed off the train car and wandered into the station then exited the opposite door onto the streets of Gering. The town offered two saloons, a boarding house, and one legitimate hotel used by most travelers on the Union Pacific line. Cody and Rosalyn dragged their feet across the street and entered the lobby of the Compton Hotel.

Cody looked at the high ceiling wooden beams and the tall staircase leading to the second floor and rooms of the hotel.

Two deer heads and one large elk head with antlers were mounted on the wall above the staircase. To the right of the lobby desk, a wide archway opened to a dining area. Tables and chairs were arranged against the walls and along one center aisle. Delicious smells floated from the room, enticing the hungry travelers. Cody spun on his heel intending to follow his nose and satisfy his growling stomach.

Rosalyn pulled on his arm, pausing him. "Wait. You need to see a doctor about that arm."

"Madame, my arm can wait. My hunger can not. Join me if you wish," Cody said as he shrugged off her slight hold and walked into the hotel restaurant. He plopped down onto the first empty chair at a table along the left wall.

"Are you always this stubborn?" Rosalyn asked as she followed in his wake and took the other empty seat.

A waiter hurried to the table and greeted them both. "Howdy folks. May I bring you some coffee or tea?" He handed them each a single sheet of paper containing the dinner selections.

"Coffee for me and a tea for the lady," Cody ordered.

"Coming right up." The waiter pointed to the menu items on the sheet. "Chicken is fresh tonight; comes with some mighty fine biscuits too."

"Sound good to me. Bring me a plate of that and whatever else comes with it," Cody said.

Rosalyn nodded that she'd have the same.

She sat back in her chair and studied her companion. Creases at the corners of his eyes increased when he narrowed his look over a gun sight or squinted into the blazing sun. She marveled at his brilliant blue eyes which appeared calm as a deep lake now but which she'd seen turn to ice when confronting danger. His skin was tanned from being outdoors but still smooth, not leathery, under the dark whiskers covering his jawline. As her thoughts returned to the image of him without his shirt, she knew his body appeared muscular and lean.

Several scars showed evidence of past violence in his life. Her perusal of the man in front of her made her blush lightly. She smiled and tried to hide her thoughts as she broke the silence between them.

"Well, Mister Jarvis, I must say … you're a handy man to have around. No one else on that train tried to stop those robbers. What made you jump into the fray? Wouldn't it have been safer if we had all just handed over our money rather than risk being shot?"

Cody snorted as he considered her words. "And what would you do the next time when your money is gone? What are you willing to hand over then? Your virtue? There will always be someone who thinks they have the right to take what doesn't belong to them." Flashes of Zachary Logan's face appeared in his mind. He shook his head and attempted to explain more.

"I've seen mothers killed while defending their children; folks driven off their land and others die fighting to keep it. Should I stand by and ignore that kind of greed and evil? Call it instinct or call it stupidity … call it what you like. I have to act. I don't know how to explain it to you."

She listened to his words and recognized the anguish behind them, submerged within a deep well of emotion. Cody Jarvis' past life would make an interesting tale, it intrigued her and she'd like to learn more. He'd make the perfect candidate to introduce to her boss. Yes, she definitely liked what she saw.

The arrival of their food saved Cody and Rosalyn from saying more. Their moods lightened as they consumed the delicious fried chicken, mashed potatoes covered in thick gravy and flaky biscuits that melted in their mouths. The meal more than justified the waiter's boast.

Doctor Moore finished cleaning the wound and applied a fresh bandage to Cody's arm. He snapped his case closed and gave one final instruction to his patient.

"You're lucky the bullet just grazed the flesh, no serious damage done. Keep it clean and change the bandage in a week. That'll be one dollar, young man," the doctor said as he held out his hand.

Cody drew a silver dollar coin from his pocket and handed it to the man. "Thanks for your help, doc."

The doctor tipped his hat and picked up his black bag. "Good night to you."

Rosalyn stepped back from the bedroom door, where she had stood watching the treatment. She nodded to the departing doctor, closed the portal, then turned to the man before her.

"I, um, guess I'll say goodnight too. We leave early tomorrow."

Cody had removed his boots; his shirt lay draped across a chair and his gun belt hung on the bed post. When his hands reached for the buttons of his pants, their eyes met. His challenged. Hers flashed indignantly as she turned and fled to her own room. Cody chuckled, listened to the resounding thud of her door shutting and the bolt slamming in place.

Breakfast was a hurried affair as passengers gulped hot coffee and downed fried eggs and toast in the hotel dining room before boarding the departing train. With a rumble of its engine and a lurch forward, the locomotive pulled its load down the tracks, leaving Gering behind. There would be no stops or breaks in the route from this point onward except for a quick water stop for the steam engine. For the next eight hours the train chugged along to North Platte where they stopped briefly.

Passengers stepped out onto the train platform, stretched limbs, sought food and water for themselves or saw to their livestock. Cody slid the stock car door open, climbed in, he refreshed grain and water for both Rosalyn's horse and

Lightning. He brushed the stallion and fed him an apple he had saved from the hotel.

"See you tomorrow, boy." Cody rubbed the steed's nose then left.

A second engineer climbed aboard to offer relief and a shift change. While one man slept, the other kept the train moving toward their destination. The Union Pacific prided itself on keeping a tight schedule on its East and West bound routes. Chunks of wood filled the tender and the boiler overflowed with water; they were ready to go. Next stop Grand Island, Nebraska and then finally Council Bluff, Iowa. Passengers would sleep and eat on the train until they connected with Omaha at the end of the line. It was a grueling forty-eight hours but faster than any overland travel.

Cody stood and stretched his arms above his head, his back muscles kinked from sitting on the hard train seat. He picked up his saddle bags and slung them over his shoulder as he prepared to leave the train for good. He needed to buy a ticket for the next leg of his journey from Omaha into St. Louis, Missouri.

Rosalyn collected her carpet bag and belongings then carefully made her way down the aisle toward the train exit. Spotting Cody waiting on the train platform, she smiled as he stepped forward and offered his hand to her as she stepped down from the car.

"I don't know about you, but personally, I'll be happy not to ride another train any time soon. My butt never hurt this bad from riding a saddle that many days," Cody said with a laugh as he rubbed his posterior end for effect. "Begging your pardon, ma'am," he apologized as he watched Rosalyn's embarrassed blush.

"Quite all right. Believe me, I understand. I suppose we better check the schedule for the next train to St. Louis. It will feel so good to get home."

Chapter 36

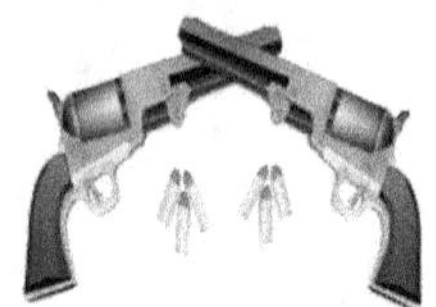

St. Louis

Planters House Hotel occupied the entire square block between Fourth Street and Chestnut. Its majestic front colonnades rose four stories high. The grand hotel offered three hundred rooms to weary travelers, businessmen, and politicians who came to gather within its popular setting. Among the notable visitors were Abraham Lincoln, Jefferson Davis, and author Charles Dickens. Dickens had even included a passage in his *American Notes* about the Planters House and its rich appointments and bountiful comforts.

Feeling decidedly out of place, Cody Jarvis walked across the plush red carpeting and admired the gilt-framed paintings adorning the walls as he waited to be acknowledged by the busy desk clerk. He was never more conscious of his soiled clothing and unwashed body as well-dressed people walked past him, with hands covering noses and expressions of reproach on their faces.

"Can I help you, sir?" asked the reservation clerk.

"Yes. I need a room. Can you tell me if Walter Burns has checked in yet?"

The clerk scrutinized Cody's appearance and considered his request before replying. "We have a vacancy; would a single room be sufficient? I can put you in room 203. Would you like to leave a message at the desk for Mister Burns? I'm not at liberty to say whether he's a guest or not." He slid a note paper toward Cody with a pencil.

"Yeah, that'll do. How much for the room?"

"How many nights will you be staying with us?" asked the clerk.

"No more than two. Here," Cody scribbled a short note and folded the paper in half, "give this to Burns when he arrives."

"Two nights with meals will cost four dollars, please."

Cody raised an eyebrow at the steep cost. He could have stayed a month at Clara's for close to that price. He shook his head as he counted out the necessary coins. Might have been cheaper to bed down with Lightning in the livery up the street.

The clerk handed him the room key. Cody put it into his vest pocket then slung his saddlebags over one shoulder and tucked the rifle into the crook of his arm as he ascended the stairs to the second floor and searched for room number 203.

"Hello Miss O'Hara. Nice to have you with us again," greeted the desk clerk with a wide smile as Rosalyn stepped forward. Her attention was drawn to the man trudging up the stairs.

She faced the clerk and returned the welcoming smile. "Nice to see you again too, Mister Clark. May I have my usual room?"

"Of course. How long will you be staying with us this time?"

"I'm not sure. Let's anticipate a week," she stated as she counted out the necessary bills to procure the room. "Any mail for me?"

Clark handed her the room key. "No ma'am. Shall I send the boy to deliver any messages to your room?"

"No. That won't be necessary, I'm not expecting anything urgent. I'll check back at your desk tomorrow. Thank you just the same."

The clerk jingled the bell on the counter. A bell hop quickly answered its call and picked up the tapestry carpet bag. He followed Rosalyn up the staircase to her familiar room on the second floor, paused as she inserted the key into the lock then placed the bag on the foot of the bed. Rosalyn pressed a coin into his palm and nodded.

"Thank you madam. Enjoy your stay."

She closed the door behind him then tossed her purse onto the bureau. Rosalyn shrugged out of her jacket and raised her arms above her head, stretching and relaxing after the long journey. She pulled pins from her hair and allowed the luxurious auburn curls to fall to her shoulders. Shaking her head lightly, running her fingers through the mass, she massaged her scalp. *Ah that felt good. Now all she needed was a long soak in a hot bath.*

Rosalyn unbuttoned her blouse and stepped out of her skirt; yards of fabric puddled onto the floor. Sitting on the edge of the mattress, she kicked off her shoes and rolled down her stockings. Wearing her chemise and pantaloons, she walked toward the bathing chamber; its door connected with hers. Her room cost a bit more but the convenience of having the connecting bath was worth the price to her. Like most hotels, it was a shared bath with the adjacent bedroom but it still afforded more privacy than guests having to walk to the end of the hall to use the communal conveniences.

Easing the door open to peek inside, Rosalyn assured herself that the room was empty. She began to run water to fill the deep tub and liberally added fragrant bath salts to the water. Stripping off her clothing, she eased into the hot water and sighed in pleasure. Reclining in the soothing water, she laid her head against the back of the tub, her hair floated around her and bubbles tickled her chin as she closed her eyes.

"Uh, excuse me! I thought the chamber unoccupied."

Rosalyn's eyes flew open. She had forgotten to lock the other connecting door. Sinking lower into the bubbles, her face flamed in embarrassment as she gaped at the man standing near the foot of the tub.

"Cody?"

"Rosalyn? Sorry to intrude. I didn't realize the bathroom was shared." Good manners dictated that he at least turn his back and afford the lady some privacy. "I take it you're in the room next door?" he spoke over his shoulder.

"Yes, it would appear we're sharing accommodations. If you'd be so kind as to leave, I'll finish my bath and allow you yours."

"Don't bother emptying the water; I don't mind lukewarm and it'll save time." He sniffed the air appreciatively, one hand on the doorknob as he turned to leave, "Although I'm not sure roses go with my cowboy image."

Rosalyn laughed. She shampooed her hair and hurriedly rinsed the bubbles from her skin then wrapped a fluffy towel around her body to dry off. Picking up her underclothes, she knocked on the adjoining door to signal Cody before slipping through her own. She turned the lock in the connecting door before removing the towel and preparing to dress for dinner. *Was it a coincidence or fate that threw them together again?*

Cody shucked his pants and stepped into the tepid water. A light rose scent still clung to the water. He grinned at the thought of seeing Rosalyn submerged in the frothy bubbles and the sight of her where the bubbles parted. Glancing around the room, Cody marveled at the indoor plumbing that produced a flow of hot water without needing to carry buckets from a hearth. Truly modern convenience. Scrubbing away days of grime and dirt he allowed his mind to ponder the confrontation awaiting him with Director Burns.

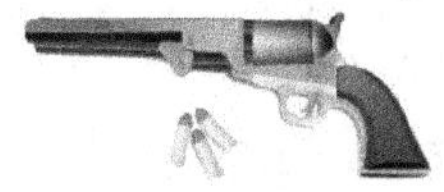

It was early evening when Cody answered the light knock on his door. A hotel bell-boy handed him a folded piece of paper. Cody flipped open the note and scanned the message.

"Thank you." He pressed a dime into the boy's outstretched palm.

The director demanded a meeting in a private room off the hotel lobby. Now. Cody glanced at his pocket watch, tucked it back into his vest pocket, then picked up his hat and left the bedroom. He strode unhurriedly down the grand staircase, resolved to carry out his decision. Cody stopped at the reservation desk.

"Which way to the conference room?"

"Through the entrance on your left, sir, down the hall and first door on the right," the clerk informed him.

Cody nodded and headed toward his appointment with Burns. He rapped once on the conference door to announce his arrival as he opened it and stepped into the room.

Director Walter Burns sat studying a file of documents before him, not glancing up to acknowledge Cody Jarvis as he took the chair opposite him. His silver hair was slicked back, gray sideburns extended downwards to his earlobe. Next to him, a pipe burned unattended in a metal ashtray; thin smoke spiraled upwards, cherry scented the air. Cody breathed in the aromatic smell and watched the smoke rise as he waited.

Finally, Burns raised his eyes to his agent. He picked up his pipe and puffed on the stem before laying it down in the dish.

"Been a long time, Jarvis. Heard you got shot preventing a train robbery enroute to here, but you don't look any worse for wear. Now bring me up-to-date on your findings in Wyoming. What happened out there?"

Cody took a deep breath before he began. He removed his Stetson and set it on the corner of the walnut conference table.

"What happened is nothing. I couldn't prove Zachary Logan created counterfeit currency although I found and destroyed his printing press, but not the engraving plates. So no evidence there.

"For the last three years I made myself part of Logan's gang and managed to witness the transactions involving the bogus money. Deer Springs has a small assay office, run by a fella named Clyde Olson, that accepts silver and gold ore from local prospectors. The miners receive a voucher for their ore. The mineral is transported to Fort Laramie to the primary assay office run by Adam Trent where it is legitimately graded and weighed and sold to the government mint. Olson brings back the money from those transactions and redeems the prospector vouchers. Problem is... the miners receive the bogus currency because Olson switches the legitimate money for counterfeit and that's how it gets passed around town. Without the engraving plates, I couldn't prove that Logan was behind the counterfeiting. We could haul in Olson for swapping and distributing the stuff, but he's just a flunky taking orders from Logan."

"What about local law enforcement? Couldn't you have had Olson arrested?"

Cody snorted in a disgusted half-laugh. "Sheriff Ned Connor is the local law and he's just a puppet of Logan's. The man is afraid of his own shadow. Local law is a joke."

The director rubbed his chin, deep in thought. "Hmm, I was afraid of that. What about the land fraud? The President wants an answer before he throws his weight behind the petition for statehood."

"I don't know what to tell the President. Wyoming will likely become a state with or without evidence of land fraud. Logan's got everything tied up. Sure, I've seen homesteaders scared off their land and forced to sell for pennies on an acre. Deeds are bet on crooked poker games with the loser lying dead on the floor. The deals are far from being fair, but the circuit judge in the territory approves the deed transfers or manipulates his hearings to side with Logan making the swindles all legal."

"Why would he do that? What's in it for the judge?" the director asked.

"The judge that I witnessed was Logan's brother. Need I say more? I'm telling you; he's got it all locked down. Anybody that questions Logan or defies him, winds up dead," Cody stated.

"So, you're telling me that you failed to charge him either with land fraud or counterfeiting. You completely failed in your mission. I expected better of you than that, Jarvis. I can't tell you how disappointed I am in this outcome and with you."

"Sir, you aren't any more disappointed than I am." Cody's chest tightened as he handed the director a folded sheet of paper. "You don't have to ask; here's my letter of resignation. Effective immediately."

The director read the brief statement, looked up at Cody and nodded. "Very well. I accept. Perhaps this is best."

Cody saluted the director, then spun on his heel, left the room and headed back toward the lobby and dining room beyond. Upon entering the restaurant, he stepped up to the bar and ordered a whiskey, knocked it straight back and ordered a second.

Hours later, Rosalyn found him seated at a table with a half empty whiskey bottle, one hand clutching a shot glass. Cody slumped forward in his chair; his head rested on the crook of his arm. Bloodshot eyes squinted and tried to focus on the face of the woman standing near him.

"C'mon cowboy, let's find you a bed. Can you walk?"

He slowly rose and stumbled over his own feet, but she propped a shoulder under his arm and held him upright as he attempted to climb the stairs. Cody clung to the banister with one hand and the woman with the other and somehow made it to the second floor without breaking his fool neck. She opened a door into the small bedroom next to hers. Propelling him toward the bed, he flopped face down onto the pile of covers, his booted feet still scraping the floorboards.

"Lucky for you, I found you first or you'd be robbed and left for dead in the back alley fella. Man, I haven't seen anyone this stinking drunk in a long time. Don't know what your problem is buddy but drowning it in booze won't help."

She stepped between his legs to straddle each one as she tugged and pulled and finally managed to remove his dirty boots.

"Whew, that was a chore. All right let's see if I can roll you over and get that gun belt off," she spoke to the silence in the room. Bending over the bed, she pushed hard on his left shoulder and arm until he rolled onto his back.

Unbuckling his gun belt was easy however it took two strong tugs to pull the leather strap out from under him. She studied the smooth tan leather and the pair of Colts in the holsters. They looked well used. If he sobered up by morning, she wanted to introduce him to her boss. He could use a man good with a gun.

Chapter 37

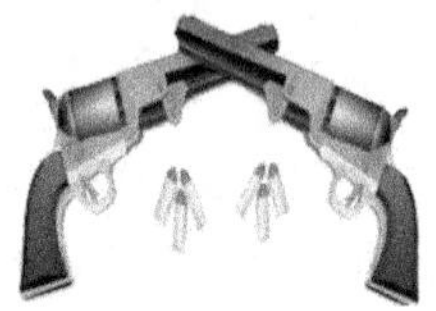

Pinkerton

Sounds of splashing water within their shared bath alerted Rosalyn that Cody had awakened. She knocked lightly on the bathroom door then cracked it open enough to peek inside. Cody stood with his head hanging over the sink. Water dripped from his hair and beads clung to thick whiskers along his jaw. He raised his head carefully and pried one eye open to glare at Rosalyn. Even that slight movement made his head spin and throb at the same time.

"Aargh! Leave me alone to die in peace."

"What you need is a steam bath and a strong cup of coffee. That'll sober you up."

"How'd I get to my room? The last thing I remember is sitting at the bar."

"I found you and dragged you upstairs. Good thing I did too, because there was a pair of characters setting their sights on you and your wallet."

Cody gingerly rubbed a towel over his face and hair. "Thanks. I owe you one."

"Get cleaned up and meet me downstairs in the dining room. I'll order some coffee for both of us. I want you to meet someone," Rosalyn said then returned to her own room.

Cody stood staring at the closed door wondering what the woman was up to. *His head hurt like hell and she wanted him to act social. Aargh. He'd seen men try to drown their sorrows before, but last night was the first time he'd ever tried it. No more whisky, better stick to beer.*

By the time he had consumed three cups of strong coffee and two slices of toast, Cody felt more like himself. His eyes were still a bit blood shot, but he was sober and ready to face the day without wincing. Rosalyn's eyes met his above the rim of her tea cup. She grinned at him as she placed her cup on its saucer and waited expectantly. Cody tried to read her mood of suppressed excitement.

Her smile widened and she waved in greeting to a short man approaching their table. He wore a gray three-piece suit with a burgundy silk tie and a crisp white shirt despite the humidity of the summer day. His dark hair was neatly clipped and he toyed with the waxed end of a curled mustache before extending his hand in greeting.

"Miss O'Hara! I trust your journey back to St. Louis was a comfortable one."

"Good morning, Mister Kennedy. Thank you for agreeing to see me today," Rosalyn said as she shook his hand and waved him to a seat at their table.

Cody exchanged glances with the man as he pulled up a chair. Curiosity on Cody's part and definite speculation shone in the eyes of Kennedy. Rosalyn watched the two men, sizing each other up like two dogs before a fight.

"This is the gentleman that I wanted you to meet. Mister Patrick Kennedy this is Cody Jarvis. Cody, Mister Kennedy is with the Pinkerton Agency." Rosalyn made the introductions. Cody raised an eyebrow, his only outward sign of surprise and interest. Kennedy nodded, summing up his assessment of the strong cowboy.

"Pinkerton's are always on the look out for talented people. Miss O'Hara suggested I meet you and she is one of our most successful agents." He saw the disbelief on Cody's face and continued, "Oh yes, Pinkerton hires female agents for undercover work. I believe we are one of the few law enforcement agencies to do so. Miss O'Hara seems to think you would make a good agent for us. Would you be interested?" Kennedy asked. He had an instinct for reading people and his senses told him now to hire the man.

"Just like that. You don't know anything about me," Cody said. He had heard of the Pinkerton agency in the past but was suspicious of any offer that sounded too good to be true.

"I know that you single-handedly stopped a train robbery in progress, killed two bandits and apprehended a third with no injuries to any of the passengers and no loss of property. You will be surprised to learn that I am also acquainted with your Director Burns and that I had a long conversation with him yesterday. I've read your file and I'd like to hire you as an agent." Kennedy sat back in his chair and studied the expression on Cody's face as he waited for an answer.

Cody tried to keep his face blank while he considered all that the man had told him. It would be a fresh start for him. He could put his failure with the service behind him. Maybe.

"What would my assignment be? Where would I work?" asked Cody.

"I'd like you to be an agent protecting the Union Pacific railroad working alongside Miss O'Hara. You'd be domiciled in St. Louis as your home base. I can assure you that Pinkerton offers a salary well above what you received with the Treasury department. Your travel expenses are covered by the agency as well."

"Can I take some time to think it over?"

"Of course. Let me know tomorrow if you're willing to join our team. We need men like you to protect the railroad and the traveling public from criminals threatening the line," Kennedy said as he stood, shook Cody's hand and kissed Rosalyn on the cheek before he sauntered out of the room.

"Why didn't you tell me who you were?" Cody asked Rosalyn when they were alone.

"I'm not permitted to divulge my mission and identity. That is part of what it means to work under cover. You do understand that, right?"

"So what was your mission on this last train ride? Why didn't you step in to stop the robbery?" asked Cody.

"The robbery attempt was unexpected. My mission in Wyoming focused on you … make contact with you, observe you in action, and assess you as a possible agent," she said.

Shock and disbelief widened Cody's eyes, his mouth gaped open and he stared at Rosalyn. Her mission, as she described it, surprised him more than anything he had ever heard.

She laughed at his expression. "Better close your mouth before you swallow a fly."

Chapter 38

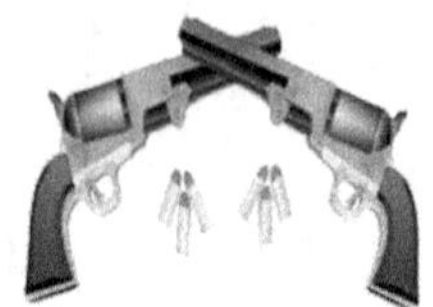

Choices

A pleasant breeze blew across the river. Its cool fingers ruffled Cody's hair and caressed the back of his neck as he stood on the quay watching riverboats negotiate the mighty Mississippi River and prepare to dock in St. Louis. Kennedy's offer rolled about in his mind. His thoughts were conflicted. Should he take the job and ride the rails or mount up on Lightning and ride West and never look back? He was no dandy to wear three-piece suits and bowler hats. The plains were his home and along with it the hardships of cowboy life living rough, just him and his horse. Working for Pinkerton would mean a whole new way of life. Cody wasn't sure he was ready for it, but what else did his future hold now that he had severed relationship with the Treasury Department? And then there was the money... Kennedy offered him a salary twice what he had earned with the service. With that kind of money, he could quickly save enough to fix up the ranch and make a future for himself where he belonged.

He strolled along the riverfront. People lay on blankets with a picnic lunch spread out before them. Children laughed and played as they ran along, dragging a kite behind them, to rise into the air. He paused next to a bench where an elderly couple contemplated the birds soar above the water then dive toward the ground in search of bread crumbs. His eyes gazed at the flight of the gulls then shifted to the skyline of the city. The tall rooftop of the Planters House Hotel stood prominently only two blocks away. Rosalyn waited at the hotel for his answer. He glanced at the boats gliding on the water and the gulls flying high, then abruptly spun about and headed back to the hotel, his decision made.

"Where do we start?" asked Cody as he and Rosalyn strolled down Chestnut Street.

"The haberdashery."

"The what?"

"We need to buy you a new set of clothes. You can't expect to wear cowboy duds all the time. Remember, you'll be working incognito; that means we may need to pretend to be a wealthy married couple and must look the part," said Rosalyn.

Cody grimaced, "Please tell me I won't have to wear one of those silly round bowler hats. I just can't do that."

One look at his stricken appearance and Rosalyn broke into laughter. She saw the annoyance building in his eyes and laughed again.

"Come on. I promise you it won't be so bad and no bowler hat. Deal?"

"I'm gonna hold you to that," Cody said as they entered a fine clothing store for men. The bell above the door chimed as they stepped inside.

Harold Stein had served as tailor and salesman for over ten years at Greenfield and Company, the finest clothier, hatter and tailor shop in St. Louis. He scrutinized the man and woman as they entered. She was beautifully garbed in a deep ruby red silk day dress, however, the gentleman appeared to have stepped out of a cattle car. The clerk looked at him with disdain and turned up his nose at the heavy denim jeans and the chambray shirt. He all but sneered at the Stetson hat that completed the costume, for that is what it appeared to be. Surely, no one dressed like that nowadays in the city. Heavens!

"Good afternoon," Rosalyn greeted with a smile. "My, ah, husband is in need of a proper frock coat and waistcoat with matching trousers. Perhaps something in a dark pin stripe fabric, fashionable but durable. Suitable for day wear or an evening social function. Can you fit him for attire like that?"

"Certainly madame. Harold Stein, at your service. I'd be happy to assist you. If the, uh, gentleman would remove his gun belt, I can take proper measurements. Perhaps you would like to inspect our bolts of fabric while I measure your husband? I suggest you choose from the selection on the left," Stein said as he pointed to shelves full of material. "Those fabrics are more what the madame has described."

Rosalyn fingered the various fabrics, testing the weight and texture of the material. She set aside a dark navy blue bolt and also a slate gray with a thin pin stripe. No black. She couldn't picture Cody wearing solid black except as a western gunslinger. That image sprang to her imagination and lingered there.

Cody's lack of patience showed as he swatted at the tailor's hand when the man began to measure his leg inseam.

"Hey there! Watch where you're touching," growled Cody.

"Begging your pardon, sir."

Rosalyn hid her chuckle behind a hand pressed to her mouth and delicately looked in another direction. She focused on appropriate shoes and hats while the tailor finished his measurements.

"Will the gentleman be wanting footwear as well?" asked Stein. He rolled up his tape measure and tucked it into his pocket.

"Yes, I believe so." Rosalyn answered him as she led Cody toward the bolts of fabric she had set aside. "What do you think of this material? Have a preference for color?"

Cody rubbed a corner of the blue cloth then did the same with the gray. "Blue reminds me too much of my cavalry uniform. Let's go with the gray stripe. Guess that'll be all right."

Rosalyn nodded, "Mmm-hm, my choice too." She handed Cody a Wellington top hat to try on.

"You've got to be kidding—an Abe Lincoln hat? No. Find something else."

She nodded and placed the hat back on a shelf, reaching for another. A black wool felt Homburg, trimmed with a wide band of black leather around the crown. "Maybe something more like this? It would look nice with the gray stripe suit. Very stylish and business-like. Distinguished."

Cody turned the hat over, looked at the hat band inside, rolled the brim between his fingers then placed it on his head. He played with the position of the hat until he felt comfortable and satisfied with the fit. Stein and Rosalyn both eyed his actions as Cody stood in front of the mirror.

"This will do."

Rosalyn let out a sigh of relief. One hurdle crossed.

"Most of my gentlemen wear this footwear. The ankle boot has a blunt square toe that is comfortable and the side elastic gore allow the boot to slip on or off easily with no laces or buttons to do up," Stein explained as he opened a shoebox with a pair of black leather boots. "Try these on for size."

Cody sat on a short bench then pulled off his calf-high brown leather boot with its intricate stitched patterns, the leather patina worn smooth and supple from wear. With a glance at the anxious pair scrutinizing him, he slid his foot into the short ankle boot, wiggled his toes a bit then reached for the other shoe. Cody strode across the room and back, testing the feel of the new shoes. They were surprisingly comfortable.

"Yeah, I'll take them and the hat. You don't think I'll look like a dandy, do you?" He asked Rosalyn with a worried expression as he checked his image in the mirror once more.

She laughed as she reassured him, "You'll cut a very distinguished figure. That's what we want... prosperous and confident."

The salesman nodded, satisfied with the large sale he had just made. "I can have the suit ready in about three weeks time."

"Oh no, Mister Stein. That won't do. The suit must be ready in five days hence. It's imperative that it be ready quickly. We'll take the hat and shoes with us today and will return in five days for the suit."

"But, but—madame, I can't possible have it ready in that amount of time."

"I'm certain you can. I do understand and appreciate the effort it will take to finish the garment so quickly and I'll most certainly award those efforts with a suitable bonus when it is finished. Do we understand each other?" Rosalyn stated her terms in a voice that brooked no disobedience. Cody witnessed her negotiation with the tailor and wisely stayed silent.

"Very well. Five days hence, it will be ready. I'll have to bring in an extra tailor to assist me and we'll still need to sew around the clock but the suit will be ready as you wish," Stein agreed.

Rosalyn opened her reticule and withdrew several large bills, placing the money on the counter. "This should cover the cost of the shoes, hat, and half of the suit. The balance shall be paid upon completion."

Cody yanked on his cowboy boots then accepted the large shopping bag holding his new shoes and hat. He tipped his Stetson to the salesman and they left the store. Stein watched the couple depart then rushed to gather up the bolt of gray striped fabric and sought his patterns and scissors. There was work to be done and no time to lose.

Chapter 39

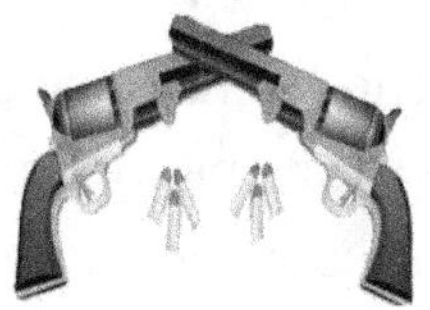

The Heist

Days flew by as Cody and Rosalyn spent every hour together discussing train routes, schedules, their next planned trip, and the recent threat to the Union Pacific. The Hole-in-the-Wall Gang had robbed a payroll delivery hauled by wagon to the Centennial Ridge mine operating on the eastern flank of the Medicine Bow Mountains in Wyoming. The owner swore he'd seek revenge on the robbers and outwit them by shipping his payroll by train and then by armed guard. It was rumored that the gang had its eye on the railroad as its next target.

"Who's running this gang?" Cody asked as he sorted through mounds of paperwork spread out across his bed. He dragged a hand through his recently cut hair and rubbed a smooth jawline nude of his usual whiskers. When he looked in a mirror, he hardly recognized himself.

"I'm still trying to learn that; my contacts mentioned someone named Butch Cassidy but then I've heard other names floated about too, even the Sundance Kid. The next payroll delivery is in five days and we are supposed to be on that train to protect it," Rosalyn said as she pushed a strand of hair out of her eyes. She sat cross-legged on the bed, her skirts tucked under her knees, and leaned back against the headboard.

"Let's get something to eat before we pick up my new clothes." Cody jumped off the end of the bed; his movements bounced piles of papers and caused a few to float to the floor.

"Just give me a moment to freshen up and I'll meet you downstairs," replied Rosalyn as she untangled her skirts and slid off the bed. She left by way of the connecting door between their rooms and the bath. During the last few days, she and Cody had made use of the private entry between their rooms to come and go unseen by the hotel staff or patrons as they met to discuss the mission at hand.

Rosalyn splashed cold water on her face and combed her hair. She stared at the woman in the mirror. *What's gotten into me? Spending days with Cody, alone in his room, listening to his voice, sharing stories... she was growing closer to the man than she'd ever been before with any other agent. She couldn't deny it; she was attracted to him. Her thoughts constantly envisioned an image of the two of them, intimate, and doing more in that bedroom than just reading documents.*

Mentally chastising herself, Rosalyn grabbed her purse and headed down to the dining room where she found Cody already devouring a plate of food. A cup of hot tea waited for her that he had thoughtfully ordered for her. The waiter quickly came to their table upon seeing her presence and accepted her request for a chicken salad on a bed of lettuce. She couldn't match her partner's appetite and still fit into her narrow waisted corset.

Cody saw Rosalyn's mouth curve into a smile as she pointedly stared at his plate. He raised his eyes and met hers.

"What? You think I'm getting fat?"

"I think if you keep eating that quantity of food, we'll have to ask Mr. Stein to let out the seams in your new pants before you even wear them." She chuckled then sipped her tea and glanced away from his piercing blue eyes.

"I'll have you know, madame, that a grown man requires a fair amount of food to sustain his energy, besides, we leave tomorrow and I'm not sure where I'll get my next meal. It certainly won't be of this quality."

"I sent a message to Mr. Stein that we'd be by at two o'clock to pick up your suit. I trust you'll be finished eating by then?" she asked.

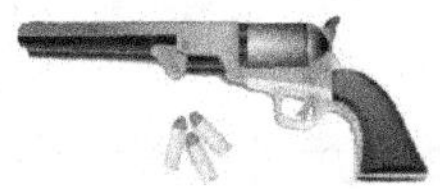

The Union Pacific train left the St. Louis station right on schedule, its destination Cheyenne, Wyoming. Cody, wearing his new suit of clothes, and Rosalyn shared a table in the new dining car of the Overland Flyer. Shifting in his seat and rubbing a finger inside the stiff shirt collar, Cody tried not to look as uncomfortable as he felt.

"Will you relax? Stop fidgeting." Rosalyn whispered from behind her menu. "What's wrong?" She sat in perfect posture; her silk skirts spread about her. The bodice of her jacket opened to reveal a white silk blouse adorned with lace.

"Too damn much starch in this shirt collar. It's stiffer than a board and scratchier than a cactus." He pulled his collar away to reveal a red, chapped neck.

"Oh my! I'm sorry. That does look prickly. When we get into Cheyenne, I'll see about getting that shirt laundered. Maybe the starch can be scrubbed off."

"Good. Won't be soon enough."

Rosalyn shot him an understanding smile. She moved her head; the gold and emerald earrings dangling from her ear lobes danced with the movement. She felt for her own lacy collar and touched the emerald necklace nestled in the frothy lace. Rays from the setting sun shone through the window and warmed their table, causing the jewels to sparkle like green fire.

Cody watched the shimmering display and considered the woman before him. "What makes a woman like you want to do a man's job? Why aren't you married?"

His question wasn't unexpected; she'd heard the same thing in the past from other men. "I suppose I've always wanted to do something different, go places, and be my own person. My two sisters are dutifully married with little babies that keep my parents happy, and some day I might desire that life too, but not yet."

Her answer surprised him. He'd never known a woman who appeared so fragile and feminine while so determined and independent.

"What about you? You must have some dream for your future?" Rosalyn questioned softly.

Cody shrugged then gazed at the passing scenery again as he voiced out loud a dream he had never shared before, "Some day I'd like to build a ranch, a place for my family and future generations. I own a piece of land, a small ranch really, that I'd like to run some cattle and work the land. A place to call my own. Must sound foolish to someone like you."

Rosalyn studied the play of emotion that crossed his face as he spoke of the ranch and land he owned, the hint of pride that colored his words. "It sounds like a wonderful dream."

The attendant approached the affluent couple. "Good evening folks. What can I bring you for dinner tonight?"

"I'll have the pork loin roast with potatoes and perhaps the sauteed green beans," ordered Rosalyn.

The waiter nodded and looked to Cody; his pencil poised above an order pad.

"I'll have the same. Bring me a beer and a cup of tea for the lady."

"Very good, sir." He tapped his pencil on the paper and moved on to the next table to repeat the process.

The Overland Flyer boasted of a full scale kitchen to serve travelers on board meals comparable to any restaurant. It was a far cry from the bland sandwiches and left over meats provided on other routes that were little more than accommodating stock cars. The flyer was definitely plush in comparison.

"Two more days. This is the fastest I've ever traveled between Omaha and the West," commented Rosalyn.

"Got to admit, I'm impressed."

"Have you always lived out West?" asked Rosalyn as she sipped her tea.

"No. Actually, I was born and raised in Missouri until my parents were both killed in the war. Then I went to live with an aunt for a few years. That only lasted until I ran away and joined the army. After that, I suppose my duty took me into the West."

"Duty or destiny?" asked Rosalyn in a voice so soft it might be a whisper.

Cody's eyes met and held hers.

"Do you believe in destiny? Think our lives are predetermined from the time we're born?" Cody turned a thoughtful gaze out the window as shadowy scenery slid by in the dusk.

Reaching for his hand, she answered in a firm voice, "Perhaps. I do believe we each have a purpose in life, but maybe we make our own destiny. Were you very young when your parents died?"

Her abrupt question made Cody pull back his hand and stare at her. Rosalyn watched an ominous cloud enter his eyes and close his expression. She hastened to apologize. "I'm sorry. I shouldn't stir up sad memories."

Cody mentally shook himself. "Don't worry about it. Ancient history. Pop died in the battle of Shiloh. My mom was killed by a Confederate deserter looking for food and money. Like I said, it was a long time ago." He returned his gaze out the window as the train sped down the tracks.

Rosalyn considered the dark emotion that colored his expression and his silence now spoke volumes. She thought of the horrors he must have witnessed as a young boy; it explained a lot about the man he had become.

The waiter delivering their dinners brought a halt to any additional conversation. Both Cody and Rosalyn breathed in the delicious aromas that teased their appetites and made them eager to dig into their food with gusto.

The Overland Flyer offered a limited Pullman sleeping car. Following dinner, Cody and Rosalyn made their way out of the dining car, through several passenger cars then into the Pullman car near the back of the train. Only two stock cars and the caboose were linked behind it, bringing up the rear. The sleeping accommodations carried a hefty ticket price, affordable by only a few passengers. Pinkerton Agency reserved the sleeping berth for its new *married couple*, in keeping up the ruse. The porter had already made up the two narrow berths in the private car when Cody and Rosalyn entered. Cody glanced at the two beds and raised an eyebrow to Rosalyn. She simply shrugged in answer and pulled a nightgown from her carpet bag.

"I'll take the upper berth," Cody offered.

"Thank you. That will do nicely. Perhaps you could step outside to allow me to undress...?" The question hung in the air.

Cody stood with a hand on the doorknob. "How would it look to anyone if the husband stood waiting in the aisle?"

Rosalyn considered his words and the dilemma of the close quarters. A faint blush colored her cheeks. He solved the problem for her.

"Turn around and I'll help with that row of buttons."

Avoiding eye contact, she lifted her hair and presented her back to him. "Thank you," Rosalyn giggled nervously, "having a man share your room can be useful at that."

She clutched the gaping bodice to her as she reached for the modest nightgown and slipped it over her head while the silk dress fell in a heap. Stepping out of the voluminous skirt, Rosalyn bent to pick up her traveling gown and draped it across the only chair.

"What should I do with the jewels?" She had removed the ear bobs and held the necklace in her hand.

"Put them on top of the dresser. They'll make tempting bait for our suspected thieves. Are you sure you spotted the pair?"

"Positively. Two men, both slim, but one slightly taller. They walked past us in the dining room three times; I could feel their eyes on my necklace. They practically drooled over the jewels. Do you think the gang discovered there was no payroll on the train and this was only a dry run? It would explain their interest in the jewels."

"I'm wondering how they came to know. They wouldn't bother with a small heist if there was a hefty payroll to be had."

"That makes sense. Maybe someone in the railroad office?"

"Hmm, second thought... maybe you better climb up into the upper berth and leave the lower one to me. If they visit us tonight, I'll need to be ready."

Cody pulled off his ankle boots and removed his coat and vest but left on his pants and shirt. With one quick movement, he ripped the stiff collar open, tearing it from the shirt neckline and took a deep breath.

"Ah! That feels better. How's a man supposed to fight trussed up like that?"

"For someone who had been so concerned over ripping an old chambray shirt, you don't seem to have any compunctions for destroying a more expensive silk one." She shook her head and looked at the ruined shirt in dismay.

He shrugged, flashing her a boyish, impertinent grin, "It can be fixed, with a better collar next time." Cody spun the cylinder of his Colt, checked all chambers were loaded then set the gun on his own bed.

She sighed, knowing she had lost that argument. "I suppose so."

"All right, put your foot in my hands and I'll give you a boost up," Cody said as he crouched and laced his hands together.

Rosalyn placed a foot in his hands and in one fluid motion he propelled her body upward, to land on the upper mattress.

"Can you toss up my purse, please? If I have to be up on this thing, I plan to defend myself if need be."

"Madame, you wound me. Don't you trust me to defend you?" Cody said with a laugh and a hand over his heart then handed her the reticule. He watched her draw out a two-shot derringer from the purse.

"Be careful where you aim that pea shooter. Don't mistake me in the dark for your target," Cody warned as he inspected the small but lethal weapon.

"Humph, I assure you I'm quite accurate."

"Let's hope it doesn't come to that, but I'd rather we're both prepared," Cody stated as he turned down the oil lamp and raised the window shade enough to allow a sliver of moonlight to illuminate their room.

Rosalyn yawned loudly, "I don't know why I feel so sleepy."

"Know what you mean. I can't seem to keep my eyes open."

He tried to lay awake listening for any suspicious noises but kept nodding off. Slowly the rhythmic sound of clickety-clack on the tracks lulled Cody and Rosalyn into a deep sleep. Cody didn't stir when the lock on their door was forced open and the pair of thieves entered the cabin.

One thief quickly scooped up the necklace and earrings from the dresser top. The other grabbed Cody's jacket and searched its pockets, finding a slim leather wallet but not much cash. He angrily tossed the jacket onto the floor after stuffing the money into his pocket.

"Be quiet!" the taller man cautioned.

"He ain't gonna wake up, not with the amount of sleeping powder Jake put in his food." The robber poked his partner and chuckled to himself. "Like stealing from sleeping babes."

The pair rummaged through Rosalyn's valise, giggling foolishly over the frilly female garments until their hands touched upon a velvet jewelry case hidden underneath. They claimed the gold chain and locket plus gold ear bobs from within and dropped the case onto the pile of clothes.

"Where's the ring? I saw a ring with a big stone; she was wearing it at dinner."

"Dunno. Maybe it's on her hand." He moved toward the upper berth, reaching across the prone man beneath and tried to grab the woman's arm.

Rosalyn stirred. Her eyes opened and stared at the unknown man hovering near her. Her hand still clutched the derringer as she raised it and fired at the thief. In her drugged state, her aim was poor but she hit her mark.

The robber howled. Blood gushed from a hole in his left cheek pierced by the tiny bullet. A hand clutching his face, he jumped around squealing, not caring if the noise woke the dead. His partner quickly took stock of the situation and in the meager light, grabbed any cloth, a pair of pantaloons, to press against the wound.

"We gotta get out of here!" The wounded man whined.

"I ain't leaving behind a witness, besides, she might be worth a tidy ransom from that dandy husband of hers."

The taller bandit reached up and roughly hauled Rosalyn off the upper bed. She fell onto the floor then saw stars seconds later as the robber's fist made contact with her face, knocking her out. He slung her across his shoulder like a bag of grain, her head and arms dangled behind him.

They left the cabin and sprinted toward the outside connecting door. Just like they had planned, the train slowed to a stop at the watering station. The pair of robbers with their captive hopped off the Overland Flyer unseen in the dark of night then mounted horses waiting for them along with their brother, Abe.

Chapter 40

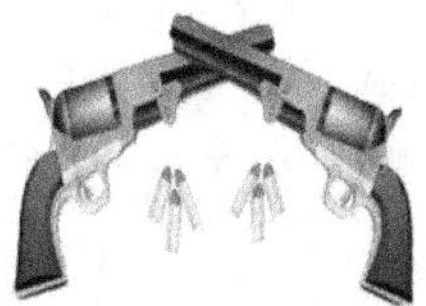

Kidnapped

Cody awoke with a sense of dread. Sunlight streaming through the window pierced his eyes and his head throbbed as if he'd been kicked by a mule. As he pried his eyes open, he saw clothing strewn about the room and blood spattered on the floor. He instantly looked to the bunk above him and found it empty. Where was Rosalyn? Her derringer lay among a tangle of sheets. Cody picked it up and sniffed the gun barrel; it had been fired. All his senses sprung to alert.

A quick glance at the dresser confirmed the jewels were gone, no doubt stolen during the night. Cody snorted as he spoke out loud, "You clowns are gonna get a nasty surprise when you learn the emeralds are only green glass, not worth more than a few dollars."

The thieves had obviously searched for more valuables by the look of their cabin, but whose blood covered the floor. What had happened?

The cabin door hung open. As Cody stood in the middle of the small room surveying the damage, a conductor stopped and stuck his head in.

"My goodness, sir, what happened? Do you need assistance?" the conductor asked in alarm.

"Have you seen Miss O'Hara, err, I mean my wife? Did the train stop at any time during the night?" Cody asked as he stripped off the torn shirt and shucked his trousers in front of the gawking man. He thrust his legs in a pair of jeans and donned a plaid shirt then tugged on his leather cowboy boots, feeling normal once again.

"I'm sorry, sir, but I haven't seen the lady anywhere on the train. She's not in the dining car. Only stop the Flyer made last night was for water for the boiler, just fifteen minutes, no longer," the conductor confirmed.

"When was that? How long ago?"

"Maybe about four o'clock; guess three hours ago."

Cody mentally calculated the distance and amount of head start the robbers had. As much as he hated to consider the prospect, Rosalyn must be with them. Why would they take her? Ransom. It was the only logical reason. He strapped on his gun belt and slid both Colts into their holsters.

Adjusting his Stetson on his head, Cody turned to the conductor and flashed the Pinkerton badge in his hand, "I need the train stopped right now so I can get off. Give me five minutes to get my horse and you can be on your way. Do it now!"

The conductor hurried from the cabin and raced up the aisle, moving from car to car as he made his way toward the front car and the emergency brake cord.

The train suddenly screeched to a halt. Passengers screamed, shouted and lost their balance as breakfast dishes, luggage and possessions went flying. Cody jumped from the pullman car and ran to the stock car, throwing open the door and climbed inside. He quickly hoisted his saddle and rig and tossed it over Lightning's back. The horse snorted in surprise as Cody tightened the cinch.

"I need you boy. We've got some ground to cover."

Lightning pawed his stall, eager to go, matching his master's energy and mood. Cody urged the big stallion to jump through the open door onto the ground, then he slid the door closed and mounted up. In less than five minutes he raced toward the front of the train where the conductor clutched the railing and hung out from the car platform.

"Have someone pack up our stuff and leave it at the Cheyenne station. Get this train moving and don't stop until you reach Cheyenne," ordered Cody.

"Good luck!" The conductor shouted as the engine belched steam and began to rumble as it moved forward on the tracks and headed away.

Cody turned Lightning and galloped off, following the tracks eastward, back to the watering station where, with any luck, he could pick up the tracks of Rosalyn's kidnappers. It would take him hours to cover the same ground, even going through the streams and across the hills that the train tracks had to go around. Rosalyn's life might depend on him finding her; he was determined not to fail her as he pressed Lightning forward.

The sun rose high overhead by the time Cody reached the watering station. He hopped off Lightning and led him to the water trough while he quenched his own thirst then bent to inspect the ground surrounding the water tower. There they were... the trace of several horse prints that led north.

"C'mon boy, let's go get 'em."

Rosalyn's head ached as she hung upside-down, tied over the rump of Abe's horse galloping across the rough terrain. Her stomach threatened to empty its content with each bone-jarring jolt. Swallowing hard, she squeezed her eyes shut to prevent the waves of dizziness and nausea caused by her position. Her nightgown had ridden up to expose bare feet and shapely calves. The sun warmed her bare skin; pale exposed flesh reddened in the heat. From her vantage point, Rosalyn could just see the tips of her toes, covered in grime from the dirt swirling under the horse's hooves.

She hoped the men would soon reach their destination while she was still in one piece. Rosalyn tried to study the ground beneath her and turned her head slightly to make out landmarks in hopes of finding her way back once she managed to get free. The thought of escape consumed her. Rosalyn tore at the cuff of her nightgown until she was able to free a scrap of lace. Spotting a stand of cacti ahead, she tossed the lace onto the prickly thorns as they rode past. The white bit of fabric fluttered in the air but stayed attached to the plant. She'd use it as a landmark, or maybe it would be a sign to any-one tracking their passage. Somehow she knew Cody followed them and would find her clues; she clung to that thought. She tore at the other cuff and deposited another piece of lace on the next cactus plant, determined to thwart her kidnappers however she could.

Men and horses began to slow as they neared a decrepit structure. An abandoned prospector's shack constructed of wood planks held loosely in place by a handful of nails with strips of corrugated rusty metal for a roof. A good gust of wind could blow it down. A short scrub pine provided the only shade. Rosalyn could hear the ripple of a nearby stream and longed for the cool water to quench her dry throat or bathe her sunburned skin.

Abe slid off his horse then with a flick of a knife cut the cord holding Rosalyn in place. She fell onto the ground; her sore body and stiff muscles collapsed under her, unable to move. One of the robbers picked her up and carried her into the hut. A single chair sat next to a makeshift table with a narrow cot along one wall. The man dropped Rosalyn onto the cot. The stiff canvas material bowed under her weight and tested its frame, but it held, giving Rosalyn the chance to lie prone, stretch and flex her sore limbs. She was finally able to feel blood pulse through her veins again.

Cody tracked three riders. By the deeper impressions in the dirt, one horse rode heavier—two riders on one horse. That had to mean Rosalyn. He needed to believe that she was still alive. They had no reason to kill her. Why take her at all unless they thought she was worth more money?

He rode along, leaning down to study the tracks again and verify their direction before coaxing Lightning into a gallop. As he headed further north, the land began to look familiar. Barren prairie held nothing but stands of cacti and scrub, not fit for man or cattle to live on. He recalled questioning a prospector once in these parts when his Army cavalry troop had passed through. The old codger had to be dead long ago by now.

Cody shielded his eyes against the glare of the sun with his hand, peering into the horizon he spotted a scrap of white. He urged the stallion forward where a tall cactus held a white bloom that on closer inspection appeared to be a piece of lace. Rosalyn. Like Hansel and Gretel she had left him a trail of breadcrumbs. All he needed to do was keep finding them. Confident now, he kept trailing the tracks and searched for more bits of white. He grinned when he saw another. That a girl! She was keeping her head, not panicking and doing what she could to help him.

Chapter 41

Rescue

Cody spotted the crumbling shack in the distance. Small shrubs and a lone pine near the structure wouldn't provide him much cover. He veered to the west, heading toward the small stream that ran through the parched land. Leading the big stallion along the banks of the narrow river, Cody approached the cabin as near as he dared. He dismounted and tied Lightning onto a shrub near the water where the horse could drink his full and be out of sight. Cody crawled up the slight rise of the river bank and searched the area for signs of movement near the shack.

Three horses were tied to the pine; wheezing, their sides coated with lather. Poor beasts appeared to have been run into the ground and would be good for little else without rest and water.

Cody crept behind the back of the shack; the tin roof hung loosely over a partial wall where wooden slats crisscrossed each other and dangled from rusted nails. He stood and listened to the disgruntled voices from within.

"Where's the payroll?" Abe demanded.

"Um, well...we didn't get it. But we got some fancy jewels!" explained the tall youth. He scuffed his boot on the dirt floor and cast his eyes downward.

"What do you mean you didn't get the payroll? That was the plan, you nimwit." Abe snarled, disgusted with his brothers.

"We heard one of the porters talking about the extra security guarding the payroll run, so we figured we better try something else. We was scared. Me and Wilbur couldn't out gun a whole passel of guards," Saul reasoned as he paced the floor.

Abe dragged a hand through his hair and stared at the pair of boys. Worthless. Why did he trust them to do the job correctly? He looked at the pair and sighed.

"Get over here and let me look at your mug."

Wilbur slid onto the chair next to his brother. He still held Rosalyn's pantaloons against the side of his face. Abe slapped his hand away and the bloody garment fell onto the floor and was kicked aside.

Abe attempted to clean Wilbur's cheek; his pudgy hands fumbled with a makeshift bandage.

"Oww!"

"Sit still. How the hell did you get shot like this?"

"She did it," he cried pointing an accusing finger at Rosalyn. "Pulled a dinky pistol on me and shot me in the face. I oughta kill her for this," whined Wilbur.

"What are we goin' to do with her?" asked Abe.

"She's our ticket to big money. That stupid husband of hers will pay to get her back," the youngest of the three brothers stated. He gave his older brother a look that said his plan should have been obvious.

"And just how do you propose to do that? Where you gonna deliver a ransom note? In case you didn't notice, the husband was on the train that's half way to Cheyenne," Abe sneered. "I swear you get more stupid every day."

"Uh, well, uh…guess I didn't think of that."

"Guess you didn't think at all," spat Abe. A sound in the corner caught his attention. He turned to study the woman in question.

Rosalyn sat on the filthy cot; her knees drawn up to her chin. Her eyes darted between the three men as she listened to their argument. Bleeding had stopped on the man she had shot but the sight of the wound was ghastly. She had never intended to shoot the man in the face, yet she could hardly be faulted for defending herself when awoken from a drugged sleep.

Abe stepped closer to the woman. She was a pretty thing, like a doll, dressed up in a frilly lace nightgown, even with its torn sleeves and soiled hemline. Desire shone in his eyes seconds before he squelched the feeling.

"What's your name?" he asked as he studied her.

Rosalyn raised her chin in mock defiance. "Rosalyn O'Hara," she answered. "I demand you release me."

Abe snorted at her nerve. "You do, do you? 'Fraid there ain't no place to release you to, ma'am. In case you didn't notice, you're in the middle of nowhere."

"You'll be sorry if you don't return me to the nearest town," she said with a bravado her trembling limbs belied.

"Lady, you ain't in any position to make demands," Abe stated as he turned his back on her and walked out of the cabin.

Cody slipped between the gaps created by the hanging slats and entered the one-room shack. He crouched behind a stack of wooden crates; he could almost reach out and touch Rosalyn on the cot.

Rosalyn swiveled her head about. Her ears heard a tiny scrape on wood and her nose twitched at a familiar scent. Cody was near. After spending days together in close proximity, she'd recognize his subtle, musky fragrance anywhere. Rosalyn nodded her head in silent communication.

Cody peered from behind his flimsy barricade. He spotted one wounded man sitting on a chair, his upper body bent over the table with his head cradled in his arms. A younger, taller man paced the floor and frequently stared out the front entrance. Cody could hear someone speaking low outside; the horses snickered and whinnied.

Slowly moving away from the stack of crates, Cody stepped into the room with gun drawn. A quick glance at Rosalyn showed a bruised cheek and the beginning of a black eye but otherwise she appeared unharmed. He shifted his attention to the two men. As he cocked the hammer of the Colt, the ominous click echoed in the vacant space. Wilbur raised his head and stared in shock but his younger brother unwisely reacted by reaching for his gun. He never cleared leather before Cody's bullet tore into his shoulder, dropping him to his knees.

The sound of gunfire brought Abe racing into the shack where is suddenly halted and raised his hands skyward as he gaped at the muzzle pointing at his chest.

"Jarvis!"

"Guess this means you left Logan. Can't say you're moving up in the world." Cody indicated his surroundings with his free hand.

"Wh...what are you doing here?" Abe stammered.

Wilbur looked back and forth between his brother bleeding on the floor, Abe frozen in place, and the dude he thought was the dandy husband. For the first time in his life, he made the right decision to remain still and silent.

"Surprised at you Abe, thought you had more sense than to rob a train and not very successfully at that," snorted Cody as he kept his gun trained on the man.

"Humph, rumor was, you went back East. Guess I heard wrong. What's it to you...a train robbery or some rich woman's jewelry? You looking for a cut?" Abe asked. "Okay if put down my arms now?" He carefully lowered his arms but kept both hands palms up in clear view.

"Pinkerton agents kind of object to two-bit thieves like you," Cody voiced in a menacing tone then pulled his badge from his pocket. "I especially object to the disrespect you've shown my partner." One eyebrow raised, his jaw clenched, he nodded toward Rosalyn as she stood next to the cot.

The expression on Abe's face was priceless as he tried to digest Cody's shocking announcement. A Pinkerton man—hey did that mean...?

Cody scrutinized the man's face as a dawning awareness came into his mind and each thought displayed on his face.

"You a lawman? You was nosing around Logan's barn that time too, huh? Knew there was something funny about you, Jarvis."

"If I were you, I wouldn't be worrying about that now. You better be thinking about what you're going to do in your current situation," Cody warned. He shook his head and glanced about the room. "Rosalyn, grab that length of rope near the door. We need to tie up this crew."

Cody picked up the discarded pantaloons from the dirt floor and handed them to Rosalyn.

"These belong to you?"

Grasping the blood encrusted garment with two fingers, she held it away from her. "Ugh. These need a scrubbing and so do I."

With a glance at his prisoners, Cody grasped Rosalyn's elbow and led her outside. "There's a shallow stream on the other side of this brush. I've got Lightning waiting there. The best I can offer is a bar of soap that's inside my gear."

"Sounds heavenly. Lead the way," Rosalyn sighed as she stepped carefully in her bare feet across the rough ground.

Seeing her dilemma, Cody turned to Rosalyn and scooped her up into his arms, pressing her against his chest. He carried her down the sloping bank and only lowered her when her feet touched the cool water. She sighed in pleasure.

"I'll go find that soap for you."

Rosalyn waded into the cool, rippling water to relieve the sting of sunburn on her lower legs. She crouched in the water until her shoulders were submerged and her hair floated around her; the wet nightgown clung to her like a diaphanous mold on her skin. She didn't care; her pleasure exceeded her modesty concerns.

Cody stood at the water's edge; his eyes fixed on the water nymph frolicking before him. Did she know the picture she made? His self-control was sorely strained.

"Ahem," he cleared his throat loudly to draw her attention.

Rosalyn plunged into the deeper water again before facing him.

He wrapped the pantaloons around the bar of soap then tossed the bundle for her to catch.

"Better wash 'em as clean as you can because you'll need to wear them, unless you plan on straddling a horse bare-assed." Cody heard her gasp at his outrageous statement then left to return to the cabin.

Standing in the doorway of the shack, he considered the three miscreants sitting on the floor, hog-tied to each other with their backs together.

Cody removed saddle bags from the three horses and rummaged through them until he located a dirty handkerchief knotted to hold the stolen gems. Tossing the bundle onto the table, he untied it to reveal the tangled jewelry. He worked to separate the gold locket on a thin chain from the bulky emerald necklace and earrings. Taking a clean cloth from his pocket, he dropped Rosalyn's locket and matching earrings onto it.

Abe observed Cody's actions, curious as to why he tossed the emeralds aside. From the corner of his eye, Cody noticed the man's interest. He held up the glittering green necklace before the captured men.

"Pretty, isn't it? You'd never guess that it's only glass, not worth more than a couple of bucks. You boys risked your lives for nothing." Cody chuckled as he stuffed the hanky with the real gold jewelry into his jeans pocket then scooped up the fake jewelry and tied it back into the dirty rag. Might come in handy again.

Abe scowled and kicked Wilbur's leg next to him. "Grrr, you damn fools, you can't do anything right! What are ya planning to do with us, Jarvis? You can't just leave us like this."

"Don't you fret, Abe, you'll be okay. I'll send a deputy over from LaGrange, reckon that's closest. He'll see to you guys."

Cody left the shack; a barrage of curses and threats followed him as he walked toward the riverbank. Rosalyn stood next to Lightning. Her wet nightgown still clung to her pantaloon encased legs. She had found his spare shirt and now wore that over the damp gown.

Coming up beside her, he watched her try to work the buttons with fingers chilled by the cool water.

"Here, better let me." Brushing aside her hand, he pulled the edges of the shirt closed and buttoned it easily. Next he rubbed his hands over her shoulders and arms, working to warm her chilled skin. "Feel better?"

"Mm-hmm, damp but warmer. At least I feel clean again. Thanks for the loan of the soap and your shirt. Hope you don't mind." Her eyes met his and held as she tried to read the spark of emotion that flared between them.

Cody was the first to break the mood. "I, ah, retrieved your jewelry...that is, a gold locket and earrings the boys must have taken from your bag. Thought you might want them back."

A wide smile curled her lips and her eyes sparkled. On impulse, Rosalyn pressed a quick kiss to his cheek. "Thank you! That locket is precious to me; my father gave it to me for my sixteenth birthday."

"What do you say we get out of here? Can you ride all right?" Cody asked as he untied Lightning's reins then unrolled his bedroll to drape it across the front of his saddle.

Rosalyn shot him a questioning look that was instantly answered as he lifted her and placed her atop the stallion on the blanket cushion. Cody placed a foot in the stirrup and swung up behind her, sitting back on the apron of the saddle. He secured Rosalyn between his outstretched arms, as she clutched the saddle horn to keep her balance. With a click of his tongue and a light thump of his heel, they were off.

Chapter 42

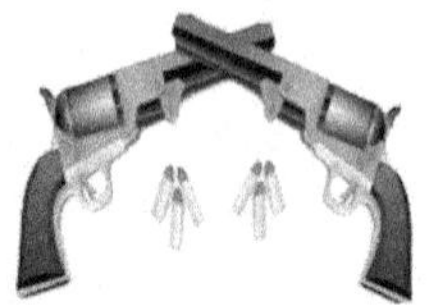

Rosalyn

"Are you all right?" Cody asked as his arms tightened around Rosalyn.

She lay her head against his chest, the top of her head tucked under his chin. Although her clothes were drying and she felt warmer, she couldn't seem to stop the slight tremble in her body.

"I will be. Just hold me," Rosalyn whispered.

Cody wished he could glimpse her face but answered her with a light kiss atop her head. They rode toward LaGrange. Cody had estimated the small town was located five or six miles further north of them. He needed to seek out the local sheriff and direct him to the shack to apprehend Abe and his brothers. They were guilty of train robbery and kidnapping.

With any luck, the next train heading west to Cheyenne would be stopping within a few days and they could catch a ride. All their belongings should be waiting on them there.

Tired and hungry, Cody and Rosalyn arrived in LaGrange close to dusk, stopping in front of the only hotel in town. Cody slid off the big bay then raised his arms to lift Rosalyn down. She glanced around, not wanting to be seen in her state of dishabille. Their appearance vastly different from the last time they had stopped here, Cody and Rosalyn quietly entered the establishment.

The clerk looked up with interest as Cody approached the front desk. His eyes roamed over Rosalyn's state of undress from her bare feet to her untidy long hair hanging down her back.

Catching his eye, Cody demanded, "We need a room... two separate rooms."

The clerk slid the register book toward Cody to sign. He checked his vacant rooms and produced one key to the couple.

"Sorry, only have one room available."

"Guess that'll do," Cody said with a questioning look to Rosalyn. She stood behind him but nodded agreement.

"When's the next train to Cheyenne due in?" asked Cody as he tossed coin onto the counter and they turned to climb the stairs.

"Probably tomorrow afternoon if it's running on schedule."

"Good. Make sure we're awake and don't miss it." He checked the room number on the key as he and Rosalyn made their way down the upper hall and paused before a door. Cody unlocked the door and swung it wide as they both trudged inside.

The room's furnishings appeared clean and comfortable with an upholstered chair, a wash stand on a single dresser with mirror, and a double bed containing a thick feather mattress.

"I've got to see to Lightning's needs and talk to the sheriff. Can you order us some room service? I'm hungry enough to eat a horse. I shouldn't be too long," Cody said.

He studied Rosalyn's expression as her eyes darted to the inviting bed then back to him. He'd leave her to make her bedtime ablutions and decision over the sleeping arrangements, hoping the floor wasn't one of them.

Cody walked Lightning to the local livery and paid for a night's care for the horse.

"Give him a brushing and an extra ration of feed, okay?"

The boy nodded and smiled broadly at the silver dollar pressed into his hand. "Yes sir!"

Leaving the stable, Cody headed to the sheriff's office where he explained about the robbery and the three suspects that he had left tied up in the prospector's shack.

"I'll have a couple of my deputies ride out there. You say one's wounded?"

"Actually two are wounded; I shot one in the shoulder and the lady shot another in the face with a derringer. Both men are bandaged and should survive their incarceration."

"Humph, a derringer you say...my, my."

Cody shook the sheriff's hand and left to find a store he'd seen near the hotel. A lamp still glowed in the front window. He entered the shop and approached a woman sweeping the floor. She looked up at the sound of his boots clomping across the wooden planks.

"I'm getting ready to close," she said as she eyed the cowboy.

"I need your help. Can you fix me up with clothes for a woman? Need a dress and whatever women wear under it plus a pair of shoes."

The woman laid the broom aside and studied his face. She began to mentally calculate the profit to be made from such a sale.

"I reckon I can put together an outfit for you. What size is the lady...tall, short, slim or heavy?

"Um, she's petite, kind of—" Cody's hands moved in front of him to outline the curves and narrow waist of Rosalyn. "This is harder than I thought," he said as he ran fingers through his tousled hair.

"Okay, I think I get the picture."

The storekeeper began to search through various boxes on the shelves, sorting through white frilly things that Cody could only guess at. She laid a corset and chemise on top of a pair of pantaloons, added a ruffled petticoat and a pair of light cotton hose then turned to a rack of dresses. Her hands tested fabrics and pushed one hangar aside after another until she selected a dress that satisfied her. The narrow green and tan striped cotton lawn cloth filled a wide bell-shaped skirt that narrowed into a trim waist edged in green ribbon, under a fitted bodice with a demure neckline trimmed with the same green ribbon. She held the dress up for Cody's approval.

"Very nice. Yes, that will do nicely. What about shoes?" He glanced at the woman in front of him, trying to judge her foot size compared to Rosalyn. "I, um, think her foot is a bit smaller than yours."

"All right, perhaps this pair might fit. The leather is soft and laces up to the ankle."

"Okay. How much for all of this?" Cody withdrew his wallet and waited to hear the tally of providing suitable travel clothes for Rosalyn. He saw the gleam in the shopkeeper's eyes as she jotted down figures on a piece of paper and added the column.

"With shoes and full set of clothes, that'll be twelve dollars." She held her hand out expectantly and watched him count out the paper currency and gold coins to equal the amount. "Thank you. I'll get these things wrapped up for you. Pleasure doing business with you." She grinned as she bundled the clothing into a brown paper parcel.

"Think I just spent a month's wages. I had no idea female clothes cost so much."

"I assure you these are the finest quality and your wife, er, or lady friend will be very pleased."

"Yeah, right. Thanks for your help." Cody tucked the parcel under his arm and hurried back to the hotel as his stomach growled to remind him of his need for food.

Rosalyn opened the door to Cody's short knock. The aroma of bowls filled with beef stew greeted him as he entered the room. Slices of thick wheat bread and creamy butter waited on a small table with the stew. Two chairs were arranged next to the table making the scene an intimate tête-à-tête.

Cody smiled at Rosalyn and tossed his hat and the package onto the bed then unbuckled his gun belt and hung it on the bed post.

"Food smells delicious," he said as he hurried to wash his hands in the basin of water on the dresser.

"This was the best the kitchen could do at this time of night. Hope it's all right."

Rosalyn perched on one of the chairs, her bare feet tucked under her. She had brushed her hair and tied it back with a piece of ribbon. Her lack of proper clothing distressed her as she gathered the loose shirt around her shoulders and rolled back the long sleeves.

Cody plunged his spoon into the bowl of stew and began eating the long-awaited meal. He swallowed several mouthfuls before he paused long enough to speak.

"I bought you a few things. A woman at the store picked out what she thought would fit. Know it won't be as fine as the clothes you're used to wearing, but it will beat that tattered nightgown and my old shirt. Besides, we can't let one of Pinkerton's best agents look like a rag-a-muffin." He slathered butter onto a slice of bread and chewed appreciatively as he waited for her reaction.

Rosalyn put down her fork. She jumped onto the bed and ripped open the brown paper parcel like a child on Christmas morning. Frilly undergarments tumbled onto the bed as she reached for the soft cotton lawn gown and spread its skirt before her. She raised tearful eyes to Cody and smiled gratefully.

"It's beautiful. A new gown has never thrilled me more. I can't believe you bought all this for me. Thank you."

He returned her smile, enjoying her happiness. "You're welcome. Um, don't let your food get cold. If you don't want it..." he teased and made to reach for her bowl.

"Never you mind," she slapped his hand away impishly as she returned to the table and resumed eating. Her eyes crinkled and held Cody's as their playful mood evolved to a different type of play, a more serious and passionate one. The feather bed beckoned.

Chapter 43

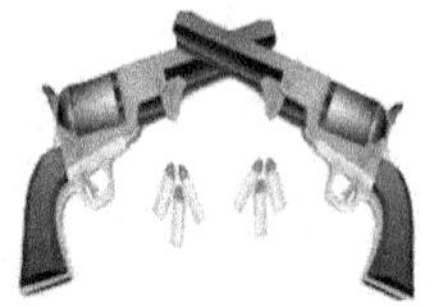

Rapture

Her torn nightgown lay in a puddle at her feet as she stood before him in all her glory, her modesty abandoned. A single oil lamp within the room cast a soft glow on her smooth skin. Cody reached out to touch the cascade of auburn curls that tumbled across her shoulders and over her breasts from her freed hair.

Rosalyn sighed, her held breath released in a soft whisper. "Oh Cody, I've dreamed of you holding me in your arms. Tell me you've felt the same."

Cody's arms encircled her and held her close against his chest, his heart racing. "You're so lovely. I want you, but are you sure?"

"Yes, yes...make love to me!" She pressed her body against his as she offered her lips in a searing kiss.

It was all the encouragement Cody needed as he swept her off her feet and placed her gently on the bed. In seconds his own clothing lay strewn about the floor as he joined her on the soft feather bed. The weight of their two bodies made them roll toward the center of the bed, sinking into the downy mattress.

Rosalyn giggled. "I think I'm falling for you."

Cody heard her words but suddenly it was another face that filled his vision; he shook his head to banish the memory. He opened his eyes and concentrated on the woman before him, shutting off all thoughts and reason while giving in to the demands of his body.

Their passion exploded with kisses and embraces as each caressed and explored the other. Cody showered kisses across Rosalyn's tender skin, nibbling and savoring her sweetness. Rosalyn's fire came to life under Cody's expert kindling as she rose to meet him, stroke for stroke. Eventually they returned from heights climbed and drifted into a content and satiated sleep within each other's arms.

Rosalyn awoke and glanced at the clock on the dresser. Nine-thirty in the morning. She'd never slept that late before, but then she'd had reason to be so tired. She turned her head and looked at the man sleeping peacefully by her side. A blush colored her cheeks as she recalled the night she'd spent in his arms.

Silently easing herself off the deep mattress, Rosalyn gathered her newly purchased clothes into her arms and headed for the bathroom at the end of the hall. Most guests had arisen earlier, allowing her the use of the room, however a later morning use also meant the remains of previous bathers in the ring around the tub. Rosalyn grabbed a rag and quickly cleaned off soap scum and other substances that she'd rather not think about before filling the large hip bath with clean water.

As she soaked in the hot bath, her thoughts turned to Cody. She loved him. She knew it in her heart. Rosalyn wasn't so foolish to think the sentiment was returned, not yet. Maybe some day. During the hours spent making love last night, Cody made no declarations of love. He made no promises to her. Rosalyn admitted to herself that she hadn't really expected any and if he had, they would've been false promises. No, she'd rather have none than to be lied to.

After quickly drying off, Rosalyn slipped on her new clothes, surprised at how well they fit. The chemise and pantaloons were soft against her skin. She managed to lace the corset easily with it's front ties and stepped into the petticoat before trying on the striped gown. Her fingers smoothed the cotton lawn material, so soft like silk but lighter and cooler. Staring at herself in the mirror, her vanity wondered what Cody would think.

Rosalyn tiptoed back to their room and quietly entered to find Cody awake and sitting on the side of the bed. She stood next to the door as his eyes raked her appearance from top to bottom, smiling at her bare toes peeking out from beneath the hem of her skirt.

"Good morning," he greeted her softly, his words a gentle caress.

Their eyes met and held before Rosalyn nervously smiled and looked away.

Rosalyn turned slowly around and modeled her outfit for him. "What do you think? Everything fits perfectly; I couldn't have chosen better myself."

"Lovely. Didn't the shoes fit?"

"Oh, I haven't tried them yet." Rosalyn hurried over to the chair, sat and pulled her skirts up, revealing shapely calves, then pulled on the white cotton hose, rolled it up above her knee and tied it with a ribbon. Next she slipped her feet into the soft leather ankle boots and stood to test their fit. She wiggled her toes in the new shoes and walked across the room and back.

"They're a bit short, but nothing I can't live with. Toes are snug. At least they won't fall off my feet."

"Good."

Cody pressed a kiss on her lips then left to find his own way to the bathroom while Rosalyn began brushing her hair and tying it into a soft chignon. Rosalyn clasped her gold locket and chain around her neck and added the pair of earrings to her ensemble. She was finished, looking quite proper, and waited on him when he returned minutes later.

Cody strapped on his gun belt, brushed off the rim of his Stetson and gathered up their meager belongings.

"Let's get some breakfast downstairs then check on that train," he said as they descended the stairs and crossed into the adjoining room of the hotel that served as both saloon and dining.

Only a couple of cowpokes leaned against the bar this early in the day while a few people sat at tables finishing their meals. Cody pulled out a chair for Rosalyn and took a seat with his back to the wall where he could face the room's activity and the door.

Rosalyn studied him as she saw his eyes scan the occupants of the room and place himself in a position to act. Cody's gaze came to rest on her and he read her raised eyebrow and silent question.

"Habit. Don't expect trouble but don't plan on being caught unaware either."

She nodded as she read the menu. A waiter took their breakfast order and scurried away before Rosalyn brought up a question that had been burning in the back of her mind.

"Those men who robbed us...you knew them, didn't you?"

Cody's eyes became guarded as he answered her, "Abe. I knew Abe, but not his brothers."

"He seemed surprised to learn you were a lawman."

"I spent the past three years or more under cover as a gunslinger in Deer Springs and Laramie. Abe worked for a man named Zachary Logan and so did I."

"This Logan...is he the mission you failed? Is he the reason you left the service and decided to come work with Pinkerton?" Rosalyn pressed for an answer.

A haunted expression crept across his face before he assumed the shuttered look that she'd seen before. His voice took on a hard edge that made Rosalyn regret bringing up the subject.

"Yeah, he was one of the reasons."

Cody presented his Pinkerton badge to the ticket agent at the LaGrange train station and was granted two complimentary tickets to ride to Cheyenne. He and Rosalyn waited in the shady train station. Within an hour, the train arrived and they climbed on board to continue their journey. With any luck, this time the trip would be quiet and uneventful.

They took opposite seats in the passenger car; each occupied with their own thoughts as the train chugged down the line. Rosalyn stole a glance at Cody, wishing he had not retreated into his cold shell. For his part he either stared out the window or sat with his hat lowered over his eyes, giving no indication of whether he slept or not. The hours dragged by as the wheels of the train devoured the miles in a clickety-clack song.

It was a relief when Cheyenne's two-colored sandstone station with its tall clock tower came into view and the locomotive blew its whistle and shuddered to a stop with a final belch of steam. Cody and Rosalyn stood and stretched cramped limbs as they joined the handful of passengers disembarking the train.

Cody retrieved Lightning from the stock car then entered the station and spoke to one of the agents to inquire about their stored belongings. He found their luggage in a locked room. Claiming the bags, he joined Rosalyn and pointed toward the exit.

"I suggest we book a room for a few days. We need to contact Clarke at Centennial Ridge Mining and find out when the real payroll will be shipped and what security arrangements have been made," Rosalyn stated as she found her reticule among the luggage and rummaged through its meager contents. She glanced at Cody as he hailed a carriage. "I need to do some shopping tomorrow too."

"Humph," he snorted and loaded their bags into the waiting carriage. Climbing into the hansom cab, they rested their feet on top of the luggage. The driver clicked to his horses and headed toward the Becker Hotel.

The Becker Hotel was a far cry from the luxurious Planters House in St. Louis. The rustic wooden exterior continued into the lobby with furnishings and décor, but it was the best that Cheyenne offered. Cody and Rosalyn put down their bags and approached the desk clerk.

"Can I help you?" the clerk asked as he judged the couple based upon their appearance. He smiled at the lady then focused on the gentleman.

"We need two rooms, preferably with a private bath or at least close to the bathroom," Cody directed in a firm voice.

His request for two rooms surprised Rosalyn but she kept her silence, not wanting to discuss private matters in front of the clerk.

"If you'll sign here," the clerk slid a register toward Cody, "we have two rooms on the third floor with a connecting bath. How long will you folks be staying with us?"

"A few days," Cody answered as he signed the book with a flourish and handed the pen to Rosalyn who entered her name in a dainty, constrained signature.

"Very good sir. I'll have someone help with your bags." He handed a key to both Cody and Rosalyn then watched as the pair climbed the staircase to the third floor.

When they were out of earshot, Rosalyn turned to Cody. The quiver in her voice and the frown on her face displayed her displeasure and hurt. "Why two rooms? I thought...I mean, after we..."

"That was a mistake. You don't want to get hooked up with somebody like me. I'm just a gun for hire. For a while, you made me forget, but I'm no good for you. There are things in my past you don't know. Let's just keep our relationship business-like. Better this way."

A tear slid down Rosalyn's cheek, her hand paused on her iron doorknob as she watched him enter his own room and close the door, callously shutting her out of his life.

Chapter 44

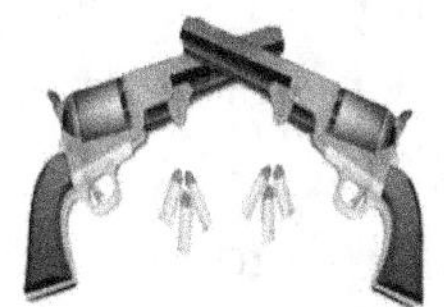

Separate Ways

Two days later they were finally able to speak with Clarke at Centennial Ridge Mining Company by riding out to the mining office near the entrance to Medicine Bow. It was a small management office with the actual silver mining operations and foreman's office miles away located deep in the mountains and wilderness of Medicine Bow.

The one room office contained only two items: a battered wooden desk and a huge vault that took up half the floor space in the small structure. Cody and Rosalyn found Clarke working at the desk. He greeted them suspiciously until they were able to dismount and show him their badges and prove their identification.

"Can't be too careful, you understand," he said as he looked the pair over.

"That's quite a safe you've got there. Nobody's gonna haul that away. Course they might try blowing it up," Cody speculated as he inspected the massive steel vault.

"I'd like to see them try," huffed Clarke.

"Do you still plan on shipping your payroll money from Omaha to Cheyenne by train and when will that be? Pinkerton Agency has committed to protecting those funds and has guaranteed safe delivery," Rosalyn stated.

"Yeah, I heard how well your protection detail went on the last train. How to do plan on protecting my money when you can't even stop jewelry thieves?" He scoffed and stared at each of them.

Cody hooked his thumbs in his pants pockets as he returned the man's scrutiny. "Who did you talk to about the payroll delivery? Who knew the Cheyenne train was a test run?"

"What do you mean?"

"Well the robbers sure weren't concerned about grabbing a hefty payroll, cause they knew there wasn't any onboard. That's why they went after whatever they could find. Means that when they got on that train, somebody tipped them off. So, again I ask you, who did you talk to about the plan?"

Clarke's face took on a reddish hue as he cast his eyes downward then mumbled, "My foreman knew and we might have talked to the station master in Cheyenne. You don't think one of them might have...? But I've worked with Clyde for years; he's my foreman at the mine."

"What's the name of the superintendent at the train station? Maybe he's our leak."

Rosalyn spoke up as the two men glared at each other, "No one should know on what train or what date you are sending that payroll. Secrecy is essential. We can't do our job if we can't count on you to cooperate."

Clarke scribbled the station master's name onto a scrap of paper and handed it to Cody. He rubbed his whiskered jawline as he thought over their warnings.

"All right. When do you want to do this? I'll arrange shipment on whatever day you tell me."

"We need four days to get back to Omaha where we can oversee the security of the payroll and the loading onto the Flyer, then it should be another four days for us to return to Cheyenne. Once we arrive with the money, we'll need a wagon and four armed guards to accompany it to your office. Is that agreeable?" Rosalyn glanced between Cody and Clarke as she counted down the travel days.

Cody offered one more word of caution to Clarke as they turned to go, "Don't circle your calendar or write down that date where someone can see it and guess what it means. Nobody should know when that money is arriving. Clear?"

"Got it. I'll telegraph the bank to release funds to Pinkerton's receipt in say five days hence."

Cody and Rosalyn each mounted their horses and galloped back toward Cheyenne. There were tickets to be purchased for the Overland Flyer and a quick telegram that needed to be wired to Kennedy at Pinkerton.

Patrick Kennedy waited in the bank manager's office of the First National Bank of Omaha. He spied Rosalyn O'Hara and Cody Jarvis as they entered the double doors of the stone structure and walked toward the corner office. Something was wrong; he knew by the expression on Rosalyn's face and the way she carried herself. Kennedy had worked with the woman for too many years not to recognize a change in her behavior.

Rosalyn pressed a polite kiss on Patrick's cheek before taking a seat before the manager's desk. Cody gave a firm handshake then sat in the other chair, sliding it slightly apart from hers. Kennedy observed the movement and raised an eyebrow but waited to hear the account from his two agents.

"Hello, Patrick, how are you?" greeted Rosalyn stiffly. "Were you able to make the arrangements with the bank?"

Kennedy glanced between the two before replying. "Yes, the manager, McPearson, received a telegram from Clarke and has all the money counted and ready to go. You'll accompany a small stronghold box to be placed within the safe onboard the Flyer that leaves in two hours."

"What about that station master in Cheyenne?" asked Cody. His voice had an edge to it but Kennedy attributed that to being tired.

"The Union Pacific decided that if they replaced him it might alert whoever he was working with, so the railroad installed a second man to work alongside him and to report everything he does and who he speaks with. The best we can do is float a few red herrings and lay a false trail of information to disguise the date of the real shipment." Kennedy leaned back in his chair and toyed with the waxed end of his curled mustache as he spoke. "Now, suppose you tell me your plans."

Rosalyn leaned forward, her hands in her lap, as she outlined their proposal. She kept her focus on Kennedy, not daring to meet Cody's eyes for fear she would lose her composure. It was important that she remain in control and honor her promise to maintain a strictly business relationship. Trouble was...she wore her heart on her sleeve and tears threatened each time she looked at Cody.

"I plan on making the trip back to Cheyenne inside the stock car with that vault. No one will get by me; I promise you," Cody stated.

"If you think it's necessary, but I don't expect you to bed down with the livestock," Kennedy said as he tried to read the stoic look on Jarvis' face and the carefully controlled expression on Rosalyn's.

"Only livestock in that car will be my horse. Lightning and I prefer each other's company. Won't be any hardship."

Ah...that said it all, thought Kennedy. *His agents are in a deeper relationship than just partners, one of the heart if his instincts aren't mistaken. He didn't approve of personal complications, but he'd let them work it out for the time being.*

Kennedy glanced at his pocket watch, "You better get going; the stronghold box will leave with you to the train."

Rosalyn and Cody both rose. Cody paused as Rosalyn began to leave the office.

"A word, sir." Cody glanced at Kennedy. His boss nodded.

"Miss O'Hara, please instruct that guard near the door that you're ready."

She glanced between the two men but nodded in agreement and continued across the lobby, her heels clicking on the marble bank floor.

Cody swallowed and cleared his throat as he turned to the man waiting patiently, "When we get to Cheyenne and delivery is complete, I'd like to be transferred to the Ogden run or the Pacific Express. Just put me to use on the western routes, Frisco maybe, as long as I can operate alone. Understand?"

Kennedy tried to read the younger man's thoughts and failed but agreed in a low voice, "All right. I think I understand. Miss O'Hara is a grown woman and makes her own decisions, but I can't help but feel the two of you are in an emotional entanglement. I rather feel like an older brother to that young woman and would take it amiss if she were hurt."

"Believe me when I say, I don't want to hurt her either. She's better off without me in her life."

Kennedy shook Jarvis' hand. "Good luck. I'll send a telegram to you in Laramie with your next assignment."

Chapter 45

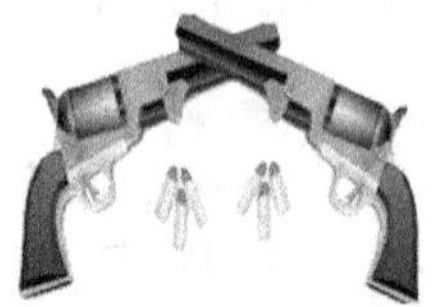

Farewell Maggie - March 1896

Years flew by spent riding the rails and living in hotel rooms. His mission remained the same: uncover any crime that threatened the railroad's expansion and stability plus protect its assets. With his regular runs between Utah and California, Cody witnessed San Francisco bloom into a bustling city on the west coast. Between the gold rush in the hills plus the influx of immigrants brought by the transcontinental railroads, the city of San Francisco and the state of California grew like no other state in the union since colonial days.

Cody was tired, but more to the point, he was bored. Sick and tired of riding shotgun on some train trudging over the mountains and plains from Ogden to Frisco or providing bodyguard duty for a rich miner or banker who felt threatened by the rift-raft population they had probably fleeced.

Jaded. Cody knew he had become jaded with life and had begun to think of himself as one of Pinkerton's whores sent out to do the bidding of any wealthy patron that could pay the fee. He longed for a change and spent lonely hours in the dark of night thinking more and more of his ranch and land that he had left behind in Deer Springs. And Maggie. What of her? Would she agree to a life together now? He had to know.

Stepping from the train at the Ogden station, Cody entered the railway building and bought a ticket for the next Central Pacific eastbound to Laramie. He spent the hour- long wait walking to the telegraph office where he sent a message to Patrick Kennedy in St. Louis and tendered his resignation. Knowing Kennedy, he probably had been expecting it.

Cody's thoughts turned to Rosalyn and wondered how she was or, for that matter, where she was. He had learned from Kennedy a while ago that Rosalyn had been promoted two years past and now directed several agents under her. She remained domiciled in St. Louis with the occasional trip to various destinations when needed. Cody smiled as he thought of her, glad she enjoyed success in her career. He felt bad about the way they had parted. She deserved better than that.

He gave himself a mental shake. Today seemed to be one of those morose days where he dwelled in the past. Time to stop that and turn his life onto a new direction, a new track.

Cody walked Lightning down the ramp of the stock car at the Laramie station. He led the horse to a watering trough then tied his gear onto the saddle and mounted up. Pulling the collar of his heavy coat up to cover his neck and ears, Cody also settled his hat tighter on his head as the cold winter winds of March blew icy shivers down his spine. March meant spring in California but not in Wyoming where winter still had a hold.

"C'mon boy, let's go see what's left of my ranch and Deer Springs."

After two days of riding hard, Cody entered the outskirts of town. He noticed a few storefronts boarded up, while the main street included a couple new saloons. Morgan's general store appeared to be in business as folks came and went. Cody reined in at the mining office. Tying the stallion's reins to the post, he noticed a young man seated at the desk of the assay office; Clyde Olson had been arrested some years back for fraud. Slippery Zachary Logan got away.

Cody stepped to the faded blue portal next door and knocked.

Clara cautiously cracked the door open then swung it wide as she recognized him.

"Hello Clara! How are you?" Cody greeted, grinning from ear to ear.

"Come in, you fool, out of the cold," she scolded in a loud voice then wrapped him in a bear hug as she closed the portal.

"Good to see you again. Is Clem here?" He asked, glancing around the room.

A shadow fell over Clara's face. "Poor old Clem died two years ago. He took cold that winter and just couldn't shake it. He never did get his strength back after that beating."

"I'm real sorry to hear that. He was a fine man. There'll never be another like him. Wish I had known he was sickly; I'd have come back." Cody took a chair near the fire, staring into the flames, he recalled the many checker games played with the old codger and long talks with sage advice.

"You look like you've been eating all right. I see a few more lines in your face, but otherwise appears life has been treating you well" Clara commented as she poured them each a mug of coffee.

"Yeah, I've been riding the rails as a Pinkerton agent from St. Louis all the way to San Francisco over the past years. Hey, got a room for an old friend for a couple days?"

"I told you when you left you'd always have a room here. Give you your old room back, top of the stairs on the left."

"Thanks, Clara. What's been happening around here? Logan still running the town? Have you, uh, seen anything of Maggie Dunlap? I've been wondering how she's been."

"Hmm, haven't see her much lately but her boy's been in town picking up supplies. Can't say how his ma's faring."

"Guess I'll find out tomorrow. I plan on paying them a visit." Cody finished his coffee then left to take Lightning down to the stable and settle him for the night.

A young girl about twelve years old paused in mucking out the stalls as Cody entered. She eyed him and the big stallion that he led into an empty stall.

"Howdy," she greeted as she watched him remove his rig and toss the saddle across the stall partition.

"You running things now?" asked Cody. "I used to do business with Clem a long time ago."

"Yep. I keep the stable clean and the horses fed and watered. You wanna keep this fella here overnight or longer?" She flipped a long, blonde pigtail behind her shoulder and waited on an answer. "Two bits for tonight or a dollar for the week."

"How about I pay for tonight and let you know how many days I'll be here," Cody said as he handed coins to the girl. "What's your name?"

"Sally." She slid the coins into a pocket of her overalls and resumed her work as Cody left.

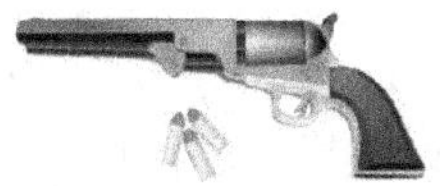

Maggie Dunlap grew weaker each day. She didn't need a doctor to tell her that her time on this earth was not long. Fever raged her body like the fires from hell while other days she shook with icy chills. She prayed Alex would stay healthy and begged him to not come close. Maggie needed to protect her precious son.

Maggie's mind drifted in and out of consciousness, like clouds floating in the blue sky that she glimpsed from her window. She recalled angry words spoken and quickly regretted, too late to dismiss. James' ghost stood in the corner with a finger pointed at her, accusing her of being a harlot. Scrunching her eyes closed, she banished him to mere memories.

Maggie ached for Cody...to be held in his strong arms again, to feel his kiss upon her lips. Her greatest regret was sending him away and wondered what their life would have been like together. Would they have suffered the town's criticism and caused a scandal if they had married? Who knew.

Years of toil and depravation endured by Alex and Maggie saved their ranch but took a toll on her health. Alex has secured his inheritance and holds his head up with pride. No man can take this land from him.

He's so young and yet at times seems so old for his tender years. Maggie sees a man in a boy's body. Michael and Rose Canavan promised to look after him when she passes and will honor the pledge of uniting their two families with the marriage of their children. Katie will be good for Alex; it should be a good match.

Maggie's strength dwindled. She struggled to keep her mind clear. There was so much she needed to tell Alex. Where does a mother begin?

Alex paced restlessly, frustrated at being so helpless. Maggie watched him but knew a far greater being was in control of their lives. There's very little that a human being can do to alter the outcome.

"Alex, please come sit down. We need to talk while there is still time."

"Mama don't talk like that. You'll be well soon. Try to eat more, you'll feel better."

"Alex, there are many things that I regret in my life, but you are not one of them. I love you with all my heart and you've been my greatest joy since the minute of your birth."

Maggie paused to gather her thoughts and ease her shallow breathing. "I don't know what to tell you to guide you through manhood. Don't make my mistakes. When you love someone, love her with your whole being and give her the greatest gift that you can – your trust. Trust her with your heart and your feelings and share your thoughts with her."

"Like you did with Papa or are you talking about Cody Jarvis? When are you going to tell me the truth Mama? When are you going to trust me? I think I have a right to know who my true father is." Alex spoke in such angry words, it surprised her. She never suspected his conflict.

"James Dunlap is your father; who is telling you otherwise? You have no reason to question that fact."

"I've heard Mike Canavan talking about you, James and Cody Jarvis; how the three of you lived together for an entire winter. Jarvis was always threatening James until the day he finally killed him. So you tell me, Mama, why did Jarvis hate James Dunlap so much unless he wanted you?"

"You're wrong Alex! Don't listen to Michael Canavan, he doesn't know what he's talking about. I'll swear on the Bible, you are James Dunlap's son. Cody Jarvis and I loved each other, that's true, but we never did anything wrong. He did not shoot your father. You must believe me.

"I won't have you thinking that you're a bastard. You need to be proud of your family roots—the Dunlap name dates back generations in Scotland and God willing, you will start a new Dunlap dynasty here in America."

"I'm sorry Mama. I should have talked to you sooner. It's just that people look at me funny when I'm in town and I hear the whispers behind my back. I've had fights with kids in school when they've called you a whore. I don't know what to believe any more." Alex cried and sat on the floor with his head resting on her chest.

Maggie stroked his hair and patted his back, comforting him as she did when he was a baby. Her heart broke to learn she'd caused such anguish in her young son's life.

Cody drew near the familiar cabin. His hat in his hand, he stepped into the shadowy room. He heard muffled crying from the frail figure reclined on the pile of quilts as he quietly approached the bed.

"Hello Maggie," he whispered as he knelt beside her bed. His warm hands grasped hers.

Maggie tried to smile as his lips brushed her cheek, forehead and claimed her lips.

"I'm sorry I left you alone all these years. I should have followed my own instincts and come back to you. Do you forgive me?" he asked in a hushed voice.

Maggie squeezed his hand to reassure herself that he wasn't a figment of her imagination, fearing her mind played tricks with her.

"I've missed you so. I should have trusted you all those years ago. I can't decide whether God is rewarding me or punishing me by bringing you to me one last time before I die."

"Hush darling. Don't say that. I love you Maggie Dunlap for all eternity. I swear I didn't know you were ill or I would've come sooner."

Cody moved to sit on the bed and lifted her limp body to cradle within his arms, her head rested on his shoulder. Maggie sighed, content. *Thank you, God, it was a reward after all.*

Maggie touched his arm as Cody tilted her face to accept his lingering kiss. He tried to share his body's greater strength with her; infuse his life spirit into her failing one. If only it could be so... but too late.

"I love you Cody Jarvis. Promise me that you'll watch over my son Alex. He needs you in his life."

"I will Maggie. I promise."

Cody picked up the worn journal that he had seen Maggie write in so often. He turned to the last blank page and made a final entry.

March 9, 1896

"We laid Margaret Dunlap to rest beneath the large aspen tree that was her favorite and among her beloved flowers. Her few friends attended the private burial along with her son Alexander and me- Cody Jarvis.

I make this entry into Maggie's journal for her. I hope that in years to come, her son and mayhap her grandchildren will find comfort in her words, memories and life story.

I only wish that I had been there for Maggie. I failed her. I pray she forgave me."

Chapter 46

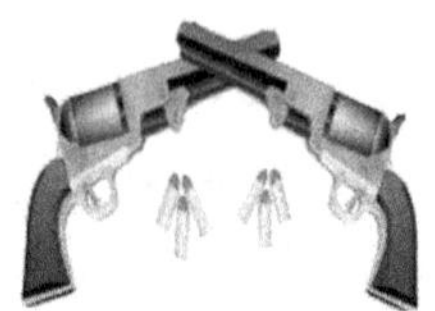

New Beginnings

The sturdy log structure still stood. Cody slowly dismounted and walked toward his house. The door stood ajar and the oilcloth hung ragged on the open window frames. He stepped inside, a hand poised over his gun hilt, as his eyes darted about the empty room. Tumbleweed and several inches of dirt covered the floor. A slithering movement caught his eye; he drew and rapidly fired, killing the rattlesnake that had taken up residence.

Cody moved about the cabin, searching for signs of more snakes or unwanted critters. He poked the toe of his boot into corners and nudged the bed frame. Wind whistling through the open windows claimed his attention next. Picking up a piece of firewood from the stone hearth, Cody used it as a makeshift hammer to pin the scrap of oilcloth back onto the wooden window frame. Except for the torn corner, the flapping cloth blocked the majority of the cold air.

He repaired both windows and managed to secure the door latch then broke up the tumbleweed and tossed it into the fireplace to use for kindling. Striking a match, he got a fire started in the stone fire box and carefully added pieces of dried wood to the meager flames.

Finding a corn husk broom standing in a corner that Carver's wife had left behind, Cody used it to knock down multiple cobwebs laced about the room then attempted to sweep layers of dirt into a pile. He needed to stay busy. His mind wouldn't dwell on the loss of Maggie if his body became too tired to think. That was the idea. It wasn't working. Waves of guilt washed over him.

Cody sat next to the hearth on the lone wooden chair in the room and stared into the flickering flames. Bent forward, his arms resting on his knees, he hung his head and wept. Wept like he'd never done before in his life. So much loss—he grieved for the mother torn from him as a lad, now his old friend Clem forsaken, and finally, Maggie.

If he was honest with himself, he'd admit that it was all his fault. Why couldn't he have saved his mother? Why couldn't he protect the ones he loved? He didn't deserve Maggie's love; she was never his. Even Rosalyn...he had thrust her from his life and future. She deserved more love and loyalty than he was capable of.

A thumping noise woke him from his stupor. His breath floated before him within the frigid room. Cody glanced at the cold fireplace with its handful of embers and burnt ash. The pounding on the door sounded again. He rose, drawing the Colt, and cautiously opened the wooden panel. Lightning stood in front of the door, loose reins dangled from his head, snorting his displeasure as he pawed at the ground.

Cody exhaled and patted the bay's head then picked up the reins. "Sorry boy, guess I sort of neglected you. Let's see if we can get you fed and out of the cold."

Lightning whinnied his agreement and trotted into the corral and what was left of the lean-to. Cody inspected the fallen timbers, assessed what repairs and supplies were needed. He'd have to make a run into town.

A week later the ranch looked more habitable, evidence of Cody's hard work. The cabin floor throughout had not only been swept but cleaned with a bucket of soapy water. Canned goods filled a shelf near the hearth and a kettle hung on an arm above the hot fire. Cody had added a feather mattress across the rope bed frame while two kerosene lamps provided light.

His hammer rang out as he secured roofing to the lean-to. Cody then turned his talents to nailing legs onto a square piece of plywood to create a decent table for the house. Using scrap lumber, he decided his limited carpentry skills could build a short bench but nothing more complex. Still, he smiled at his accomplishments, satisfied that his home would contain a few pieces of furniture. He didn't mind rustic but he didn't want to live like a caveman either.

The sound of horse beats made him raise his head. Shielding his eyes with his hand, he peered into the distance and looked twice, not believing what his eyes told him.

Rosalyn slowed and reined to a stop near the corral fence. She waved and offered a tentative smile as she slid off her horse. Her eyes met Cody's. She stood unmoving, waiting for some sign from him to welcome her. Rosalyn took a step forward. His silence was maddening on her nerves.

"I thought I'd find you here. Kennedy told me you had resigned." She took another hesitant step. "I figured you'd come back to your ranch. You did say that was your dream," Rosalyn's soft voice explained her reasons while her eyes questioned as she continued advancing toward him.

Cody put down his hammer and took off his hat, running a hand through his hair. He wiped sweat off his forehead with a crumpled bandana then stared at the determined woman.

"What are you doing here, Rosalyn?"

"I...just wanted to see how you were. Maybe I was curious to see what a dream looks like up close." She reached for his hands and clasped them firmly within hers.

Her touch cracked the ice he had carefully encased around his heart. His eyes searched hers, tried to read her mind, and delve into her soul as he felt a spark of the old connection surge through them.

"Are you going to show me around?" asked Rosalyn, dropping her hands to her side. She nervously glanced around, noting the corral with Lightning inside happily munching clumps of grass and the spirals of smoke rising from the stone chimney of the small cabin.

"Sure." He paused, unmoving.

Cody studied the gray clouds floating across the horizon, peered at the wintry sun shining high above then focused his gaze on the woman before him. He shifted his stance. His eyes briefly displayed a window to the war of emotions raging in his mind and heart, feelings of disloyalty to Maggie's memory, and a heart haunted by his lost love. What could he possibly offer Rosalyn? What kind of life could they have together?

He swallowed hard. Maggie's gentle voice whispered in his mind, *"Go on. Get on with your life."*

Rosalyn studied her image in the mirror then turned to stare out the bedroom window with its new glass insert. Lost in thought, she didn't hear Cody enter the room until his arms wrapped around her and pulled her against his chest.

"Penny for your thoughts," he said.

"Hmm, just thinking what a difference a few months have made. Look how pretty the wild flowers are blooming in the meadow. I woke this morning to the sound of birds chirping and the soft rippling sound of the river. The land is so pretty, awakening to the warmth of summer. Even the cabin looks different."

"You've made the difference," Cody said as he looked around the bedroom with its bright quilts on the bed and warm rag rugs spread across the floor. The main room also welcomed them with the added comfort of a Franklin stove to both provide heat and a cooking surface. Cody recently surprised Rosalyn by hauling home a comfy upholstered chair that he had purchased through mail order at Morgan's general store. It was delivered by train and finally picked up at the Laramie station. The sturdy cabin had become a home.

Rosalyn smiled as Cody turned her in his arms. "I've got something to tell you."

Cody nuzzled her neck and pressed a gentle kiss on her lips as he waited.

"I'm pregnant. We're going to have a baby by Christmas."

Cody took a step backwards. He stared at her, searching for signs, noticing for the first time her fuller breasts and the slight widening of her waist. How could he have been so blind? He grinned and hugged her to him.

Rosalyn exhaled; she had held her breath waiting for his response.

"Marry me, Rosalyn." He held her delicate hands between his own larger ones, smiling at her, the corners of his eyes crinkled.

"Are you sure?"

"Yes. I'd like my child to bear my name."

"Is that the only reason?" asked Rosalyn with a catch in her voice. She hastily wiped away unwanted tears.

"Of course not. You know I care for you."

Rosalyn pulled her hands free. She looked at Cody, tried to read his expression as she stated, "You've never told me you love me. Do you? How do I know what you feel if you don't put it in words?"

"I'm sorry. I loved someone once. When she died, part of me died with her. I'm offering you as much as I can right now. We can build a life together, Rosalyn, and I'll do my best to be a good husband. I'd be dishonest to promise you more." He faced her, seeking an answer.

Rosalyn paced the floor. With her back turned to him, she considered his words and accepted the truth behind them. She always knew in her heart that there was another reason he had left Deer Springs in the past, and that it was a woman. Now she knew for certain. She could accept his terms or walk away; it was her choice to make.

"All right," she answered in a voice just above a whisper.

Chapter 47

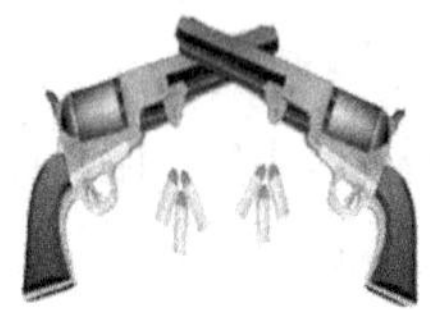

Family

Fall leaves had begun to change colors and the early morning air contained a nip of frost. Cody finished feeding the animals and glanced toward the storm clouds building in the north. He strode back to the cabin, grabbing an armload of firewood to stack near the stove before entering the cozy house. He was greeted with the aroma of coffee perking on the stovetop and the delicious smell of fresh bread baking in the stone hearth.

Rosalyn smiled at him as he hung his coat on a peg by the door. When she turned toward the table with two mugs of coffee in hand, Cody watched her protruding belly lead the way. She caught him staring at her rounded middle; he coughed before putting into words thoughts that weighed heavily on his mind.

"Sit down please. You don't have to wait on me. I've been thinking...you need to go back to St. Louis." At her gasp, Cody hastened to continue, "looks like winter might be early this year and I'm worried about you and the babe. You don't know what it's like during a harsh Wyoming winter stuck in the middle of nowhere. What if something goes wrong with the birth? I want you safe and cared for and St. Louis can provide that."

Cody reached for her hand; his thumb rubbed the slender gold band on her finger. Her eyes flashed in anger at his proposal and he knew he had sparked her Irish temper before she opened her mouth to speak.

"Now Rosalyn, you know what I say is true. Just listen. Please." He tried to make her see reason. "You're used to silk gowns and hotel room service, not frontier living. I know what you're going to say; you've managed to make this place a home and have done your best to fit in on the ranch. And I'm very proud of you for doing so, but we need to think of the baby now."

Her eyes searched his. "What about you? Are you going to stay with me or the ranch? What kind of family will we be?"

"I'll stay with you until after the babe is born, then I'll come back here to take care of things during the winter. When summer comes and it's safe, you can come back."

"You've given this some thought, I see."

"I have. I want you to get your things together and be ready to leave by the end of the week. We've got to ride down to Laramie, that'll be hard enough on you, then four or five days on the train. Maybe we'll get lucky and can catch the Flyer for the trip East. I'll try and reserve a pullman suite for us."

"I better telegram my parents from Laramie; let them know we're coming. Guess we can stay with them. Is that what you had in mind?"

Rosalyn sipped her coffee and let her gaze wander around the little cabin that she had begun to think of as her home. She'd worked so hard to make it cheery and comfortable. She was going to miss it.

Cody nodded, relieved to hear her acceptance of his plan. "Okay, it's settled then. I'll hitch up the wagon and we can leave on Friday."

The hansom cabbie stopped in front of a stately Victorian home with steep marble steps that led to a wide wrap around porch. Panes of decorative leaded glass adorned the front entry. A pair of tall elm trees graced the front yard and rose taller than the three-story rooftop. Their russet and golden autumn leaves carpeted the cobblestone street of St. Louis.

Cody turned to Rosalyn, disbelief and worry etched on his face as he stepped down from the cab. "This is where your parents live? You never mentioned that your folks were rich. Holy cow! What does your father do for a living?"

"Didn't I? Sorry. I'll let Papa tell you about his business. Come on, they'll be waiting on us." Rosalyn stood before her childhood home, her gloved hand resting lightly on her burgeoning belly. She recalled happy memories of playing with her sisters and parents in this house. Now she returned, not quite the independent and free-spirited girl that was determined to make her mark on the world but rather a new bride and expectant mother fearful of her parent's reception. What would they think of her hasty marriage and to a man they knew nothing about?

With bags in hand, Cody and Rosalyn climbed the front steps, both feeling trepidation but for different reasons. Before they could ring the bell, the door was thrown open.

Kate and Sean O'Hara stood in the threshold to welcome the weary travelers into their home. Sean O'Hara, a distinguished gentleman with a mane of silver hair and a well-groomed mustache, exuded an air of authority and respect. He and Cody locked gazes, assessing each other silently before Sean extended his hand to Cody in a polite handshake. Kate O'Hara appeared elegantly attired in a silk day dress, with auburn hair so like her daughter's with the exception of a few silver strands. Her face lit up with a broad smile at the sight of her daughter. Cody looked on as his wife wrapped her arms around her mother and both women cried unabashedly.

"Come in, come in. Why are we all standing in the vestibule?" Sean O'Hara gruffly directed his daughter and new son-in-law into the parlor.

Tall, ornate windows adorned with heavy brocade curtains filtered the warm afternoon sunlight, casting a soft, golden glow upon the polished hardwood floors. A comfortable, velvet settee sat beneath the front windows and a pair of plush wing-back chairs flanked the fireplace with its roaring fire. A Chippendale sideboard was positioned on the opposite wall, laden with trays of sweetbread and crystal decanters containing brandy and whiskey. The scent of fresh flowers lingered in the air, mingling with the faint aroma of brewing tea. Cody's glance roamed about the room, taking in the posh furnishings and obvious signs of wealth. He squirmed in his seat then looked up to find he was the object of speculation by Sean. Both men nervously cleared their throats as they continued to stare at each other.

"So you're the man who has stolen my little girl's heart," Sean stated with a pointed stare at Cody. His words brought immediate silence between the two women.

Rosalyn rose and went to stand next to Cody's chair with her hand upon his shoulder.

"Papa, let me introduce my husband to you properly. Cody Jarvis, this is my father... Sean Michael O'Hara."

Cody nodded to the gentleman, "Nice to meet you sir. Thank you for welcoming us into your home and extending your hospitality to Rosalyn and me while she waits on the birth of our child. It was very kind of you."

Rosalyn's mother quickly broke into the conversation, "Why of course! We wouldn't have you go any where else."

"Tell us how you met our daughter, Mister Jarvis," Sean asked in a formal drawing room manner.

Rosalyn raised an eyebrow at her father's tone. Her mother caught her look and shrugged. Before Cody could answer, she hastened to explain, "I'm sure I mentioned to you that Cody and I both worked for Patrick Kennedy with Pinkerton Agency. We were partners for quite some time before Cody transferred to the San Francisco region."

"Is that a fact? And what did you do before that, Mister Jarvis?" Sean persisted.

"Please, feel free to call me Cody, sir. In answer to your question, sir, I was a treasury agent and before that I served a hitch in the Army."

"I see. What do you do now? How will you support my daughter?"

"I own a small ranch in Wyoming, just north of Laramie, about one hundred and sixty acres that I plan on expanding and will raise beef cattle. We probably won't make any big money for years to come, but it'll be a good life. The ranch will provide everything we need. All it takes is hard work."

"And you're not afraid of hard work; I can see that. But what of my daughter? Do you expect her to have calloused hands and grow old working this ranch of yours?"

"Papa! Really! Why don't you ask me what I want?" Rosalyn stepped forward as she waved her hands in a gesture of frustration. "Cody is my husband and we've created a home on that ranch. I'd still be there but it was Cody who insisted that we travel back to St. Louis for the baby's birth. He was more worried about me and my welfare than the ranch. You do him a disservice."

Sean stood and approached his daughter, draping an arm about her shoulders and kissing the top of her head. "Forgive me, my dear, I only want what's best for you. Your mother and I were quite hurt to learn you had married without our attendance but I can, ahem, see why the haste. You are both welcome to stay with us as long as you'd like."

Kate O'Hara clapped her hands in glee, "Oh Christmas will be so joyous this year! The family all together again and a new baby too; it'll be wonderful."

Cody slipped out of bed, careful not to awaken his sleeping wife, and dressed in the suit of clothes Rosalyn had laid out for him. The gray pin-striped suit the tailor had sewn for him years ago still fit but with the addition of a new shirt and comfortable collar. Cody would never feel completely at ease in the formal clothing, but to please Rosalyn he had promised to set aside his western attire while in St. Louis. Now he ran a brush through his unruly locks and rubbed a hand over the light whiskers covering his square-cut jaw.

He tried to step silently as he descended the stairs in the early morning hour and made his way to what he hoped was the kitchen in the back of the huge house. Following his nose and the aroma of fresh brewed coffee, he stepped into the kitchen and was surprised to find Sean O'Hara seated in the breakfast alcove of the cozy kitchen. A faint dawn pinkened the sky visible through the room's frosty bay window.

"Good morning," greeted Sean as he took a sip of coffee then set his cup back onto its saucer. "Couldn't sleep?"

"Morning. Actually, I slept well, thank you. I'm used to getting up early to tend the animals on the ranch. Thought I was the only one who woke at dawn, what's your excuse?"

"Hmph, spent my youth rising early to catch the morning tide. Guess the habit stayed with me."

"Were you a fisherman, then?" asked Cody, curious as the to occupation of his host.

"No, not fishing...shipping. I grew up in Ireland; we're an island nation. Sailing the seas, shipping freight, is something that I learned from an early age. When we came to America and moved here, I quickly learned that moving cargo on the great Mississippi was where the money could be made. I own a shipping company and a fleet of barges that carry bales of cotton, crates of produce, lumber, even cattle up and down the river. There's always a market in demand for goods and my barges supply them."

"I'm impressed." Cody poured himself a cup of coffee and stared out the window as he recalled the day he had decided to join Pinkerton. "One time I sat on the docks here in St. Louis and watched a barge coming up river, the captain had to maneuver around a bend in the river and other boat traffic. Fascinating."

"I know the place; there is a tight turn in the river and many a boat or barge has hung up on a sand bar there."

The two men sat in silence enjoying their morning brew and watched the sun rise higher in the sky.

"I'll be going down to my office today. I'd like you to come along if you've nothing else to do," Sean invited.

"All right. I'd be happy to. When do you want to leave?"

"Oh, I suppose we can wait until the women are up or they'll wonder where we disappeared to."

The housekeeper entered the kitchen, accustomed to greeting the master of the house in the morning but raised an eyebrow to find the newcomer at the table. She hurried to fetch eggs and a slab of ham from the ice box and began cooking the breakfast meal.

Sean glanced up from reading his morning newspaper. "Matilda, this is my new son-in-law, Cody Jarvis. He and Rosalyn will be staying with us for awhile."

"Yes sir. Nice to meet you Mister Jarvis. Is there anything special that you would like for breakfast?" she asked as she cracked eggs into a bowl.

"What you're fixing will do nicely, Matilda. Thank you."

Two hours later, the men had finished eating their food in silence and Sean had given Cody a tour of the property outside when they returned to hear the excited conversation flowing between the three women.

Sean chuckled and nudged Cody, "The peace and quiet alone is reason enough to wake at dawn."

Cody nodded in agreement. He joined Rosalyn in the kitchen and pressed a kiss onto her cheek.

"Morning."

"I see you and Papa are getting along okay. He hasn't threatened to shoot you yet, has he?"

"As a matter of fact, he's offered to show me his business and office on the riverfront. We waited to leave until you ladies were down."

"Sean, I'll need some money. I'm taking Rosalyn shopping today; we need so many things for the baby," Kate told her husband and held out her hand.

Sean O'Hara smiled indulgently and looked between his wife and daughter. "Somehow, that doesn't surprise me. Here," he said as he pressed several folded bills into her hand, "if this doesn't cover it tell them to put it on the account and bill me."

"Thank you, dear." She gave her husband a quick peck.

"Be careful and be home before late afternoon; it gets dark early now and wouldn't be safe for you ladies to be out alone."

"Don't worry, Papa. I still have my derringer," Rosalyn said with a mischievous grin at her father's scowl.

"Rosalyn, you're in no condition to start brandishing a gun. I hope you're only joking," Cody admonished her.

"Of course, dear. Have a good day," she smiled in return.

Chapter 48

Maureen

Christmas preparations kept the household staff busy as fragrant pine garlands were draped across the mantle and around the front entrance. Holly wreaths decked with bright red bows adorned each of the windows and the front door. Matilda spent hours baking numerous Christmas treats, plum puddings and delicious roast turkey to celebrate the holiday.

Invitations had gone out for a special Christmas Eve party. Matilda and the maid, Claire, scurried about the house whisking away any speck of dust and arranging floral centerpieces and glowing candles along the long dining room table. All of the O'Hara girls would be coming home with their husbands and children to celebrate the special holiday.

Just before noon time, Rosalyn moaned and bent in pain as the newest member of the family decided to make its entry into the world, just in time for the Christmas feast and celebration.

"It's time!" Rosalyn called to her mother as she grabbed for the newel post of the railing and tried to climb the stairs.

Cody rushed to her side and swept her up into his arms and took the stairs two at a time as he carried her into their bedroom and laid her gently down on the large bed.

Kate quickly joined him and threw back the covers on the bed then began to remove Rosalyn's shoes and hose and helped her to undress.

"What can I do?" asked Cody in a worried voice.

"Go find Claire and tell her to fetch a kettle of hot water and plenty of towels. Don't worry, Rosalyn will be fine. I'm with her."

Cody raced downstairs and alerted the rest of the house. The commotion grew as Rosalyn's sisters arrived in the afternoon with their families and were informed of the pending birth. The women hurried upstairs to join their mother and sister leaving their husbands and children to fend for themselves and make their own introductions.

Cody paced the floor in the parlor, struggling with the desire to do something and concern over his wife's well-being. He looked up to find that Sean had joined him as he pressed a glass of Irish whiskey into his hand. Cody tossed back the shot in one gulp; the fiery liquid seared his throat and warmed his stomach. Shadows grew as the two men paced side by side until a scream rent the silence and turned their blood cold. Minutes later a new sound could be heard...the wail of a newborn infant. Cody stood still as he listened to the sound of his child; he glanced at the mantle clock and saw the hour was nigh on midnight, Christmas Eve. He'd been given a very special Christmas gift.

Sprinting up the stairs, he pushed past the group of women gathered around the bed and bent to Rosalyn holding the blanketed baby. He gazed upon the sweetest, tiniest face with a fuzz of reddish hair covering its head.

"You have a daughter," Rosalyn whispered in a tired voice.

"Are you all right?" Cody asked as he brushed the damp tendrils of hair from her forehead and claimed her lips in a soft kiss. "She's beautiful." He lifted a corner of the blanket with one finger, afraid to touch the baby, mewling like a kitten.

"Come on girls," Kate commanded as she ushered her daughters and servants out of the room. "Let's give them some time together."

Rosalyn watched her mother and sisters leave the room, so thankful to have had her family with her during the birth of her daughter.

"You were right. Thank you for insisting that we come back here. I don't know if I could have managed without my mother. Having everyone here gave me the strength and confidence I needed."

"You're a special woman, Rosalyn Jarvis." Cody pressed another kiss on her lips as he gingerly sat on the side of the bed. He wrapped an arm about her and sat holding his wife and baby in awe of God's miracles.

"I'd like to name her Maureen. Maureen Anne Jarvis. What do you think?" asked Rosalyn as she cuddled the infant.

"Perfect. Sounds like a good name."

The first week of February, Cody started packing his gear and prepared to return to Wyoming. Rosalyn watched her husband as he folded his clothes and stuffed them into the crammed leather gladstone bag.

"Do you have everything?" she asked in a hushed voice.

Cody squeezed her hand then pressed a kiss to her palm. Their eyes met in silent communication. The hour when they must part was rapidly approaching. Time had become their enemy.

"Are you sure it's wise to leave now? Wyoming winters are so harsh, you said so yourself, and February is still the middle of winter there. What if the snows are deep? How will you manage?" Rosalyn persisted in her argument; the same one they'd already had.

"I've got to get back. It's close to four months that I've been gone. For all I know the house could have fallen down or a pack of animals taken up residence. Besides, now I've got to build another room onto the cabin for our daughter."

"Maybe I should leave with you?"

"Absolutely not. I want you here safe and cared for while I do what needs to be done. You can join me this summer after I've got the house ready and Maureen is old enough to travel. It's better this way," he explained again.

"I know, but I'll miss you terribly. I don't like being separated like this."

"The time will pass quickly. C'mon, let's make the best of our time together before our daughter wakes from her nap," he suggested with a wink and a lecherous grin.

Rosalyn smiled seductively then locked their bedroom door.

Cody kissed his wife goodbye then climbed aboard the westbound train. Huddled in her warm cloak, Rosalyn stood on the platform with her mother and father who had come to see him off. They waved goodbye as the train slowly chugged out of the station. Hanging out of the passenger car, Cody waved a final salute to them, then leaned back into the compartment and closed the car's window.

Once again he was on his own. It would be a lonely trip back to Deer Springs. He began to make a mental list of all the lumber and supplies he would need to buy and load into the buckboard wagon he'd left stored in Laramie. His thoughts turned to Lightning and Rosalyn's mare Daisy and hoped Sally was taking good care of them at the livery stable. Lightning will either be happy to see him or more likely annoyed with his master for leaving him behind the past months. He'll act cantankerous just to show his displeasure.

Relaxing against the seat back, Cody let his mind recall the conversation they'd had with Patrick Kennedy the day before. The Pinkerton agent had called on the O'Hara residence to extend his congratulations to the happy couple on their marriage and birth of their daughter. Rosalyn seemed very pleased by his courteous attention but Cody was suspicious of the man's motives.

Kennedy had affectionately held Rosalyn's hands and made a point of telling her that he'd always be available if she needed help. And what was that business about him telling her she could return to work at Pinkerton whenever she was ready? Did the man forget she was a mother with duties to her child? The nerve of the man! And right in front of her husband too. Cody noticed that Kennedy didn't offer him his old job back. The more he thought about the man's solicitation to Rosalyn, the angrier Cody became. He should have confronted him but that would have upset Rosalyn so he let the matter lie. Kennedy was lucky there'd be several hundred miles between them.

Light snow continued to fall and quickly turned to ice on the already frozen surfaces. Twice Cody had to pull back on the mules' reins as the buckboard wagon slid on the ice-packed roadway leading into Deer Springs. He was almost frozen himself despite the blankets wrapped around his legs and across his shoulders after being on the road three days from Laramie. *Maybe he should have listened to Rosalyn and waited another month.* He pulled up his woolen scarf across his nose and mouth against the freezing temperatures. For once the sight of Deer Springs outer buildings was a relief, almost there.

Cody stopped the buckboard near the stable then pounded on the wide doors before pushing them open and driving the mules and wagon inside. The stable's warmth felt like a welcome hug to his frost bitten body. Cody stomped his feet to knock off snow from his boots and to gain some circulation again in his toes. He glanced around the barn and saw the source of the welcome heat radiated from a pot-belly wood stove inside a small enclosure on the far wall of the stable.

Sally stood in the doorway of the newly built room. She watched Cody as he unwrapped his layers of snow encrusted blankets.

"You look like the abominable snowman. Didn't figure I'd be seeing you again until spring," Sally said.

"You're a sight for sore eyes. You living in here now?" Cody asked her as he moved closer to the stove and held out his stiff hands over the heat.

"Yep. Only way I can prevent the thieving going on. You woulda lost that big stallion if'n I weren't here. Caught two boys trying to lead him away but they won't be back, not after I filled their backsides with a load of buckshot," Sally told him with a cackle that reminded Cody of Clem.

"Guess I owe you Sally. Appreciate you taking extra care of Lightning for me. I'm gonna take him and Daisy with me back to the ranch tomorrow. It's too late tonight and I'm too damn cold."

"Figured as much. You can bed down in here for the night. I've got extra blankets, dry ones. You better hang yours across those stalls to dry out before they harden into boards."

"Good idea," Cody said and with shaking fingers tried to drape the sodden material across the partition. Sally rushed to help him and between them they managed to get the chore done.

"Here, you better drink this," Sally said as she offered him a mug of steaming coffee.

"Thanks." He took a gulp of the hot liquid and savored the heat as it slid down his throat and filled his empty belly. "Know anybody looking for work? I'm gonna need some help at the ranch. I plan on building an extra room on the house. Can't pay much but it'll be steady work for three or four months plus room and board." Cody reached for the pot to refill his cup.

"Maybe. When you gonna need him?"

"As soon as he can start. Tomorrow I plan on buying some food stuffs to add to my supplies then head out to the ranch. If he can follow me, that'd be great or at least in the next day or so. I got a lot to do and could use an extra pair of hands. Who is this fellow you have in mind?"

"My brother Tommy. He's a year younger than me but he's a good worker. If Ma says it's okay and he wants to do it, he oughta be able to strike out with you tomorrow."

Cody considered her offer. If her brother was half as industrious as Sally, he'd be an asset.

"That's great. I can use his help."

Sally retrieved a couple of heavy blankets and spread one across a pile of sweet-smelling straw close enough to the stove to enjoy its heat. Cody lay down and covered up with the second blanket and soon was sound asleep.

Chapter 49

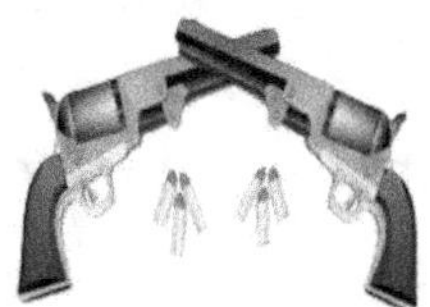

Revelations

Spring bloomed in a riot of colors erupting within Rosalyn's flower garden. The air contained a mixture of scents. The clean, freshly milled lumber blended with the damp soil and delicate fragrance of sweet crisp young vegetables poking their heads through the rich earth in the warm sunshine.

Cody paused in his work, resting his hands on the rake handle, he surveyed with satisfaction the new addition to the house and the animals grazing in the corral. It had been a productive time. Hard work, grueling at times, but they got it done and he had to admit he wouldn't have been able to accomplish all of it without the assistance of Tommy Olster. Cody smiled to himself as he thought of what Rosalyn's reaction would be when she spied the vegetable garden that Tommy had planted. Tommy had insisted that every homestead required a decent garden to supply the kitchen with fresh food so he set about planting one. With each season, fresh vegetables would be ready to harvest.

Cody pulled Rosalyn's last letter from his pocket and read again the date she promised to travel with Maureen to Laramie. In a few more days, she'd be home. Cody scanned the sky, trying to forecast signs of rain and calculating how long it would take to ride from the ranch to Laramie and back. He was eager to see his wife and baby.

He had rented a more comfortable carriage from the town's livery and had hitched Lightning to pull it. The big bay chafed a bit under the harness, but Cody wanted his strength and power to pull the conveyance that would carry his precious cargo.

"All ready?" asked Tommy as he wiped his hands on the seat of his pants.

"Just about. Hand me that feed bag of grain for Lightning and I'll put it in the back. I've got a packet of food for us to last a few days. Think that's all I need."

"When do you think you'll be back?" Tommy asked as he closed the gate to the corral and stood back while Cody maneuvered the carriage.

"Four days, five at the most. You'll be okay here on your own?" Cody asked as he readied to flick the reins and start his journey.

"Yep. Good luck to you." Tommy waved to his employer as Cody guided Lightning down the path and headed south.

Cody had made good time and now stood on the platform of the Laramie train station waiting for the arrival of the train from Omaha. He paced back and forth then peered into the distance as he listened to the train whistle round the bend. A plume of black smoke from the engine announced the arrival of the powerful train into the station. The conductor lowered steps in place at each of the passenger cars. Cody moved to each car as he searched among the crowd of descending passengers until he spotted Rosalyn stepping off the train. She held the baby in one arm with a large bag dangling from the crook of her other arm while she clutched the hand rail. Cody rushed forward and grabbed the tapestry bag from her arm as he enfolded her in a welcome hug.

"Welcome home," Cody said as he pressed a quick kiss to her soft lips then hurried his family away from the noisy train and its belches of steam.

"I've missed you so much," Rosalyn cried as they entered the station. She shifted Maureen against her shoulder and wrapped the baby's blanket tighter as they waited for the conductor to finish unloading the passenger luggage. Rosalyn pointed to two large bags and Cody quickly claimed them. Exiting the train station, Cody led the way toward the waiting carriage.

"I thought you'd be more comfortable riding in this than that rickety buckboard," explained Cody as he held the baby while Rosalyn climbed up into the carriage. He handed her the baby then hoisted their bags into the back of the carriage; it was a tight fit.

"Whew! Glad you packed light, dear," Cody said with a laugh then climbed aboard and took the reins. "C'mon Lightning, let's go home."

Two months later, Rosalyn hummed a gay tune to herself as she pinned wet clothes onto the line to dry. Maureen slept peacefully in her new crib that Tommy had built and Rosalyn had only to peek into the bedroom window to check on her daughter. The summer weather couldn't have been more perfect; for once the plains had received enough spring rains to produce lush green vegetation and the temperatures had remained moderate. She looked over to the plot of vegetables and made a mental note to pick the handful of tomatoes ripening nicely before the animals got to them.

Rosalyn paused in her chores to watch Cody and Tommy balance precariously on the tall beams of the large barn under construction. Tommy seemed to be a natural carpenter and had convinced Cody that the two of them could build a barn for the horses and livestock that would protect them better than the lean-to in winter months. They'd been hard at work on the structure for almost five weeks. The four sides had been built and now they struggled to attach the cross beams for roof pitch. Rosalyn held her breath each time she saw the men climbing the A-frame so high off the ground.

If the completed barn was half as nice as the new room addition to the house, she and Cody would be pleased. Coming home to the spacious bedroom that had been added plus the new shelving and cupboards build along one wall of the kitchen thrilled Rosalyn and she had clapped her hands in joy. The cabin had been transformed into a more formal structure. Cody had even removed the original door and in its place a thick, solid wood door had been hewn from a single tree trunk to protect and insulate the entry.

The men climbed down from their perch and jumped onto the ground. They both needed drinks of water and a break in their labor. Cody pulled on the rope to raise the bucket from the well to the surface. He hauled up the full bucket so he and Tommy could quench their thirsts with ladles of cool water.

"Hungry?" asked Rosalyn as she walked past them into the house. "How about some sliced tomatoes and buttered bread? Just picked the tomatoes; they look delicious."

Both men nodded then plopped onto a bench in the shade to relax strained muscles. Cody groaned. "I don't think I've ever worked this hard. That barn should stand a hundred years, it's so solid. Where'd you learn carpentry skills like that?"

Tommy wiped his hands on his pants before reaching for the plate of food offered by Rosalyn. He grinned shyly at the sincere compliment from Cody. "Guess I just learnt by watching and helping since I was no taller than a tot. Working with wood was a way of life. My folks came out west from Lancaster, Pennsylvania. Like others before us, this was as far as we got."

"Are you Quakers or Amish then?" asked Rosalyn as she joined the men and bounced Maureen on her lap.

Tommy appeared embarrassed. He lowered his eyes as he admitted, "Mennonite. We were shunned. That's why we left. My family keeps to themselves. Sally tends the animals in town; she's got a way with critters. And now I'm here. My Pa died last year and my mother takes care of the young ones while my brothers and me work the land."

"Is that where you go every day, back home?" asked Cody.

"Yes sir. When I finish here I go home to work my chores and plant our crops."

Rosalyn reached for his hand in an affectionate squeeze. "You've done an amazing job here. The vegetable garden and the work on the house—now the barn. Cody and I are both very grateful. You can be proud of what you've accomplished."

"No ma'am, pride is a sin. It would be wrong of me not to give you my best work. You've been kind to me and pay me a fair wage."

Cody patted the lad on the shoulder. "You deserve it. Guess we better be getting back at it. And Tommy, Rosalyn and I meant it when we said we wouldn't have the home we do without your help. If there is anything we can ever do for you or your family, we're in your debt."

Later that night, as they lay in bed listening to the sounds of crickets and night owls hooting in the distance, Rosalyn spoke softly, her head pillowed on Cody's shoulder.

"I need to go into town tomorrow. Maureen is growing out of her clothes; I'd like to buy some bolts of cloth to make her larger ones. Maybe I can find shoes for her too, or at least order ones from the catalog. She'll be walking by winter; today she tried to crawl across the floor. You would have laughed if you'd seen her; she looked more like an inch worm, scooting forward on her belly. She actually got up on her knees once but then fell flat and cried."

"Crawling already? We'll have to be careful when the stove is hot and remember to close the door so she doesn't crawl outside. You keep an eye out for snakes when you're moving about the yard too. Don't forget where you are. This isn't St. Louis; there are dangers on the prairie."

"I promise, I'll be careful, but can we make a trip into town tomorrow?"

"Yes...Missus Jarvis, you talk too much," Cody joked as he silenced her with a searing kiss.

Morgan's store hustled with customers buying everything from farm implements and plant seeds to mason jars filled with canned vegetables or jam. Rosalyn held Maureen in her arms as she inspected the colorful bolts of cloth along one wall of the store. Cody browsed through a selection of hand tools and had decided on a new claw hammer when he heard a familiar voice.

"If I hadn't seen it with my own eyes, I wouldn't have believed it. So it's true...you've turned into a homesteader." Zachary Logan laughed a harsh sound. A sound filled with cruelty, not humor.

Cody took a step closer to him and noticed Sarah Logan standing behind her husband. The meek woman stood silently as her husband continued to cast jibes at Cody. Her eyes darted about the room but her mouth was drawn in a tight line. She resembled a frightened mouse.

Logan stepped backwards and stumbled into his shadow of a wife. Looking like a fool, he awkwardly bumped into a table full of produce.

"Move out of my way," he growled and raised his hand to slap his wife. Suddenly he found his wrist caught in an iron-like vise as Cody held the man's arm and twisted it viciously away from the cowering woman.

"I don't abide hurting women," Cody warned through clenched teeth. He released Logan's wrist as he faced the man.

A deadly silence filled the store. Onlookers held their breath. Rosalyn clutched her baby as she waited on the outcome of the encounter.

Logan locked eyes with Cody. Finally, he shifted his feet and directed his wife, "Get outside." Turning to Cody he threatened, "We're not done here."

"Any time Logan. I'm not done with you either," Cody stated in a calm, lethal voice. His right hand lightly rested on the Colt's handle.

Early the next morning Rosalyn opened the door to a timid knock from an unexpected visitor. Sarah Logan. Rosalyn immediately ushered her into their home. Sarah held a pie pan covered with a gingham cloth. When she saw Cody walk out of the bedroom, she held out the dish to him.

"I remember you; you came to the house once. You were different. I wanted to thank you for yesterday. No one has ever cared about my well-being before. Accept this housewarming gift... I think you'll find it to your liking." With that Sarah Logan turned and left Rosalyn and Cody staring after her in stunned silence.

Cody placed the pie pan on the table and lifted the cloth. He raised shocked eyes to Rosalyn as they both stared at a pair of engraving plates for hundred dollar bills nestled in the pan.

"Oh my God," whispered Rosalyn.

"I searched years for these. Finally!" Cody stated as he fingered the intricately engraved copper plates. "I've got to go to Laramie and wire Director Burns."

Chapter 50

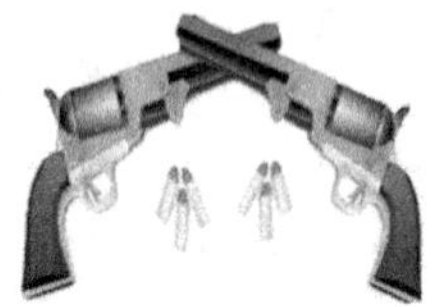

Revenge

Winter struck with a vengeance upon the land. Wind howled and blew snow into deep drifts. The windows rattled, struck by gusts of snow and wind, the glass frosted over. Cody stomped his feet, depositing several inches of snow onto the floor as he entered with an armload of chopped wood. A puddle of melted snow quickly formed.

"Now I understand what they mean when they say that weather is not fit for man nor beast. If this keeps up, we'll have the makings for a true blizzard," Cody said as he hung his coat and scarf on a peg.

Rosalyn wrapped a woolen shawl around her shoulders against the cold. She already wore as many layers as she could without ripping out seams and had dressed Maureen with extra layers of clothing to keep her warm as she toddled about the house.

"I've never witnessed a storm this bad," said Rosalyn as she mopped up Cody's puddle then went to stir the pot of porridge on the stove.

"I warned you once that Wyoming winters can be unforgiving; I should know, I almost froze to death one winter. If this keeps up, Burns will wait until spring before he sends out any agents to arrest Logan and confiscate those counterfeit plates."

"Do you think it's safe, having those plates here?"

"Safe enough, I guess. I've got them hidden in case Logan or his men come searching. Frankly, I'm surprised he hasn't tried yet."

"Do you think he suspected his wife took them? I was really surprised when Mister Morgan told me about her death last month. I mean, I didn't really know the woman, but it made me sad to think of someone killing herself like that."

"She must have decided her life wasn't worth living any more, putting up with Logan's violence and abuse. A pity. Logan is the one that deserved to die but he'll get his just rewards when he's looking through a set of jail cell bars."

Cody held Maureen as he and Rosalyn stood chatting with Clara on the sidewalk. Cody tilted his daughter's sun bonnet forward to shade her eyes from the brilliant noon day rays. After a long cold winter, the warmth of the summer sun felt good.

"Can't get over how big she's grown," Clara said as she handed the little girl a lollipop. "Okay if she has a treat?"

"Just this once," replied Rosalyn as she looked on indulgently. It made her heart swell to watch Cody proudly hold their daughter. He'd changed so much during the past year. No more dark days with sullen moods. Rosalyn could tell that he didn't dwell on the past any longer. Maybe it was knowing he had finally completed his mission where Logan was concerned, or maybe it was just accepting the role of being a father. It was hard to tell, but she was happy witnessing the smile in his eyes and the easy affection they shared.

A trio of riders kicked up a cloud of dust as they galloped into town and stopped in front of the Silver Spur. They dismounted then paused as they stared at the scene across from them. Abe and his brother Wilbur strode toward the happy family. Wilbur held his gun in hand.

Cody noticed the riders, but too late. His instincts had dulled by domesticity. He should have been more alert and on guard. He started to react as the cowhand shouted and began advancing toward them.

"You bitch!" Wilbur yelled as he marched closer to Rosalyn and raised his gun. "Look what you did to my face! I waited ten years in prison hoping I'd find you. I'm gonna make you pay."

Cody suddenly thrust Maureen into Clara's arms as he pivoted and tried to get between his wife and the gunman. He saw Wilbur fire just as he leaped in front of Rosalyn, drawing his Colt from its holster and firing off a round as he collapsed onto the ground.

Gunsmoke hung in the air. It had all happened in seconds. Rosalyn crawled toward the dropped Colt; picking up Cody's revolver, she pointed it at the wounded gunman, firing twice before she saw him drop to the ground near her husband. The second man stood with hands raised as he backed away.

Rosalyn dropped to the ground and held Cody's head in her lap as she pressed her hands on the gaping hole in his chest. Tears flowed from her eyes, blinding her.

"Please, someone, get a doctor!" she shouted to the onlookers that had gathered. "Cody, Cody...hold on darling. Help is coming. Please, stay with me."

"I love you, Rosalyn. I'm sorry..." He coughed; red spittle bubbled in the corner of his mouth. One finger reached to wipe away her tears before his hand fell to the ground, lifeless.

Epilogue

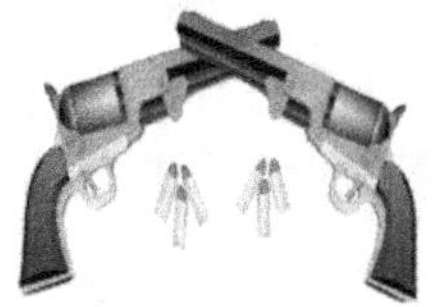

Cedar Hill

Maureen slipped her hand through her mother's arm as they slowly walked up the church aisle. Her mother's eyes glistened with moist, unshed tears as they approached the altar. Maureen kissed her mother on her cheek before Rosalyn moved to sit in the front pew.

The minister greeted the seated guests then asked, "Who gives this woman to be married?"

"I do. Her mother," spoke Rosalyn in a clear voice, proud of the beautiful daughter she had raised.

Maureen kissed her new husband, Daniel Hartman, as the ceremony ended. In her cream colored satin gown and her long auburn hair adorned with baby breath flowers, Maureen was the portrait of a beautiful bride.

The happy couple followed Rosalyn with his parents back to the large Victorian house on Elm Street, that was once Rosalyn's childhood home and where she had returned to raise Maureen. Rosalyn directed them all into the dining room. A wedding cake and champagne awaited them.

Lifting a flute of champagne to toast the newly married couple, Rosalyn said, "May you have many years together and be as happy as your father and I had been. He left a special gift for you to be opened on your wedding day."

Rosalyn handed Maureen a paper scroll tied with ribbon. She watched as her daughter untied the ribbon and read the certificate that deeded to her a parcel of land in Deer Springs, Wyoming with all buildings and improvements.

"Your father put your name on this deed when you were just a baby. He wanted you to share his dream. I hope you and Daniel can build a new life and generations to come on Cedar Hill. That was the name Cody gave to his ranch, and now it's yours."

Daniel and Maureen held the deed then each kissed Rosalyn on the cheek.

"Thank you, Mama. I love you very much. We promise to honor Daddy's legacy."

APPENDIX A

DUNLAP FAMILY TREE

Circle-D Ranch

JAMES JOHN DUNLAP –
Born 1861, Died Jan.10,1887
Married – Nov. 2, 1883
MARGARET DOHERTY -
Born 1863, Died Mar. 9,1896
Son: Alexander John Dunlap - B. 1886
Daughter: Anna M. - B. 4/12/1885; D. 4/13/1885
ALEXANDER JOHN DUNLAP
Born June 18,1886, Died Oct.6,1945
Married - 1903
KATIE ANN CANAVAN
Born Aug. 2, 1886, Died Jan.8,1944
Daughter: Peggy Ann, B. 1906, Died 1913
Son: Alexander John Dunlap, Jr.,
        B. 1916, Died Oct. 8, 1943
Son: Samuel James Dunlap, B. 1920
SAMUEL JAMES DUNLAP
Born Oct. 17, 1920, still living
Married – Mar. 1944
MARY K. BARNES
Born Apr. 4,1922, Died 1989
Son: Alex J. III, B. 1946, D 1946

Son: Brian James Dunlap, B. 1947
BRIAN JAMES DUNLAP
Born Aug. 5, 1947, Died 7/21/1997.
Married - 1973
SARAH CUMMINGS DUNLAP
Born Feb. 1, 1949, Died 7/21/1997.
Daughter: Andrea Brianna Dunlap, B. 1977

APPENDIX B

HARTMAN FAMILY TREE

Cedar Hill Ranch

CODY JARVIS
Born 1859, Died Aug. 8,1898
Married - 1896
ROSALYN O'HARA
Born 1862, Died 1918
Daughter: Maureen Anne Jarvis - B. 1896
MAUREEN ANNE JARVIS
Born Dec. 24,1896, Died 1971
Married - 1913
DANIEL JARROD HARTMAN
Born 1889, Died 1968
Daughters: Deborah A. Hartman- B. 1915, Died 1996
Patricia Sue Hartman – B.1913, died 1998
Son: Christopher Cody Hartman - B. 1919
CHRISTOPHER CODY HARTMAN
Born May 3,1919, Died 1990
Married - 1941
DIANE M. BECKETT
Born 1926, still living
Son: Jarrod C. Hartman – B. 1946
Daughter: Ruth D. Hartman – B. 1949, still living
JARROD CHRISTOPHER HARTMAN

Born Aug. 5,1946, still living
Married - 1969
INGRID SCHMIDT HARTMAN
Born Nov. 9,1950, still living
Daughter: Jessica Hartman, B. 1975
Son: Jason Cody (J.C.) Hartman - Born 1972

APPENDIX C

LOGAN FAMILY TREE

Diamond Bar Ranch

Zachary Logan -
Born 1859, Died Oct.10,1898
Married - 1878
Sarah Murphy
Born 1861, Died 1897
Son: William Henry Logan, B. 1880
William Henry Logan
Born Jan 2,1880, Died 1948
Married - 1905
Kathleen Morgan
Born 1884, Died 1935
Son: Avery Harold Logan, B. 1915
Avery Harold Logan
Born July 3,1915, Died Oct 6,1945
Married - 1939
Clara Lee
Born 1923, Died 1983
Daughter: Annabelle Logan, B. 1940
Son: Brent Logan, B. 1941
Brent Logan
Born June 2,1941
Married – 1965

Iris Parker
Born Sept. 18,1946
Daughter: Veronica Lynn Logan - Born 1976

Award winning author, **Nancy M. Wade** combines a love for travel with the joy of reading romance and mystery novels since childhood. She fills her writing with warm characters set in exciting locales. She and her husband resided in central Ohio for over forty years; now retired, they claim the hills of Tennessee as home. An honors graduate of East Tennessee State University, Nancy studied film and criminology.

Nancy M. Wade's works include The Circle-D Saga trilogy of western romantic suspense novels: *Endless Circle* and book two *Moment in Time,* and the third book *Gun For Hire.* A rich family drama, *Reflections: A Sentimental Journey*; a colonial historical romance novel, *Frontier Heart*; plus, a contemporary short story called *Courtship of Laura.*

Nancy also pens an exciting cozy mystery series *A Meadowood Mystery* with four books *Scarecrows and Corpses, Reunion with Death, Deadly Bones, and Berry Little Murder.* Watch for a fifth book in the series called *Deathly Wedding Woes* to be released in early 2024.

All of her works are available for order in both paperback or E-book formats on Amazon.com, or online in Barnes & Noble Books, Books-A-Million and IngramSparks.

Follow the author on Instagram or her Facebook page: https://www.facebook.com/authorNancyMWade/ and on her web site https://nancymwade.com .

Endless Circle

Circle-D Saga, Book One

An American West dynasty tale of struggle and violence as dramatic as *Yellowstone* or Janet Dailey's *Caulder* family—*Moment in Time* tells a story of conflict, love, and hate between three families who each staked their claim during the late 1880s in the wild west of Platte County, Wyoming. One family always demanding more, forcing the others to fight for their existence and future.

Do the ghosts from our past speak to us? Can we right the wrongs committed a hundred years ago?

Andrea (Andy) Dunlap is determined to save her family's financially struggling Wyoming cattle ranch. She'll need to summon all her strength as she copes with the loss of her parents in a suspicious plane crash. Was it an accident? Andrea is helped by her childhood friend, Sheriff Jason C. Hartman, as together they become embroiled in murder and treachery while following the clues to solve her parent's death and uncover secrets from three generations ago.

Jason and Andrea discover the path to justice may be found within the writings of Maggie Dunlap, Andy's great-great grandmother, as they read her remarkable diary and story of survival in this rugged land; the betrayal, heartache and loss she suffered of her own true love. Maggie's resilient pioneer spirit guides them as they unravel the mystery of an 1887 land swindle and murder.

The young lovers are caught in a mystery of deception and family legend as past meets present in this romantic suspense set in the rugged west. Jason must prove to Andy that his love is strong enough to bridge the gulf between family feuds and suspicions. Andrea and Jason draw their strength and determination from their pioneer stock, but little do they know that their lives were destined to be intertwined, proving that the **Endless Circle** of love remains unbroken.

Moment in Time

Circle-D Saga, Book Two

An American West dynasty tale of struggle and violence as dramatic as *Yellowstone* or Janet Dailey's *Caulder* family—*Moment in Time* tells a story of conflict, love, and hate between three families who each staked their claim during the late 1880s in the wild west of Platte County, Wyoming. One family always demanding more, forcing the others to fight for their existence and future.

The Circle-D Saga continues...follow the Dunlap brothers from their struggling cattle ranch on the plains and rugged mountains of Wyoming to the green countryside of war-torn England where they experience both the thrill and dangers of serving on the mighty Flying Fortresses of the Eighth Air Force. Their sibling rivalry comes to a head when both brothers vie for the heart of a pretty English WAC. Can Samuel prove himself worthy? Can he measure up to his older, admired brother Alex? Will tragedy or triumph await them as each man struggles to survive the battles of a world at war?

Past conflicts with the sprawling, neighboring Diamond Bar ranch will haunt the young veteran and his new war-bride when they return to the Circle-D ranch. They must confront cattle rustlers and murderers as they fight to save their home and forge a bright future for themselves and generations to come.